YIELDED CAPTIVE

BY DALAINA MAY

Yielded Captive
a novel by Dalaina May
copyright ©2012 by Dalaina May

Trade paperback ISBN: 978-0-9852192-3-9
Ebook ISBN: 978-0-9852192-4-6

Cover design by Eric Powell
Cover photo by Jenna Masters

Yielded Captive is also available on Amazon Kindle and Apple iBooks.

BottomLine Media, an imprint of Pioneers, publishes materials that celebrate the "bottom line" of God's covenant with Abraham: "I will bless all nations through you." To purchase other BottomLine titles, visit *Pioneers.org/Store*.

Pioneers is an international movement that mobilizes teams to initiate church-planting movements among unreached people groups. To get involved, visit *Pioneers.org*.

This book is lovingly dedicated to Isaac William Sward, August 8, 2006–February 4, 2008. I will never have all the answers to why, but you helped me better know God, whose goodness makes the answers not as necessary.

ACKNOWLEDGEMENTS

There are several people whose love, encouragement, and critique made *Yielded Captive* worth sharing. My first reader and greatest cheerleader, my husband Dan, thank you for believing that I could do this and for your honest (though sometimes painful) criticism. Thank you helping me carve out time to write in the middle of full-time ministry and raising four babies.

Karene, you made this book readable, and I shudder to think what it would have been like without your pink pen and your great ideas. What a joy to have found a friend in you through the process!

Traci, Kelli, Devona, Kimi, Dad, and Andy, your encouragement was what I needed, and your openness about what you liked and hated was what the book needed. Thank you. Jenna and Megan, you were a delight to work with. Thanks for getting excited about this project and for lending your creative minds and beautiful faces.

Matt and Caryn, I doubt I'll ever know how much work it took to get *Yielded Captive* in print, but I'm thankful for your dedication and for your vision.

My Caquinte family, not one of whom will ever actually read this, it is an honor to know you and call you friends. Thank you for providing a rich supply of ideas to help create the Shampiri culture. May you grow in your knowledge and love of Creator God.

Finally, to my Jesus, who is everything to me. I'll never know what You are going to do next, but I know You.

CONTENTS

CHAPTER **ONE**

"**I**s there anything new out in the gardens this morning?" Allison asked her husband. "Nope. Nothing," Eric replied. "It's driving me crazy. There was a ton of activity last month, and now there are no signs of the Shampiri at all."

"Well," Allison said as she put her arms around him, "There is always tomorrow."

Eric grinned down at her. It was her standard line. Nearly every day for the last three years she had voiced the hope that they all felt about their endeavor. The Carters, along with their missionary teammates, had been living in a little camp on a small tributary of the Amazon River around 150 miles from Iquitos in the Amazon jungle of Peru. Their intention was to make contact with the Shampiri tribe that was said to travel through the area seasonally. It had been three years of little success and a lot of boredom. Occasionally their gardens were raided, and once in awhile the men of the team found foot tracks while hunting out in the jungle. They were positive that the Shampiri knew they were there, but it was up to the tribe to decide when and how they would show themselves.

Just a month ago, some of the team's efforts had been rewarded. The cooking pots they had left in the gardens as gifts went missing. A few days later, the tribe had taken the knives that had replaced the pots. It was a great sign to the missionaries, and they all dreamed that the day they had been working for was in sight. The Shampiri would be contacted, and the team would be able to befriend them, learn their language, and eventually share the gospel with them.

Eric held his wife in a tight hug and smiled into her adoring, green eyes. "What are you up to today?" he asked.

"After Isaac wakes up Jamie and I are going to the river to do some laundry. It's unbelievable how much clothing a little kid goes through." Allison motioned through the doorway to the bedroom of the two room, palm bark home where their thirteen-month-old son was asleep in his homemade crib.

Eric kissed his wife's cheek and gave her long, auburn ponytail a tug before walking toward the door. "I'll be working on the strong house with Kyle and Tim if you need me. I noticed some of the boards are rotting in one of the corners, so we'll probably have to replace them."

The strong house was the very first structure the team had built when they arrived - even before they built the airstrip at the edge of their base. It was a small building, but large enough for their entire team to fit comfortably inside. It was stocked with enough food and water for all of them for three days and was also where the shortwave radio was kept. In the unfortunate event that unfriendly natives attacked the camp, the team would gather inside and call for help on the radio.

Luckily, there were nearly always warning signs before such a thing happened. Broken gifts left in the garden, arrows shot into the camp, and other threatening messages were all reasons for the team to go on high alert. They had seen nothing but positive responses, few though they were, and were hopeful that the Shampiri would soon attempt friendly contact.

Allison washed up the breakfast dishes in a bowl of boiled river water while she waited for Isaac to wake up from his nap. She thought about the missing gifts and wondered how close they really were to the next phase of their ministry. *Lord, help us to be patient for Your timing. I know you love the Shampiri and have a plan to bring them the Good News about Jesus. Let it be Your plan and Your way, and not ours.*

With a smile on her lips, Allison continued praying for the people that she had never met, but loved nonetheless. She had loved the Shampiri since she had sat in her adult Sunday School class in Texas five years ago and listened to Kyle Huntington explain that no one in the tribe had ever had the chance to hear the gospel. He told the class that he and his wife, Jamie, would soon be returning to Peru along with another family to begin working toward making contact with the group. They were based out of the jungle city of Iquitos, but spent the bulk of their time at a camp they had carved out of the jungle.

A quiet knock broke Allison out of her reverie. She opened the door and smiled at her blond haired best friend. From the moment they had met, Allison felt a deep connection to Jamie Huntington, almost as if they had known each other their whole lives. Jamie had taken Allison under her wing when the Carters had arrived in Peru and patiently showed her how to survive in a place totally foreign to someone raised in the modern world. Cooking over a fire, doing laundry by hand, and preserving food without refrigeration were among the chores that Allison had quickly grown accustomed to.

"I think you are starting to show." Allison patted Jamie's pregnant belly.

Her friend beamed. "I know!" she said excitedly. "I can hardly button these jeans. It's about time. I've been ready to look pregnant for years." Jamie's was a long awaited pregnancy. The rest of the team had been almost as thrilled as the Huntingtons with the news that a fourth child would soon be added to the team. For several years, Tim and Kathy's twin girls were the only little ones running around. Isaac had come along as a surprise two years after the Carters' arrival. Jamie's baby would make the number even again.

"Is Kathy washing today too?" Allison asked.

"Maybe later. She told me that she wants to finish up the girls' math lesson and get them started on their homework first. Are you ready to go?"

Allison pointed to a bucket of dirty cloth diapers soaking in bleach. "Yes, and I have a ton to do. I hear Isaac babbling in the bedroom. Let me grab him, and we can go."

Walking toward the bedroom, Jamie said, "Oh, let me get him. I need the practice."

Allison followed her to the crib. "Fine. I'll carry your laundry. You shouldn't carry both."

"I would argue, but the truth is, I am already tired from my morning chores." Jamie picked up the baby who immediately snuggled his dark curls into her shoulder.

After Allison had retrieved the laundry from the front room, Jamie held the door open. Allison used both buckets of laundry to keep her balance as they walked the trail through the tall grass down the hill to the river. The rainy season had only just started, so the river was still receded, creating a wide, sandy bank full of washed up logs and branches that Isaac loved to explore. Allison had long ago lost her fear of germs and allowed him to play with the rocks, sticks, and leaves as much as he liked.

The women set their buckets in the shallow water of the shore and began to scrub detergent into the dirty clothes. They chatted while they worked and kept watch over Isaac's explorations. He had recently begun walking, but was still unsteady on his feet.

After an hour, both women had finished the scrubbing and rinsing, and together they wrung out the clothing to carry back to the camp to be hung on the clothes lines strung next to their houses. It was a hard, hot job, but doing it together made it much more enjoyable for both of them.

Jamie yawned. "I think I am going to go catch a nap before lunch. I am beat." She picked up her bucket of laundry and started for the trail up the hill to the camp. "Are you coming?"

"Go on ahead. I am going to play with Isaac for a few minutes and wash him off. I'll see you later."

Allison waved her friend away and turned to her son who was stuffing pebbles into his mouth. She gently swept her finger inside his cheeks to rid them of the stones before she picked him up and carried him to the river. "Don't eat rocks, Isaac."

The two lingered at the water's edge for a long while, tossing sand into the slow current and looking for tadpoles in the small puddles of water that had formed by the retreating river. For Allison, it was among the sweetest moments in her days. She had loved the years she and Eric had together before Isaac came along, but there was something indescribable about having a child to watch grow and begin discovering what was around him. She delighted in seeing his dark green eyes light up with the introduction of the new sights and sounds landscaping his little world.

"Hey, guys!" Allison looked up to see Kyle making his way down the trail to the riverbank. "Where's my wife?" he asked.

"She went home to take a nap. We were just playing for awhile before we head back. Are you guys done with the strong house floor already?"

Kyle stooped down at the edge of the river and began washing his face with the cool water. "Yes." he replied, "We decided that it's not as rotted as we thought. We replaced one board, but that's all we're going to do with it for now. I left the guys to put all of the tools away. I thought I would take a dip in the river and carry Jamie's laundry back for her, but, since she isn't here, I'll carry yours if you'll wait for me."

"Take your time. We're having fun, although I think Isaac is getting hungry." As if to confirm his mother's words, the toddler began pulling at her blue T-shirt.

Kyle chuckled. "You know, when your kid starts asking to eat, it might be time to quit nursing," he teased.

Allison turned her son's attention to a short, fat stick before saying, "He is still a baby. He isn't ready to give it up yet, and neither am I."

"Fair enough." Stripping off his filthy short-sleeved, denim shirt, Kyle waded into the river. He ducked under the water a few times to wash the grime off of his body and to cool off his steaming skin.

After several minutes of relaxing in the water, he sloshed to shore and began re-buttoning his shirt. He paused with his head cocked to one side. "Do you hear that?" he asked.

Even as the words left his mouth, Allison heard loud whoops break the peaceful sound of the river. Then screaming began. Her eyes lit with understanding, then fear. "Do you think—?"

"The strong house. Hurry. I think the camp is being attacked." Kyle grabbed Allison's arm and propelled her to her feet. He shoved her forward, and they both dashed toward the trail.

Allison clutched Isaac tightly as she ran the path back to the camp. He began crying, but she scarcely heard. *Oh, God, please don't let them be in the camp. Protect Eric and Jamie and—*

Allison stopped and a terrified scream gurgled up her throat. With Isaac dangling from one arm, she dropped to her knees. Eric was lying unconscious on the trail near the clearing of the camp with one long arrow pierced into his back. Blood was seeping from his wound and into the dirt below him.

"There's no time," Kyle said firmly and forced her up again, "Take Isaac and get into the strong house. *Now!*" Barely breaking his stride, Kyle dragged Eric's body into the tall grass beside the trail and ran after her.

Isaac. Save Isaac. Run. It was all Allison could do to command her body to leave her husband and scramble toward the strong house fifty yards away. Clasping her screaming son to her chest, she focused on the door of the strong house, but still she saw chaos all around her. There were half a dozen native men, their faces smeared with red paint, wielding long, drawn bows and yelling to one another in an incomprehensible language. It was clear to her, however, that they were very angry.

Thud. Allison looked over her shoulder to see Kyle on the ground, an arrow through his shoulder. "Go!" he shouted, his face twisting in pain.

Thirty yards, twenty-five yards. Allison's chest heaved in exertion and terror. Then an arm reached out and plucked Isaac from her like fruit from a tree.

"No!" she screamed, charging at the warrior who had stolen her son. He pushed her to the ground, but she was back on her feet a second later. She dove for the strong brown hand that held Isaac by his arm as if he were nothing more than a rag doll. She scratched and bit at him as a fury like she had never experienced filled her soul.

His eyes glittering with rage, the warrior dropped the child onto the dirt and grasped her by the throat. He pushed her to the ground with one hand, and, in a heartbeat, had an arrow loaded into his bow. As the warrior pulled back the bow, Allison scrambled to cover Isaac with her body. She waited for the impact of the four-foot long arrow that she knew could easily impale her and her son's bodies at such a close range. *Lord, this was not how it was supposed to end. Please, don't let Isaac feel any pain.*

To her surprise, she was yanked back to her feet. She whirled around to find herself staring into the face of another native man. This one's eyes lacked the fury of the first man's. The second warrior held her tightly by the elbow and began arguing animatedly with his comrade. Though she could not understand a word of their language, she knew that they were speaking about her. The warrior that held her fast motioned to her and to Isaac who was still sitting on the ground wailing.

Whatever was said angered the first man who again drew back his bow and pointed it at her chest. Smoothly, she was pulled safely behind her captor's back.

Before the argument could continue, a third man joined the pair. He was taller than the first two, a little older, and obviously in charge. He listened as the two warriors yelled simultaneously. Finally, he put his hand up and uttered one word that ended the discussion. Allison was handed to him, and he began dragging her back toward the trail that led to the river.

Her heartbeat was wild with panic, and she could not seem to catch her breath. She had no idea what their plans were for her, but she knew that they could not be good. Kicking and flailing, she tried to wrench her arms from his grasp. It was futile. Though not much taller than she, he was broad shouldered with thick arms corded with muscle.

He continued pulling her toward the trail. When they passed by the mouth of the trail where Eric's body had lain, Allison struggled to catch a glimpse of her husband in the grass, but she was unable to see him through the foliage.

At the river, Allison managed to break free from the strong arms that held her. She ran back to the trail, toward Eric, toward Isaac. Not even three steps to freedom, she was seized from behind and thrown onto the ground. On the way down, her head came in contact with a rotting log that was sitting on the bank. A searing pain ripped through her temple, and the world went black.

CHAPTER **TWO**

Allison's eyes fluttered open against the pain in her temple. She looked at the trees above her and noticed that the sun was low in the sky. How had it gotten so late?

In a rush, the memories assaulted her. The attack on the camp, Eric prone on the trail, being dragged to the river, Isaac... She sat up and, despite her throbbing headache and dizziness, struggled to her feet. Looking around, she realized that she had been lying at the base of a tall Kapok tree in a bed of wet, fallen leaves.

The crunch of footsteps startled her as the native man who had saved her from death by his companion's arrow walked toward her. Isaac was in his arms, and the baby had clearly been crying for a long time. Relief washed over Allison like a wave. Her child was alive, and he was here.

With a whimper, she reached tentatively for her son. The native man uttered something unintelligible and gladly allowed the child to fall into his mother's arms. "*Hambre*" he said motioning to Isaac and then putting his fingers to his lips.

Allison's eyes widened at the familiar word. She immediately began speaking in Spanish, asking the man where she was and why she had been taken, but he shrugged and turned away. He squatted on the ground next to the tree under which she had awoken. "*Hambre*" he repeated and again pointed at the baby.

Isaac cried against Allison's shoulder, and she felt her breasts—heavy with milk—begin to leak. Sitting down with her back to the warrior, she lifted her shirt to nurse her son. He latched instantly and began sucking voraciously.

Tears fell from her eyes as the implications of all she had just lived through rose in her mind. Eric was dead. Kyle might be as well. And, as far as she could tell, she had been abducted by the very people she had dedicated her life to win for Christ. What would Eric's parents do when they found out that their family was gone—one murdered and the other two disappeared. His father had been correct; coming to Peru was a big mistake. Allison remembered his words well.

"*You can't possibly be serious,*" *David growled across the table at his son. Though Eric looked remarkably similar to his father, handsome with dark, curly hair and dark eyes, the two held very different expressions on their faces. David's features were pinched in anger, but Eric's expression was one of stubborn confidence.*

Allison watched her husband close his eyes in what she knew was a prayer for patience. They had invited Eric's parents over to tell them of their decision to become missionaries in Peru. Eric had quietly explained why they both felt called to go and that they had been approved by both the team and the mission agency to join the Shampiri work.

Jean had listened in silence with tears running down her cheeks. Eric's father, on the other hand, had exploded.

"Dad," Eric pleaded, "I know this is hard for you to understand. You don't believe like we do, so I don't expect this to make sense to you. But we would like your blessing."

David shook his head before erupting. "I can't support such an absurd plan. I did not send you through law school for you to run off to play Indians in the rainforest."

"No, you sent me to law school so I could be just like you." Eric rubbed his eyes, *"I wish you could understand that practicing law has never stirred me the way the anticipation of this ministry does. I don't feel that I am missing out; I feel like I am gaining the world."*

"Son, I can promise you one thing. This is a decision you will live to regret."

David had been wrong about one thing: Eric had not lived to regret their decision. But she had. A sob escaped Allison's throat, and her tears fell against Isaac's now sleeping face. For all of his anger, David deeply loved his son and would be broken by the news of his death.

Eric's mother, Jean, would also be devastated, but she had already counted the cost of sending her son and daughter-in-law across the world. A few days after they had broken the news to his parents, Eric and Allison met Jean at a local coffee shop. There she explained that she had wrestled with God over their decision, but had come to believe that the potential for God's work among the Shampiri was worth the price of the pain of sending her loved ones away. She had given them her blessing and remained their most involved supporter.

Allison turned at the sound of deep voices. The other native men had returned and were settling down against the trees. Realizing that they must have decided to remain in the clearing for the night, she began to contemplate the possibility of escaping after they had fallen asleep. Yet, she knew that running would be akin to suicide. She had no idea how far away she was from the jungle base, much less which direction it was in. Even if she found a river to follow, there was no telling where it would lead. The Amazon River was fed by hundreds of small tributaries, many of them flowing from as far away as the Andes Mountains in the west. She had no protection, no food, and little knowledge about how to survive alone in the jungle. She was simply at the mercy of her captors.

The tallest man who had dragged her to the river sat cross-legged on the ground, silently observing the others who were talking around him. He was a good-looking man, but there was a hardness to his round face underneath the smeared red paint. His nose was short and flat, and his full lips were drawn into a frown. His dark eyes were almond shaped and missed nothing. As they rested on her, Allison caught her breath. It was as if he knew of her desire to run, almost as if he was waiting for her to do so. They stared at one another for a moment, his gaze issuing a challenge.

She turned her eyes instead to the other men who had begun eating. They were also covered in red paint and each had a number of necklaces made from seeds and some kind of animal teeth. Bands of some kind of fabric were wrapped around their upper arms. Most notable was their lack of clothing. Each man had a wide, dark belt of material around his hips and another above each knee. Their black hair was straight and cropped short across their foreheads. Allison tried to estimate how old they were, but could not. Their ages could have ranged from eighteen to fifty.

Laughing and talking with one another, the warriors enjoyed their meal, until one by one they leaned against the trees with their eyes closed. Though they appeared to be sleeping, their hands were curled around their long bows as if ready to jump into action in an instant.

The man who had held Isaac made his way to Allison and held out a closed fist. He motioned as if to give her something, so she reached out hesitantly. He dropped the gift into her hand with a slight smile then returned to his position under the Kapok tree.

She looked down at her hand and nearly dropped its contents. It was a wiggling mass of fat white larvae. She knew many natives in the Amazon enjoyed such delicacies, but she had never been in the position to try any. She was thankful for the shared dinner, but unsure if she could even eat it.

She looked down at her son and realized that her milk supply would dry up quickly if she did not eat. She swallowed the bile that rose in her throat and forced herself to put a larva in her mouth. It was easier to consume them whole than to bear the thought of chewing them, so she gulped them all down as quickly as possible.

Soon the sun set and darkness engulfed the group. Familiar jungle sounds of frogs, insects, and rustling leaves rose with the night. The bright moon could barely be seen through the thick trees. The darkness was lonely and matched the shadows in Allison's heart. She was frightened and felt completely vulnerable.

God, where were You today? How could You let this happen to me... to Eric? These men killed my husband and could... force me to do anything they wanted. I know You are in control, but I am so afraid.

Allison's fear eased from consuming terror to dull anxiety as she continued to pray. She still had no idea what the morning would bring, but she knew she was not alone. The Creator of these very men who had shattered her life was present and comforted her with a tentative peace.

It had been a long night. Though she had dozed off a few times, Allison had jumped at every sudden noise. Isaac, exhausted from the previous day's trauma, slept deeply until the sun lit the rainforest canopy above.

The warriors wasted no time in getting started on their hike. As soon as it was light enough to safely walk through the trees, the leader motioned for her to follow.

The trek was grueling, and she marveled at the natives' ability to navigate the jungle without a trail. Within a few hours she was completely exhausted and disoriented, yet unable to communicate her need for rest. She continued on, Isaac growing heavier and heavier in her arms.

Eventually the group came to the bank of a small stream where the men refreshed themselves in the water. Allison set her son down beside her and knelt next to the stream. She cupped her hands beneath the water and drank deeply. The coolness of the water cramped her empty stomach, but she drank as much as she could simply because she did not know when her next meal would be.

Isaac splashed happily at her feet, so she took the opportunity to bathe him as well. She had long since removed his cloth diaper from the day before. She quickly rinsed it and his cotton shorts in the water, wrung them out, and laid them across her shoulders. With any luck they would be dry before nightfall, and she could use them again while they slept.

Before she was ready to go, the warriors began walking away from the river. She quickly replaced Isaac's dirty shirt and hurried to catch up with the group. They traveled for several hours upstream and eventually turned inward at a fork in the river.

By the time the warriors decided to camp, Allison could barely keep her eyes open. Two of the men wandered off and soon brought back a feast of guavas, cashew fruit, and more white grubs. She ate her portion of the fruit and shared some with Isaac. Once full, Allison leaned against a tree and nursed her son. They were both asleep within minutes, though the night seemed entirely too short when they rose the next morning to continue their journey.

For four more days, the eight travelers trekked through the jungle at a remarkable rate. Allison wondered how far away their village was and how long she would be able to keep up the pace they had set. In the late afternoon of the fifth day, when she was so weary that she thought she might literally drop in the middle of the trail, she realized that they had arrived at a village.

There were only a handful of houses within view, all set back against the jungle around a small central clearing. Down a trail she could see there were more homes further into the jungle. The rectangular houses were scarcely seven feet tall and made of stalks of bamboo fastened together with handmade fiber ropes. The roofs were thatched palm leaves. Each had a single doorway, but no windows. Fires were burning near the front doors, and naked children played together in the dirt around them.

Soon the children noticed the return of their warriors and scampered inside the houses to inform the occupants of the arrival. Within minutes, dozens of natives were gathered around Allison, touching her matted hair and examining her green eyes.

Isaac was quickly scooped out of her arms and passed around while the native women giggled over his milky skin and brown, baby-fine curls. Unlike his mother, the baby enjoyed the attention and, much to the pleasure of all, babbled and waved his arms gleefully. Each woman had her turn holding him, and Allison struggled to keep an eye on her son. Eventually, he came to rest in the arms of an older woman.

Despite the fact that she was dressed only in a rough cloth skirt, the woman held herself with dignity, and her presence commanded the respect of those around her.

The native woman began a thorough appraisal of Allison. She ran her fingers over her hair and skin, examined her eyes and teeth, and made a full circle around her taking in every detail.

"*Quero pipajita?*" she asked suddenly. Allison stared at her blankly.

Trying a different approach, the woman touched a finger to her chest and said, "*Inani.*" She then pointed at Allison.

"Oh, my name!" she exclaimed, "You want to know my name? Allison." She repeated her name several times.

Inani attempted to pronounce "Allison" again and again, but each time it came out more like "Aditso." Finally, she declared, "*Imeshina.*" Several of the other women standing nearby nodded in approval.

Inani reclaimed Isaac and gave him back to his grateful mother. Putting her arm through Allison's, she led her to the warriors, now joined by several other men at the fire in front of one of the houses. They were all sitting on log benches, laughing and drinking a pink liquid from wooden bowls. A woman stood nearby ready to refill their bowls as they were emptied.

Allison waited as Inani approached the tall warrior and began conversing quietly with him. The man listened without expression or word for a few moments. Finally he nodded, and Inani again took Allison's arm and led her to one of the small dwellings. Standing aside, the older woman waited at the doorway for her to go in before turning to leave. Hesitantly, Allison looked around the house not sure what she would find.

It was a dark, stuffy little room with a dirt floor. A platform constructed of the same bamboo poles as the outer structure sat three feet off the floor in one corner. Underneath the platform were woven, grass baskets and a variety of crude tools. On top of the platform lay a pile of coarse, cotton blankets similar to the women's skirts. A hammock of the same fabric was strung in the corner.

Allison's eyes widened as she took in a familiar sight. One of the cooking pots that she and Jamie had purchased months ago as a gift to try to lure out the Shampiri was overturned on the ground. Her eyes stung with unshed tears at the memory. In her wildest dreams, she could not have imagined that she would see that pot again in this context.

She did not know whose house she was in or why she had been placed here, but she appreciated the opportunity to be alone. Few times over the past five days had she allowed herself to think about all that had taken place. Instead, she had focused on caring for Isaac and surviving the grueling trek through the jungle. Now, however, she could not seem to stop the tears from falling.

She remained in the house for a long time waiting for someone to come for her. Eventually she nursed Isaac and laid him down on a blanket on the platform against the wall. Exhausted herself, she curled up next to him and was soon asleep.

CHAPTER **THREE**

The next morning Allison and Isaac both slept until well after the village came alive. When Isaac's babbling woke her up, she was surprised at how late it was. She picked him up and stood in the doorway watching the native women scurrying around—cooking over fires, preparing food, and chattering to one another as they worked. Many of them had babies strapped to their bodies with a wide cloth forming a sling across their chests. Allison noticed that not many men were present, although a group of three old men sat together around one of the fires.

She stood there observing, fascinated with the inner view of a tribal village. However, as soon as she was noticed, many of the women came to greet her. They tried repeatedly to get her to speak to them, but she could do nothing but smile and shrug her shoulders. Eventually the women gave up and returned to their work.

Inani appeared on a trail between two of the dwellings with a large clay pot of water balanced on her head. She set the jar down beside a house a few doors down and then beckoned Allison to join her.

Propping her son on her hip, Allison walked between the houses to the fire in front of the house. Inani was squatting next to it over a pile of long, tapered dirt-crusted tubes. She held one of them up, and Allison realized that it was a yucca root. *"Caniri,"* Inani informed her.

Much to the older woman's pleasure, Allison repeated the word a few times. She watched as Inani skinned and cut the roots. She washed them and put the pieces back into the pot of water and over the fire to boil.

After completing her task, Inani took Isaac from his mother and cooed at him. Isaac giggled and reached for the streak of gray in the woman's long black hair. After playing with the child for another moment, she called to a young girl who was playing nearby. The girl walked over, took Isaac, and scampered off before Allison realized what had happened. Before she could decide to chase after the girl to retrieve her son, she was given a pot and summoned by the older woman.

Allison followed Inani down a narrow path into the jungle. The rainforest was thick all around, but the trail was obviously well used and easy to follow. Soon the sound of running water met her ears, and the jungle opened to reveal a narrow river. The river's bank was sandy and the water full of sandbars. A flock of children played happily, some on the shore and others splashing in the water. Allison smiled as they all stopped to gape at her. Inani waved her hand at them and with a word sent them back to their games. Inani pointed to the river, *"Ojaaki."* She lifted a palm full of water and, as it tricked through her fingers, said, *"Nija."*

A group of women wandered down the bank and watched the language lesson with amused expressions. Pointing to various things, they indicated that Allison should try to repeat the names. They seemed pleased with her efforts, but mostly laughed at her attempts to pronounce words in their language. One of the women was much quieter than the others and did not laugh as they did. Instead she smiled in support and kindly corrected Allison's inaccurate pronunciations.

"Um. What are your names?" she asked. She pointed at herself and, remembering what Inani had called her the day before, said, "Imeshina."

The women giggled, but understood her question. One by one they told her their odd-sounding names. She immediately forgot everyone except for the quiet woman's name, Amita.

Eventually, the women left, and Inani led the way back to the village. The native woman easily carried her pot of water on her head, but Allison could not bear the weight of it on her neck when she had tried to emulate. Instead she awkwardly lugged the heavy pot of water against her hip, spilling half of it by the time they arrived back to the clearing.

For several hours, Allison shadowed Inani as she went about her daily chores, watching how the native woman was able to complete tasks without the benefit of any modern technology. She used sharpened palm blades to cut, handmade grass baskets to store, and sheer muscle power to break off tree branches to feed her fire.

In the afternoon, after her lunch of boiled yucca, the men began arriving from many directions. Most had game or fish lying in grass baskets strapped around their foreheads and hanging down their backs. After dropping the baskets at the feet of the women, the men sat down to eat and soon slept under trees and in the few rough hammocks strung around the village. The women also took a break from active labor, although many continued working on quieter tasks. Deciding that a rest was a good idea, Allison retrieved her son, fed him, and took him to nap inside the house she had used the night before.

After he was asleep, she slipped around to the back of the house and sat against the bamboo wall, looking out into the jungle. She sighed deeply. Her spirit was still so heavy with grief and anxiety. She longed to have a Bible in her possession to soak in the peace and hope of the Word. As she tried to pray, she remembered a passage of Scripture that she had long ago memorized. *"The Lord is my rock and my fortress and my deliverer. My God, my rock, in whom I take refuge, my shield and the horn of my salvation, my stronghold… He drew me out of many waters. He delivered me from my strong enemy and from those who hated me, for they were too mighty for me. They confronted me in the day of my calamity, but the Lord was my stay. He brought me forth also into a broad place. He rescued me because He delighted in me."*

Falling face forward to the earth, Allison sobbed. "Oh God, oh God," she cried as her tears began turning the dirt underneath her to mud, "Your Word says that You delight in me, that you love me, then why have You allowed this to happen? Eric and I came here to serve You. How could You not protect us?"

She was completely overwhelmed with sorrow and unable to even continue praying. Her body heaved, and she wept without relief. She knew that God was sovereign and never allowed anything to happen that was not a part of His ultimate plan, but the very idea brought anger instead of peace. How could God, who was in control, be so cruel?

In her heart she heard a sweet, familiar voice. **There is no one like Me among the gods, nor are there any works like Mine. All nations whom I have made shall come and worship before Me, and they shall glorify My name. For I am great and do wondrous deeds. I alone am God.**

"God, this can't be Your plan for bringing the Shampiri Your Word. Not like this. Not through me… alone." she whispered.

Beloved, years ago you said, "Use me in any way that brings You glory—no matter the cost."

Allison protested aloud, "But I didn't mean *this.*"

Beloved, I have chosen you for this time, for this work, to give you a heritage among this nation. Love these people, teach them who I am.

Weeping in broken surrender, Allison tried to make sense of the things that she felt God had revealed. It made no sense to her. In fact, the very notion that God could use her for such a task was ludicrous. Yet part of her latched on to the idea that there might be a purpose for all of this pain. A seed of hope was planted.

That evening Allison and Isaac were brought to the fire in front of Inani's home. There was a group of Shampiri talking and eating, and she was surprised at how many faces she recognized. In addition to Inani, Allison recognized Amita, another woman and several children from the river, and three of the men who had attacked the jungle camp. One was the kind man who had fed her and taken care of Isaac while she was unconscious, and another was the tall, quiet warrior.

Allison took her place at the fire and accepted her food gratefully. It was boiled yucca again, along with cooked bananas and some sort of tough meat and the pink beverage she had seen many of the villagers drinking throughout the day. She tasted the drink from a small bowl and was surprised at the strong alcoholic flavor. It was actually good—it tasted a bit like fruity beer, but concern for her still-nursing son forced her to put the drink back down.

Amita noticed right away what the others did not. She left the fire momentarily before coming back with another bowl that she traded with Allison for the pink beer. In the bowl she had brought was cloudy, hot water mixed heavily with mashed bananas.

"*Iracagaja*" Amita explained with a smile. Allison smiled back with appreciation and drank it down.

The conversation swirled around her, but she understood none of it. Instead she studied the others around the fire, particularly Amita who moved with such grace that she almost seemed to be dancing. Amita's face was as gentle as her manner. The soft curves of her high cheekbones widened often in a quiet smile. Her eyes were almond shaped and dark like those of the rest of the tribe. She was a beautiful woman, petite but curvy in all of the right places. The shiny, jet-black hair that fell to her waist was the perfect crown to her loveliness.

Realizing that the group had gone completely silent, she looked around. The food she was chewing lodged in her throat as she realized that they were all watching her.

"*Imeshina.*" She looked at Inani with a question in her eyes.

The older woman again said, "*Imeshina.*" She then pointed to the tall warrior. "*Majiro.*"

Allison nodded with understanding at the introduction though she was unsure of its purpose. Majiro simply looked at her with that intense stare that sent shivers down her spine.

Inani continued, "*Majiro. Pijime.*"

The word meant nothing to her, so she shook her head in explanation of her lack of comprehension. Inani tried several different approaches to no avail. In frustration, she rattled off a string of Shampiri to the group.

"*Esposo.*" That word Allison understood. It was the Spanish word for husband. Her eyes narrowed at the warrior who had said it. It was the same man who had told her Isaac was hungry. She wondered how much Spanish he really did know.

"*Imeshina,*" Allison turned her attention back to Inani. "*Majiro, esposo.*" She pointed to Majiro and then back to Allison.

Shock jarred her as understanding dawned in her mind. She shook her head violently, "No. No, I have a husband already." She repeated herself in Spanish looking at the warrior who had initially spoken the Spanish word, hoping that he understood. He did not, or if he did, he pretended not to. Most of the group continued on in conversation as if the matter was settled, but Amita smiled at her over the fire with sad compassion.

Allison's mind swirled with the implications of what she had been told. She hoped that they had been simply asking her if she was interested and that her reaction had been enough to squelch any other proposals.

Thinking perhaps avoidance was her best recourse, she stood up, smiled awkwardly at the group, and returned with her son to the small house she had come from. Isaac was ready for bed, and she was ready to be alone with her thoughts.

Not even an hour later, Majiro walked into the house. Alarmed, she immediately jumped from the platform where she had been sitting and pressed back against the far wall. Her heart in her throat, she watched as he took her sleeping son and laid him in the hammock. The baby did not even stir.

Then he faced her. There was fire in his eyes and a challenge. "*Majiro, esposo.*" He declared firmly as if the matter were settled.

"No. No *esposo*. No, no, no!" Allison shook her head and crossed her arms across her chest.

A shadow of anger darkened his expression, and she surmised that he neither expected nor appreciated being defied. He grabbed her shoulders and pushed her to the blanket-laden platform.

Allison fought, but was overpowered. She screamed, hoping that just maybe someone would intervene, but the noise only served to awaken Isaac who wailed pitifully from the hammock. Majiro's heavy forearm pushed against her throat and forced her to silence. Ignoring the baby, he unfastened her jeans with one hand. Her air was nearly cut off, and all she could do was scratch at his arm and gasp for each breath. Majiro was quick but cruel, using her body for his own pleasure.

For the most excruciating moments she had ever endured, Allison lay whimpering under his weight and listening to her son cry. Every time she moved to go to him, she was forced back down by Majiro's heavy hand. Eventually, Isaac fell asleep, and Majiro's body went limp across her own.

Allison extricated herself from beneath him, quickly re-dressed, and ran from the house. Barely out of the doorway, she doubled over and retched repeatedly into the tangled, jungle grass. Her insides felt like they were on fire, and her heart was seared. Spent, she sat down in the tall grass behind the house, rocking back and forth with her head resting on her knees.

Thinking of Eric, Allison's stomach heaved again with the realization that her husband had not been nor would ever be the only or the last man to touch her. The ache of Eric's death was all the more excruciating, and she wept with anguish.

The tentative hope from that afternoon was shattered. In its place was fury. *No, Lord. I absolutely refuse. I want no part of this horrible plan.* She spent the rest of the night under the stars.

CHAPTER **FOUR**

Allison, having not slept at all during the night, watched the dawn break over the village. The sweltering heat had taken a break for a few hours, and she enjoyed the night's cool moisture. As the darkness faded and the beauty of the morning surrounded her, the events of the previous evening almost seemed like a bad dream. Almost. She had cried for hours the night before and wished that somehow it would all be over soon. However, she had the sneaking suspicion that her ordeal was only beginning.

Startled by a noise nearby, she looked up to see Majiro emerge from the corner of the house. He was clearly upset. Looking around, his eyes quickly locked on Allison's form huddled beneath a tree a few feet from the back wall. He strode purposefully to her and began speaking quietly. She sensed his agitation, but had no idea what he was saying.

Finally, he took her by the arm and pulled her back inside the house. Once there he raised his voice and began gesturing wildly. By the motions he made to her, the bed, and the doorway, she deduced that he was unhappy about finding her outside that morning.

He continued raging in Shampiri until she finally interjected, "Okay. I got it. I'll stay inside at night."

Majiro's eyes narrowed angrily. As if insisting on having the final word, he repeated all that he had just said. This time his loud, deep voice woke Isaac who began crying from the hammock.

Side-stepping Majiro, she leaned over the hammock to pick up her son. Majiro's muscular arm shot out and held her back as he lifted the baby into his arms. Isaac was as startled as his mother and screeched even more loudly. Allison stood helplessly, hoping that he would tire of the crying and return her child, but he ignored her and bounced her son gently. By talking softly in a comforting tone, the warrior soon had the baby calm and playing with one of the beaded necklaces that lay across his broad chest. Looking up from Isaac, he reached for a discarded water pot in the corner and handed it to her. He motioned to the corner where a basket of yucca lay and then to the door.

Understanding the dismissal, Allison took the pot and left the house. The village was still quiet, though the sounds of talking and babies crying came from many of the homes. Soon the Shampiri would rise to face another day much like the previous one. For her, however, everything had irrevocably changed.

Once at the river, she looked around and realized that she was alone with the dawn sky. She laid the pot aside and stripped to her underwear, snorting at the condition of her blue T-shirt, jeans, and athletic shoes. The shirt and pants had been torn during the hike to the village and were discolored with unidentifiable stains. Her shoes were completely caked with mud and beginning to grow mold inside.

She waded slowly into the icy water, her breath catching as she forced herself deeper into the river. She was grimy and smelly, and the water was marvelous. Though she would have paid a hefty price for a bar of soap, she was glad for the chance to rinse off the filth of the past week. And what a week it had been. Though too numb to weep again, she wondered how her family and friends had reacted to the news of the tragedy at the jungle base. She wondered if her teammates had managed to make it safely into the strong house, or if their lives had ended as abruptly as her husband's had. *Eric, I wish you were here. You would know what to do and how to protect me.*

She had to get away. Away from the village, away from Majiro. She looked across the river and for a moment contemplated simply walking into the jungle. Better to starve or get eaten by a jaguar than to face going back to the reality that awaited her. Just as she prepared to swim to the other side, she remembered the one thing that kept her prisoner here. She could not leave her son, and she could not take him into the jungle, knowing that to do so would surely lead to his death. With a sigh, she swam back to her clothes and put them on again.

Dreading the return to the house, Allison sat in the sand and tried to pray. This morning, it seemed, her prayers went nowhere. Instead, she cried in despair and frustration.

She was still in tears when a voice behind her called, "Imeshina." Allison recognized her Shampiri name and turned to see Amita walking toward her, a water pot balanced on her head.

"*Ari,* Imeshina."

Allison understood the greeting, and responded with, "*Ari,* Amita."

Amita cocked her head to one side and studied the other woman's pale, tear-streaked face. She smiled the same sad smile from the night before and gently reached out to wipe away the tears on Allison's cheeks. She spoke a few quiet words, and though Allison did not know what they meant, they comforted her.

Setting her own pot on the sandy shore, Amita picked the other one up and began filling it with river water. She gave it to Allison, filled her own pot, and motioned for her to follow her toward the trail to the village.

Allison walked behind the small woman back toward the clearing, but a fork in the trail led them to a different house. The home was very similar to Majiro's, but this house had three young children around the already blazing fire in front. The eldest, a girl who looked to be around seven years old, stood stoking the fire. At her feet were two boys playing naked in the dirt. They were small, probably three and four years old.

Amita poured the water from her water pot into the one sitting on the fire that was filled with soaking bananas. She gave her daughter the empty pot and directed her to put it away in the house. As the girl went inside, a man came out. It was the warrior who had spoken Spanish to her. Allison looked at him in surprise, and he smiled kindly.

"*Ari*," he greeted and walked off into the jungle behind the house, likely to relieve himself as that was the only place to do so.

Noting Allison's surprise, Amita said, "*Manitari, esposo.*" Allison nodded her understanding.

For a few moments, she enjoyed watching Amita's family. They were a happy group. The children were obedient and loving toward their mother, and Amita managed them with a firm tone and a smile. Manitari played with his boys with obvious pleasure. Allison ached over the brokenness of her own family as she thought about Isaac who would never remember his father. Finally, realizing she could dawdle no longer, she carried her water pot back toward the trail.

When she arrived, Majiro was outside with Isaac and did not acknowledge her. She pretended to ignore him too, but she was conscious of his every movement. He was such a difficult man to read. Obviously strong of will and intelligent, he took in everything around him without expression and responded to his environment with iron determination. The events of the previous night were far from forgotten, but Allison knew that for her own peace, she had to learn to perform the tasks he set before her efficiently.

She stoked the ashes of the fire and eventually got it to flame. Then, she began making breakfast as she had seen Inani do the day before. Luckily, the dish was simple, and her first attempt at preparing yucca was successful. Allison stood back watching Majiro eat it ravenously near the fire in front of their house. After a few pieces, he looked up from his meal and smiled at her. She stared back at him, her face stony.

As Majiro ate, little Isaac toddled near his feet. He had cared for the child the entire morning while Allison had completed her chores, and Isaac now seemed perfectly content with the warrior. Majiro broke off a piece of his boiled yucca and handed it to Isaac who immediately began gumming the treat. The yucca fell into the dirt, and Isaac began sobbing. Chuckling, Majiro picked up the food and rinsed it in the leftover water in the cooking pot before returning it to him.

Allison pulled her own portion of yucca out of the pot and sat down to eat it. Watching Majiro with her son was at least interesting. The differences between them were almost comical. The Shampiri warrior was as dark as mahogany, with straight, black hair cropped straight across his forehead and eyes so dark that the pupil nearly disappeared. Isaac, in comparison, had creamy skin, brown curls and the same green eyes as his mother's.

Isaac pulled at Majiro's knee after he had finished his yucca, and the warrior reached to pull him into his lap. He spoke to the baby in a quiet voice as Isaac laid his head against the man's naked chest and yawned. For a few minutes, Majiro continued speaking softly as if telling a story. As Isaac's eyelids fluttered closed, he grinned triumphantly at Allison across the fire. Expressionless, she stood and left the house.

CHAPTER **FIVE**

Every morning for the next three days, Inani arrived soon after breakfast and ushered Allison off to a new lesson in Shampiri survival skills. Usually, she allowed Allison to keep Isaac with her, but on the third morning, she brought Amita's daughter, introduced as Micheli, and sent the girl away with Isaac on her hip.

Using the awkward form of charades they had adopted to communicate, Inani motioned for Allison to get a woven basket from the corner of the house and join her outside. Stepping into the bright sunlight, Allison shielded her eyes and saw that the older woman had a basket of her own.

"*Jaame*," Inani said, indicating that she should follow along. The two walked into the jungle on a path that Allison had never been on before, going in the opposite direction of the river. Wondering where they were headed, she sped her pace to keep up with Inani who was walking along the narrow trail as easily as if it were an empty ten-foot-wide sidewalk.

Not able to see well underneath the basket she held in front of her, her foot caught underneath a root snaking along the soil's surface on the trail, and she sprawled out, face in the dirt.

Inani clucked her tongue and scurried back to offer her a hand to help her to her feet. She jabbered something that Allison took to mean "be careful," and started back up the trail.

Quickly checking herself for injuries, Allison rubbed her scratched hands against her filthy jeans. She grabbed her basket from the ground and hurried to catch up.

They walked in silence for over an hour until the jungle suddenly opened up to reveal a small plot of land with plants of all kinds and in all stages of maturity dotting the area haphazardly. Some trees grew in the field, but they were mostly banana trees of some variation or another.

Inani waved her hand around at the garden. "*Ianequi Majiro,*" she said, and Allison looked around appreciatively at what must be Majiro's garden.

"Very nice," she replied, smiling to convey her meaning.

Inani put her arm through Allison's and led her around the garden pointing out various plants and urging her to practice their Shampiri name. Many of the plants Allison recognized by the vegetable growing amid the green leaves. There was a small section of skinny corn stalks and another of yellow gourds growing like pumpkins along a thick vine. There was also an impressive array of fruit growing in the garden. Aside from the bananas, she saw a cluster of pineapple plants, a row of melons, and even a few pepper plants growing near the north edge.

However, the plant that was most abundant was one that she did not immediately recognize. It was a short bush with skinny stalks ending in clusters of seven slender leaves.

Inani squatted next to one of the plants. "*Caniri,*" she said.

Remembering the often used word for the Shampiri main staple, Allison bobbed her head. "*Caniri,*" she repeated. "Yucca! No wonder there is so much of it."

Pulling a short knife from the bottom of her basket, Inani quickly sawed through the few stalks attaching the plant to the earth. She tossed the branches and leaves aside and stood, pulling firmly on the trunk. The ground gave way as long tubular roots appeared in the turned-up soil. The women bent down and dug the yucca roots the rest of the way out and tossed each one into the basket. They harvested the roots of only three plants because each produced a half-dozen foot-long roots, weighing several pounds each, which quickly filled their two baskets. After each harvest, Inani cut off a section of one of the stalks and thrust it back into the ground where it had been before.

Finished with the yucca plants, Inani also cut a stalk of ripe cooking bananas and added them to the top of her basket. She motioned for Allison to lean over so that she could strap the basket onto her head. Allison eyed the basket doubtfully, but complied. Once it was laid on her back, she very nearly toppled over.

Seeing her struggle, Inani grinned and took a couple of yucca from Allison's basket and added them to her own. In one fluid motion, she strapped the basket to her forehead, stood, and began walking back toward the trail, her body leaning forward and hands gripping the top of the basket at her shoulders.

Allison mimicked Inani's posture, but still found the basket cumbersome and uncomfortable. Yet, to the defense of the ancient transportation method, she could not fathom a better way to get that much weight over the little trail and back to the village.

At first, Inani rushed up the trail, but after realizing for the third time that Allison had stopped for a break, she sent the younger woman ahead to set the pace. The trip back took them twice as long as going to the garden had, but eventually they made it to Majiro's house.

Allison slipped the strap off her forehead, and the basket fell to the ground with a thud. She arched her back to stretch the kink out of her lower back and rubbed her head where the strap had dug in painfully.

Just as she was thinking about finding Isaac and nursing him until they both fell asleep, Inani put a water jar in her hands. "*Ojajaqui. Nonigue nija.*"

Allison nodded dully and walked slowly to the trail to the river. She hoped that this was the last chore for the morning because in lieu of an aspirin, she was in desperate need of a drink and a nap.

The river bank was deserted, and she lingered only long enough to wash her sweaty face and fill the water jar. She toted the jar back up the path, thankful that it was not as heavy as the basket of yucca had been.

At the edge of Majiro's yard, she set the jar down and lifted her hand to brush the sweaty hair from her eyes. All of a sudden a foot appeared in her line of vision, kicking the jar at her feet and tipping it over. Water ran into the dirt making a wide puddle of mud.

Astonished, she looked into the glaring face of the warrior who had nearly killed her during the attack. He looked no less threatening today.

As she took a fearful step back, Inani appeared in Majiro's doorway. "Sema!" she called out to the warrior. Before turning to Inani, he carefully rearranged his features into a pleasant smile.

Sema chatted with the older woman for a few minutes until he said goodbye and walked away. Warily, Allison watched him go wondering why he had tormented her and how soon it would be before she saw him again.

"Imeshina!" Allison looked back at Inani, who was shaking her head and sighing in disgust. She pointed to the puddle of water and the empty jar and rambled something in Shampiri.

Allison shrugged, unable to explain. Inani picked the jar up off the ground and gave it her again. "*Otsepa,*" she said firmly and pointed to the trail.

Trudging back to the river, hot tears of frustration ran down her face. She was not sure if she could go on much longer living with the Shampiri, but, unfortunately, it did not look like she had any choice.

The evening finally came, and Allison was grateful to be done with Inani's lessons. The little village quieted as people began to prepare for the night. Without any source of light other than the fires in front of the houses, the natives rose with the sun and went to bed soon after dark. She hastily rocked Isaac to sleep in the hammock and climbed onto the sleeping platform while Majiro was still outside speaking to another man. She scooted as close to the wall as she could and closed her eyes hoping to at least look like she was sleeping.

Soon enough Majiro came inside. She felt his eyes on her as he stood next to the platform and soon felt his hand on her hip. White-hot rage boiled her blood, and she sat around and slapped him full on the face. "Don't touch me!" she hissed.

A second later, his fist slammed into her mouth, cutting her lip against her teeth. She cried out in pain, but that did little to deter his rage as he pulled her off the platform and onto the dirt below. Adrenalin surged in her veins along with fearful desperation. She struggled with him, ignoring every blow, and soon drew his blood as well. They rolled around on the floor, crushing baskets and knocking over jars.

Finally, Majiro pinned her to the ground, kneeling over her with both of her wrists held above her head in his strong grip. With the other hand, he assaulted her, ignoring her ongoing protests and weeping.

At long last it was over, and Majiro stood up. Ignoring her, he dusted himself off and settled onto the platform to sleep. Allison remained on the ground, curled on her side in the dirt. It seemed that the tears would not stop coming until a soft giggle caught her attention. She looked across the room and saw her son, wide awake and watching her. A wave of revulsion spread through her as she realized what he had just witnessed. She joined him in the hammock and sang to him quietly until he fell back to sleep. One thing was clear to her, fighting Majiro was not an option any longer—at least not when her son was around. It made her furious that she would have to allow Majiro to have his way with her whenever and however he pleased, but she refused to expose Isaac to that kind of violence again. At least she could protect her son, even though it seemed that there was no one around to protect her.

CHAPTER **SIX**

During the following days, Allison walked around numb. It felt as if life was moving all around her, but she was not participating. The Shampiri, for the most part, welcomed her into their community with kind curiosity. Of course, there were those who ignored her and others who watched her fearfully from afar, but many sought her out and tried to draw her into conversations that she could not follow.

Though thankful for the distraction of those new relationships, her mind constantly turned to home, and she wondered about her family and friends. What did they think happened to her? How were her teammates handling the aftermath of the violence that had erupted on that day? She also frequently fantasized about being rescued or escaping, each time in a different way. But as the days turned into weeks, her hope dwindled.

Maybe that was why she did not really notice when the fever started. It was muggy in the jungle anyway as the rainy season brought daily downpours, and her depression made her listless. Her head throbbed, but she simply tried her best to ignore it. After all, it was not like she could go pull an aspirin out of the medicine cabinet. Her first inclination that maybe there was something else amiss was when she tried to stand up from weeding in Majiro's garden and immediately dropped back to her knees.

Putting her hand to her sweaty forehead, she took a few deep breaths and waited for the spinning to stop. Unfortunately, the garden was far enough away from the village that she was not sure she could make it back alone without getting lost.

Majiro was also in the garden plowing up a section of corn that had already been harvested, but she did not want to speak to him. He did not often accompany her to the garden because he spent many mornings dealing with problems and conflicts among the tribe. From observing this, she had deduced that he must be the village chief. The truth was that she loathed the man, hated the very sight of him. During the day he was mostly helpful, though occasionally indifferent, as she learned to navigate life among the tribe. But each night he obliterated every speck of warmth that might have grown between them. She would rather crawl across glass than ask him for anything.

Instead she gathered up Isaac who was happily toddling in the dirt nearby and settled under a shade tree to nurse him. Soon they were both dozing, though she did not realize it until Majiro's deep voice jolted her awake.

She peered up at him, but could not see his face through the hazy drizzle that had started while she slept. However, she could understand his hand gestures, so she stood on wobbly legs to return to the village. Majiro had a heavy basket laden with freshly harvested corn and yucca on his back, so the only load she carried was her son. Allison looked at the basket doubtfully. It was not likely that she could have gotten more than a few steps with it even on her best day.

They made their way slowly, and she felt her legs grow heavier each step. Isaac, fresh from his nap, was wiggly and required all of her attention to keep him from jumping out of her arms.

"Majiro," she gasped, stopping suddenly in the trail. He turned and looked at her with a question in his eyes, but she did not know how to explain to him that she was suddenly dizzy and that there was a strange fuzzy haze around her.

He paused for a moment, and then seemed to decide that whatever was wrong with her was better and started walking again. With a soft groan, she followed. Finally, they broke through the edge of the village clearing. Having the forethought to set her son down first, Allison fainted into a heap on the dirt.

For a while, all she was conscious of was alternating fire and ice. The fire would consume her body, and she would writhe, trying to free herself from its fangs. In the next moment, cold settled in her bones, and she would shiver so violently that her teeth would chatter.

Kind hands held her, bathing her flaming face with cool water and tucking blankets under her chin after she kicked them off again with her thrashing. Soon, however, she began to be aware of sound. Voices, both soft and deep, conversed unintelligibly. Then the steady beat of a drum pounded inside her skull. At first, she thought it was just her headache, but soon she realized that there really was a drum beating not far from her head.

She managed to pry one eyelid open just enough to see Inani seated on the ground next to her holding a small drum and swaying as she hit it rhythmically with a closed fist. Occasionally she would chant softly for a moment, but mostly she let the dark cadence of the instrument reign. The eerie sound raised the hair on the back of Allison's neck, but she had neither the strength nor the knowledge to ask the woman to stop.

For what seemed like hours the rhythm continued, and she struggled against the weakness of her body. Finally, a slow trickle of strength began to flow into her bones, and she was at last able to raise her head off of the mat.

Inani, seeing the movement, quickly laid aside the drum and knelt next to her. She moved a hand from Allison's forehead to her stomach and smiled slightly.

"Please, help me up." Allison pleaded through cracked lips. Inani looked at her curiously, then slid an arm around her shoulders and helped her sit.

The house was dark as all the Shampiri houses were, but the sunlight peeking through the cracks on the wall assured her that it was still daytime. However, her aching breasts also hinted that she had been under Inani's care for a long time.

Allison groaned in pain. Every joint in her body, from her hips to the tiny bones in her fingers and toes, ached. For that matter, so did her stomach. She pushed back the blanket from her legs and stood. "I have to go to the bathroom," she explained, despite knowing that her English words were useless. Without waiting for help, she rushed outside into the jungle a few feet behind Inani's home.

She had always thought that being sick anywhere away from home was one of the worst feelings. All of the traveling that she and Eric had done had left her quite an expert in that regard. But this experience topped them all. She could think of no price too high for a clean bathroom—or even a dirty one, a pillow, and access to a pharmacy.

Once the heaving in her midsection diminished to a quiet gurgle, she stumbled back around to the front of the house. She looked at the cloudy sky, surprised that it was mid-day. She must have been unconscious at least overnight. As she dawdled, Inani stuck her head out of the door and ushered her back inside like a concerned mother hen.

"Where is Isaac?" Allison asked motioning.

"*Ashi Majiro.*" Well, at least he was in good hands. Majiro had proven himself to be a surprisingly capable babysitter.

"I need to feed him." She turned to go back outside, but the older woman blocked her way and pulled her back down onto the sleeping mat.

Propping herself up on her elbows, she watched Inani scurry around the one room house pulling bits of dried herbs from bundles hanging from the rafters into a wooden bowl. She set the bowl down next to Allison. A little of the water was added to the herbs, enough to turn it into a gooey, pungent paste. Allison wrinkled her nose at the smell.

"*Pimaaque.*" Inani ordered and motioned for her to lie back.

Allison complied, curious about the native woman's intentions but not very concerned about them. The herbs seemed innocuous enough.

Surprisingly, Inani put a wad of the herb medley into her own mouth and chewed it for a few moments. However, instead of swallowing, she tugged Allison's shirt up around her rib cage and spit the green goo onto her stomach.

Allison yelped in surprise as the mess hit her belly, but Inani ignored her and continued her work. She rubbed the herbs in wider and wider circles, as if trying to work them into Allison's skin. She continued on spitting and rubbing until the bowl was emptied. Then she took up her drum and began anew the chant from before.

Realizing that she was in the middle of some sort of healing ritual, Allison tried to decide what, if anything, she should do. On one hand, she did not want to insult the woman that had been so kindly caring for her. But on the other, she was completely uncomfortable with this foreign custom.

She sat up and pulled her shirt back down, leaving it to stick on her stomach. "I really need to go find Isaac," she said, hoping that Inani would not be offended.

Despite her weakness, she was determined to go, and she walked out with more vigor than she felt. Thankfully, Majiro's house was only a few buildings down. She spotted him sitting peacefully under one of the trees in front of the house. Isaac was napping in his arms, his long, dark lashes brushing across the tops of his pudgy cheeks.

Majiro saw her coming and stood with the baby. Allison reached for him and was glad when he was given up without a word. Nursing would have to wait until he woke, but at least she could enjoy the comfort of holding him close.

For a few more hours she rested, first dozing with her sleeping son and then nursing him until they both sighed with relief. Then she realized that she had better prepare dinner if they were to have anything to eat before nightfall.

Majiro was nowhere to be found, so she carried Isaac with one arm and her water jar with the other and walked slowly to the river. She felt some better, but still her head ached and her stomach lurched every half hour. She was looking forward to a quick dip in the river to cool off and wash the green crust from her shirt and her body.

The river was refreshing, however the hike back to the village with her son and the heavy water jar nearly did her in. It was sheer determination that kept her on her feet long enough to get home and get a pot of yucca boiling on the fire.

Hands shaking, she sat next to the fire. As sweat dripped down her neck, she realized that her fever must be up again. She would have to manage as best she could until Isaac fell asleep.

Once the yucca was cooked, she poured out the hot water and offered Majiro his choice of the pieces of root. The thought of eating made her nauseated, so instead she drank as much boiled banana juice as she could because she knew that getting dehydrated would only make her feel worse.

Her son waddled back and forth between her and Majiro, stealing bites of yucca and sips of juice. Fortunately, he was ready for bed soon after the meal. Like all the other native children, he had grown accustomed to sleeping as soon as the sky darkened.

She settled him into the hammock and flopped onto the sleeping platform. Completely exhausted, she could do nothing but roll over and fall into a fitful sleep.

Her rest was light enough that she was aware when Majiro laid next to her a few hours later, his body, thankfully, rolled away from her. She was also aware of the aching chill in her bones, and she tossed and turned for hours trying to find a comfortable position.

Majiro sat up on the platform and put a hand to her forehead. "Imeshina!" Though conscious that he was shaking her shoulders, she was unable to open her eyes for the pain in her head. It felt like a spike was being driven through each eye. Instead she groaned and rolled away.

She felt herself being lifted and carried into the cool night. The moist air cut through her thin shirt, and she began to tremble. Soon she was brought inside and laid gently on the floor. Inani's voice issued orders and a scurry of activity ensued as she slipped in and out of consciousness.

The crackling of a fire finally roused her to open her eyes. She was surprised to see that the fire was only a few feet from her head, right inside the home. The roof above was dried grass that would surely burn down within minutes if a stray ember were to fall on it. However, no one seemed terribly concerned.

After Inani added some fragrant herbs to the fire, the drumming began again, bringing with it an overwhelming darkness. Suddenly death terrified her like it never had before. She had no fear of what would happen to her after she died—she was completely convinced that heaven awaited her—but she was frightened at the thought of leaving her son.

Surely Majiro would continue to raise him as his son, and Isaac would be loved and provided for. Yet, the weight of his spiritual upbringing rested solely on her shoulders. There would be no one else who could teach him about the God who created him, loved him, and offered him eternal hope. If she were gone, he would grow up in a position of honor as the chief's son, but would never know what it was like to be a child of God.

She began to pray earnestly for Isaac and for her own healing, pleading for God to spare her for his sake. At last, the shadows lifted and she slept.

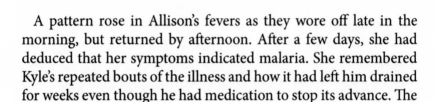

A pattern rose in Allison's fevers as they wore off late in the morning, but returned by afternoon. After a few days, she had deduced that her symptoms indicated malaria. She remembered Kyle's repeated bouts of the illness and how it had left him drained for weeks even though he had medication to stop its advance. The cyclical fevers, headaches, and diarrhea could lead to dangerous dehydration and even death if not treated.

For this reason, Allison rested. Even after she returned to Majiro's house, she refused to get up for more than a few minutes. She drank until she felt like she was going to explode and even decided to begin weaning her son. And she prayed. For hours every day, in between naps and visits from Inani and Amita, she prayed for her loved ones back home, for Isaac, for the Shampiri, and for herself.

In the middle of one such prayer, she heard the chattering of familiar voices outside.

"*Ari*" Amita greeted as she entered the dark room.

Smiling, Allison motioned her inside. She was glad for the visit for she was growing restless with nothing to do but think, pray, and sleep all day.

"You look good," Amita noted.

Pausing to think of how to form her words correctly in Shampiri, Allison replied, "A little."

"Where is Isaac?"

"With Majiro. What are you doing today?" These were some of the very few simple phrases that she could speak, but, as Amita launched into a detailed explanation of her chores, she realized that she could actually understand some of what was said. Being inundated daily with Shampiri was paying off.

Amita broke off as deep voices approached the house. They were not loud, but clearly in an argument. Grabbing Allison's arm, Amita hissed, "It's Sema!"

The women froze and listened to the conversation outside. She wondered what business Sema had here, for he had avoided her since their last confrontation in front of Inani's house. The only interaction she had with him was receiving icy glares whenever their paths accidentally crossed.

"I don't understand what they are saying," she whispered.

"Shhhh! Sema is angry."

"Why?"

Before Amita could answer, the door slammed open, and the two men entered. Pointing at the women, who were sitting wide-eyed on the sleeping platform, Majiro said, "See for yourself! She is well." Sema ground his teeth, spun around, and went out the door without another word.

After Majiro had returned outside, Allison asked her friend to explain what had happened. Unfortunately, despite Amita's repeated explanation, all she understood was that Sema had tried to convince Majiro that her illness was a sign and that she should be taken out of the village and left to die. The fact that she was recovering was enough to send the angry man back home. What she could not understand was what kind of sign her illness was supposed to be or why Sema was so intent on getting rid of her.

"It's okay. You'll explain it to me another day," she finally said.

Amita rose to leave. "Don't worry, Imeshina," she said patting Allison's arm. "You are safe here. Majiro is the chief, and you won't be sent away unless he agrees." The corner of Allison's mouth rose at the irony, but she appreciated the other woman's comfort. It was nice to hear the reassurances, even if they were hollow. She did not think she could ever feel safe again.

CHAPTER SEVEN

"Good morning," Allison greeted Amita. As had become their routine over the past few months, they met in the early hours of the morning at the river.

"Hi," Amita replied, reaching out and tickling Isaac's tummy. "What's he doing with you this morning?" she asked.

After pausing for a few seconds to think of the words Allison explained, "Majiro is hunting."

The two sat down companionably in the sand and watched Isaac explore the shore. He had changed dramatically since their arrival. His walking was sure, and his curiosity about the world around him had enlarged as Majiro toted him around the village and allowed him to investigate to his heart's content. Allison had discarded his shredded clothes and allowed him to go naked like the other children. The only cloth diaper she had was washed daily, dried, and used during the night.

"He is getting brown like a Shampiri," Amita commented.

Allison laughed, "Yes." She wished she knew how to explain that he had also begun speaking a few Shampiri words. Thinking about his quick adaptation to a new language was also sobering as it reminded her that many of her child's first words were in the language of a foreign people. In the midst of the joy of seeing her son grow was the constant pain of realizing she could not share his accomplishments with Eric.

Amita observed the change in Allison's face. "You are sad," she stated.

"Yes."

"You are thinking of Isaac's father?"

Allison sighed and replied, "Yes. He was... hunted?"

At first, Amita's expression was puzzled, but then she realized what Allison was trying to explain. "You mean killed." She motioned as if to draw back and shoot an arrow.

"Yes, when I came here."

Instead of responding, Amita reached for Allison's hand. It was something that Allison appreciated the most about her new friend. The only other physical contact that she had with another adult was the nearly nightly torture she silently endured, counting her own heartbeats while Majiro took his pleasure. Amita's hugs and caresses were comforting and reminded her that some touch made no requirement of her.

Allison stood, gathered her full water pot and son, and said, "I must go. Majiro will return soon." They walked together until the fork in the trail sent them each to their respective homes.

She was glad that she had come back, for Majiro's hunting trip had been successful, and, shortly after she arrived, he returned with a heavy basket of wild pig. He walked back into the village with Sema, who had gone on to his own home while Majiro brought the game to Allison to deal with.

He dropped the basket to the ground with a thud and reached for the banana drink that she offered. She heaved the pig out of the basket without even a flinch. At the jungle base, Eric had always done the nasty job, but Allison had learned to dress game competently under the tutelage of Inani, who she learned was Majiro's mother.

With a few well-placed strokes of a sharp, pona-wood blade, Allison removed the pig's skin and laid it upside down across a tree branch. The natives used nearly every part of the animal. The skin was converted into a lining for baskets to make them waterproof. The teeth and bones were used for tools and decoration, and most of the organs were eaten.

She butchered the animal quickly. It would be divided between Majiro and Sema, though they would both give most of it away to others. Because there was no refrigeration, food spoiled very quickly unless it was dried into jerky. When meat was available, it was shared among as many as possible.

After wrapping half of the animal in banana leaves to protect it from flies, she returned the rest to the basket and walked to Sema's house. It was ten minutes into the jungle down a nearly invisible trail.

Neither Sema nor his wife or children were outside his home when she arrived. She called out a few times, but no one answered her. She decided to just leave the basket inside the house to protect it from any nearby animals. Pushing the tired door back on its wooden hinge, she said one last time, "Hello? Sema? I've brought you your meat."

She was surprised to hear a soft voice summon her inside. "Come in."

As she entered and her eyes adjusted to the dim light inside, she saw an old woman reclined on a mat in the corner. The woman's ancient face was lined with pain, but still she smiled in delight. "You are the foreign woman."

"Yes. Who are you? I've never seen you before."

The corners of the woman's eyes crinkled with good humor. "Well, I can't really get up, and you haven't been here to visit me before. I'm Onijaa, Sema's mother."

Allison left the basket next to the door and walked over to the mat. "Are you sick?" she asked, kneeling next to Onijaa.

"For a few months now." She motioned down at her abdomen. "It hurts inside when I try to walk." She took Allison's hand and pushed it against her belly. There was an obvious mass underneath the skin. "The spirits put something inside me, and it is growing." she explained.

Before she could say anything, Sema appeared in the doorway. "What are you doing here?" he demanded.

She hastily explained, "I... I was just bringing you the meat from your hunting trip. Your mother invited me in."

"Get out."

Inclining her head to Onijaa in a silent goodbye, Allison quickly complied. As she reached the doorway, Sema's wife entered. Her eyes grew wide at the sight of the foreigner, but she said nothing nor did she return Allison's smile. Sema shoved the little woman rudely out of the way and motioned for Allison to leave.

Once outside, he stood in front of her, his nose nearly touching her own. "Stay away from my mother and my house. I don't want a foreign witch smelling up the place."

"I'm sorry. I was just trying to—"

"*You* should not even be in this village," he growled. "It was my mistake for not killing you when I had the chance, but I won't make that mistake again. Now go!"

Her eyes wide in shock and fear, Allison hurried back up the trail. She had no doubt that Sema meant what he said. There was murder in his eyes.

A few days later, the village buzzed with excitement, though for what reason, Allison did not know. Late in the morning, Amita arrived, carrying a water pot full of frothy, pink beer.

"This is for tonight," the native woman said, setting the pot in the shade of a tree near the house.

"Tonight?"

Amita explained, "It's a party. At the end of every harvest, the Shampiri celebrate before we leave our village with the end of the rains. Each family will bring beer tonight, and we will celebrate all night long."Allison understood most of what was said, and the rest she was able to put together. Wishing she was able to ask all of the questions swirling in her head, she simply nodded and thanked her friend.

By the time the sun set that night, all the Shampiri gathered around a bonfire built in the center of the clearing. Many she had never seen before were there, and she surmised that they lived further up the trails in the jungle. The night filled with laughter and the noises of children as they chased each other and played games. The men brought split logs and placed them in a large ring around the fire.

Allison sat next to Amita's family with Isaac wide-eyed in her lap. She smiled at the villagers as they approached her, many asking her questions that she could not understand. Manitari and Amita tried their best to help her communicate with the others, but the noise made it nearly impossible.

Majiro stood and began speaking, and immediately the other conversations quieted. The children settled near their parents, listening respectfully.

Amita whispered, "He is talking about the good harvests we had this year. The earth was good to us."

Majiro did not speak for long, and when he returned to his seat, the merry-making began again. The women brought out the beer in pots and jars of all sizes and poured them into a hollowed-out log. Clay bowls were filled and passed around to each person, first to the men and then the children. Finally the women served themselves.

One of the warriors brought out an intricately carved drum with a thin gray skin stretched across the top and held in place with bone nails. He held it under his arm and began a slow beat. He chanted softly to the cadence, his husky voice picking up volume as the rhythm increased. It was a mournful sound. Allison could not understand the words that he was singing, but, nevertheless, the song made her sad. After a long while, the drum beat out a livelier tune, and many of the Shampiri began to sing in unison. Others danced to the side of the fire, their feet stomping the earth and hands clapping along.

Fascinated, Allison and Isaac watched together as the people celebrated. As the level of beer in the log dropped, the crowd became more animated. Manitari, who was seated on the other side of Amita, leaned over his wife and pointed to Allison's half-empty bowl. "Why do you not drink more *cachojari*?"

"I'm not thirsty," she responded, which made him laugh.

"We drink *cachojari* to celebrate, not because we are thirsty."

Allison smiled at him. "Yes, and tomorrow all Shampiri will be sick, but I will feel fine."

The people around who were observing the conversation thought her answer was hilarious and shared it with the others next to them. Manitari shook his head in wonder. "Imeshina, you may be smarter than all of the rest of us! Many of us will not even sleep in our own beds tonight. We will sleep where we are."

She did not realize what exactly he meant until a few hours later when the first man passed out. His daughter rolled him away from the fire while the rest of the tribe made fun of his inability to hold his liquor. Within another hour, a half dozen other men and women had joined him. Allison decided that she was finished with the party as it had degraded into raucous jokes and drunken games. Carrying her sleeping son, she picked her way over the bodies around the fire and through the crowd. No one seemed to notice her leaving.

It was very dark once she left the circle of the fire's light, and she had to watch the ground carefully to avoid tripping over the rocks, branches, and debris that littered the clearing. Inside the house, she laid Isaac in the hammock and sat on the edge of the sleeping platform wiping the dust from her feet.

Suddenly the door banged open, startling her. "Majiro! You scared me! Isaac was asleep, and I am tired. I thought..." The shadow moved toward her, and she realized that it was not Majiro but one of the natives whom she had not met before. He was not very tall, but like all the other Shampiri men, he was thick-chested and roped with lean muscles.

"Who are you? Leave my house!" she commanded, her voice more fierce than she felt.

Ignoring her, the man advanced and reached for her. She screamed and slapped his arm away. He did not seem surprised by her reaction, but all the more determined to have his way. His fingers grasped her hair and pulled her still screaming to the ground. She fought him, kicking and flailing, desperate to at least be outside, away from Isaac, who was now awake and crying. However, she quickly realized that she was no match for his strength. Just as she was prepared to give up her fight, the door flew open for a second time. As quick as a snake-strike, Majiro rushed in and flung the man across the room.

The man scrambled back against the wall, his eyes showing his confusion. "Chief, I just wanted to use your woman."

"*No one* touches my woman or my son," Majiro growled. He plucked Isaac out of the hammock and passed him to Allison, who still lay on the floor, gasping for breath. He hauled her to her feet and then grabbed the other man by the hair and half-dragged them both back outside to the crowd.

A hush settled over the group as they saw their chief shove the man to the ground. He motioned to Allison. "This is my wife. No man but me can have her. This is my son. You will all treat him with the respect due a chief's son."

No one said anything as Majiro led Allison back to their house. "No one will bother you now. Go to bed." He left the house, closing the door softly behind him.

After finally getting Isaac calmed down and back to sleep, Allison laid on the platform for a long while listening to the sounds of the party outside. The rage that Majiro had shown both scared and reassured her. She had little doubt that his order would be followed, but she also feared being the object of such wrath. Shivering, Allison prayed until her mind calmed and she fell asleep.

CHAPTER **EIGHT**

"**D**o we have enough fuel to make another pass over that river bend?" Eric asked into the speaker of his headset. He was seated in a small, six-seat airplane that was owned by a mission agency and used exclusively to fly missionaries in and out of their jungle bases.

The pilot next to Eric checked the panel of the airplane. "We have enough fuel," he replied. "I'm just worried about it getting dark on us... I think we can make one more pass over the area, but then I have to head straight back."

"Thanks, Jack." Eric offered a smile to his pilot buddy.

Eric was anxiously hopeful about finding his family now that he was a part of the search team. Allison and Isaac had been missing for nearly six weeks, but he had only just been released from the hospital in Lima, Peru's capital city.

The attack had caught them all by surprise. When the first arrow was shot into camp and the chaos began, he was shocked. Once he realized what was going on, he ran to the river to find his wife and son. Unfortunately, an arrow pierced him from behind before he even got close, and he immediately passed out. Though he regained consciousness while the attack was still going on, he was too weak to move. To his horror, he helplessly watched through the grass as Allison was carried screaming down the trail to the river. Soon thereafter his teammate Tim found him. He was carried into the strong house where the rest of the team was gathered. Kyle was injured as well with a flesh wound to his shoulder and was preoccupied with Jamie who was critically wounded.

After radioing for help, Tim broke the shaft of the arrow near Eric's skin and used rags to stifle the flow of blood. Hours later Eric was loaded, again unconscious, into the mission airplane on the base airstrip and flown to Iquitos. There he was stabilized, given a blood transfusion, and sent to a more equipped hospital in Lima.

In Lima, he required surgery to repair damage done to his colon, but, to the surprise of many, was otherwise unharmed. The recovery from surgery was entirely too long, in Eric's opinion, because a nasty infection of the surgical site prolonged his stay.

During his recovery, he heard of the many missionaries in Iquitos who had put their own work on hold in hopes of rescuing one of their own. Volunteers scoured the area around the jungle base on foot for any sign of the tribe they believed had taken Allison and Isaac. The pilots with the mission agency graciously donated their time as well as the airplane whenever it was not in use. As the story made its way back to the United States, strangers sent donations for Eric's medical bills and words of hope for the recovery of his family. Eric's parents immediately flew to Peru when they had received the news. Jean took on the role of advocate and caregiver for her hospitalized son, but, at Eric's request, David went on to Iquitos to join the search. Over a month later, Eric was finally free to join the ongoing search for his wife and child.

Eric turned his attention to the window and gazed down at the landscape below. They were a few miles east of the jungle camp, following the river. Unfortunately, the water's bank was the only break in the thick, green foliage dotted here and there with the occasional red or orange flowering tree. Usually Eric loved watching the jungle. It always filled him with reverence as he contemplated the vastness of God's creation. Today, however, it seemed like a leafy prison holding his family captive.

The plane circled around the river bend before heading back toward Iquitos. Eric and Jack were silent, both wishing their return was with good news.

Jack finally spoke up, "I'm sorry, Eric. Do you want to go out again tomorrow morning? It's Saturday, so we have no scheduled flights."

Eric blew his dark hair out of his eyes—it had grown long during his hospital stay. "Yeah, but I have to get my mom to the airport first. She has been here for a month. My dad left a couple of weeks ago to go back to work, but my mom was able to get a leave of absence from her job. I told her she should go back home now that I am out of the hospital."

"A blessing they could come," Jack observed.

"I just wish it hadn't been necessary. It makes me so angry that I couldn't do more…"

"It wasn't your fault."

Eric turned his tortured brown eyes to Jack's face. "You've never had to watch your wife being kidnapped and been unable to do a thing to help her." He slammed his fist against his knee. "I am supposed to be the one to protect her!"

"Do you think they are still alive?"

Eric muttered forcefully, "I *have* to believe that."

Jack focused on flying the plane. Luckily they were near Iquitos now and would be on the ground before the darkening sky made their landing dangerous.

The remaining minutes of the flight ticked by slowly as each man was lost in his own thoughts. When they landed, Eric waited patiently in the plane while Jack went through the post flight checklist. As they emerged from the airplane, he was surprised to see his mother sitting on an old metal chair in a corner of the hangar.

"What are you doing here?" he asked, giving her a quick hug.

Jean returned the squeeze. "I thought maybe we could go to dinner together tonight since I'm flying home tomorrow morning."

"That would be nice," Eric replied. "I haven't eaten since this morning. Let me say good-bye to Jack, and then we can go."

Eric thanked the pilot and made plans with him to fly the next day. He helped his mother into the dusty, diesel pickup truck and drove the few miles back into town. After suggesting several restaurants to Jean, he drove to the one she chose that specialized in Peruvian jungle meats. It was a favorite for many of the tourists that visited the area because of both its tasty food and its reputation for cleanliness.

When they arrived at the crowded restaurant, the pair chose a semi-private table in a back corner. Silence dominated as they each struggled with what to say to the other. Jean's upcoming departure highlighted the length of time it had been since the abduction and the lack of progress in the search for Allison and Isaac.

It was not until they had ordered that Jean broke the silence. "Son, I'm concerned about you."

Eric's dark eyes were guarded. "What do you mean?"

Searching for the right words, his mother paused for a moment before explaining, "You are not eating well. I know that you're not sleeping because I hear you walking around at all hours of the night. You're... obsessed with the search—"

"Mother, my family is lost out in that jungle somewhere. Do you really expect me not to be 'obsessed' with finding them?" he asked.

"Of course you want to find them. I'm not saying that you shouldn't be..."

"Then what exactly are you saying?"

Jean sighed, "It's been over a month."

"So..." Eric trailed off as their food arrived. Though *paiche* was one of his favorite river fish, Eric could hardly stand the tantalizing smell of the plate in front of him. His mother was right; he had no appetite these days. It was hard to enjoy a meal when he knew that his family might be going hungry.

Jean took a few bites of her strip steak and grilled plantain bananas. "I spoke to Marshall Herring today," she said.

"You're changing the subject," Eric said.

"Actually I'm not. You know that Marshall has lived in South America nearly his whole life. His parents worked in a primitive tribe much like the Shampiri." Jean stopped speaking until Eric looked into her sad eyes. "Eric, he believes that after such a long time with no sign of them... He doesn't think that the Indians would have allowed either of them to live."

Eric's fork clattered on his plate. "What is wrong with you people?" he cried. "First Jack, and now you and Marshall! My wife and son are not dead, and I will not give up looking for them because it's taking longer than we expected!" His raised voice caused several heads to turn, and eyebrows rose at the two Americans. They both sat silently for a few moments, embarrassed by Eric's outburst.

Jean would not give up. "But how long until you realize that they won't be found?" she asked. "How long will you wait until you decide it is time to move on?"

"Mom," Eric whispered. "This conversation is over."

For the remainder of the meal the two tried to talk of other things, but the gulf between them was wide. He knew that his mother simply wanted to take his hurt away. What she did not realize was that without the possibility of his family's return, he could scarcely face the idea of living.

The next evening, Eric returned to his house in Iquitos despondent. It had been another uneventful day in the sky and now his mother was not even around to distract him. Unable to muster the energy even to heat the leftovers she had stocked in his refrigerator, he simply grabbed a soda and sat down at the dining room table.

Where are they, Lord? Can You give me some help here, some guidance? I know You know exactly where they are. Could You just point me in the right direction?

But there was only the tick of the wall clock to break the silence around him. He got up and walked into the living room only to flop back down on the couch. Directly across from him was a picture from his wedding day. It was Allison's favorite, and so she had it enlarged, framed, and placed in a prominent place in their home.

He stared at the image, at his bride. She looked in the photo exactly how he remembered her a couple of months ago—beautiful, sweet, and full of joy and optimism, exactly the way she had been since the first time he saw her. That day was forever a bright spot in his memory.

He had been a junior partner at his father's law firm and, along with an entourage of paralegals, had gone with his father for a meeting at a marketing agency.

The secretary opened the door and motioned for the legal team to enter the conference room where several of the marketing executives were already waiting. He knew most of them by name from his earlier interactions, so he greeted them cordially. One face he did not recognize, and it was pretty enough that he was sure he would have remembered.

"Hi. I'm Eric Carter," he said, sticking his hand out.

"Allison Wainwright." She stood, and he noticed appreciatively that her navy suit fit flawlessly over her trim figure, its modest skirt skimming the tops of her calves. She had a pair of killer legs, accentuated by high-heeled pumps.

Introductions completed, the group sat and the meeting started. More than once, Eric caught himself being distracted by the woman across the table from him, though she seemed to be oblivious to his stares.

It was something that she held his attention so easily, given the high emotions in the room. The negotiations were at a standstill, had been for weeks, with neither side willing to bend to the other. His father carried the bulk of the conversation, cajoling, manipulating, and even flat out threatening.

Finally it was over, with very little accomplished. The group gathered up legal pads, stuffed documents back into briefcases, and quietly shuffled to the door.

Eric managed to skillfully work his way around the room so that he ended up standing next to Allison at the doorway. However, his mouth went dry and uncharacteristic shyness took over as she glanced up at him in question. "Uh… I guess I'll see you next time—" he stuttered. "I mean, at our next meeting. Um…" He resisted the urge to smack his forehead.

Allison's green eyes danced, and her easy smile encouraged him. "Yes. I'm looking forward to that," she said.

It was just the shove he needed. "Do you want to catch lunch with me sometime?"

Her smiled widened. "Sounds like fun."

"How about tomorrow?" She agreed, and they made plans to meet up the next day at a restaurant between the two offices.

Realizing that his colleagues had already departed, he rushed to catch up. His dad held a hand out to stop the closing elevator door, and Eric dashed inside.

Keeping his gaze on the door, David asked, "Well, what did she say?"

"She said yes." Eric grinned and glanced over at his father. "How did you know I was asking her out?"

David laughed and clapped a hand across his shoulder. "You couldn't take your eyes off her the whole time we were in there. Why do you think I did all the talking?" Eric felt his face go hot as David continued to chuckle. At any rate, she had agreed to lunch, and he supposed that was worth making a fool of himself.

The next day, Eric was very late for their lunch date, so he was running by the time he made it inside the restaurant. Allison was already seated at a table, sipping lemonade. She was just as lovely as he remembered. Her cinnamon hair was in soft layers framing her heart-shaped face. And those eyes… as green as the sea and just as deep. He knew when she saw him because two spots of pink rose on her cheeks.

"Hi," she squeaked.

"Sorry I'm late."

"I thought maybe you changed your mind."

Eric pulled out a chair and grabbed the menu that was still sitting unopened across from her. "Not a chance." He smiled at her above the menu, and the color on her face deepened.

"Actually, I was on a conference call with a client. He had to repeat everything about six times before letting me hang up," he explained as the waitress arrived.

They gave their lunch orders, and Eric waited until the waitress left before asking, "So are you new to the marketing firm? I haven't seen you there before."

"Fairly new. I had a six-month probation period that kept me doing grunt work. They decided to release me from my cubicle a few weeks ago, and I got put on this project since Laura will be taking maternity leave soon."

"I see."

"I was kind of surprised to see you there too," Allison noted, and she rushed to explain. "I mean, you are really young. Usually the execs are pretty adamant about having the partners themselves for the meetings."

"I am a partner, actually. It helps to have your dad as the boss."

"Eric Carter. Got it. Family business, huh?"

Eric snorted. "Something like that. I guess it was just always assumed that I would follow in Dad's footsteps. Besides, I couldn't come up with anything better."

"I know exactly what you mean."

"Not a fan of marketing?"

Allison shrugged. "It's interesting and challenging. My parents died a few years ago, and I wanted to make sure I had a good job. Something stable, something safe. A business degree seemed like a good idea." She paused as the waitress arrived with their food.

Eric grabbed the ketchup bottle and squeezed a healthy dollop next to his fries. "What about other family? Do you have brothers or sisters?"

"Only child. No grandparents. My dad has a brother somewhere in the north, but I haven't seen him since I was little."

He said, "That must have been so hard. I can't imagine losing my parents."

"It was awful. But, you know, it was the thing that brought me to the Lord, so, in a way, I am thankful as well." Eric looked at her curiously. She seemed a bit shy, so it surprised him to hear her speak so easily about her faith to a stranger. It also delighted him.

"Were your parents believers?"

"Very much so. But it wasn't until they died that I made a decision about it myself."

Eric studied a drop of condensation rolling down the side of his glass. "My mom raised me and my brother in the church, but it didn't really mean a lot to me until a few years ago."

"What changed?" Allison asked.

"Nothing huge, like your experience," he replied, "I was assigned a roommate my first year of college. He never got into the parties and girls like I did. After that first year, we went our separate ways. He roomed with a buddy from his church, and I pledged to a fraternity. From all appearances, I had everything. I was on the football team, had good grades and a pretty girlfriend. But when I saw him around campus, I could see that he was the happy one. One day, I ran into him and asked him why he was so satisfied with his life. He told me about his relationship with God and how I could have my own."

"Your mom must have been thrilled."

"She was."

"And your dad?" Allison asked, as she set her spoon down over her empty soup bowl.

Eric snorted cynically. "Not so much. My dad has been apathetic toward Christianity at best. He was not at all excited about my decision, but as long as I didn't mess up his plans, he didn't intervene."

"Your dad does seem very... um, tenacious."

"Tenacious?" He laughed. "He's as stubborn as a mule in quicksand. Though, I guess that is what makes him so good at what he does."

Allison tapped the table with her forefinger thoughtfully. "Hmmm."

Watching her suddenly guarded expression, he asked, "What aren't you telling me, Allison Wainwright?"

She smiled. "It's just my observation..."

"Go on." he urged.

"Well, it seems like both of our offices are in a competition to see who can strong arm whom, which is a little silly since we are both supposed to be on the same side. I think my bosses are afraid of Mr. Carter taking advantage of them, so they are holding ground that they don't really care about anyway. I wonder if your dad took a more… gentle approach, if the issues would resolve on their own pretty quickly."

Eric stared at her, wondering if the answer to months of deliberations was that simple. If it was, she had just saved both sides countless hours of meetings and a bundle of money. "Do you really think that will do the trick?"

"You didn't hear anything from me."

Their third date was a week later. The weather report predicted sleet, so he invited Allison to his apartment for a cozy night complete with pizza and movies.

He opened the door in response to her knock and stood letting his gaze sweep over her. Wearing tattered jeans and a faded college sweatshirt, with her hair swept up in a messy ponytail, she was breathtaking.

"I brought hot chocolate," she said, holding out a box of Swiss Miss.

"With marshmallows?"

"Of course." She stepped inside, surveying the living room. She kicked off her shoes by the door and walked a slow circle around the room, looking at the art on his walls and photos on his shelves.

He held out three DVDs. "Here. Take your pick."

Taking the movies from his hand, she shuffled through them and held up the first one, a romantic comedy. "You don't really want to watch this. It's just safe because I am a girl." She tossed it onto the coffee table and held the other two for him to look at.

"This one is the one that you really want to see, but you figured you could settle for this old favorite if I refused the gory one."

He was both surprised and impressed with her deduction. "All right, Miss Smarty Pants, how did you figure that out?"

"Well, this one isn't a rental and has been watched a million times, and I don't know any man in his right mind that would want to watch a Hugh Grant movie. That leaves this one." She held up the winning DVD.

They settled down on the couch for the action film. The pizza arrived partway through, and they paused the DVD just long enough to pull gooey slices onto their plates. Eric wondered how much attention Allison was paying to the movie because he had difficulty focusing on the plot. Every move she made drew his attention, from her soft sighs to stretching those perfect, long legs across the coffee table.

Barely even conscious of doing so, he reached out and pushed a stray piece of hair behind her ear. Her hair was as soft as it looked, and he wanted to bury his face in it for a deep breath.

Allison reached for the remote and flipped the television off. "You're not paying much attention to the movie," she said.

"Sorry. I'm distracted. You are very beautiful."

She ducked her head and blushed. Sensing her need for a redirection, he pulled her closer to his side and put his arm around her shoulders. "My dad made a call to your boss today," he said.

"Oh?"

"Looks like you were probably right on. They are having lunch tomorrow, but from what my dad says, things should proceed smoothly."

"I'm glad." They lapsed into silence, but it was comfortable. He was just enjoying the feel and smell of her next to him.

"Eric?"

"Hmm?"

"Do you ever feel like God must have something more than this for you?" she asked.

"What do you mean?"

She looked up at him. "I mean, going to work, going to church, seeing friends… it's all great, but is that all there is? Don't we have a greater purpose?"

"I've heard people say that God gives everyone a purpose. It's just up to us to figure out what that is and then fulfill it."

"Do you know what your purpose is?"

"I guess I've always just thought it was to serve God however I can in my day to day life."

She nodded. "Yeah. Me too. But I wish there was something bigger, so that…" she trailed off as if unsure how to finish her thought.

"So that when your life is over it will have mattered that you lived?"

"Exactly!"

Eric nudged her sock-clad foot with his own. "How about it, Alli? Want to go save the world with me?" he joked.

Deep green eyes met his own, and he swallowed for the intensity of her gaze. It was as if she was reading his very soul. "Yes," she said softly.

That was the very beginning. Only a few months later, they were engaged, and a few months after that they left for their honeymoon in wedded bliss.

Closing his eyes against the image across from him, Eric leaned his head back against the couch. Maybe tonight he would see her in his dreams.

CHAPTER **NINE**

"**Y**uck," Allison muttered to herself as she wiped her bare foot off in the dirt. She had stepped in a wood ant nest in front of her house. The bugs scattered, each attempting to carry off a slimy egg that looked like an overcooked grain of rice. The Shampiri were arriving back in the main village after spending several months split into small groups and working in far away gardens. Now back at the main village, they would cultivate their local gardens until after the harvest at the end of the rainy season the following year.

Looking around her yard, she was baffled by how abandoned it looked after only a few months. The grass and vines had grown halfway up the house's walls, and in several places, the palm frond roof had caved in.

She sighed and decided to start a fire before tackling the bigger chores. After a brief stop in their garden, she had come straight home with Isaac while Majiro went hunting. With the tribe having been gone from the village for a while, he was sure that there would be plenty of game in the area.

After gathering dry branches from behind the house, she stacked them skillfully and dragged a flint rock against another stone. A spark flew from the rock and caught on the kindling at the bottom of the heap.

Nodding with satisfaction, she threw another branch into the fire and watched to make sure it lit up with flames as she wanted. It did. The lessons from Inani in the early months after she arrived in the village and those she had been given on the trail as they traveled around to other gardens paid off, and she now possessed most of the skills she needed to keep house. The only thing that she had yet to master was the intricate weaving by which the women made the skirts, hammocks, and baby slings that every family used. She helped the older woman pick the cotton from the garden and learned how to comb and twist it into threads. Finally, she helped dye the fibers with the sap of different plants, but that had been as much of the process that she could manage.

She had watched as Inani sat beneath a hand-made, wooden loom and made a skirt for her like the other women wore, as well as a shirt to match. It was a project that had taken the woman three months to complete. But the effort had been worth it when the beautiful teal, black, and white garments had been completed. The zigzag pattern that was used resembled that of the other fabrics in the village, but was unique to her skirt just as all fabrics varied according to the dies available and the imagination of the seamstress at the loom.

"Imeshina! You must come quickly!" Allison's head snapped around to see Amita's husband, Manitari, hurrying toward her.

"Is it the baby? Is the baby coming?" she cried, already rushing toward him. Amita's pregnancy had been difficult, and she was looking forward to its end almost as much as her friend.

"No, not the baby. It's Amita. She won't stop crying, and I don't know what to do with her. Can you come see what is wrong with her?"

"Of course, I'm coming now!" Allison moved the pot of yucca that sat on the fire to the side so that it would not boil dry and called for Isaac, who was playing nearby. She took her son by the hand and the two followed the worried warrior back to his house.

Manitari motioned through the doorway, and Allison entered the dark home to find her friend weeping on the sleeping platform. Her daughter stroked her hair with a worried frown. "Micheli, will you take Isaac?" Allison asked the girl. "I'll stay with your mother." Micheli, looking relieved, picked Isaac up and left the house.

She sat quietly next to her friend and held her hand. Amita did not look up but squeezed Allison's hand to acknowledge her presence. For several minutes the two women sat together, saying nothing. Eventually Amita's sobs died down to hiccups.

"What is going on, my friend? Manitari is worried about you." Apparently it was the wrong thing to say, for Amita's cries began again with fervor.

Gaining control of herself eventually, Amita said, "I hate that he is so kind to me."

Allison's eyebrows shot to her forehead. "I don't understand," she said.

"He loves me, Imeshina, but I cannot love him because I cannot forgive him."

"What are you talking about? Forgive him for what?"

Amita's tear-filled eyes met her own, and she said, "For taking me from my family. I am my mother's only daughter, and she will never even know her grandchildren."

Allison was puzzled. She knew that Amita's family did not live in the village, but there were many families that lived alone in the jungle and even more had died from the many diseases that swept through the tribe. "I don't understand," she said again. "How did he take you from your family? Where are they?"

"Ten years ago, a group of Shampiri warriors raided my village, Paamari. I was taken along with two other women," she explained.

"You were taken… like me?"

79

"Yes, like you."

Shaking her head, Allison asked, "Why didn't you tell me until now?"

"I do not speak of it. Everyone knows, but it is not something that we talk about. It is not uncommon for warriors to take wives from different tribes when there are few to choose from among their own people. That is why you were taken—to replace Majiro's dead wife. She died after giving birth to their first baby."

Allison processed the information about Majiro, but put it to the back of her mind, determined to concentrate on her friend. She asked, "Then you are not Shampiri? But you speak perfectly!"

"My people are the Oneata, but we share ancestors with the Shampiri. Our languages are nearly identical because only a few generations ago, we were the same people. After the clans split, there was much bitterness, and we have been at war ever since." The explanation was intriguing. It also helped her understand the compassion that Amita had consistently shown since her arrival a year ago. Her friend had lived through a similar situation.

Hating the question, yet feeling the need to know, Allison asked, "Were you taken from a husband too?"

"No. I was not married, but my cousin was working in the garden with my father." Allison understood her vague explanation. In order to gain approval to marry, a man demonstrated his ability to provide for a family by working alongside a girl's father for a time. Also, cousins were the preferred marriage partners among many Amazonian tribes. Though other marriage partners were acceptable, marrying a cousin was considered the best choice.

Shocked by the disclosure, Allison sat silently, trying to sort out what she had heard. One thing that stood out to her was Manitari's obvious affection for his wife. His tenderness toward her was unusual among the native men. At best, many of the Shampiri men were indifferent to their wives, seeing them as property. Others were simply abusive. Manitari, in her opinion, was one of the kindest husbands in the village.

"Is there another reason that you cannot forgive him? I mean, besides the fact that he took you away from your family?" she asked.

Amita shook her head. "No. He is a good man, a good husband. He loves my children and provides for us. I just can't forget how I came to be his wife. What should I do?"

Allison replied hesitantly, "I know that we are supposed to forgive those that hurt us and love our enemies." She had spoken of her faith to Amita on several occasions, but mostly as an explanation of her own beliefs, not as an answer to her friend's personal problems. "When Jesus died on the cross, he forgave the men that killed him. He told his followers that they were supposed to do the same."

"But aren't you a Jesus follower?"

"Yes, of course."

Amita looked confused. "But how can you be? You have not forgiven Majiro."

"That's not the same thing!"

"How is it not? We were both taken from our homes and families, and our loved ones were killed in the raids. Both of us were given to good men, even if they were men that we did not want."

Allison sat back, stunned. In her mind, the issue was not nearly so simple. Yet, Amita's observation cut through all of her complicated rationalizations. Since the first night with Majiro, she had struggled with feelings of hatred and bitterness toward him. Though in the past year she had come to respect him in many ways, she had never been able to forgive him for bringing her here or for forcing her to sleep with him time after time. And, if she was being honest with herself, she had not really forgiven God for putting her in the situation either. Her inability to forgive was glaringly obvious, and it shamed her to examine it so closely.

Sighing, Allison murmured, "I should forgive Majiro. I just don't know how."

"When you learn, you must tell me, so that I can forgive my husband too." Amita wiped her eyes and slid off the platform. "Thank you, Imeshina. You are a true sister. You have helped me today."

"You have helped me too, Amita," Allison said, and she meant it.

Back at home, Allison put Isaac down for his nap on his little sleeping mat in the corner and settled down in the hammock. It had become her favorite spot to think and pray. She thought about Amita's revelation and her observation of Allison's hypocritical admonition to forgive when she could not do the same herself.

Well, Lord, I can't really ignore this anymore, can I? Amita is completely right about how I feel about Majiro. I simply don't understand how I can possibly forgive his cruelty. Maybe he is a good man in many ways, but none of that seems to matter when I think about what he has done to me and my family. Am I supposed to just let that go?

Seventy times seven.

She laughed bitterly. *I have been here for a year. I think we are approaching that number quickly.*

Beloved...

Sorry. But seriously, Lord, how could You allow this to happen? You could have stopped this. At any point You could have prevented it all. I have only ever tried to serve You, and You can't even protect me. Tears began falling down her face as the hurt she had buried welled up. She had loved the Lord with all her heart, dedicated her life to Him, but He had failed her.

For to this you have been called, because Christ also suffered for you, leaving you an example, so that you might follow in His steps.

I know that Christians often suffer for their faith, but I don't see how You can love me and allow this to continue.

I am jealous for my glory.

She sniffed. *What does that have to do with anything?*

Beloved, love these people. Teach them who I am.

Allison was angry, confused, and tired of arguing. Why did God seem so unreachable and cryptic? Her relationship with him spanned a decade, and she had grown accustomed to being able to discern His voice and know His will. It seemed that in many ways, she had grown distant from God during the past year. Amita's comment had finally shed light on the situation. Her inability to forgive Majiro had stuck a wedge between herself and the Lord, but she had no idea how to remove it.

CHAPTER **TEN**

The next morning Allison made the hour-long hike to the family garden. Inani had taken her there the first few times she had gone to make sure that she did not get lost along the trail. Now, a year later, after having traveled it a least a couple of times every week to retrieve food for the family, she could practically walk the path in her sleep.

Often Isaac and Majiro came with her to harvest yucca, plantains, or sweet potatoes, but today she was alone. Majiro was hunting, and she had left Isaac in Inani's care. She looked forward to the solitude. Her conversation the previous morning with Amita still weighed heavily on her mind, and she felt like Jacob must have when he wrestled with God. She was determined not to return home until the matter had been settled between her and the Lord.

She walked quickly to the garden and dug up several sweet potatoes for dinner. Delighted, she spotted a few ripe pineapples and cut them off the plants holding them to the earth. She added the fruit to her basket. Isaac would be thrilled with the treat.

Once her task was completed, Allison selected a small pineapple and cut it open. It would make a perfect, juicy lunch since she had a limited amount of banana drink with her in a wooden jar. She settled in the shade and nibbled on her lunch. She waited silently, but for what she did not know. All that she could think of was a psalm she had heard years ago, "*Seek My face. My heart said to you, 'Your face, Lord, I will seek.'*" Her spirit was heavy and, from past experience, she knew it was a call from God to find rest in Him. For months she had maintained only a casual interaction with the Lord because she could not bear to tell Him the things that were truly on her heart. It was time for that to change.

As she sat, overwhelming feelings that had been pushed aside since soon after her arrival began poking their way through her stony heart. Grief had not been useful in her efforts to adjust to life among the Shampiri and to learn their language. For the first time in nearly a year, Allison allowed herself to feel, and she doubled over, holding her arms across her chest as if to keep her heart from breaking. She thought of Eric and grieved for his life. She still missed him and found herself furious at his being taken from her in such a sudden, violent way. She was angry with God, angry with Majiro, and angry with the Shampiri for maintaining such cruel practices. Her greatest regret was simply that Isaac would never remember his father's easy smile and tenderness. Majiro had become Isaac's father. But, though the Shampiri chief and Eric shared a stubborn strength and determination, Eric's faith had made him gentle in a way that Majiro was not.

Over the year, Allison had grown accustomed to performing as Majiro's wife, with all of the duties that were required of her. She no longer fought him, but there was clearly no love between the two of them. Majiro seemed satisfied with the arrangement, but Allison longed for the intimacy she had shared with Eric.

She began to pour out her complaints to God. This time, she held nothing back. "Do you see me? Have you forgotten me? I am right here!" She stood up screaming at the sky with her arms outstretched and pain etched in her face. "You are supposed to be a savior. Why have You not saved me from this place?"

Beloved, I know the plans that I have for you. Plans for a future and a hope.

"What future?" she yelled, enraged. "With Majiro? No, thanks."

Every good and perfect gift comes from Me.

"You have given me no gift."

Your life.

Allison laughed bitterly. "It's a life that I despise. I wish I had died."

And your son?

That stopped her cold. She realized that if she had died as well, Isaac would be left with no parents at all and with no hope of ever hearing about the Lord.

Majiro is a gift to you.

"How is *he* in any way a gift to me?" Not sensing an answer, she began to ponder God's response. Aside from Majiro's nightly demands, she was forced to admit that he had been good to her and to her son. He consistently provided for them, and he clearly saw Isaac as his own child. In contrast to the cruelty many men in the village showed their families, Majiro was usually just, and his discipline of Isaac had been fair and never brutal. She also realized from conversations with Amita that his position as chief had sheltered her from the rough treatment that many other captured wives had experienced at first. According to her friend, it was not unusual for a man to "loan" his new wife to his friends, and as a non-member of the community, she had no right to refuse. As he had at the harvest party, Majiro's position allowed him to refuse such a tradition without challenge.

Allison sat back down in a heap as the Lord revealed blessing after blessing that she had overlooked in her anger. Amita's friendship, Isaac's health, her uncanny quickness in understanding the language, and so many more were brought to mind. She felt chastised and a little embarrassed over her rage as she began to see God's mercy through her whole experience.

"God, I'm sorry. I still don't understand why You are allowing all of this to happen to me, and I still hate that I am forced to be the wife of a man I don't want. But I'm thankful for the way that You have cared for us," she said. In that moment, the peace that she had been lacking for so long flooded her heart, and for a long time she simply sat and enjoyed it. Then she realized that more was required of her.

"What do I do now?"

Love these people. Teach them who I am.

"Okay, but You are going to have to help me with that. I can't do it on my own."

I am always with you, Beloved. I was with you in the beginning, and I will remain with you for the duration. I will show you the things that you need to know.

With that assurance, Allison gathered her food basket. The sky was already beginning to darken, and she would have to hurry to get back home before nightfall. Her heart was so light that she nearly skipped down the trail. Unfortunately, her lack of attention kept her from seeing a small, deep hole in the trail. Her toes caught in the hole, and the basket strapped to her back threw off her balance. She fell roughly on the ground. Groaning at the immediate pain that shot through her foot and up her ankle, she lay still on her side for a few minutes until her breath came back and the ache in her ankle dulled a bit. She pulled the basket from her back and tried to stand. When she put her weight on her right leg, the sharp pain returned.

"Oh, great. It's going to take me forever to get home now." Allison was frustrated but also nervous. She knew the dangers of the jungle at night and had no desire to be here alone with no light and no weapon but her wooden spade. She settled the basket strap back across her forehead and began hobbling down the trail, being much more careful to watch where she was going.

Each step was agony, but she focused on the thought of getting home to Isaac. She needed to get back soon in order to get him to bed on time. As the glimpses of sky above the canopy turned from orange to purple, she knew that she was in trouble. Nightfall was soon, and she was only halfway home.

She kept walking until the night overtook her. Debating whether or not to go on, she chose to stop where she was. If she got off of the trail, she might become hopelessly lost. She decided to try to climb a tree next to the trail and remain there for the night. Jaguars and snakes could get to her easily, but at least she was out of the way from the wild pigs that scavenged the jungle floor. They could run incredibly fast, and the natives feared getting caught in their strong, quick jaws.

It took her a few minutes to climb the tree through the pain that had increased over the walk. She finally settled on a low branch. It was uncomfortable, but she doubted that she would actually sleep that night anyhow. Indeed a few hours later, she was still wide-awake and singing softly to herself in order to keep her overactive imagination from rehearsing the possibilities of her death. The sounds of the jungle—the birds, frogs, and insects—were usually a comforting symphony, but tonight they just scared her.

Her eyes narrowed when she saw that there was a light moving in the distance. As it bounced toward her, she realized that it was attached to a person. It looked like one of the native torches, a thick branch rolled in tar and lit.

"Hello!" she called. The torch moved more quickly toward her, and she could soon make out the face behind it. Sema! She groaned, for he was the last person that she had hoped to see. She contemplated letting herself disappear in the dark and taking her chances through the night, but he had already seen her waving hand and was moving steadily toward her.

"Why are you in a tree?" Sema demanded, with no warmth in his voice. Not that she expected anything else. He had proven himself to be incapable of kindness toward her.

Allison bit her lip before answering, "I hurt my foot, and I couldn't make it all the way back. I was afraid to keep walking and lose the trail." She hated admitting her weakness to Sema.

"Stupid woman. I should leave you here, but Majiro would find you and wonder why I didn't bring you back."

"Majiro is looking for me?"

"He sent me to his garden to search there. He is making his way up the trail."

"I'll wait for him."

Sema growled, "No. You'll come with me." He grabbed her arm and pulled her from the branch. Even though it was only a few feet down, Allison cried out when her feet hit the ground and her ankle gave out beneath her.

"Get up, stupid woman," Sema growled. He moved toward her, pinning her against the tree she had climbed. "Perhaps I will find out for myself what reason Majiro has for not putting you out to rot with the other garbage."

Allison gulped, her eyes wide with fear. She did not move or speak because she knew that any show of fear would encourage his cruelty. Running was futile. Even if she was not injured, she could not escape his speed or hunting abilities. Instead she prayed for a miracle.

Sema pressed his body roughly against hers and brought his lips down hard on her mouth. His hand made its way under her skirt, caressing her legs. She shivered in disgust and squeezed her eyes shut, awaiting what was surely to come.

"Majiro." Allison opened her eyes to see Sema spit on the ground in disgust. She spotted Majiro's glowing torch in the distance and nearly wept with relief. Sema kissed her roughly again and then whispered in her ear. "If you speak of this to anyone, you will find your son floating face-down in the river." She paled knowing that he would gladly keep that promise.

The warrior picked up his torch and met Majiro on the trail. "I found her here. Her foot is injured."

Majiro looked at her, but she turned her face away, fearing that he would read what had just happened in her eyes. "Can you walk?" he asked. She nodded her reply.

The three began the trek home, the warriors slowing their pace for her injured one. Majiro carried the basket, and no one spoke until they entered the village. At the doorway to their home, Majiro bid Sema goodnight before closing the door behind them. "I am glad you are home," he said simply.

"Thank you for coming to get me. I did not want to sleep in a tree."

Majiro cocked his head to the side. "A tree?" he asked with a confused expression. She told him the tale of her fall and decision to sleep in a tree, and he chuckled. "You are still not Shampiri. A Shampiri woman would not have waited until so late to come home. Next time, you must leave the garden sooner." He stooped down to examine her swollen, dirty ankle.

"Does it hurt very much?" he questioned.

"Not as long as I am not walking."

"Good. It will be sore for a day or two. You must rest. I will tell my mother that Isaac will stay with her tonight."

Allison protested, "I'm fine. I'll go get him—"

"No," he replied firmly and left the house.

Allison found a jar of clean water and washed the grime from her face and feet. She was relieved to be home, and it was a strange feeling. For so long she had seen the village, and particularly her house, as a kind of prison. For it to feel like home made her realize that truly God had done a deep work in her heart that day.

CHAPTER **ELEVEN**

Allison clicked her tongue in Shampiri fashion and called out, "Amita, are you home?" It had been a few days since her eventful trip to the garden, and she had been praying frequently about having the opportunity to speak to her friend. This morning she had felt peace about approaching Amita to talk.

The small native woman appeared in the doorway and smiled when she saw who was there. "Do you need something, Imeshina?" she asked.

"I was just wondering if you have time to talk."

Amita nodded. "I do. Sit. I will get something to drink." Allison sat as directed next to the coals of the fire pit in front of the house. Soon Amita returned with two bowls of *cachojari*, the bright pink beer. The alcohol content of the beer varied according to the time it had been given to ferment.

Allison accepted the bowl graciously and drank from it. Amita's *cachojari* was weak enough that she did not mind sharing it with Isaac. "I thought a lot about the other day when we spoke in your house," she began. Amita peered at her with big, dark eyes and waited for her to continue.

"You were right about me not forgiving Majiro, and I was wrong. If I am going to be a Jesus follower, I have to obey everything He has said. I cannot just choose what I want to obey and ignore the rest."

Her eyebrows rising in surprise, Amita asked, "Then you have forgiven him?"

"Yes."

"But how could you do that so quickly and so easily?"

Allison laughed, "Well it wasn't easy! And it wasn't really quick either. I have been angry with him for more than a year. I know that it was not by any power that I have, but Jesus gave me the strength to choose to forgive. I just kept thinking about how God has forgiven me for the many terrible things that I have done against Him, and I could not accept His forgiveness and offer none to Majiro."

"But, Imeshina," Amita protested, "you are a good woman, a good wife and mother. What could you have done to offend your God?"

It was a struggle for Allison to answer spiritual questions because the Shampiri had no history of the gospel in their culture. She had found that they understood the concept of a Creator God, but many saw Him as indifferent to the struggles of human beings. To them, the world was controlled by spirits that had to be appeased and manipulated. The idea of having any interaction with a loving God was one that she had struggled to explain to her friend. So far Amita had accepted that it was plausible for God to choose to be involved in human affairs, but how that worked was still a mystery to her.

She prayed silently for wisdom and the right words to adequately convey such important theology. "God is perfect. He is all good, and there is nothing bad in Him. When we die we will either go to be with Him where everything is good and beautiful, or we will go to the place of fire where there is nothing but darkness and pain. God wants us to choose to be with Him, but He cannot allow us in there with any badness on us because there is nothing bad there. Every time we lie, hurt one another intentionally, or try to have our own way, it stains us."

Amita had been listening carefully, and as Allison spoke, understanding lit her face. "We have all done bad things like that," she stated. "Even my children are guilty of those things… Then how can we ever join God when we die? I cannot undo what I have already done."

"Exactly! That's why God came to earth by sending His Son. Jesus was God Himself and at the same time, a man like any other. He was born, lived a life without doing wrong, and died to take all of the badness from everyone with Him to the grave. Then God raised him back to life! He told us that we just have to accept that the living Jesus came to take our badness away, and He will wash us of our guilt. When He does that, we become clean and can go to be with Him when we die." Allison paused before continuing, "And it's not just that we can be with him when we die, He also says His Spirit will live in us while we live and will teach us and comfort us and help us."

"Many of our people have spirit guides too, but sometimes the things they tell us to do harm us."

Allison said, "The Holy Spirit is not like that. Everything He does is for our good."

"Our spirits will not like to share their territory."

"They can't share. When God's Spirit lives in you, He sends all of the other spirits away."

The pair sat silently for a long time while Amita considered what she had heard. Allison knew that it was a radical change of paradigm. A personal, saving God who offers hope was like nothing the native woman had ever heard before. Finally Amita said wisely, "This is a hard teaching. It is very different from our way, and it will change how we live. A decision to believe in your God cannot be made quickly."

"No. It will take much thought." Allison took her friend's hands and smiled at her. "I will ask Jesus to show you that believing Him is the very best thing you can do." With that she stood and, with a little wave, walked back home.

A few days passed, but Amita did not bring up their conversation again. Allison waited patiently as her friend processed what they had spoken about and resolved to faithfully pray for her in the meantime. She was doing just that as she walked the short distance to her mother-in-law's house with a handful of sweet potatoes she had brought from her garden the day before. She found Inani inside her house, grinding ginger root between two stones at a table in the corner. The pungent odor filled Allison's nostrils and made her eyes water.

"Good morning," she greeted as she came to stand over the older woman's shoulder. "What are you doing?"

Without looking up, Inani explained, "I am making tea to take to Ogatsita's youngest daughter. She is dying."

"Dying? The baby?" Allison was surprised, for the child had seemed healthy the week before when she had seen her with her mother at the river. "What is wrong with her?"

Inani shrugged. "The spirits are trying to steal her."

Thinking she might have some helpful medicinal insight to offer, Allison asked, "Maybe I can help. May I come with you?"

Inani looked at her doubtfully, but agreed that she could tag along. Soon the women were walking on the overgrown trail toward the one-room house in which Ogatsita lived with her husband, elderly father-in-law and half a dozen children. It still was mind-blowing that so many people could live together in such a small home, but since the tribe spent the bulk of their time outdoors, no one seemed to mind.

Inani called out a greeting before stepping into the dim house. Allison followed her in, and as her eyes adjusted to the darkness, she saw Ogatsita sitting on her sleeping platform. Her eyes were rimmed with red, and she did not seem to hear the whimpers coming from the child that lay on a grass mat next to her. Allison moved in for a closer look.

The baby was around nine months old, though she was grossly undersized for a child that age. Like most of the children in the village, she was naked and covered in fleabites. Her eyes were matted shut and sunk into her skull. She was the most pathetic thing that Allison had ever laid eyes on, and her heart broke with compassion both for the infant and the mother who seemed to have accepted the coming reality.

After taking a quick look at the baby, Inani was all business. "I brought some ginger tea. Let's see if we can get her to drink, and then we will dust her." The baby refused to swallow anything. Each of the three women tried to coerce her to take some of the tea, but it all seemed to dribble out of her mouth as she choked and gagged.

Ogatsita sat back in frustration. "She won't nurse either. She's had nothing to eat for two days."

Giving up, Inani brought out another jar that she had brought along. She removed the lid and began to sprinkle white dust over the baby.

Allison was alarmed. She wondered what kind of germs lived in the dust and how it would affect the little girl's lungs that already seemed so fragile. However, she remained silent and observed the ritual, all the while praying for God's mercy on the child and her family.

Inani finished the dusting and asked her daughter-in-law with a sideways glance, "Your people do not dust the dying?"

"No. What does it do?"

"It tricks the spirits into believing that the person is already dead. If there is no one to steal, they will leave." The older woman motioned to the infant who did indeed look deceased with the white powder caked to her tiny body.

The women kept their vigil over the baby for a long while, until Inani rose from the platform. "I must go. Onijaa is not doing well, and I promised I would stop in this afternoon."

"Onijaa? Sema's mother?" Allison asked. "What's the matter with her? I thought she was doing better."

Inani shrugged. "She was, but she is ill again. There is a lot of swelling in her stomach, and she is in pain." Offering the stone-faced mother a squeeze on the shoulder, Inani quietly left. Allison remained at the home for a while longer, unwilling to leave Ogatsita alone. Finally, early in the afternoon, the baby whimpered and then died quietly.

She expected that the child's mother would weep, but after allowing herself only one muffled sob, Ogatsita covered the child with a blanket and turned away from the still form. The woman reached for a knife lying in the corner with the cooking pots and began sawing off her long black hair close to her head. Allison gaped at her with surprise, but the woman's face showed no emotion. Soon, all of her hair was in a heap at her feet.

Allison followed her outside and watched as she began to cut the hair of each of her children as she had her own. The children received the haircuts solemnly and then joined their father inside the home where he was gathering all of the family's belongings. The children disappeared down the trail with their heavy loads, and Ogatsita's husband took a burning branch from the fire and lit the bottom corner of the house.

"What is he doing?" Allison cried out, as the dry bamboo quickly burst into flame.

Ogatsita replied quietly, "Now that the spirits have come for my daughter, they will remain in that house. We must burn it or they will take another one of us."

"But where will you live?"

She pointed down the trail after her family. "My husband has already begun making another house."

Allison awkwardly took the woman's hand. "I am so sorry about your daughter. If there is anything I can do—"

"There is nothing anyone can do. We are all born, and we will all die." The fatalistic words were spoken harshly, but Allison saw a lone tear make a muddy path down the woman's cheek before she turned away from the burning building.

After Ogatsita had gone, Allison watched the flames as they licked the green leaves above. Her own face was streaked with tears of sorrow as she tried to understand what she had seen that day. Her heart ached for the family that had hopelessly accepted life's reality and for the little girl who was now nothing more than a memory.

That evening she held Isaac for longer than usual as she rocked him before bedtime. She had stopped by Amita's house to tell her about the baby's death, and her friend had explained that nearly everything she had seen had been an attempt to fool the spirits that the Shampiri believed were constantly waiting for an opportunity to harm their people. Even the hair cutting was a way to keep the evil spirits from grabbing hold of another as they took the baby's soul away.

"There is so much fear, Amita." she had observed sadly.

"Yes, of course. We all fear what is stronger than us."

"But what if you were under the protection of the God who made all of the spirits, the One who is the most powerful?"

Amita's eyebrows pinched together as she had mulled over that idea. "Then we would have nothing to fear at all."

The conversation had ended then as Manitari came home with a basket full of game, but Allison remained prayerful as she also returned home to her evening chores. She knew that the Holy Spirit was revealing truth to Amita, but she also knew that the enemy would not give up his bastion of evil easily.

A week later when Amita did not arrive at the river as she usually did, Allison knew that something was amiss. She quickly went to her friend's house, stopping only to drop off her water pot and tell Majiro where she was going. As she had expected, she found Amita inside her house, doubled over with a contraction.

"How long ago did your labor start?" she asked after it passed.

Amita sank down to the ground. "In the middle of the night."

Allison chided, "Why didn't you come get me?"

"The pains were not strong yet. And I knew that you would figure it out when I didn't go to the river this morning."

After confirming that the birth was not imminent, Allison took Micheli to gather large banana leaves to use as a birthing mat. They returned quickly, and she arranged them on the floor in a corner of the home with a thick blanket on top.

Amita chose to walk around outside for much of her labor, stopping only when the hard contractions forced her to. By the early afternoon, she was exhausted. Manitari had stayed seated next to the fire where he could observe his wife. His wide mouth was turned down with worry, and occasionally he would send Micheli after food and water for her mother.

Laboring through one particularly difficult contraction, Amita cried out in pain. Manitari jumped to his feet and rushed to his wife's side. "Is it time? Do I need to carry you inside?" he asked anxiously.

"No. The baby isn't down enough yet. Just leave me be, husband. This is a woman's work." Though not unkind, Amita's tone was firm and sent her husband scurrying like a scolded dog back to the fire. Allison bit her lip to keep from laughing.

"You are getting tired. You need to save your strength for pushing later," Allison coaxed, until Amita agreed to rest on the leaf mat inside against a stack of blankets.

The afternoon continued on in much the same way as the morning. As the sky began to light up with the colors of sunset,

Allison grew worried by Amita's lack of progress, particularly when she was told that the woman's previous labors had been much shorter. As her concern grew, so did the intensity of her prayers. Never before had she so longed for a doctor.

The door to the house opened, and Inani stepped inside. "How are you, Amita?" she asked, leaning over the pregnant woman.

"This baby won't come. It will kill me." The older woman's question had unleashed a torrent of fear, and Amita began to sob.

Inani squatted down and held Amita's head to her chest. "Don't speak such words! We will have this baby out before the sun rises. I will bring you some herbs. It will make your pains stronger, but the baby will come."

Inani left and, as promised, returned a while later with a jar of hot, foul-smelling liquid. Amita drank from the jar greedily, wanting to do anything she could to end her labor. Soon the contractions increased in intensity, and Amita said, "Oh, I think I can push now!"

After several more contractions passed, it was clear that the pushing was doing nothing but frustrating the mother and draining her strength. Allison suggested a different position, and for the next hour Amita tried squatting, lying on her side, and kneeling on her hands and knees. Still the baby would not come.

Finally Amita flopped back against the blankets and wept. "Tell my husband that this child has killed me, and have him bring my children so that I can say good-bye," she said miserably.

Allison crawled behind her crying friend, spread her legs on either side, and pulled Amita back until she was leaning heavily against her. "My friend, rest against me. You will not die. You will deliver this baby. Let me pray for you to my God, okay?" Amita nodded, and Allison began to pray aloud, her hands splayed against Amita's swollen stomach. "God, you have woven this child in Amita's womb. The time has come for the baby to be born, but his mother has no more strength to bring him out. Give Amita the strength to do this task that you created her body to do." She continued praying and soon felt Amita's body relax against hers.

Then, with a start, Amita cried out and began pushing. Allison held her hands and helped her brace herself until one strong contraction brought the baby's head. "One more push, and he will be here!" she encouraged.

A moment later, a little boy slid onto the blanket under his mother. Inani carefully picked the child up and placed him against his mother's breast.

"It's over," the new mother quietly said with a sigh.

"Yes. Congratulations. Your son is beautiful." Allison pulled herself from behind Amita and helped her settle back to nurse her son. Inani cut the umbilical cord with string and a knife that Allison had talked her into boiling.

Allison said, "I will go tell your husband that the baby is here. He has been worried about you."

Amita looked up from her baby's pink face. "Thank you, Imeshina. Tell him that your God has brought us a new son."

Allison found the new father by the fire, where he had continued his vigil through the night. "Manitari, you have a new son. Your wife is feeding him right now."

The warrior's pinched face relaxed, and a single tear rolled down his cheek. "She had a hard time." It was more of a statement than a question.

"Yes." Allison joined him by the fire and related the story of his son's birth, including what Amita had said.

"Then we are thankful to you and to your God. You must be the one to give him his name."

Despite her protest, Manitari insisted that Allison have the honor of naming the baby. She thought for awhile before saying with a smile, "*Iquemisa*." He hears.

CHAPTER **TWELVE**

Eric heaved the last cardboard box out of the car and slammed the trunk closed. For a moment he stood next to his vehicle, looking at his newly leased apartment. He sighed and carried the box through the front door and left it in the heap with all the others. A strange feeling of closure accompanied the sound of his front door clicking shut, and he felt more than a little anxiety over what his next step should be.

When he left Peru a few weeks ago, his only goal had been to move out of his parents' home and regain his autonomy. Now that was completed, and he had no other goals in mind for the future. The truth was that he still had trouble separating himself from the search for his wife and son that had consumed him for so long. He had lost weight, and his eyes showed his lack of sleep and hope.

Walking into the kitchen, he found a coffee mug in a small box and poured himself some water from the tap. The sound of the running water reminded him of the day that he had decided to call off the search and return home.

He flopped down on the ground next to the river that he had bathed in, watched his son splash in, and seen his wife dragged to. Today was the anniversary of the capture, and aside from that very day, it was the worst of his life. He felt like a dismal failure. For a year he had searched in some way nearly every day for the location or condition of his family. He had been on wild chases of phantoms based on unclear memories of natives in the area. For over a month, he had tracked down a tribe said to have a white woman among them only to find an old albino woman. He had searched for miles around the jungle base in every direction and was now simply out of places to look and leads to go after.

Rubbing his hands through hair that had grown long and unruly, Eric watched the river silently. "What now?" he whispered to the wind. Though his heart told him otherwise, he knew that there was no way he could continue looking as he had been. The volunteers had long since given up the search, and his parents pestered him constantly about returning to Texas. The truth was that he had drained his savings and simply had no money to go on. And they were probably all correct, after a year of no signs and no information, the chances that Allison and Isaac were alive were minuscule.

He thought through all of the possibilities and tried to pray for direction. It was odd to pray anything other than the "help me find them alive" prayers that had been singularly on his mind for so long. Like a hurricane that begins with a soft breeze, confirmation of his next step welled in his heart, gaining strength and giving him confidence with each passing moment. It was time to accept what had happened and go home. There was nothing more for him to do here. Indeed, he could not fathom continuing in ministry so near to where he had lost so much. Whatever God had for him next was not in Peru.

And so, to the delight of his friends and family, Eric had officially completed his search and begun the process of returning to the home he had left five years before with his dreams still intact. His mother had the self-imposed task of seeing him settled in and nearly smothered him with motherly interference. It became clear to him early on that he would have to find his own home soon, and far enough away that she could not drop by every hour just to "check on him."

His father, inserting his own kind of pressure, invited Eric to return to the law firm, even offering several lucrative contracts to entice him. Law held no interest for him any longer, but he agreed to put in a few weeks to appease his father. It also enabled him to save up enough money to lease a furnished apartment an hour away from his parents' home. Neither Jean nor David was pleased when Eric announced his intention to move, but both knew their son well enough not to challenge the decision he had made.

He now found himself alone in a place he had never lived before, jobless and aimless. Concern for the future was not something that he struggled with any longer, for he now had no one to take care of. His attitude was simply one of curiosity. What would God do with him now? Obviously there was something in store for him or he would not have lived through the attack a year ago. He figured that he would just keep moving, hoping that God would point him in the right direction.

A few days later, Eric entered a coffee shop down the street from his apartment armed with newspapers and his laptop. He had already halfheartedly filled out a couple of applications for positions in town that he was not really interested in. It was time to get back to work; he would have bills in his mailbox at the end of the month. The problem was that he had no idea what he wanted to do. He was not going back into law, and he realized that beginning a new career in missions overseas was out of the question without a partner. He knew and admired many single missionaries, but he did not have the fortitude to deal with a new culture, language, and people alone.

After paying for his coffee, he set up a workstation at one of the shop's tables. He looked through the ads and circled a few requesting business managers. He sighed loudly, catching the attention of an older man seated nearby.

"Eric? Eric Carter?" the man asked, his white eyebrows coming together so that it looked like a big caterpillar sat on his forehead.

Eric's face broke into a wide smile. "Pastor Denny! How are you? What are you doing here?"

Pastor Denny rose and rushed over to shake Eric's hand enthusiastically. "I could ask you the same thing, son. I work at a church just a couple of miles from here. My secretary called in sick, and I never got around to making coffee this morning."

"You are pastoring again?" Eric was surprised. Pastor Denny had been the pastor of his church while he was growing up and was the one to perform his wedding years later. Shortly after he and Allison had married, the pastor's wife had died, and he had stepped down from the pastorate, saying that he felt it was time to retire from ministry.

A twinkle in his eye, Pastor Denny replied with a chuckle, "I didn't expect it either, but God wasn't done with me yet! I think He just let me think so to get away from the church I had been in and loved for so long. I would not have looked elsewhere. When I moved here to be closer to my grandchildren, a new church was forming and, well, they seemed to think God had brought me to them to lead."

"I think that's wonderful. They are lucky to have you."

"That's kind of you." The pastor's smile faded as he searched Eric's face, "But what about you? My friends back at the old place have kept me up to date about your situation. I know about Allison and your boy. I'm sorry, son."

Eric appreciated the older man's simple sympathy. He did not try to lessen the reality of Eric's pain or offer a useless platitude of attempted comfort. "Me too. I miss them," he replied simply. "I've moved back now, called off the search. I live just a few blocks from here."

"From here?"

"Yes. I moved in a few days ago. My mother was starting to pack my lunches and make up my bed for me, so I figured it was better for all of us if I got a little farther away."

Pastor Denny chuckled. "And I can just see Jean doing that! Well, I don't suppose I can expect you for church on Sunday?"

Eric nodded slowly. "It will be strange to be back in church. I haven't really gone this past year—I was always too busy with the search. Since I've been back… well, I guess I just couldn't face the questions and pity."

"That is certainly understandable. You'll make a fresh start of it here. I think you will find the members of Antioch to be friendly, but also discreet." Before he left, the pastor wrote down the service times and directions to the church.

Eric tucked the directions into his wallet with a smile. Having Pastor Denny around again was a wonderful blessing. While his own father had not shown any interest in the Lord, the pastor had been a spiritual mentor for years. It was exciting to think about being back under his leadership. He was looking forward to Sunday, but, for now, he needed to find a job.

The cell phone on the table rang, startling Eric from the book he was reading. Few people had his new number, and his mother would already be in bed. He looked at the phone's display but did not recognize the number on it.

"Hello? This is Eric."

"Eric, I hope I am not calling too late. This is Denny."

Eric put his book down and sat up straight, "Pastor Denny, no it's fine. What can I do for you?"

"I've been thinking about you since we ran into each other this morning. I couldn't get you off my mind. So I pulled your poor mother out of bed and got your number from her. Eric, are you still interested in being in the ministry?"

After a momentary pause, Eric stuttered, "I… uh… Yes, I suppose, but I don't want to go overseas. Not without a wife. I am just not cut out for that."

"What about being a pastor here in Texas?"

"Pastor Denny, I went to law school, not seminary. Allison and I took some Bible classes before we went to Peru, but I couldn't be a pastor. I am not even a good speaker."

The pastor replied, "Maybe not a senior pastor, but what would you think about being a pastor of missions."

"I don't guess I have ever thought of it before."

"You see, Eric, our church is looking for someone to oversee our outreach programs, both local and international. All day I've felt the Lord putting you on my mind for the job. Would you be willing to pray about it? If we don't scare you off on Sunday, you could meet with me next week for an interview."

Eric sat thinking for a moment while the pastor waited patiently for his answer. "There's no harm in that. The whole idea is a surprise to me, but I am certainly willing to pray about it and visit the church. Can I get back to you before you schedule an interview?"

"Of course." The two exchanged pleasantries before they bid one another good night. Eric remained seated on the couch, telephone in hand, for a long time after they had hung up. Back in ministry and with a focus on missions without actually leaving the United States. It sounded… well, perfect. Staying true to his promise, Eric prayed long into the night for God to show him if this was the direction he was to go. By the time he fell asleep, it seemed to him that it just might be.

CHAPTER **THIRTEEN**

This interview made Eric nervous. It was his second this week. On Sunday, he had agreed to interview with Pastor Denny after being delighted by the service that morning at Antioch Bible Church. The congregation was enthusiastic in their worship and had gone out of their way to make him feel welcome. There had been over five hundred people at the church that morning, and he had been surprised by how many had greeted him, asking if he was visiting and inviting him to return. Pastor Denny had explained in the subsequent interview that the church was passionate about missions and believed that each person held the responsibility to share Christ in word and in deed with those around him. For that reason the church was growing rapidly.

During his interview with the pastor, Eric had learned much about the history and people of the church, but this interview with the elder board was about his personal beliefs and experiences. It would be the major determining factor for whether or not the church would accept his application as their pastor of missions.

Eric opened the door to the church office and was led by an elderly secretary into a room where Pastor Denny was waiting at a long conference table with the seven men comprising the board of elders. Introductions were made, and Eric made an effort to remember the names of the men before him. Luckily, Pastor Denny had a knack for putting people at ease, and soon the group was laughing at his stories. The men began the interview with basic questions about Eric's education and job history. The line of questioning soon moved to his ministry in Peru.

One of the elders said, "Pastor Denny has filled us in on what happened to your family in Peru last year, and, frankly, we have some reservations about bringing you back into ministry such a short time after what happened."

Eric replied honestly, "I can understand that. And the truth is, I am not 'over it,' whatever that means. But I do believe that God has pretty clearly led me back to Texas."

"You've only been back for a couple of months. Why did you stay in Peru for so long after your family's death?"

"I still don't know that they are dead." Eric sighed and explained what he had seen during the attack on the jungle camp. "After a year of looking for my family, I knew that God was closing the door on the search. Everyone tells me that Allison and Isaac are gone, that the tribe would not let them live. Even though we have found no evidence that they are alive, I haven't found any evidence that they are dead either."

The man wrote a few lines on his notepad and then continued, "Do you feel you will be able to complete the requirements of the ministry while you are still grieving for your family?"

"I do," he responded. "What happened to my family has not detracted from my passion for missions, here or abroad. In fact, I am even more convinced how crucial it is to give people an opportunity to know the Lord. I can't help but think that if the people who took my wife and son had known Christ, it would have made for a very different ending."

The conversation continued for awhile as the elders outlined the expectations for the position of missions pastor. As the discussion neared its end, an elder who had been mostly silent during the interview casually threw out the most difficult question that Eric had faced for years. "Would you have gone to Peru knowing what would happen to your family, if you believed that it was God's will?" he asked, and the room became silent as all eyes focused on Eric.

Feeling his face pale slightly, Eric looked directly at the man who had voiced the question. He said slowly, "No. If I could do it all over again, knowing what I know now, I could not put my family through that—even if I thought it was God's will. I wish I could say that I would. I guess my faith is just not strong enough." With that, the interview was abruptly over. The men shook hands, and Eric left with a casual promise that he would be contacted again soon.

After getting into his car, he sat in the parking lot with the engine off reliving each question and answer during the previous hour. He groaned. It had been going so well until that last zinger. But his answer had been honest. Though he did believe that God was in control and that somehow what had happened to his family was part of God's plan, he would not have chosen to go to Peru if he had foreseen the pain that the future would hold.

With a deep sigh he decided to pick up a newspaper on his way home. Hopefully, he could send off a few more resumes before the mail was picked up in the afternoon.

The mood was light, and Eric was hesitant to share the news that he had brought with him to his parents' house. Tonight was the weekly dinner that had become a habit and something that they all looked forward to. Jean used the meal as an attempt to feed her son enough to last the week, while David always took the opportunity to try to entice Eric back to the law firm. This week, however, it was Eric who had an agenda.

A few days before, Pastor Denny had called with the unexpected news that the elder board had unanimously voted to offer the missions pastor position to him. If he accepted, he would be officially hired after a month-long probationary period designed to allow the congregation to get to know him before a church vote at the next business meeting.

Eric had been shocked by the offer and had even mentioned to Pastor Denny that he had thought his answer to the final question of the interview had tossed him out of the running. The pastor had merely laughed and replied that it had been an honest answer that the elders had deeply sympathized with. "A pastor who is willing to look truthfully at his faith is far more valuable than a pastor who thinks he has it together," he had said.

Eric cleared his throat, and his parents looked at him expectantly. "Is there something that you want to tell us?" his perceptive mother asked.

"Uh, yes, actually." Eric paused before launching into the story of meeting Pastor Denny in the coffee shop and the subsequent interviews. "All that to say, last Friday I got a call with the job offer, and I've decided to take it. I start tomorrow."

Jean jumped to her feet and ran around the table to embrace her son. "Oh Eric, I am so proud of you! What a wonderful opportunity! You will do a fine job."

"Thanks, Mom," he replied, all the while keeping his gaze on his father who had yet to say a word. He waited knowing that it would not be long before his father would issue his opinion like a verdict.

"A pastor's salary isn't nearly what you were making at the law firm," David observed.

"No, Dad, but it doesn't really matter to me. Money doesn't buy happiness."

David snorted with disdain. "And I suppose your religious notions do? It seems to me that all your God ever did for you was get your family killed."

"David!" Jean gasped, horrified.

"It's true, Jean, and it's something he needs to hear. I thought that after his failure in Peru, he would come to his senses and realize what he had given up back home."

"Dad—"

"No, you listen to me, son. Get this do-good notion out of your head. Even if your God is real—which I see no reason to believe— He has not done you any favors. Do you really want to follow a God that kills off His own servants?"

Eric tried to explain patiently, "God did not 'kill off' anyone."

"He certainly didn't protect them!" David retorted.

"Dad, I don't know what went on that day. Who knows what He protected them from? I do know that what happened doesn't change who God is. He is still good, and He is still sovereign."

David shook his head, but quieted down as he recognized his own stubbornness in his son. "Eric, I won't believe that your God is any of those things unless I can see with my own eyes that my grandson and daughter-in-law are safe."

The trio sat for several moments in an awkward silence until Jean, ever the peacemaker, patted her son's hand. "We're just so glad to see you getting your life back together. The church is lucky to have you. Now, who wants dessert?"

Eric got up to help his mother clear the table and set out plates of chocolate cake and mugs of steaming coffee. The remainder of the evening was spent discussing everything but Eric's new job.

The next morning came quickly. Eric arrived at the church early and was greeted with coffee by Helen, the elderly woman who served as receptionist and office manager for all of the full-time staff. He carried a couple of boxes of books into his new office and proceeded to organize them on the shelves. The office was roomy and brightly lit, and he was pleased with the oak desk and comfortable wing chairs arranged in a corner.

Throughout his first hour at the church, different members of the church staff dropped in to say hello. Many of them brought along church members to personally introduce to the new pastor. He had met several members after the church service the week before when he had been presented as the provisional missions pastor. There would be an all-church meal on Sunday where he would hopefully meet the remainder of the congregation.

After lunch, the office quieted down and Eric began working on the short speech he was asked to give on Sunday, both to introduce himself and to cast his vision for the direction of the church's outreach programs. Before he had even begun writing, he was left in a quandary. How much of his background should he reveal? He did not want his history to be the focus of the morning, but he also wanted to be the one to share his story and not leave it to the grapevine to fill in the blanks.

He decided to briefly describe his ministry in Peru but was unsure how to proceed from there. Realizing that mentioning his return was precipitated by the capture of his family would simply raise more questions, Eric decided to tell the congregation what he had been unable to tell himself until this moment. His family had died on the mission field.

The computer screen blurred as Eric read over his words. The pain of those first days, when he woke up in the hospital and had nothing to do but agonize over the disappearance of his family, came back in a rush. It seemed that he would never heal from his loss. Just when things seemed to be getting better he would see a woman who reminded him of Allison or catch a glimpse of a toddler playing with his father, and his heart would break all over again. He was a widower and a childless father. It was an identity that he had never wanted.

CHAPTER **FOURTEEN**

Life had settled into a normal routine. Of course, that she considered her life normal at all was strange to Allison. More months had passed, and her third rainy season in the village had begun.

While her relationship with Majiro had become a workable one, the chief's temper still flared easily. She had learned to keep most of her thoughts to herself and pacify him with her diligence and obedience. Isaac was the one joy that they shared. At three years old, he was talkative and remained curious as always. Majiro, whom Isaac called "father," still insisted on Isaac's company most days. For this reason, Allison coveted the moments that she had alone with her son and used the time to talk to him of her faith, his family, and the world outside of the village.

Today was such a day. Majiro was out of the village at the garden of his cousin, clearing a new section of land for eventual planting. Since the cousin's wife had gone along to feed the men, Allison had not been required to go. Isaac had remained home with her.

After finishing up her daily chores, she sat on the low bench next to the fire with Isaac between her knees, enjoying the new roof that Majiro had built above it to keep out the rain. Using a long stick, she helped her son draw letters into the dirt and practice their names. For each letter she told him two words beginning with that letter, one familiar and one not. "A is for apple. That is a fruit, Isaac. It's red and round, and it crunches when you bite it." She yearned for her child to be able to identify with her world, and so she described it to him using his own experiences as a comparison.

For a long while, they sat together reviewing letters and then singing nursery rhymes. Finally, Allison began telling Isaac's favorite story, Noah and the Ark. As she depicted each pair of animals going into the ark, Isaac mimicked the animal's sound. Soon they were both in a fit of giggles.

The smile faded from her face as she realized that they were being watched. Sema stood a few feet behind them, his expression twisted into an ever-present scowl. Isaac, unaware, continued talking about the animals on Noah's ark, but she met Sema's dark eyes.

"Have you no respect for our people? You use this foreign language in our village, and you teach it to this boy that our chief calls 'son,'" he snapped pointing at Isaac whose eyes were wide with surprise at the interruption.

"I respect the Shampiri, but I want my son to know the language and ways of his mother as well. I teach him about Creator God who—"

"Your spirit is an enemy of ours. Our spirits have warned us for many years that the words of foreigners would bring quick death to our people and way of life. Majiro would have been wiser to kill you all." Not waiting for a response, Sema stormed away.

"Mommy, why is he angry?" her son asked, moving close to her for reassurance.

She hugged him. "He doesn't know Jesus in his heart, so he is not a happy man." The explanation was sufficient for the child, and he soon scampered off to play with Amita's children, who came walking up the trail with their mother.

After greeting her friend, Allison reached for little Iquemisa who was now a bouncy six-month-old. She cuddled the baby close as she told Amita of her confrontation with Sema. Amita, clearly more disturbed than she was, said, "Be careful of him, Imeshina. He is a dangerous man. It's not just you that he hates. He hates me and everything and everyone that is not Shampiri."

"But why?"

Amita shook her head. "I don't know. Manitari told me that his father was a powerful shaman and felt the same way. In fact, if his father had not died, I doubt that you would be alive. His father always said that a village mixed with foreign blood would be cursed by the spirits."

"He was a shaman? Like Inani?" Allison asked curiously.

"No." Amita explained, "Inani is a medicine woman. Her magic is only to cure people from disease and curses. A shaman is much more powerful. The strongest shamans can kill a person from miles away by magic."

"Then why would anyone want a shaman in their village? It sounds like it would be dangerous to have him around."

"A shaman uses his power against the enemies of his tribe, though I don't suppose much would stop him from using it against anyone he wanted."

"Does the village have a shaman now?"

"There are a few men—Sema is one of them—that have the shaman's spirits. But none are as powerful as Sema's father was," Amita answered.

"Wow. I didn't realize all this."

Amita put her arm around Allison's shoulders. "You must be careful of what you say and who you are around. Because my people shared ancestors with the Shampiri, many do not see me as foreign. But there is much fear in the village because of you."

"People are scared of me?" she asked.

"No, not scared of you," Amita clarified. "Scared of what will happen because you are here. Most are too intimidated by Majiro to say anything. You are fortunate that the chief is your husband."

Allison's head was reeling at the new information. She had often felt like a bit of an outcast in the community, but had always believed it was a simple matter of being unable to communicate well. The idea that she was seen as a bearer of a curse was both stunning and sickening. Fear was rampant in the tribe, and she hated that she was the reason for even more.

A few days later Allison met Majiro as he came toward the house in the late afternoon. He had gone hunting early in the morning while she was bringing up water from the river. He had been gone for most of the day but had returned with a couple of wild turkeys.

She took the birds from his basket and began plucking them quickly in order to cook them for dinner. "Where is Isaac?" she asked absently.

Majiro looked at her strangely, "What do you mean 'Where is Isaac'? I've been gone all day."

"Didn't he go hunting with you?"

"No. When I left he was playing by the fire."

Allison rose, her eyes wide and her heart sinking. "I thought he was with you because the house was empty when I returned from the river... Majiro," she said slowly, "I haven't seen him all day."

The two stood motionless, staring at one another as they realized the seriousness of the situation. Her own fear reflected in Majiro's eyes, and he immediately let out a loud bellow that brought those that heard running to find out what had happened. He quickly explained Isaac's disappearance and began issuing commands to search for the boy around the area.

The Shampiri scattered, all as intent on finding the lost child as if he were their own son. No one had to explain the dangers of a child lost in the jungle, especially as night approached.

Grabbing his bow and arrows, Majiro started toward the trail to their garden. "Stay here," he ordered without pausing in his step.

Allison protested, "No. I am going back to the river. He may have tried to follow me there." Majiro nodded his assent and wordlessly hurried into the jungle.

As she ran for the river, her body quivered with anxiety. Terrible thoughts of all that could have happened to her son raced through her mind. Her immediate concern was that Isaac had encountered a predator. Poisonous snakes and frogs were plentiful in the Amazon, and wildcats and alligators hunted their territory without mercy. However, she knew that even if he had managed to avoid dangerous creatures, becoming hopelessly lost and perishing from exposure or hunger was a genuine threat as well.

As her feet pounded against the packed dirt of the jungle floor, her heart beat wildly with panic. *Please, God, be with him. Don't let anything happen to my son! Please, please...*

Suddenly, as if she had run into a wall, Allison stopped on the trail listening to a familiar whisper. **Do not be anxious. Where can your son go that I am not with him?**

The truth in the words did little to reassure her. "I know you are with him, but he is so small. It will be dark in a few hours."

The darkness is not dark to me, and the night is as light as the day.

Thinking of her little boy alone in the night, she burst into tears. She dropped to her knees in the middle of the trail and sobbed into her shaking hands. "I just want to know that he will be okay," she pleaded hoarsely.

As a soft breeze caressed her cheek, she felt the tears cool on her face. An inexplicable certainty flooded her soul, and she knew without a doubt that Isaac was safe and would return home unharmed. There was no logical reason for her conviction other than that God Himself had filled her with His own clear knowledge.

She wept again, but this time in relief as her anxiety ebbed away. "Please, help us to find him soon so that he does not suffer. Show me where to look. I trust You."

She continued toward the river, still hurrying, but unafraid of what she would find. As she approached the river's edge, she saw Amita standing beside the water, her hand shading her eyes as she looked downriver.

Noticing Allison's arrival, Amita called out, "Has anyone found him yet?"

"No." Allison strode to her friend and laid a hand on her shoulder. "But don't worry. I don't know where Isaac is, but I know that he is all right. We will find him, and he will be alive."

"How can you be so sure?" Amita demanded, her fear written all over her face.

"I don't really know how to explain other than that God told me, and I believe Him." Allison quickly told her about her experience on the trail.

Amita looked at her doubtfully. "If you say so."

The two women continued walking along the edge of the river, being careful to look behind the few scattered boulders on the bank. Before too long, they encountered Amita's daughter, Micheli, playing in the water with her younger brother.

"What are you doing?" the girl called out.

"Looking for Isaac. He's been gone all day. Have you seen him, daughter?"

"I saw Isaac this morning going into the jungle with Sema."

Allison gaped at the girl as the blood drained from her face. "With Sema? But..."

Amita grabbed her friend's hand. "Sema came back to the village this afternoon. I saw him myself. He was alone."

"We have to go tell Majiro! What if Sema has done something to him? Come on!"

As she turned to run back to the village, Amita's hold on her hand tightened. "Wait, Imeshina! We don't know anything yet. If Sema is responsible for trying to harm your son, Majiro will kill him. You know that he will! Our village will divide over his death. And if we accuse Sema falsely, he will hate us even more than he does now."

Allison tugged her hand away. "I can't just do nothing!" she cried, "You know as well as I how cruel Sema is. Isaac wouldn't be able to defend himself. He could be hurt!"

"You just told me that your God promised to protect him."

"But—"

"Do you believe it or not?"

Allison stared at her friend for a full moment as fears paraded through her mind. Finally, she sighed. "Yes," she decided. "Yes, I believe it."

"Then we will say nothing."

They continued searching around the river bank until dusk was imminent and then returned to the village. When they arrived, most of the others were returning as well, but no one with news, good or otherwise.

Allison retreated to her home and finished preparing the birds she had dropped on the ground earlier. They were roasting over the fire when Majiro appeared, a defeated frown on his face.

"No one found him," he said glumly.

She gently touched his arm in a gesture of comfort, and the warrior looked up in surprise. "No," she said softly. "He will be found soon, Majiro. God told me that he is alive."

"Spirits can deceive," he scoffed.

She smiled. "Not God. He cannot lie. Isaac is safe."

Not having anything to say, Majiro sat by the fire and ate. Allison served him, but did not eat. She was too busy praying for her son. While she believed with all her heart that he was safe, she also knew that he was probably hungry and, most of all, terrified of being alone in the dark. She prayed that he would be warm and full and peaceful through the night.

The next morning came slowly and with it, a rainstorm. Ignoring the storm, both Allison and Majiro were outside before it was completely light out. Neither had slept. She had spent most of the night sitting in the hammock praying, while he had kept watch by the fire hoping that somehow Isaac would appear.

Now that day had come, they were joined by many of the Shampiri to search the trails around the village. Allison focused her pursuit of her son around the trail where Micheli had seen Sema and the boy the day before.

By lunchtime, she was exhausted and shivering from the long trek through the soggy jungle. The rain had stopped, but the ground was slick and muddy. She retraced her steps toward the village, feeling less hopeful than when she had started. Her trust that Isaac would be found safe and alive had not wavered, but she agonized over what he would suffer through in the meantime.

As she walked toward her house, she recognized an unusual clatter of activity and instinctively knew that it had something to do with her son. She raced toward the noise coming from the house at the very end of the clearing and found a crowd laughing and talking excitedly. When they saw her coming, they parted to reveal Majiro holding Isaac, who was munching voraciously on boiled yucca.

"Mommy!" Isaac called out, scrambling out of Majiro's arms and into her own. Relief flooded her heart, and she wept without shame as she examined him from his toes to the top of his brown, curly head. He was covered in mud and scratched all over where briars had caught his skin. His knees were scraped from an apparent fall, and he had an impressive array of mosquito bites. But otherwise, he was completely fine.

"Who found him?" she asked the group as she hugged him close.

"Tsipavi. He was asleep in a ravine," Majiro said.

Scooping up her son, Allison stood in front of the grizzled warrior that had brought him home. "Thank you for bringing him home safely."

Tsipavi nodded solemnly. "He must have wandered off when no one was watching and fallen down the ravine."

"I doubt that is what happened." Allison turned to see Sema shouldering his way into the crowd. "The spirits likely took him away," he said. "For years we have been warned of what would happen to our people if we allowed foreigners to live among us. You are just lucky that he was not killed."

Majiro interjected, "He may not be my blood, but he is my son. He is Shampiri."

"You are deceived, Chief. Even if he is your son, your wife is teaching him foreign ways. She told me herself that she is raising him to follow her spirits, not yours." Sema looked around and seemed to draw strength from several who were nodding in agreement.

Allison watched Majiro's face as his eyes narrowed in controlled rage. He was angry, but he was a capable enough leader to know when to speak and when to remain silent.

"Ask your people," Sema continued. "We've all seen the evidence. Surely even your own mother has seen it."

Majiro looked over at his mother for confirmation. The woman looked between him and Allison and sighed. "I've seen them praying together to their spirit," she admitted reluctantly.

Majiro's jaw tightened. "It will not happen again," he vowed. Turning toward Allison, he said, "You will no longer speak of your God to anyone."

"But, Majiro—"

"Enough, woman. You will do as I say." Majiro glared at her and then stalked away in the direction of their home.

With a sigh, she followed him home with Isaac still in her arms. As she passed by, Inani reached for her hand. "You will see. It is better this way," the woman said. Allison smiled weakly, thankful for the words of comfort, though she did not see how they could possibly be true.

That night Allison sat next to Isaac on his sleeping mat as he fell asleep. A whispered conversation confirmed that Sema had indeed been the one to lead the boy out of the village. She implored him not to say anything about it to anyone, but she was not too concerned since no one seemed interested in asking him what had happened. They all seemed content with the explanation Sema had provided that afternoon. Finally, Isaac slept. She pulled the blanket to his chin and kissed his cheek as she breathed another prayer of thanksgiving for his safe return.

Standing, she approached Majiro, who was sitting on the floor carving an arrow out of the heart of a long, straight tree branch. "I want to talk to you about this afternoon," she said.

He replied without looking up, "There is nothing to talk about."

"Yes, there is," she said firmly and sat down across from him.

Majiro's jaw set stubbornly. "You will not speak to my son about your spirits or the ways of your people. He is Shampiri now."

"He is still my son—"

"Sema is right. I have been too soft with you since you came. You are a *captive* and a woman. Our people have been in this jungle for generations, following our spirits and performing our rituals. To defy them is to invite destruction to the Shampiri. You will obey me and do all you can to become Shampiri—and only Shampiri."

Majiro did not raise his voice. But the intensity of his gaze and the hardness of his tone almost caused her to drop the matter. Instead she tried another tactic. "If it really was your spirits that took Isaac, why were they unable to kill him? Maybe because my God protected him?"

"Or maybe it was just a warning as I am now warning you."

"Majiro, won't you even let me tell you about God? He is stronger—" A powerful blow struck her on the face, and she grabbed her stinging cheek as hot tears gathered in her eyes.

Dropping his carving knife, Majiro leaned toward her until their faces were nearly touching. "Never speak of your God again, Imeshina. Not to me, not to Isaac, not to my people. We are Shampiri, and we will have nothing to do with Him." The chief went back to work on his arrow, completely ignoring her.

She sucked her split lip, trying to decide what to do. Her sense of justice screamed at her to put him in his place, to tell him exactly what was in his future if he refused to acknowledge the Creator God. However, she knew that her anger was not righteous but full of vengeance, so she said nothing and went to bed with a prayer that she could forgive this man yet again.

For much of the night, Allison laid awake considering the predicament she was in. It was clear to her that acquiescing to Majiro's demand of silence was against the Lord's direction, but how to go about sharing her faith was not so clear any longer. She pondered ways to reach the Shampiri until, finally, she felt the Lord's assurance that He would lead her to know when and how to speak of Him. With her next breath, Inani came to mind. After praying for her for a few minutes, she recalled the older woman's shame as she was forced to confess that she had seen Allison praying with Isaac. She decided that the next morning she would go to her so that she would know that she did not blame her for the scene that day.

After sleeping for only a few hours, Allison woke up to the sound of Isaac giggling in the hammock. She looked over from the sleeping platform and laughed as she watched him swinging wildly.

"You are such a monkey! Maybe you should live in a tree," she teased him. She got down and hugged her son for a long moment before sending him outside to look for firewood. Once she had stoked the fire's ashes back to life, she cracked open a few yucca roots and set them in a pot of leftover water to boil for lunch. Soon the family had eaten a breakfast of sweet bananas, and Majiro and Isaac had gone to look for the feathers to attach to Majiro's new arrow.

Wasting no time, Allison hurried to Inani's house and found the woman quietly working at her weave. "Good morning," she greeted. The woman smiled tightly, and Allison continued on as if she had not noticed Inani's discomfort. "Isaac hasn't stopped eating since he came home. Would you believe that he ate five bananas this morning?"

The native woman listened as Allison carried on the one-sided conversation. Finally, Allison broached the subject she had come to talk about. "I want you to know that I am not upset about what you said to Sema yesterday afternoon. I'm glad that you didn't feel you had to lie for me."

"You are not angry?" Inani asked, as she paused from her loom to study the younger woman's face.

"No, of course not."

"Then you will do what the chief has said?"

Allison smiled and shook her head. "I will obey him as much as I can, but not if it makes me disobey God."

Laughing at Inani's perplexed expression, Allison explained, "I know that God wants me to tell the people about Him. I can't keep silent about my faith, even if it makes Majiro angry."

"What are you supposed to tell us?"

"That He is the one, true God. And that He loves you."

"Spirits do not love," Inani said.

"God does."

Inani was still not convinced. "Imeshina, I have served the spirits my whole life. They are powerful and vengeful. If they are angry, they kill and destroy. The best we can do is keep them content, and if that doesn't work, we deceive them just like they deceive us."

"They are powerful and evil," Allison agreed. "But Creator God is more powerful than all of them, and He is never cruel or deceptive. He is always good and loving to His people. Do you know that when Isaac went missing, God told me that he would be safe? I know that God watched over him. Would one of your spirits do that for your children?"

Regarding her for a moment, the older woman replied, "No. Never. But you do not know these spirits. They are strong."

Though she wanted to continue the conversation, something in her heart held her back. She knew that generations of belief would not be changed in a single morning, so she let the subject drop. She visited for a while longer until she needed to return home to do her chores. Before she left, her mother-in-law implored her to follow Majiro's order. "You are his wife now," she said, "Leave your spirits behind and become Shampiri." But Allison knew that was simply not an option.

CHAPTER **FIFTEEN**

"How are things at the chief's house?" Manitari asked his wife as she walked through the door of their home after her visit. "Tense," Amita replied. "Ever since Isaac went missing, Majiro won't let Imeshina speak of what is closest to her heart."

"What is that?"

"Her God. She doesn't say anything to him, but she has told me that she has spoken to Inani about her faith too. I am afraid of what the chief will do if he finds out."

Manitari nodded pensively. He and Majiro had grown up together, and he knew the man better than most. "Majiro will never allow her to defy him publicly. He will send her away or he will kill her."

Amita sat next to him and grabbed his arm. "What should I do? I'm scared for her."

Surprised by her offered touch, the warrior rubbed her soft cheek with the back of his hand. "Warn her. Tell her to keep silent. She will listen to you, Amita."

Just then, the children burst through the door arguing, and Amita rose to referee the squabble. Manitari watched her, his heart filled with sadness and hope. This woman he loved more than any man was supposed to love a woman. However, for all of their years together, she had seldom shown any love in return. This was the first time she had ever approached him with a personal problem that did not involve their children. Maybe, just maybe, she was finally softening her heart toward him.

A few days later, Amita offered to go with Allison to her garden to do some heavy weeding. It was the chance she had been waiting for to speak privately to her friend about her concerns. The pair walked amicably down the trail, laughing over the recent antics of their children. Once at the garden, Amita set little Iquemisa on a mat of wide leaves and gave him a dried guava to play with. The baby was sitting on his own now, but had not yet figured out how to crawl. He fussed over not being with his mother, but was soon distracted by the flowers she tossed in his lap.

As they bent over the earth and began to pull the weeds that were choking the food-producing plants, Amita shared her concerns about Allison's situation.

"Amita, you don't have to worry about me."

"Don't you know what could happen to you if Majiro finds out that you have defied him? I would never tell him of our conversations, but I know that it is not just to me that you speak about these things. Aren't you afraid of the consequences?"

"I'm more afraid of not saying anything," Allison replied.

"What do you mean?"

Allison sat back on her heals to explain. "In the two years that I have been here, I have come to love the Shampiri. You are my dearest friend, and your children are as precious to me as Isaac. I love Inani like a mother, and so many of these men and women like my sisters and brothers. For me to not tell you about my faith would be like having the only producing garden and only set of arrows in the village and not sharing the food that I have. How can I love you all as I do and not share what gives me life and peace?"

Amita pulled another weed and tossed it aside. "You think we have no peace?"

"Do you?"

Amita blew the hair from her eyes and thought for a moment. "We're born, we live, and we die. But much of our life is lived in fear. Fear of starvation, fear of the death of our children, fear of raids. You've endured many terrible things, yet you remain confident in your God. How can you still trust Him?"

"Following God doesn't mean a life free of pain or difficulty," Allison answered. "It just means that I know that my pain has a purpose because I know that the God that allows it is good. When my husband was killed and I was brought here, I was hurt and angry with God. But I am beginning to understand now that He let those things happen not because He enjoys my suffering but because He is a God of love." She reached for Amita's hand and said softly, "It is because He loves *you* so much that He brought me here to make sure you knew about Him."

"It's hard to believe that the Creator God would care that much about anyone."

Allison took the opportunity to tell her again about Jesus, the God-man and proof of God's abounding love for humanity. Amita listened without comment, her eyes never straying from Allison's face.

"Imeshina, how do I follow this Jesus God like you do?"

"He says that we only have to believe in our hearts that He is who He says He is, and tell Him with our mouths that we accept His forgiveness and want to follow Him with our lives."

Without waiting for any prompting, Amita began spilling her heart out to God and asking Him to be her one and only spirit guide. In a matter of minutes, Allison looked with joy upon the first believer in the Shampiri village. She could not contain her tears, and they spilled freely down her cheeks. Throwing her arms around Amita, she said, "Now we are sisters! Daughters of the true God."

The two women went back to their work in the garden, but their conversation remained on what had taken place. Amita was full of questions about her new faith, and Allison was only too excited to answer them. Already she could see a change in the small woman. Her voice evidenced her joy, and her face was finally filled with the peace she had been craving for so long.

Manitari watched from nearby as his wife hummed softly to herself while she nursed their son. She had been acting strangely for the past few days, lighthearted and, well, giggly. She was unlike the stoic woman he was used to seeing working around their home, and he wanted to know why.

"Are you feeling well?" he asked, coming up behind her and causing her to turn and smile.

"I feel wonderful."

"You've been… different this week."

Amita laughed. "I feel different this week." She finished feeding the baby and went inside to lay him on the children's sleeping mat on the floor. Manitari followed her in and stood in the doorway with his hands on his hips. It crossed his mind that she had taken a new lover like many of his tribesmen did. Divorce was unheard of, but infidelity was common.

"Are you with another man now?" he asked, bracing for the news that would rip his heart out.

Again his wife laughed. "No, husband," she responded walking to him and taking his hands. "I made a decision to put away all of my old spirits and follow only the Creator God."

"You mean Imeshina's God?"

"Yes!"

Alarmed, Manitari gripped her shoulders. "No, Amita! I can't let you do that. You know what the chief says about her religion. You will be an outcast among our people if anyone finds out."

"It doesn't matter. I've never been so… -*free* in all my life! This God loves me, Manitari. He protects me and speaks to me all day with words of hope and direction. I want to keep learning all I can about Him!"

"You do seem happy," her husband said slowly. "I just wish I was the one you felt this way about, not some foreign God."

"This 'foreign God' has helped me do what I have never been able to do before. I've forgiven you."

Manitari was dumbfounded. "For what?" he asked.

"Ever since you took me from my family, I've despised you. No matter how kind you were to me or how good you were to our children, all I could think about was that you stole me from my family. God has shown me that He allowed the pain of being taken from my family, so that I could know the happiness of making a family here with you… -Manitari, I want to start over with you, but this time I want to be your wife by choice, not by force." Amita put her hand softly on her husband's tanned chest and smiled into his unbelieving eyes. He lowered his mouth to hers, and her lips softened underneath his. For the first time in their marriage, she responded to his caresses eagerly as she pressed against him.

Manitari raised his face just high enough to see her eyes. "Amita, I have loved you since I saw you the first time. All I have ever wanted to do is make you happy."

"You never had a chance. But now we will make each other happy."

"I still don't want you to talk about this with anyone but Imeshina and me," Manitari insisted.

"All right. Only with the two of you. Now come, I have a lot to tell you." Amita led her husband to the fire, and there they sat for hours as she told him all about Jesus.

CHAPTER **SIXTEEN**

It felt strange driving into work after nearly three weeks away, but Eric was glad to be back. The two weeks he had spent leading a group from the church on a mission project in Iquitos had been taxing both physically and emotionally. The team had worked diligently on constructing a new hangar for the aviation ministry that served missionaries from Iquitos and had left feeling satisfied that their project had been a success.

All the while Eric had toiled alongside his team and the missionaries, his thoughts had been on Allison and Isaac. Not many days went by that he did not think of them at least in passing, but usually he no longer dwelled on their disappearance as he had in the beginning. Returning to Peru had brought back the old nightmares, and he had found himself waking up in his bunk in a cold sweat, ready to run after his wife and son. Even after returning to Texas, renewed doubts about their whereabouts remained.

The evening before the team left for their trip, he had attended a retirement party for Helen, the church's secretary. Pastor Denny had been concerned for him from the moment Peru was nominated as the location for the mission trip. He had tried to persuade Eric to take the group elsewhere, but Eric had simply pointed out the practicality of taking his first trip as missions pastor to a place he was familiar with, working alongside old friends.

"I know this might be difficult for me, but I can't just avoid a section of the globe because of painful memories. Besides, it's been almost two years since I was in Peru. It will be different for me now," he had pointed out. Though he still believed the trip to be a good idea, it had been more upsetting than he had expected. Now, he was just glad it was over.

Eric parked his car and took his time making his way to his office. Everyone he passed asked about the trip, so he paused to give each person a synopsis of the team's work in Iquitos.

While he was standing in the middle of the front office talking to another pastor, an unfamiliar face caught his eye. She was around his age and positively stunning, with huge, dark eyes framed by heavy lashes and jet-black hair cut into a trendy style just under her jaw-line. Her high cheekbones and caramel-colored skin suggested Native American descent. She was carrying a heavy stack of files and smiled as she walked around him and set her load down on the front desk.

"Hi!" she chirped cheerfully. "You must be Eric. I've heard a lot about you. How was your trip to Peru? I'm Julia Ayer by the way—the new secretary."

Eric blinked a few times, feeling slightly overwhelmed by her bubbly manner. "I... uh... yeah, hi. Nice to meet you. Peru was good. The pilots were very excited about the new hangar we built."

She smiled again, showing off a row of straight, white teeth. "That's great! Well, I had better get back to work. I am putting together an updated church directory. Let me know if I can help you with anything!"

After thanking her, Eric retreated to his office. Work had piled up in his absence and he spent most of the day locked away, returning calls and approving outreach announcements for the following Sunday's bulletin. Toward the end of the day, he emerged for the first time since lunch with a sheet of paper in his hand. It was time to put the new secretary to the test. Helen had been proficient in meeting most office needs, but her age showed when it came to current technology. He wondered if the younger woman would have more to offer.

"Julia, are you busy?" he asked stepping up to her desk.

She looked up from her computer screen and shook her head. "Not with anything too important. What can I do for you?"

"Well, there is a new program some of our church members are getting involved in. They are working with Social Services and the Department of Corrections to start a Big Brother/Big Sister program with some of the kids in juvenile hall. Anyway, I'm trying to get a brochure put together for an informational meeting on Sunday. How good are you at that sort of thing?"

"Good, actually," she laughed. "But it might take me a few days."

"I'd like to see it by Thursday morning."

"Not a problem."

Eric grinned, glad to have the project off his hands. "Perfect! Thanks. I'll e-mail you a few pictures and the information that needs to be included. You'll just have to make it look nice."

"I'll get it printed by Wednesday. That way, if there's a problem, we'll still have time to make changes."

"Good thinking. I'll go send those files to you now." Eric returned to his office and sent the promised e-mail immediately. He hoped Julia's abilities were as good as she seemed to think they were, because his own creativity for things like that was fairly limited.

He finished a few more things before deciding to call it a day. On the way out of the office, he passed the new secretary's desk, but she was already gone.

On Tuesday night, Eric finished a microwave dinner in front of the television, which was turned up to drown out the sound of the rain. He walked into the kitchen to throw away his tray and decided to make coffee to finish off his meal. As he filled the filter with coffee grounds, the doorbell rang. He put the coffee can back into the cabinet and flipped off the television on the way to the door.

Looking through the peephole, he stood back, surprised. He opened the door, and Julia smiled up at him sheepishly. "Julia, hello. What can I do for you?"

"Hi, Eric. Sorry to drop in on you. I was looking at the brochure for the big brother program after you left today and realized that there's a problem with it," she explained. "Pastor Denny gave me your address, and I thought if we can get it fixed tonight, I could get everything printed tomorrow morning."

"Of course. Come on in. You're getting soaked out there." Eric opened the door wider so she could pass by him.

She stood in the living room looking around. "I like your place. It's very well decorated," she complimented.

"Thank you. My wife's doing, not mine."

Julia's brows knitted together in confusion. "You're wife? I heard that… that she…" she trailed off as if unsure how to explain what she had been told.

Eric rescued her quickly. "She died, yes. In Peru. But most of the stuff that is here we had in storage. I just kind of put it back the way it had been before we left."

"I get it. Well, she had great taste," Julia said lamely, and they looked at one another awkwardly.

"Uh, I was just making coffee. Why don't you have a cup with me while you tell me what's going on with the brochure?" Julia followed him into the cozy kitchen and sat on a high stool at the counter. He added more coffee grounds to the filter and flipped the coffee maker on. Within minutes, the coffee was brewed. He filled their mugs and set out a bowl of sugar and a carton of milk.

"So what's the problem?" he asked as he took a seat next to her.

Julia pulled a copy of the brochure from her purse and handed it to him. "Take a look. I printed this up at the office," she said.

Glancing at the document, Eric looked up in surprise. "This is amazing. It looks professional."

Ignoring the compliment, she said, "Look closer at the pictures." She pointed at one of them. "See how grainy they look? That will look worse when it is printed professionally. I just realized that the JPEG files you sent me were automatically compressed by your e-mail."

"Do I need to resend them?"

"You could. Do you know how to override the compression command in your e-mail?"

"Um..."

Julia grinned at his baffled expression. "I figured as much. All I need is to get the original files. If you still have them on your laptop or camera, I can just copy them onto the memory stick I brought."

"Now, that I can do. I'll be right back." Eric hopped off the bar stool and retrieved his laptop from its case by the front door. He handed the machine to Julia and said, "They are in the 'Big Brother' file on the desktop."

In a matter of moments Julia had the files copied and the computer shut down. Eric watched her work silently. Her efficiency spoke of practice.

"So how do you know all of this stuff?" he asked.

"I almost graduated with a degree in graphic design."

"Almost?"

"I decided it wasn't what I wanted to do with my life, so I switched to education. I have just a few more on-line classes to go to finish my master's degree in special education."

Eric asked, "You plan to teach?"

"Hopefully. I just moved here a few months ago," Julia explained. "I don't know a whole lot about how the school districts are set up yet. But it will be a while before I am ready to apply."

Moving to refill their coffee mugs, he observed, "You won't be staying at the church then."

"No. Pastor Denny knew that when he hired me. Helen highly recommended me for the job, and I am buying him some time while he finds someone permanent."

Eric paused his line of questioning, unsure if he was making his guest feel interrogated, but her open, friendly eyes assured him that she did not. "How did you come to know Helen?" he asked.

Julia waved her hand nonchalantly. "Oh, I've known Helen since I was a kid. My mother moved here with my older sister and me when my parents divorced. I followed my sister to college in Chicago, but when my mom died at the end of last summer, I came back to settle her estate and deal with her house. At some point I just decided to stay." She laughed at herself, and Eric had to smile back at her contagious humor.

"What about you, Eric? I mean how did you end up here after your—" Julia broke off and covered her mouth with her hand. "Oh, I probably shouldn't ask that. I can be really nosy sometimes."

"It's all right. I'm originally from Dallas, but when I came back from Peru I wanted to start over someplace new."

Julia wagged her head sympathetically. "That makes sense."

"It's actually kind of nice that you asked. Most people don't want to bring it up, even though they are curious. It just becomes the elephant in the room."

"Hmmm. Subtlety is not on the list of gifts the good Lord gave me. My mother called me 'tactless.'" She made a face, causing Eric to laugh heartily.

"Whatever you call it, it's refreshing."

"Glad to be of service. Well, I guess I will head home. I'll make sure to get the picture files replaced on this first thing tomorrow. It should be back from the printer's before you leave in the evening." Julia took their empty coffee mugs to the sink, washed and dried them, and put them back in the cabinet she had seen him take them from. She then threw out the used coffee filter and grounds and washed the glass carafe, completely unaware of Eric's amusement as he watched her putter around the kitchen as if she had done it a hundred times before.

"Thanks for cleaning my kitchen, but you didn't have to," he said dryly when she finished her task.

Her high cheekbones turned pink as she realized what she had been doing. Covering up her embarrassment, she retorted, "I'm the secretary. I always clean up after you guys. And you're welcome." With that she grabbed her purse and made her way to the front door. Eric followed her. He bid her good night and shut the door behind her. Standing in the entryway, he laughed out loud. Julia was definitely a breath of fresh air—a whirlwind really, and he decided that he liked her. A lot.

Over the next few weeks, Eric found himself often working on projects with the new secretary as he took advantage of her computer skills and creativity. She seemed eager enough to help him and continued to entertain him with her witty personality. Perhaps that was why he found himself seeking her out on a Friday morning.

"Hey Julia, do you like basketball?" he asked approaching her desk.

"Watching or playing?"

"Watching."

"Live or on TV?"

"Live."

"Pro, college, or high school."

Eric could not keep himself from laughing. "Pro."

"I like it. Why?"

He explained, "My dad gave me two tickets to the Mavericks game tonight in Dallas. Roger was going to go with me, but he forgot it was his daughter's birthday sleepover tonight. Do you want to go?"

With her lower lip stuck out in an exaggerated pout, she said, "If I am only your second choice... absolutely! What time do we leave?"

"Right after work. The game starts at 7:30. Traffic will be in our favor, but I want to give us plenty of time."

Julia nodded. "That's fine, but can we swing by my place first? I don't really want to wear heels to the stadium."

Eric eyed her pencil skirt and pumps. "I'll just follow you to your house, and then we can take my car."

"Perfect." The two made plans to meet by the front door at five o'clock, and Eric returned to his office.

As promised, they stopped by Julia's house, and she changed into jeans and a blue cardigan set. By the time they were on the road, it was later than he had hoped, and he was a little worried about getting to the game on time. However, traffic into the city was light, and they were parked and in their seats well before the game started.

"I want a hot dog," he announced. "What would you like for dinner—my treat?"

"A hot dog sounds great, thanks. Just make sure you put a lot of mustard and jalapeños on it."

Eric made his way to the concession stand and was back just as the game began. He gave Julia her soda and hot dog, and she took a huge bite of her food. "Mmmm," she sighed. "That is awesome."

Grinning at her exaggerated delight, Eric settled into his seat and ate his own food. They watched the game, both cheering for the Mavericks. It seemed to him that everything about Julia was unexpected. While she dressed impeccably and was beautiful enough to turn heads wherever she was, she was oblivious to the stares and did not seem at all interested in trying to impress people. She was overtly feminine, but at the same time ate her spicy hot dog in man-sized bites. It surprised him that she was familiar with basketball, as she rattled off NBA statistics and argued with the referees' calls. For the most part, Eric watched the game with as much interest as he watched his companion. It was hilarious to see her stand up and shake her fists and yell down at the players as if their game depended upon her coaching.

Julia seemed to enjoy herself as much as Eric did. When the game ended in a solid victory for the home team, she let out a loud whoop. Quickly, they gathered their jackets and joined the flow of the enthused crowd streaming out of the stadium. In the car, Julia chattered a play-by-play of the game. Finally she let out a satisfied sigh. "That was a great game," she stated.

"How do you know so much about basketball?" Eric asked.

"I played in high school, but mostly I'm an NBA junkie. My dad played in college, and it was always something I could talk to him about. Did you play sports?"

"Football in high school. I played for a year in college, but I realized that I couldn't keep the training schedule if I wanted to get into law school."

She glanced at him in surprise. "You went to law school? How did you end up a missionary?"

That question launched Eric into his testimony. He explained that as his relationship with God deepened, his dissatisfaction in his law career grew as well. For the first time in over two years, he found himself describing how he and Allison had decided to move overseas and what a joy it had been to them both to be involved in the ministry of reaching the Shampiri.

As he drove toward home, he nearly forgot that Julia was sitting next to him. She was uncharacteristically quiet, and he continued his story. The pride in his voice was evident as he spoke of Isaac's birth and first few months of life. When he finally got to the day that changed his life forever, his voice dropped to nearly a whisper. He finished by saying, "I still have days that I wonder if they are still out there, but I know it is probably just grief and guilt. I wish I had been able to protect them."

"I can see why you would feel that way," Julia said softly. Eric glanced at her and was surprised to see tears in her eyes. He was also surprised and grateful that she did not say anything about the situation not being his fault. Though he knew instinctively she believed that it was not, he appreciated that she gave him the freedom to feel as he did.

After a few silent moments, Julia reached over and touched his arm lightly. "I'm so sorry about your family, Eric."

"Thank you. I still don't understand why God allowed it to happen, and I doubt I ever will. I just keep reminding myself that God is still in control, and He is still good. Some days that can be hard to believe… I hope it doesn't bother you, hearing that from one of your pastors."

Julia cocked her head and flashed her winning smile. "What? That you are human? Sorry, I already figured that out. Right about the time you spilled water on the copy machine."

Eric laughed at the reminder of the incident. "Now don't bring that up again. I learned my lesson. Expensive electronics and liquids don't mix very well."

"I'll remind you of that on Monday when I go into your office and see you drinking your coffee over your laptop." The two continued their friendly banter for what remained of the trip back home. Soon Eric pulled into the driveway of Julia's house and put the car into park.

"Thanks for coming with me. Sorry I kind of monopolized the conversation on the way home," he said.

"Not at all. I had a great time tonight. I'll see you at church on Sunday." She got out and shut the car door. Eric waited until she had gone inside before he pulled out of the driveway to go home. It had been an unexpected night, but one that he was thankful for. He had been slow to make friends since returning to the United States, yet he could safely say that Julia had managed to become one tonight.

CHAPTER SEVENTEEN

Coming back from a trip to the river for water, Allison encountered an exuberant Isaac. "What are you so excited about?" she asked him as she set her water pot carefully against the lean-to that was serving as their house. It was her third trip to the river today, and she did not want a careless mistake to send her on a fourth. The river was much farther away from this home than it was from their house in the main village.

"Father says that we are going on a trip tomorrow!"

"He does, does he? Where to?"

"Way downriver! We are going fishing."

"I bet you'll have a good time."

Isaac put his arms around her legs and looked up at her with bright eyes. "You are coming with us!"

Allison glanced over at Majiro, who nodded. "We are going with Manitari's family. We will be gone overnight, so prepare enough food for a couple of days."

Irritated thoughts raced through her brain of all that she had to do that day and how much work it would be to get ready to go. She nearly asked him why he had not given her more warning, but the excitement on her son's face kept her from speaking. When they were not at the main village, there were not many others around, as each family tended to strike out on its own, tending to their own gardens and hunting. A few days ago they had encountered Amita and Manitari with their children and decided to camp together for a while. A trip together with their friends would be fun, no matter how much work it would be.

She put Isaac to work peeling finger-sized, ripe bananas to boil for juice and took an inventory of their food supplies. Fortunately, it seemed that they had enough to keep them fed on their trip.

A little later in the morning Amita came by on her way to look for wild fruit to make sure that Allison had heard the news and had her own preparations under control.

"Why are we going so far away to fish?" she asked Amita.

"The water downriver is still and deep and full of fish. Here the current is too swift to use poison."

"Poison? What do we need poison for?"

Amita laughed merrily. "You'll see," she answered cryptically.

Allison was still wondering what she had meant early the next morning when the group left their camp. Isaac ran ahead with the other children, while the adults followed with baskets of supplies strapped to their heads. They walked amicably, if quickly, down the trail to the river. Once at the river, they crossed, only the children taking the time to play. Majiro led them to another trail across the river, and they headed downstream roughly parallel to the river.

The trail was narrow enough that at times they had to duck their heads underneath the tangle of vines that snaked through the jungle. Since they walked single file, conversation was kept to a minimum, but Allison did not mind the chance to let her mind wander a bit.

Since Isaac's disappearance, she had carefully avoided speaking about her beliefs to Majiro and was conscientious about when and where she spoke to Isaac about them. She refused to be scared into silence with the others in the tribe, so the time out of the village was almost a relief. Soon, however, they would be returning along with the rest of the tribe, and she knew that the tension would likely escalate.

The group finally stopped for a lunch of cold boiled yucca in the early afternoon. The children received their food sitting on a fallen log next to the trail, while the adults ate where they stood. "Hopefully we will have a feast of fish tonight," Manitari said as they resumed their journey.

Only an hour or two later, the trail led them from the dense jungle into a wide, open bank of the river. Like Amita had said, the water was as calm and deep as a lake, though still only a few yards across. With whoops of glee, all of the children stripped off what little clothing they were wearing and, dropping their clothes on the sand, ran splashing into the water.

Leaving the children to their games, the women quickly made camp. Together they gathered firewood in the jungle and carried it on their backs to the river bank. Amita worked on starting a fire with two flint rocks and a tiny pile of dry, peeled bark while Allison laid blankets in a rough circle around the fire pit.

Finally, an enormous fire was cheerfully flickering, and the women joined the men, who were farther downstream stringing a wide net across the river.

"Is the bottom secured?" Manitari yelled across the river.

"Yes! Attach your side now, but don't pull too hard."

Manitari waded into the water and dove under with the net. A minute later, he popped back up with a smile. "That should hold," he said. "By the time the *cogi* is ready, we will have a nice pool of fish here."

"Cogi?" Allison asked.

Amita explained, "That's the poison I told you about. We use it on the fish."

"But won't we get sick eating fish that have been poisoned?"

"It doesn't last very long—you'll see."

Allison followed the other three back to their supplies and watched as Majiro turned his basket upside down. A number of tan-colored, tubular roots fell to the sand.

"Is that the poison?" she asked doubtfully.

"Yes." Manitari picked up a root and broke it in half exposing the white interior. "This is cogi. I believe your people call it *barbasco*."

"I don't think so. I've never heard of it before."

"Hmmm. That is what they called it in Iquitos."

Allison jerked her head up and gaped at him. "Iquitos? What do you mean 'Iquitos'? Have you been there?" she demanded.

"It's been a long time. Before I had my family, I traveled some."

"I thought that the Shampiri don't like to leave their villages."

Majiro snorted, "The smart ones don't, but Manitari has always been too curious for his own good."

"My travels brought me to my wife," the warrior retorted. "But I am old enough now to realize that there is nothing out there that I need that I can't find at home."

Allison's mouth opened and then closed again as she struggled to overcome the shock of Manitari's revelation. "Wait a second! So you really do speak Spanish, don't you? When I was cap—when I first came to the Shampiri, you spoke a few words to me, but then you acted like you didn't understand when I tried to speak to you."

Manitari shrugged. "I thought you would learn our language quicker if you didn't know that I could understand you."

Allison stared at him for a moment and then finally laughed. "You were probably right, but it sure would have made those first few days a little easier!"

Manitari chuckled but did not reply. Instead, he knelt down next to Majiro and began breaking up the *cogi* roots into smaller chunks.

"Here. Put these in that basket," Majiro said. Allison held open her hands, and he began dropping bits of the poison into her hands. Soon all of the *cogi* was broken into bits and put back into the basket.

"Children! Come over here! It's time!" Amita called. Micheli herded the younger boys onto the sand, and they all came running, naked and dripping.

Quickly dumping the contents of all of the other baskets, Amita handed them around. "Are you ready, Imeshina?"

"I guess so."

The women and children waded back into the slow current near the net, baskets held high. Each stood with water up to his hips. "What now?" Allison asked.

"Watch." Amita pointed to the men who were several yards upstream. They carefully placed the *cogi* on a large flat rock that peeked above the water near the shore. Once it was laid out, each man took a large stone and began to pound and grind the *cogi*. After the root had turned into a pulp, the men tossed it by handfuls into the river. As the *cogi* sank, the water around it turned murky gray. Soon the current carried the poisoned water further into the river and toward the rest of the group.

Plop. Allison shrieked in surprise as fish literally popped up belly up next to her hand. Amita and the children roared with laughter.

A hand on her hip, Allison accused her still-laughing son, "You knew that was going to happen!"

"Yeah. They told me about it." She laughed and then caught herself from crying out again as more fish began to pop up on the surface of the water. *Plop, plop, plop.* Dozens of fish now surrounded them.

"Quick! Grab them and put them in your basket before the poison wears off. Get the biggest ones and leave the small ones behind," Amita said, reaching for another fish.

Allison, being the tallest of the women, situated herself closer to the center of the river where most of the fish were. They shouted at one another in glee as they scrambled to fill their baskets as quickly as possible.

"Look at this one! It's huge. Help me get it in my basket, Micheli!" Isaac called.

Within minutes, the men had waded back downstream to help gather fish from the deeper water. But as promised, the *cogi's* magic only worked for a few minutes, and the fish had begun to sink back into the water.

Allison grabbed the last fish within her reach. "It's still alive!"

Majiro replied, "Of course. The poison only stuns them; it doesn't kill them. That is why the ones we didn't take went back under. They came back to life."

"How does it work?"

"What do you mean, 'How does it work'?" Majiro asked. "You just saw for yourself." They waded back to shore, each basket heavy with fish that were now suffocating in the air.

Setting her basket down next to the fire, Allison pushed her hair out of her eyes. "I know what happened, but what does it do to the fish. How does it stun them?"

"Someone told me that it makes them unable to breathe, but I don't know if that is true," Manitari answered. "All that matters to me is that it works because I am hungry!"

"You're always hungry," his wife teased with a poke in his ribs.

Everyone set to work getting the fish ready to be smoked. The children ran off into the jungle to find wide leaves to wrap the fish in. The women cleaned the fish, and the men spread the fire's ashes out to make it the perfect temperature. Once the children returned, the smaller fish were wrapped in leaves and nestled into the hot coals to cook quickly. The larger fish were laid across a row of thin sticks propped up high between two logs on one half of the fire. The women laid leaves across them to hold in the smoke and the warmth of the fire. It would take hours for them to cook at such a low temperature, but when they did, the smoked meat would stay edible for weeks.

Soon the sun began its descent, and the temperature began to drop. At first, it was a cool relief from the stifling heat of the day, but soon everyone began to scoot closer to the fire. Allison gathered Isaac in her lap and draped a blanket around their shoulders.

"Are you warm enough?" she asked him.

"Yes. Can we eat yet?"

"Let me check." Allison speared a buried fish with the end of a narrow stick and laid it next to her leg. She carefully unwrapped the blackened, crumbly leaf until the white meat of fish was visible and a delicious steam rose up to her nose. She examined it and declared it ready.

"Just give it a minute to cool off. It will burn your tongue if you try to eat it now."

Isaac impatiently blew on his food for a few seconds and then delicately pulled off a piece of meat and popped it in his mouth. "This is the best fish ever!" he announced.

The rest of the group followed suit and dug their dinners from the ashes. They ate heartily, for there was no lack of food. Soon, however, the conversation lagged. The combination of a long hike and a heavy meal was enough to make them all drowsy. The children were each given a blanket to wrap up in, and Majiro revived the fire with fresh branches.

Isaac was asleep with a contented smile within moments of lying down. Allison smiled as she pulled the covers up to his chin. She loved watching him sleep because the years melted from his young face, and she could see his baby face again in his rounded cheeks.

Smoothing her own blanket next to her son, she curled herself on one half and flipped the other over her body. As exhausted as she was physically, her mind could not seem to slow down. It seemed that no one else shared her problem for the sounds of even breathing and light snoring soon rose from around the fire.

She flipped onto her back and stared at the sky. It was awesome. The bank on either side of the river was wide enough to give her a great view of the enormous sky. There was nothing like being outside on a clear night this far from civilization.

She watched what she thought at first was a shooting star before realizing it was an airliner flying thousands of feet overhead. A tear trickled into her hair as she watched the airplane fly across the sky until she lost sight of it in the trees. To have something of her old life so close yet so impossibly far off was a terrible reminder of what she had lost.

God, I know you are using all of this suffering for a good purpose, but sometimes I just don't care. Sometimes I don't want to walk another step, and I just want it all to be over. Will the rest of my life be like this? Trying to walk faithfully on this path that I never chose? I'm tired, Lord. I don't know if I can keep going much longer.

She just felt weary… and alone. She was weary of the silent battle of wills with Majiro, weary of being the only Christian influence in Isaac's life, and weary of always feeling misunderstood. More than anything she wanted to feel known by someone else. But how could they really know her if they had no concept of her life before the raid? Telling them would do no good. It would be like trying to describe a rainbow to the blind.

I wonder what they think airplanes are when they see the lights move across the sky. They probably have some kind of superstition to explain it. Just like disease or weather or anything else they don't understand.

Sighing, she closed her eyes against the velvet sky. A breeze blew across her face, causing the fire to flicker across her eyelids.

I see you, Beloved.

It feels like this plan of Yours is more important to You than I am. What about me? What about my life, my hopes, my plans? Am I so insignificant that You would allow me to be abused if it furthers Your plan?

I knit you in your mother's womb. Before you were born, I knew all of your days. I know the number of hairs on your head. I love you with an everlasting love, and I will continue my faithfulness toward you. Trust Me, for my plans are right and full of blessing and joy.

Allison sniffed. *I'm not feeling terribly joyful at the moment.*

Beloved, in the meantime, I am holding every tear in a bottle.

For whatever reason, that was enough for now. Her questions were still unanswered, but at least she knew that she was loved, that she was seen. She could wait for the answers.

The next morning Allison awoke to the sound of howler monkeys hooting in the trees a few yards away. Sitting up, she stretched her arms overhead and yawned.

"Good morning, lazy bones," Amita chirped from her squatting position next to the fire where she was peeking under a banana leaf at the smoked fish.

"Where is everyone?" Allison asked, looking around for the others.

"Our husbands are bringing firewood and the children are looking for fruit. Did you not sleep well last night? You didn't stir at all even with the boys running around you."

"It just took me awhile to fall asleep." she replied. "Is the fish cooked?"

"Yes. Help me get it off the fire and packed away." The women laid the banana leaves in the sand and carefully transferred the meat from the fire pit. The filleted fish had smoked into a jerky, but it was crumbly enough that they had to work together to get each one onto the mats without it falling apart onto the sand. The women then wrapped the fish carefully in layers of leaves, tucking the ends so nothing would fall out.

They had barely finished packing all of the fish into the baskets when the children came back carrying handfuls of wild oranges.

"You want one, Mom?" Isaac asked, holding out a particularly large one. "They're really sweet."

"Sure. Thanks." She dug her thumb into the thick green and yellow skin and pulled back the thick peel. Isaac was right. The fruit was sweet. And juicy. It was enough of a breakfast for her, but when the men returned, they were eager to start a fire and reheat some of the remaining fish from the night before.

"We had better eat well. It'll be a long walk back to the village today," Manitari noted, as he knelt on the ground with his face close to the ashes. He blew the fire gently until sparks from the ashes caught the bits of kindling he had placed in the pit. As soon as the kindling lit, he added small twigs, then sticks, and finally broken branches.

Even after a filling breakfast, there were a number of small fish left over, and the women added them to the baskets to be eaten later in the day.

"I am going to take down the net so that we can leave soon." Majiro announced as he stood and brushed a thin fish bone from his leg.

Manitari began to rise as well, but Majiro placed his hand on his shoulder. "Stay and finish eating," he said. "My son can help me."

The other children jumped up, pleading with Amita to have one last swim before they departed. "Go. But stay away from the net while the chief is working." Amita waved them away.

Turning to her husband, she asked, "Do you want another?" He nodded, and she placed a wrapped fish in his lap. "You would think *he* is the pregnant one the way he eats all the time."

Allison chuckled and said, "My people call it sympathy weight when a husband eats like his pregnant wife and they both get big bellies."

"I don't have a big belly!" Manitari protested.

"Yet!" the women responded simultaneously. They laughed uproariously as Manitari eyed the second half of his fish and delicately laid it aside.

"What was your village like?" Amita asked curiously.

"Well, for awhile I lived in a small place with just three families. That is where I first met your husband. But where I am from is a village of thousands of people."

"Iquitos," Manitari said.

"No, actually. My village is even farther than that. And bigger."

"Bigger than Iquitos?" Manitari's eyes widened as if he could scarcely imagine the possibility.

"Much bigger," she confirmed.

"Why did you move to the small village? Did you not like your home?" Amita asked.

"I loved it, but Eric—my husband—and I felt that God wanted us to leave in order to find the Shampiri and tell them about Him."

Manitari stared at her. "You were looking for *us*?"

"Yes. That's why we left all those gifts for you. We were trying to show you that we wanted to be your friends…" Allison trailed off, unsure what else she should say.

"You must regret ever going there," Amita said.

"Sometimes. But it was the right thing to do because to not go would have been disobeying God."

Manitari regarded her doubtfully. "Why such an allegiance to a spirit when obeying Him got your husband killed and nearly yourself as well?"

She looked him in the eye. "Because He created us and this world, Manitari. He has the right to demand our obedience, no matter what it requires of us." Manitari's easy expression filled with dread, but he did not speak. Seeing that her words had hit the mark, she added, "Besides, our being there had the exact result that we had hoped for. You are sitting here listening about the Lord, aren't you?"

"But it is not the way that you thought it would be," Amita stated.

Allison reached over and gave her hand a squeeze. "No. I always hoped that Eric and I would be together to tell the Shampiri about Jesus."

"Do you think that God sent your husband to the village just so that he would die and you would be brought to our village to tell us about Him?" Manitari asked.

"God is always good, and there is no evil in him. I don't believe that He caused Eric's death or my capture, but He did allow it. I also know that His plans will never be thwarted. What men mean for evil and destruction, He is able to use for good."

Manitari was silent for a few moments as if pondering what she had said. "My wife believes these things you tell her about the Creator spirit, but I don't understand. Why would a spirit powerful enough to create the whole world care what we do?"

"Because He loves us. He created us in His own image and chose to love us despite all—"

The three had become so involved in their conversation that no one had noticed that Majiro had returned with the children and was standing behind Allison, his face pinched with an expression of pure rage.

"Do my ears lie to me, Imeshina? Do you dare to speak of this foreign spirit after I have forbidden it?" He spoke quietly, but his words were like ice. The net he was holding dropped to the ground, but the knife in his fist glittered in the sunlight.

Allison stood, her eyes on the cold blade. "Majiro, please. I—"

"I will hear no excuses! I will not have a woman that will not obey me. I am your husband, and I am your *chief*." In an instant, he grasped her by the hair and pulled her head back, exposing the delicate flesh of her neck.

Allison felt the sharp edge of the knife at the base of her throat and heard Amita's cry.

"Mommy!" Isaac screamed, and from the corner of her eye she saw him run toward her. Amita caught him by the arm and pulled him against her. He wrapped his arms around her legs and buried his face in her stomach.

Manitari stood calmly next to Allison. "Chief, if someone must be punished, it should be me. I asked Imeshina about her God. She was only answering my questions."

Majiro's gaze flickered to the other man, but his hold on her did not waver. Allison waited, immobile. She gasped as she felt the tip of the knife cut into her skin. A drop of blood ran down between her breasts.

"Never again, Imeshina. No one will be able to save your life next time." Majiro shoved her back and dropped the knife in the sand at her feet. Not looking at anyone, he stalked away. Trembling, Allison sank to the ground. Isaac let go of his hold on Amita and scrambled into her lap.

"Shhhh. It's okay, baby. Mommy's all right." She comforted him as he sobbed hysterically.

Manitari untied the red band around his right leg and handed it to her. "Take this. Your neck is bleeding pretty badly." he said.

Accepting the strip of fabric, she pressed it onto her throat. She knew that the cut had not been bad enough to cause any major damage, but the fact that Majiro had drawn her blood both stunned and terrified her.

With very few words, they finished packing up. As Allison and Amita helped the children strap baskets of smoked fish onto their foreheads, Majiro began walking toward the trail.

Manitari took a step to follow him, but Allison placed a hand on his arm to stop him. "Thank you for what you did." The corner of her mouth lifted. "I guess this isn't the first time that you have saved me, huh?"

Not cracking a smile, he looked into her eyes. "He wasn't joking. He will kill you next time."

Allison lifted her shoulders. "My highest allegiance is to Creator God. I will submit to Majiro's authority so long as it doesn't interfere with my devotion to God. No matter the cost."

Taking Isaac's hand, she headed for the jungle. Behind her, she heard Manitari mutter to his wife, "Your friend is a fool."

Amita replied, "Is she? It seems to me that if what she says about God is true, then we owe our loyalty to the one who created us and saved us, even more than we owe it to our chief."

CHAPTER **EIGHTEEN**

Hurrying into the park, Eric saw that Julia was already waiting for him on their usual basketball court. They had been playing together most Friday evenings for the past few months, often with Roger or a few other friends from church. Tonight, however, they were on their own.

As he approached the court, he slowed his pace and watched as she dribbled the ball and shot it easily into the net. She looked too neat for the court, her hair pulled back in a soft headband and her pink tank top and gray shorts wrinkle-free. But her movements were liquid motion and obviously that of a natural athlete.

"That's pretty fancy stuff, little lady!" he called out as he dropped his water bottle and towel on the concrete bench at the edge of the court.

"Are you sure you can handle the heat?" she retorted, tossing the ball at his chest. Eric caught the ball with a laugh and bounded onto the court where she immediately went to work playing defense.

Though he was much taller and heavier than she, he knew from experience that he was no match for her abilities. They played hard and soon were both panting for breath. The Indian summer's humidity had not broken and his red T-shirt was already drenched with sweat and sticking to his back.

"Break!" Julia announced and retreated to find her water in her backpack. She took a long drink and wiped her mouth with the back of her hand. "You know," she teased, flopping down on the ground. "I really thought you would be faster on your feet."

"Me too. I might not have asked you to play with us the first time if I had known that you play so well. It's embarrassing."

"I told you I played."

"Yeah. In *high school*."

She threw him a grin. "Hmmm. Did I leave out the part about my team winning nationals my senior year?"

"Well done, Julia. Next week we're playing football," he grumbled. She simply laughed in response.

They rested for a few more minutes, but before they could return to their game, a group of five men sauntered onto the court. "Hey guys, we're still using this court. We were just taking a breather," Eric called out.

One of them looked at them critically. "We could use another player. I guess your girlfriend can be the cheerleader."

Eric reddened and looked over to see if Julia had taken offense, but she just smiled back at him sweetly. "We'll let you have the court," he said, "but you have to take both of us. She doesn't like to sit on the sidelines."

"Whatever. She's on your team. I'm Brent. This is Jeff, Jamal, Alan, and Nathan." Brent quickly introduced his buddies.

"Eric and Julia," he replied, and without further comment, the group split into teams and began playing.

The group of guys seemed to assume that Julia was useless on the court and pretty much ignored her, choosing instead to pass the ball to one another. She continued to play aggressively, waiting for the right opportunity to make her move. Finally, as Brent went to pass the ball to Jeff, she lunged, knocking the ball out of his hands. She dribbled around him and paused behind the three-point line to complete a perfect shot.

Eric caught the ball as it passed through the net and tossed it back to Brent. "You can see why she's not really into the whole cheerleader thing." He said it in good humor, but Brent's eyes narrowed with wounded pride. All of a sudden the game's stakes were higher, and the intensity of it rose exponentially. Eric was ready to call the thing off, but the fire in Julia's eyes made him reconsider. She was enjoying the competition, and he figured he would let her have her fun.

She intercepted another pass and dribbled the ball toward the basket. As she paused to toss it in, Brent's big body slammed into her left side, and she fell to the ground, her hand skidding across the cement to break her fall.

"What's wrong with you?" Eric yelled at Brent, running across the court to help her off the ground.

She had long scrapes on her right hand and arm and down her right leg. "I think I broke my ankle," she whispered. There were tears in her eyes, but she was fighting them. She leaned heavily on his arm as she hobbled to the bench beside the court and sat down to examine her injuries.

Livid, Eric strode up to Brent and demanded, "Is that how you handle being outplayed? Really manly of you to foul a woman because she's wiping the floor with you." Brent moved to fight, but his friends held him back by the shoulders. Eric shook his head and turned away.

"Come on, Julia. I'm taking you to the hospital." She protested, but he ignored her and gathered their things into her backpack. They slowly made their way to the parking lot.

Once she was settled in the car, Eric shut her door and tried to get the anger boiling his blood under control. When he had seen Brent charge her, a fierce, protective instinct had welled up in him. It was a miracle he had not decked the guy.

He got into the driver's seat and started the engine. "How's your ankle?" he asked tightly.

"It burns like fire. But I can move it a little, so maybe it's not broken."

"I'm still taking you to the ER."

She remained silent, and they did not speak until they pulled into the hospital's temporary parking lot. Eric said, "I should have stopped that game sooner. I'm sorry I let it get out of hand."

Julia looked at him, but his eyes stayed on the windshield. "It's not your fault. That guy was a jerk, and I was taunting him. I should not have been enjoying beating him so much."

"That is hardly an excuse for his behavior." Eric parked the car and came around to help her out.

They went inside, and she signed in. Fortunately the room was fairly empty, and it was only about half an hour before her name was called. She was wheeled off to x-ray and then returned to the little exam room where Eric was waiting.

"The doctor will be in soon," the nurse said as she shut the door behind her, leaving the two of them alone.

"Cute hospital gown."

"I don't know why they made me wear this thing. It's not like they couldn't take the x-ray and let me keep my regular clothes on," she complained.

Soon the doctor came in, her x-rays in hand. He introduced himself and then popped the x-rays into the display on the wall and turned on the light behind it. "No break," he announced. "Let me examine you though, and we'll see what's going on." The doctor prodded and pulled on her ankle for a moment before he nodded and pulled out his prescription pad.

"It looks like just a sprain. Ice it today and tomorrow, and then wrap it in a heating pad for the three days after that. Thirty minutes on and thirty minutes off. Here is a prescription for 800mg Motrin if you need it for pain." The doctor handed her the prescription and then proceeded to wrap her foot in an ace bandage.

After brief stops at the pharmacy and a drive-thru, Eric drove to Julia's house. By the time they arrived, night had settled comfortably around them. He ran to open the door and turn on the porch light and then came back to the car to help her out. She hobbled slowly inside and flopped gratefully on the couch.

"I'll be right back with the ice." He left her on the couch and rummaged through her kitchen cabinets until he found a ziplock bag and a towel. After filling the bag with ice, he poured a glass of water and took both of them to Julia, who was pulling burgers out of the bag. She laid the ice across her ankle, which was propped on the coffee table.

"Do you need anything else?" He reached for another pillow to slide under her foot.

"You're hovering."

"Sorry." He sat down on the chair across from her. She offered him a hamburger, but he set it aside. "I feel really awful about this. I should have just sent those guys away or taken you to a different court. I should have known—"

"Yeah, shame on you for not being psychic," she said dryly.

"I'm serious."

"So am I. It was an accident. Let it go."

He rubbed the back of his neck slowly. "It really scared me when you fell." he admitted.

"I was afraid you were going to punch that guy."

"I thought about it."

"I'm glad you didn't. Wouldn't look good, you being a pastor and all." The humor was back in her eyes, and he was relieved that she was not upset about the incident.

They sat quietly while Julia inhaled her burger. She crumbled up the wrapper and stuck it back in the bag. Taking a long drink of her soda, she peered at him through her lashes. "You are a good protector, Eric. The fact that you can't anticipate the actions of hateful men doesn't change that."

He looked at her thoughtfully for a moment before he stood with a sigh. "It's nice of you to say that. Too bad it's not always enough." He reached for the front door knob. "Get some rest. I'll have Roger drive me to the park tomorrow and drive your car home."

"Okay. Thanks. For everything."

"Good night, Julia."

CHAPTER NINETEEN

Life seemed to carry on as usual until an afternoon a few weeks later after they had returned to the main village. Allison stopped by Amita's house to say hello and noticed a group of men gathered around the fire in the front yard, talking animatedly with Manitari. As she walked past them, she heard one of the men say, "There won't be anything there anymore. All of the whites left when we brought the chief's wife back. We shouldn't count on going through those gardens again because the animals have surely eaten everything down to the last root."

Allison slowed her stride to hear more, but the men noticed her and stopped speaking abruptly. She went inside where Amita was resting from the heat of the day on the sleeping platform.

"Why are they talking about my old village?" she demanded after a cursory greeting.

"Many of the warriors go on a trip this time of the year. Don't you remember? Majiro went last year," she replied.

"I remember Majiro's hunting trip last year, but I had no idea that he went back to my old village."

"They've always traveled that way—that is how they found your village in the first place. I think they are just trying to decide which trail to take."

Allison nodded, her mind whirling with possibilities. It made sense. The very reason that her team had decided on that location was because they suspected the Shampiri came through the area on a regular basis. She had not thought of it again since arriving in the village. Of course they still carried on as usual, regardless of whether or not the base was there.

She said good-bye and marched back to her house, hoping that Majiro was there. He was. She joined him under the tree where he was half asleep. "Majiro, I would like to go with you on the hunting trip."

"No," he said, not bothering to open his eyes.

"But don't you want a woman with you to cook for all of the men," she pleaded.

"Jarono's woman is coming with us."

Majiro stood up and, with an irritated look, walked into the house. Allison would not be put off so easily. She followed him into the house still trying to argue her case. "I can go with her and help."

Majiro whirled around. "What is the real reason you want to go with us?" he growled, his dark eyes flashing. "Is it that you heard that we will be going through your old village? What do you think you will accomplish by going there?"

"I—I don't know," she stuttered, surprised by his quick assessment of her intentions. "I guess I just want to see it again."

"There is no one there. The ones that weren't killed are gone, and the ones that were have long since rotted away."

She felt sickened by his description. The thought of Eric's broken body left to the elements and animals broke her heart.

However, the emotions flickering across her face only seemed to irritate Majiro further. He took a step toward her and stared intently into her face, his hands curled tightly at his sides. "You still think about your dead husband. Have I not been a good husband to you?" he demanded roughly. "Have I not provided for you?"

Her own anger erupted, "There is more to being a good husband than putting food on the table. My husband did all that you do and more. He was kind to me; he protected me; he *loved* me."

For a moment, she thought that he would strike her, and she braced herself for the impact of his fist. Instead, he wounded her far more deeply than she thought possible. "Did you know, *wife*, that it was my arrow that killed him?"

Her head snapped back in shock. "What did you say?" she whispered.

"He was the dark-haired one, right? I saw him on the trail, running to the river. I shot him in the back, the way I would any coward running from a battle." Allison stood silently, wishing she could stop her ears against his horrible words. Majiro continued, "He's dead, and you are my wife now. If you can't accept that, I can see to it that you join him." The threat left hanging in the air, Majiro stalked from the room. When he was gone, she sat for a long time, trembling on the floor with her arms wrapped around her knees. It seemed like the horror of that day would never fade.

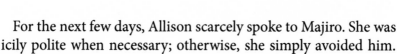

For the next few days, Allison scarcely spoke to Majiro. She was icily polite when necessary; otherwise, she simply avoided him. Isaac noticed the tension between the two of them and began clinging to her in a way that he had not done for years. It annoyed her, but she couldn't figure out why.

On the day after the hunting party left, she sent Isaac off to Inani's house and lay down on the sleeping platform. It was still early in the day, but she was exhausted. She had been run down for a few weeks. At first she thought she must be coming down with something, and then she just figured it was the emotional strain of her argument with Majiro.

With a start, she sat. Counting back in her head, she groaned. *Oh God, no. It can't be. You wouldn't do this to me.* The signs were all there. She was tired, irritable, had no appetite, and her period was late—very late. She was pregnant.

Allison ran her hands down her face and groaned. She had known this was a possibility, even a likely one, but somewhere in the back of her mind she figured that God would spare her this heartache. Surely He owed her at least that?

It was not that she feared having a child out here without medical care. Obviously, the Shampiri women did it all the time, mostly without incident. And it was not that she did not want any more children. She had always thought a big family would be fun. She simply loathed a further connection to Majiro. Bearing his child would mean that she was forever linked to him.

How could you let this happen, Lord? I don't want this baby— Majiro's child. I don't need another thing to forgive him for! Not having the energy or the emotional fortitude to deal with reality, Allison lay back down and cried herself to sleep.

The rainy season progressed to daily torrential rainstorms, and the Shampiri quickly grew accustomed to being soggy most of the time. Allison trudged through the downfall to Amita's house. She had promised to sit with her while she worked on her loom this afternoon. With Manitari gone with the hunting party, Amita was determined to finish the new hammock she was making.

Allison quietly untangled the blue, woolen threads as Amita sat before the loom moving the wooden bars with expert ease. The native woman chattered happily about different happenings around the village, but Allison scarcely heard a word. All of a sudden she realized that her friend had gone silent, and she looked up to find that she was being watched.

"Sorry. My mind was wandering," she apologized.

"I noticed," Amita responded dryly. "What's going on? You've been acting strangely for days."

Unbidden, tears ran down Allison's cheeks as she began to sob. Amita jumped up from her mat and ran to her side. "Shhhhh. Don't cry." She rubbed Allison's back, which only served to make her cry even harder.

After a few minutes, Allison's tears stopped flowing. Taking a deep breath, she explained, "I'm pregnant."

Amita's face lit up with delight until she realized that her friend did not share her excitement. "You don't want this baby?"she asked.

"Of course not! How could I? It's Majiro's child."

"It's also your child," Amita pointed out. Allison said nothing, her thoughts full of anger and self-pity. Amita sighed. "I understand. This is not a child conceived in love. It's not the same as it was with Isaac, is it? I should know." She laid a hand across her own swelling abdomen. "This pregnancy is very different from my others, now that Manitari and I…"

"… are in love," Allison finished for her.

"It was not like that with my other children. When I realized I was pregnant with Micheli, I was not sure if I could love the child that was inside of me because I did not love her father. But you will see, Imeshina, your love for your baby will have nothing to do with who the father is. Jesus will give you all the love you need for this child."

Allison smiled at the encouragement, not so much because she believed her, but because it was moving to hear of her friend's growing faith. Amita's love for Jesus had blossomed alongside her love for her husband. Listening to her talk of her simple, pure devotion to her Savior was captivating.

Still tearful and unsure of her own feelings, she mulled over what Amita had said. She wanted to believe that love for her unborn child would grow naturally, regardless of the circumstances of its conception, but she was not sure how that was possible when all she felt now was bitter disappointment.

Luckily for her, Majiro's hunting trip was scheduled to take a few weeks. His absence provided a much needed relief from the tension that had built in their home. Allison was thankful that she had time to process the news of her pregnancy in solitude, for she had not yet been able to believe Amita's promises. She knew her friend was faithfully praying for her, but she could still not seem to pull herself out of the cloud of depression that had dropped on her with the realization of her pregnancy.

One night, long after Isaac had fallen asleep, she was still tossing and turning, wrapping the blanket in tighter circles around her legs. Frustrated, she threw off the covers and stood. She tiptoed outside in search of something to drink and opened a pot of cold banana juice from its perch on the bench next to the fire. She filled a wooden bowl with juice and sat down next to the dead fire, the bowl cradled in her hands.

For the hundredth time she thought about Eric's last moments of life, and a fresh wave of anger heated her blood. She hurled the bowl savagely at the fire and watched the droplets of juice reflect the moonlight as they fell to the ground. Covering her face with her hands, she drew in a shaky breath. She wanted to cry, but it felt like every last tear inside her had already been shed. What was the point anyway? To weep for Eric, for Isaac, or for herself—it would not change anything.

Her impulse to run away was strong, and she debated about going inside, waking up Isaac, and escaping into the night. He was older now, and she was more capable. They might be able to make it… somewhere. However, with Majiro due home any day, she doubted they could go anywhere that he could not track them. And she knew the man well enough to know that he would not stop until he found them, especially when he found out that she had run away pregnant.

God, how many times will I have to forgive this man? He murdered Eric. How can I look past that? How can I not think of what he has done every time I look at him… every time I look at his child?

The gentlest of voices spoke clearly to her heart. **Walk in a manner worthy of your calling, showing humility, gentleness, patience, and love.**

She sighed. *I don't have any of those qualities. I am sick of being patient and trying to show love. I want to rip his hair out and scream at him until he knows the pain he has caused me!*

The seed whose fruit is righteousness is sown in peace by those who make peace. Forgive, Beloved. Yes, forgive again.

As clearly as if she were staring at an actual path, Allison saw her choices laid out before her. On one road, she could turn inward and allow the bitterness she felt to take root and grow, destroying all hope and peace with it. On the other, she could cling to God's promises even in her brokenness and extend mercy to the undeserving. It was not an easy decision. In the end, it was the thought of her son that moved her toward grace. If she did not show him the power of faith, who would? She would forgive not for Majiro's sake, or even for her own, but for Isaac so that he would know what grace looked like wrapped up in the grime of reality.

In surrender, she opened her hands palms up, and lifted her face to the sky. *You've allowed me to be crushed, my heart to be shattered, and all that is familiar to be ripped away. I'm broken, Lord, so that you can pour me out. Let the pieces of me bring healing and restoration to these people who remain at war with You. I relinquish my rights and ask only for the strength to walk steadfast on the path You've put before me.*

The next morning, Allison was still feeling the effects of a short night's sleep coupled with a bout of morning sickness. She trudged slowly around the house and yard trying to motivate herself to do something useful. Running from the clearing, Isaac nearly knocked her into the fire as he dashed up to her. Eager to tell her the news, he bounced up and down with excitement. "Mom, the warriors are back! They are crossing the river right now! Can I go?"

"They are? Um, sure, go ahead. Ask your father if you can help him carry something, but don't get in the way." She had not even finished the sentence before he darted toward the river trail.

Within a half hour, loud chattering and laughter announced the arrival of the hunting party, as their families gathered outside the houses to welcome them home. Allison stood in the doorway and smiled at the sight of Isaac riding gleefully on Majiro's shoulders atop an overflowing basket of game.

From several houses away, Majiro caught her eye. Knowing what was expected of her, she met him in the clearing in front of their house. "Welcome home," she said.

Majiro grunted and pulled Isaac off of his shoulders so that he could remove the basket's strap from his forehead. He dropped it at her feet and, ignoring her, walked to the pot of weak beer next to the fire. Allison sighed. It looked as if the long trip had not served to soften his anger in the least.

She half-carried, half-dragged the basket to the side of the house. The animals at the bottom of the basket had long since been cleaned and smoke-dried into jerky, but the rest had not yet been tended to. It would mean a long afternoon of work, and already the putrid stench of decaying flesh was making her dizzy.

Calling out for Isaac to bring her a knife, she set about removing the animals from the basket and laying them out across the ground. There was a wild pig and the leg of a deer to dress, plus all of the dried meat to store inside.

She was only halfway through skinning the deer, when the smell overwhelmed her and she began retching into the weeds. Majiro looked up from his seat at the fire with a puzzled expression on his face.

"Are you sick?" he asked, coming to stand beside her. Unable to speak, she shook her head and then nodded. "Well, which is it? Yes or no?" he asked, his tone indicating his annoyance.

She straightened up, hoping that the worst of it had passed. "It's just the smell…" She looked him in the eye. "I'm pregnant, Majiro."

For a long moment, his face remained expressionless, until finally a grin tugged at the corner of his mouth. "Are you sure?"

"Positive. I'm around three months along. I realized it right after you left on your trip."

He nodded, his smile coming into full bloom. "This is good. I was beginning to wonder if there was something wrong with you."

"There is nothing wrong with me," she retorted.

"Another son for the chief. He will be strong and clever like his father."

"Or *she* may be strong and clever like her mother. It might be a girl," she pointed out.

At this, Majiro laughed. "A girl would be a help for you. That would be good too." He continued to chuckle as he walked back to the fire. He poured himself another bowl of beer and lifted it in her direction. "A girl," he said, and drank it down.

CHAPTER **TWENTY**

"Eric, we only have an hour left before the doors open, and two of the parking attendants haven't shown up. What do you want me to do?" Roger's voice was calm, but Eric could see that he was on the verge of panic. It was the opening day of the church's first missions conference, and the hosts were frantically putting the final pieces into place.

"Find a couple of people to replace them until they show up. I think I saw Peter and Bill with Pastor Denny near the stage." Eric turned to walk away and then called over his shoulder, "I am locking myself in my office until 6:45."

Eric retreated to his office and closed the door. Plopping down in a wing chair, he momentarily debated the wisdom of trying to pull together such a large event. However, there was no use in considering that now as several hundred people would be descending on the church over the next hour.

Because he was leading the opening service, Eric was especially nervous. The tone of the weekend would be set by his words and attitude. For that reason, he sought out the solitude of his office so he could spend the final moments before his sermon in prayer.

Though missions conferences were nothing new, he hoped that this one would be different in terms of its honesty about the price of the call to missions. He had heard dozens of messages pleading for laborers in fields that were ripe with people headed to hell without the gospel. Though he believed that message to be true, the guilt that it produced could never sustain a missionary on the field long term. No, the message that he wished to impart during this conference was that serving in a ministry capacity anywhere came with a cost, and that cost must be considered in light of God's commands and ultimately His glory around the world.

The message hit especially close to home. As he had prepared his sermon, he had spent long hours studying Scriptures and crying out to God. For three years, it was the question of his heart: how could he reconcile the idea that God, whom he knew to be loving and all powerful, had allowed his family to be ripped apart in such a violent way?

After half an hour, Eric locked his office and walked toward the sanctuary. He was still as nervous as ever but felt a renewed sense of assurance that he was indeed bringing the message that God intended.

The room was abuzz with activity as guests found their seats and the worship band finished setting up their instruments. Eric looked for his mother, who had driven out specifically to hear him speak. She was sitting near the front next to an empty seat, so he joined her. Soon the lights were dimmed and the music began playing with accompanied words flashing on the screens to each side of the stage.

Eric lost himself in worship and scarcely realized that it was time for him to go on stage until his mother poked him in the side. Gathering his Bible and notes, he made his way up the side stairs to the podium and welcomed the audience to the conference. Spending the first few minutes spelling out what the conference would entail and other pertinent information enabled him to sufficiently relax before he began the message.

He said a brief prayer and then launched into his testimony. Though he had shared parts of it with the church in the past, never before had he shared the intimate details of the ordeal in the jungle and the days following with such a large crowd.

The congregation listened solemnly, and he saw tears in the eyes of several as he described the attack on the base and the ensuing year of desperate searching.

"After I lost my wife and son, I would have said that going to Peru was the dumbest mistake of my life. Now, I'm not so sure. The truth of the matter is that God led us there, and though I do not blame Him for the actions of sinful men, somehow His plan included allowing what took place." He paused, trying to find a way to express his point without dismissing the suffering he had endured. "Anyone who is called to any ministry—abroad or at home, professional or a lay position—has to count the cost of that call. There will likely be hardship, sacrifices, and pain. But when our eyes are focused on Jesus and our hearts set to see Him worshiped around the world, the potential for adversity is the very least of our concerns. Allison and Isaac are gone from this life, and I miss them every day. Yet, I know that God has been glorified. When I cut things down to the bare bones, that is all that really matters."

Eric stepped down from the platform to be closer to the crowd that was held in rapt attention. "Don't agree to join a ministry or go into missions because you feel sorry for the people or because you want an adventure," he admonished. "Go because you love Jesus and because He is calling you to that place. If you go with your heart set on doing His will, He will sustain you. And whatever the cost is to you personally, the sacrifice will be worth it. What more could any of us ask for than to hear at the end, 'Well done, faithful one'? That is what I know Allison heard after she breathed her last breath, and that is what I too am waiting for."

As he quietly returned to his seat, the band began playing softly. He bowed his head, his own emotions roiling with what he had said. He believed every word, but it remained a struggle to live like it. He knew God always used evil for good, but it did not change the hurt.

"Lord, continue to heal my heart," he whispered. "Let my story bring glory to You and give others the desire to follow You no matter the cost."

Soon the conference was over for the night, and Eric found himself surrounded by friends and strangers alike, some wanting to offer him condolences and others wanting to ask questions. He remained in the auditorium long after most of the attendees had gone home, talking freely with those who had waited for the chance to speak with him personally.

Finally, he turned to the last person, a young man probably not even out of college yet. The young man smiled, but his eyes were still red with fresh tears. "Hi, I'm Matt," he said, offering his hand in greeting.

"Eric. Nice to meet you. What can I do for you?" Eric asked.

"Just wanted you to know that you won."

"Excuse me?"

"I've been arguing with God for the last six months about why I can't go into the ministry, but tonight… Well, I realized that all of my excuses simply amounted to idolatry. If I really want to put God first in my life, I don't really have a choice but to obey, you know?"

"What makes it hard for you?"

Matt chuckled. "All of it is hard for me! I've felt like I am supposed to go to the Middle East somewhere as a missionary. Two years ago, my big brother was killed while he was stationed in Afghanistan. Everything in me screams that it is idiocy to go to a place where people will hate me and might even kill me. I've tried and tried to convince myself that I just need to love the Muslims more and have a greater burden for them, but tonight I finally realized that is not the problem. I don't need a bigger burden for the lost; I need a greater love for Christ. *He's* worth it!"

The young man's passion warmed Eric's heart as he was reminded of his own inner turmoil after hearing Kyle Huntington speak for the first time. "It's great when we finally get things in the right order, isn't it?"

Matt remained for a few minutes longer, asking Eric to pray for him before he left. When he was gone, Eric realized that his mother was still seated a few rows behind him. With her was Julia, and they were chatting animatedly.

"Sorry to keep you waiting," he said, walking over to join them.

Jean replied, "Don't worry about it. Julia has been keeping me company."

Turning his attention to Julia, he could not help but notice how lovely she looked in the belted, gray sweater dress that could not conceal her curves. "What are you still doing here?" he asked, trying to ignore the flush creeping up his neck. He hoped that he had not been staring.

"Oh, I'm in charge of lockup tonight."

Jean stood and gathered her purse. "Then we are keeping you here. Come on, honey. Let's get out of her hair." She shooed Eric toward the exit despite Julia's protests that they were welcome to stay and visit.

Eric walked his mother to her car, enjoying her chattering. He opened the car door and waited patiently while she settled inside. She held her hand out before he could shut her into the car and peered up at him. "Julia seems like a nice girl," she said with all the subtlety of a train wreck.

"She *is* nice." Eric replied easily.

"She says that you play basketball in the park together every week."

"Yeah, usually with some other friends too."

"She is very beautiful."

"Mom…"

Jean held her hand up in surrender. "I just wanted to make sure you've noticed." She smiled innocently at him and then closed the door.

She drove away into the night, leaving him shaking his head. Oh, he had noticed all right. How could he miss it?

All of his energy had been poured into the weekend missions conference, so when he arrived at the church office the following Monday, Eric thought seriously about turning around and going home. Instead, he bee-lined from the front door to the coffee pot in the entryway.

"That bad, huh?" Julia chirped from her desk as he poured the steaming brew into his travel thermos.

"I had to talk myself into coming in this morning," he admitted. He walked over to her desk and leaned against it. Even the strong coffee smell could not cover the sweet fragrance of lavender he had come to associate with her.

Julia looked him over critically. "Maybe you shouldn't have. You look like death."

He snorted. "Thanks a lot."

"See, now that you are smiling, you look much better."

"Julia to the rescue."

"Of course! Besides, I think you have the right to look awful. That conference was a ridiculous amount of work."

"So why don't you look terrible? You put in at least as many hours as I did, and you look as gorgeous as always." He had spoken without thinking and immediately wished he could retract his words. True as it might have been, he was not sure that he wanted to let on that he had noticed.

She brushed off his compliment with a casual wave of her hand. "It doesn't take a lot of brain power to unlock doors and tell people where the bathroom is." He breathed a sigh of relief that his words seemed to be taken as more of the friendly banter that was typical of their relationship.

Feeling the need to escape, he quickly excused himself and withdrew to his office. However, the stack of paperwork on his desk could not hold his interest, so he flipped on his computer to check his e-mail.

There were a number of new messages in his inbox from people who had attended the conference, and he enjoyed reading the mostly positive feedback. The few complaints were about minor details such as long lines in the bathroom and under-stocked materials in the bookstore. If that was the worst that anyone had to say about the conference then he could safely assume that it was a raging success. It also probably meant that another one would be in the works before too long.

Eric sighed. He would wait to think about that another day, when his energy level was higher and his thoughts did not continue to stray to the pretty woman down the hall.

A few hours later, he had finally found a rhythm, albeit a slow rhythm, for the day. But when he heard a knock on the door, he was glad for the interruption. "Come in," he called.

"I'm bailing you out of this place," Julia announced as she flung open the door cheerfully.

"Huh?"

"C'mon. It's lunchtime. I'm hungry, and you're bored."

"How do you know I'm bored?"

"Aren't you?"

Eric laughed and shut down his computer. "Yes. I'm almost counterproductive today."

The pair drove around the corner to a popular deli and chatted amicably as they waited in line to order. Once seated, Julia looked heavenward and said with a happy sigh, "Thanks, Jesus, for ham and cheese sandwiches and sweet tea."

"Amen!" Eric added and took a bite of his pastrami on rye.

"I have to be honest, Eric. I have ulterior motives for bringing you here."

His throat went dry, and he nearly choked on his food. "Oh?" he asked uneasily.

"Don't look at me like you are afraid I am going to hurt you. I'm not that scary." If only she knew. "I've been wanting to talk with you about your sermon on the first night of the conference. I figured I would be better off waiting until now instead of trying to beat your fans off with a stick."

"Sure, what's up?"

"Well, I think you are wrong."

Eric cocked an eyebrow. "About what?"

"About the whole calling thing." He simply waited patiently, and Julia rushed on. "I agree that some people are obviously called by God to certain ministries, but I don't think that is always the case. I mean, do we really need some kind of emotional experience before we decide to pursue a life of ministry?"

"Do you think we should just jump into whatever strikes our fancy without consulting God about what He wants us to do?" Eric threw back.

Julia shook her head. "No. That is not what I think at all. But do we need to walk down the aisle and surrender to a special calling to know that God wants us, all of us, in ministry? Seems to me like He gave us the Great Commission a long time ago."

Not sure that he understood her point, he asked, "Where exactly do you think I've missed the mark?"

"I think you have dichotomized those of us who are called by God to be in ministry and those who are not. I think we are all intended to be in a life of ministry regardless of any 'calling' we may or may not have received. I think you alienate a lot of Christians when you speak only to those who are called. The rest of us are left wondering why God doesn't want to use us. I think your definition of calling is too narrow."

Eric sat back in his chair with his hands tucked behind his head, his sandwich forgotten, half-eaten on his plate. In his opinion, one of Julia's best qualities was her candor. Right now, however, it packed a mean punch.

"I can't really speak for other people, but I do know that Allison and I both felt a very clear calling to go to Peru."

"Does that make the rest of us less Christian? Less worthy?"

"That is not what I mean!" he exclaimed.

Julia reached across the table for his hand. "I know that is not what you meant. But that *is* how you come across sometimes, and it's totally unattainable for some of us. For me."

He was unarmed by her tenderness and vulnerability and tried to see behind her words to the deeper issue. "This isn't just theoretical to you."

"No," she agreed. "You remember how I told you that I left the graphic design industry to get my degree in special education?"

"I remember."

"I made that decision not because of any great call that I received from God, but because it seemed logical to me. I feel I can have a greater impact on people, especially children, in education than in design. If I had waited for some call, I would never have changed my mind."

"Are you doubting your decision now?"

"No. I just think you need to realize that God's calling to some of us may simply be a logical choice or a pursuit of long-held passions."

"But by your own definition, those are still callings," he pointed out. "So you don't disagree about God being the one to call people to ministry, just that He does it in a greater range of ways."

Thinking for a moment, Julia nodded. "That sounds about right." She grinned. "I'm glad you can listen to reason."

"Right," he replied dryly.

"Anyway, now would probably be a good time to tell you that I gave Pastor Denny my notice this morning. I got a job at Clear Creek High School, teaching this fall in their special-ed program. I figured that I would let him know now so that he will have the whole summer to find and train my replacement."

Eric's heart gave a strange flip. "No kidding? Congratulations. That's… really great."

"Don't sound so excited for me or anything."

"I *am* excited for you. I'm just going to miss having you around the office." They looked at each other for a long moment, and Julia's cheeks turned pink.

"I still live around the corner from the church, and you have my phone number," she pointed out. "Besides I'll still trounce you on the basketball court on Fridays."

Seized by impulse, Eric said, "I don't know if that will be enough for me anymore. Maybe I can take you on a date this weekend?"

Julia beamed. "I was hoping you would ask!" She smacked her hand over her mouth. "Good grief, was I that obvious? I am so embarrassed. If this is a pity date, then forget it. I have my pride."

Eric chuckled. "It's not a pity date, and you've been the definition of subtle. I guess the idea of not having you around all the time makes me realize how much you are a part of my life now. Seems like asking you out is a *logical* step, though I can't say I feel *called* to do it."

"Foul play!" she protested, joining his laughter. "I'll forgive you, but it might cost you two dates."

Eric's brown eyes held hers. "I think I can guarantee at least that many."

CHAPTER **TWENTY-ONE**

"**A**m I glad to see you!" Allison called out to Amita from the river's edge. "Will you help me wring these out?" She sat back in the shallow water and pushed a sweaty piece of hair from her eyes while she waited for Amita to make her way from the trail to the river.

Without comment, Amita reached for one end of the heavy, wet hammock. The cotton fibers had soaked up so much water that lifting it was difficult, even with the two of them.

Twisting the fabric, Allison studied the other woman. Amita's usual smile was gone, and her dark eyes were troubled. "What's the matter?" she asked.

Amita gazed at her sadly. "The men are leaving tomorrow morning on a raid."

"A raid?" Allison's eyebrows shot up. "What are you talking about? Who told you that?" she demanded.

"My husband. He just came back from talking with the chief and a group of warriors. The plans have been made. They will leave at sunrise."

The women spread the hammock over a fallen log to dry in the sun and then sat down next to it. "Why?" Allison asked.

"Why else? They want more women in the village, and there are rumors that the Oneata are trading for foreign goods now. They'll attack them and take as many of their things and women as they can manage."

"Wait. Aren't the Oneata your people?"

Amita burst into tears. "Yes! They are going back to my village, Paamari. I begged my husband to go somewhere else, but he said that it was out of his hands. The warriors have already decided." Amita covered her face with her hands. "I am so afraid for my family there. What if they are killed in the raid?"

Allison laid a comforting hand on Amita's shoulder, but her mind whirled as she thought about the upcoming raid. Majiro had not spoken a word about the plans, and likely would not have until the moment he left, especially if he guessed that it would result in her vehement protests. Well, now she knew and protest she would.

"Come on," she said, hauling Amita up with her. "I want to go talk to Majiro."

"There is nothing you can do. You will just make him angry."

"That won't be anything new. You and I both know that this is wrong. It's murder and theft."

"It's been done for generations."

"That doesn't make it right."

Allison turned to march back to the village, but Amita caught her arm. "If you are going to speak to him, at least pray first. Let your anger be the anger of God, not the sting of your own pride."

For a moment, Allison was speechless. Then she laughed. "You are a much wiser woman than I. Yes. Let's pray first."

They found both Manitari and Majiro inside Allison's house. The men were sharpening arrowheads and restringing their bows. Manitari greeted them warily when they walked in, but Majiro ignored them.

The women sat quietly at the edge of the sleeping platform for a few moments. Finally Allison spoke up. "I heard that you are planning a raid."

Majiro heaved a sigh and gave her a long-suffering look. "Yes. Not that it is a woman's concern."

"It concerns me that you are bent on stealing and kidnapping and killing anyone who gets in your way."

"You don't know what you are talking about."

"Am I wrong?"

Majiro did not answer, but Manitari said, "It's the way of our people. We have been at war with the Oneata since before our grandfather's grandfather was alive."

Pulling her gaze from Majiro's rigid form, Allison peered at Manitari. "How does that make it right?"

"We need women in our village. Jukiri's wife died last month in childbirth, and there are three warriors waiting for wives—"

"They can wait longer!"

Majiro snarled, "They are men now. Once a Shampiri becomes a man, he must find a wife to gain his rights! They will not wait any longer."

Manitari explained patiently, "Imeshina, if we don't go find wives for them from the other villages, they will have to take girls like my daughter as their wives. Is that what you want?"

Allison shuddered as she thought of the ten-year-old girl forced into marriage, but her resolve remained firm. "It's no better to kidnap and rape a woman than it is to rape a child. There has to be a way to avoid both," she insisted.

Majiro glared at her, and Manitari looked ashamed as he glanced at his wife. Amita sat next to him and laid her hand gently on his knee. "I do not want to see blood on your hands, husband. Especially not the blood of my own family."

Majiro dropped the bow onto the ground and stood. "We will leave for Paamari tomorrow." With that, he turned to leave.

Allison called after him, "I will pray that your efforts will be thwarted and that you return empty-handed." She saw the muscle tighten his jaw, but he left the house without speaking.

Manitari also stood. "Try to understand," he said gently. "This is the way that it must be."

She shook her head. "We don't get to make the rules. That was up to God. And He condemns what you are planning to do. I hope that somehow He will spare you of the sin you are running toward."

After Manitari and Amita went home, Allison stayed where she sat on the sleeping platform. As she had promised, she prayed that God would intervene in what the Shampiri warriors were about to do and that the unsuspecting women of Paamari would not have to live through the pain she knew so well.

Majiro did not reappear that night until after Allison and Isaac were both asleep. When he did finally settle onto the platform next to her, she woke up and stiffened as she waited for his inevitable, demanding touch. After a moment, she realized that the touch was not forthcoming and relaxed again. Apparently, he intended to completely ignore her for the few hours that remained until he left on the raid. That was fine with her.

She fell asleep again and did not even notice when he slipped out of bed before dawn. When she awoke, the sun was up and the warriors had already left. She quickly dressed, fed Isaac breakfast, and sent him off to play while she did her morning chores.

Despite her disapproval of the warriors' mission, it was always nice to have the house to herself. She took extra time playing with Isaac, teaching him numbers and letters, and telling him stories about their family back home. She also had more time for visiting friends.

On the second morning, she left her son with Amita and went with Inani to visit her younger sister's family an hour's walk down the trail.

Tentega, Inani's sister, was delighted by the visit and scurried around cutting up a pineapple and offering them fresh *iracagaja* to drink.

"Thank you," Allison said, as she took the wooden bowl of banana juice and sat down on the reed mat next to the fire. Tentega's house was even more rustic than those in the main village, and she wondered how the family of ten managed to sleep in the tiny room.

After greeting the women, Tentega's husband quickly excused himself to work in the family's garden. Allison suspected it was more of an excuse to leave the yard full of women, than a desire to work. The children, however, were excited about the visitors and crowded around to listen to the women's discussion.

The two sisters talked about family and friends, updating each other on all that had happened since they had last seen one another. They spoke so quickly—and often simultaneously—that Allison had trouble following the conversation and soon began to lose interest. Instead, she turned to the children and asked their names and what they liked to do during the day.

In the middle of one such question, a boy ran from around the house shouting through his labored breathing. "Mother! There are raiders on the trail to the village."

The women quickly jumped to their feet. "Opempe, what have you seen?" Tentega exclaimed.

The boy bent at the waist, his hands on his knees, trying to catch his breath. "I went to the river to fish… but as I was crossing the trail to the village… I heard voices… They were not speaking our language, so I hid. When they came around the bend, I saw that it was warriors, but they were not Shampiri."

Inani asked, "Are you sure that they are going to our village?"

"Yes."

Tentega said, "I will send Rafi to catch up with the warriors and tell them to return."

"That will take too long!" Allison cried, feeling the surge of adrenaline flood her bloodstream. "I have to get back to Isaac now!"

"They are on the longer trail next to the river. I can show you the most direct trail to the village, but we will have to hurry to make it there in time," Opempe offered.

"Let's go!" Without pausing to say good-bye, Allison and the boy ran into the jungle. She struggled to keep up with him as she jumped over fallen trees and splashed through mud puddles. Disregarding her pregnancy, she was only as careful as she needed to be to stay upright. As long as she made it back home to Isaac before the raiders entered the village, she did not care what condition she arrived in.

The run through the jungle seemed to take forever, though in reality, they made it back in a little over half an hour. Her lungs were burning, her side aching, and her legs were scratched from the overgrown brush on the trail. But the village, thankfully, appeared peaceful. Allison sent Opempe to warn each house of the impending raid while she sprinted directly to Amita's house.

She saw Isaac playing in the yard with Amita's boys and called his name while she was still running toward the yard. Amita appeared in her doorway, her eyes widening as she took in Allison's disheveled appearance. "What's the matter?" she asked.

"There are raiders on the trail. They will be here soon. Quick! We need to hide the children!"

Amita called to her oldest daughter, whose eyes were wide with fear at Allison's words. "Take Isaac and your siblings and go quickly to our garden and hide. Don't come back. I will come get you later."

Micheli took her baby brother from her mother's arms. "What if you don't come?" she asked.

"Then you can return here in two days. Someone will be here to take care of you. Go now." Amita kissed her daughter's cheek and hurried her children to the trail next to the house. Allison followed with Isaac in her arms. She whispered instructions to him and set him down behind Micheli. He whimpered, but he obeyed and disappeared into the jungle with the others.

All around them, old men, women, and children were running into the jungle as the news about the raiders swept through the village like a tsunami.

"What now?" Allison asked.

"I will make sure everyone has been warned, but you should go now, Imeshina. If they are coming for women, you will probably be the first to go."

"I'm a foreigner," she protested.

Amita shook her head. "You are exotic. They won't be keeping you for a wife. They will use you and leave you dead on the trail when they are finished with you."

"I am not afraid."

Amita gave her an exasperated look. "Don't be stupid. You—" her words were cut off as a scream pierced the air.

Going against the flow of humanity, they ran toward the end of the clearing where the terror-filled screams continued.

They stopped abruptly next to one of the homes as eight warriors broke through the trees and spread around the yard. One stood over a Shampiri woman with a wooden club, while the others continued toward the other houses.

"Please don't hurt her!" Amita cried as she dashed toward the fallen woman and threw herself between her and the warrior.

"Amita?"

Amita looked up at the warrior and gasped. "Maapi?" The warrior dropped his club and pulled her to her feet, a look of joy on his face. The woman crawled away tearfully and then staggered to her feet and ran into her house.

Holding fast to the raider's hands, Amita pleaded, "Please, Maapi, stop them. Our men are not here, there is no need to harm anyone."

Maapi searched her eyes for a moment, then stepped away. He yelled out something incomprehensible, and the other warriors soon began to reappear. A conversation of clipped syllables began, and Allison was surprised that though she could not understand everything that was said, she could follow the conversation easily. The words and sentence structure were similar to Shampiri, but the accent was very different.

As the men gathered around, they all seemed to be both surprised and pleased to see Amita, and, when her words about the lack of warriors in the village were passed through the group, they pulled their arrows from their bows and tucked their clubs back into their belts.

The last of the warriors, an older man, came around the corner, and Amita shouted with delight. She ran toward him with her arms outstretched and flung herself into his chest. "Father! Father, it's me!"

Taken aback, the old warrior gaped at her until understanding lit his weathered face like noontime. "My daughter! You are alive! I never thought to find you here. This is wonderful!" He embraced her again.

From his arms, Amita waved Allison over. "Imeshina, come. Meet my father. Father, this is Imeshina, my dearest friend. She gave me hope after I was taken from your home."

Amita's father beamed at her. "Then she shall call me 'father' as well." Allison dipped her head in recognition of the honor and tried to ignore the curious stares from the other men.

Maapi clapped a hand down on Amita's shoulder. "Cousin, I have done what you asked, but we need an explanation. Where are your warriors?"

"They are on their way to your village to do to Paamari exactly as you intend to do to here."

At the news, the men shouted in rage and shook their weapons angrily. One warrior shouted, "I say we take everything we can from here and let them find an empty village when they return."

"No," another said. "We should make our way back to Paamari as quickly as we can. We cannot let them take our women and our trade goods."

The men continued arguing back and forth, debating about what to do. One thing was clear, however: they were bent on violence.

Allison shouted over the roar of voices, "Please! Listen!" The noise died down as they gave her their attention. "Your women are safe. Our men left only yesterday, so they could not have reached your village yet. A runner was sent to alert them that you were on your way here before you even arrived. Please, sit and rest for awhile before you decide what to do."

The shouting resumed, and Allison shook her head in frustration. It sounded like they either did not understand her or simply did not care what she had to say. Finally, one man shouted with a tone of finality, "We will wait. Just as the white woman said, our rushing back to Paamari now will not change anything. We will decide what to do when our bellies are full and our minds are clear."

"As you say, Chief," Maapi said, his voice hollow with frustration. "Cousin, we will eat at your fire."

Amita nodded and led the men toward her home. Allison walked beside her. "Do you know all these men?" she asked under her breath.

"Yes," Amita whispered back. "My cousin is the one I told you about—the one I would have married. The chief is Shintsi. We were children together, but when I left, his father was the chief. The one with the long hair is my uncle, and the rest I recognize. They are good men, but I don't know that we can stop them from their path any more than we could stop our own warriors."

"We have to try."

"I know."

Amita invited the men to sit by her fire, and she and Allison began to rush about serving the men beer and boiled yucca. The danger past, the men stretched themselves around the fire, laughing and exchanging stories. By the time the women had finished serving them and sat down as well, they were half drunk and exuberant with pride over their "victorious" raid.

Maapi said, "You must be so glad to see us, Amita! We will take you back home where you belong."

Allison was alarmed by his words, but Amita did not seem moved. "I would love for a chance to see all of our family again, but this is my place now. This is where I have my home and my children and my husband."

"Surely you don't want to stay with these barbarians?" her father asked, incredulous. "They don't even have access to trade goods here."

"They are good people. Just like the Oneata."

Maapi narrowed his eyes. "Good people? You say that even as they are on their way to kidnap and kill your family?"

"And what exactly are you doing here?" Amita retorted, and Allison nearly laughed at the shock on the faces around her. Her friend's gentleness often softened the iron core inside, but her fearlessness was evident now. And admirable.

Maapi was not easily persuaded. "You know our people have been at war with the Shampiri for years."

Allison stood to refill the empty bowls with more beer. "But when does it end? What will it take for the Shampiri and the Oneata to have peace with one another?"

Shintsi spoke up. "Peace would be a wonderful reality. But it is an impossible dream. How can we have peace with people who continue to raid us?"

"Someone has to be willing to stop first. Someone has to forgive."

"We will not forgive wrongs done against us! They must pay for what they do!" Shintsi said forcefully.

Allison sighed. What was the point of arguing with men set on destruction? She knew that she did not have the right words to change generations of mutual animosity.

Having noticed earlier that the chief had his left arm tied at his side with a vine, palm facing forward and that he grimaced every time he shifted positions, Allison asked, "What happened to your arm?"

"I fell when we were crossing the gorge and smacked my shoulder on a rock." he replied ruefully.

"Can you move it?"

"Not well. And not without a lot of pain."

"Can you lift it above your head?"

"No."

"Do you mind if I take a look at it?"

"If you want."

Allison moved behind him, looking carefully at his shoulder and back. The tell-tale hump of his shoulder blade evidenced the dislocation that she had suspected.

"I think I can help you, but it will take a little while and it might hurt."

Shintsi smiled slightly. "It already hurts."

She untied the vine, holding his arm in place and directed him to lie on the ground. "Face your good shoulder. I am going to pull on your arm. If this works, you will feel a pop when the arm bone slips back into place."

He did not speak as she grasped his wrist in both hands and brought his arm into a forty-five degree angle, but she could see the muscles in his arm tensing from the pain. "It's important that you relax," she said. "I'm going to do this slowly, so there will be no sudden pain."

The other men watched in quiet curiosity as she leaned her weight back. She put her bare foot against his ribs to help keep the line of his arm at the correct angle. For several minutes she worked, keeping constant pressure against the joint. Sweat dotted her forehead and trickled into her eyes, but she did not dare stop to wipe them.

All of a sudden, she heard rather than felt the joint of his arm slip back into the shoulder socket. Shintsi's eyes widened and he let out a soft gasp.

"There. I think that worked." Allison helped him to a sitting position. "How does it feel?"

The chief rose to his feet and rotated his arm cautiously. "That is amazing! It's like I never even fell!"

"You will be bruised and stiff for a few days. Take it easy with that arm because from now on it will be much easier for it to slip out of place."

Shintsi asked, "Are you a healer in this village?"

Allison smiled. "No," she replied. "My husband had a habit of knocking his shoulder out of joint, so I learned how to pop it back in for him."

"Who is your husband?"

Amita answered for her. "She is referring to a husband who died a few years ago."

"Then you are not married?" Maapi asked.

Allison glanced at Amita, unsure if offering the information would harm or benefit her. Amita said, "Her husband is Majiro."

"The chief?"

"Yes."

"Well," Shintsi said, seemingly unconcerned about her marital status, "I am indebted to you for your help."

"Perhaps you can repay me by showing mercy to my village and seeing yourselves home now."

The warriors laughed as if she had made a hilarious joke, but she stood there letting her silence display her sincerity. Shintsi, still chuckling, remarked, "You are a bold woman to even suggest such a thing. We will do nothing tonight. Your men will not return until at least the afternoon, so we will remain tonight. Since it seems like all the women are hiding in the jungle anyway, our choices are limited. Tomorrow we will decide whom and what to take with us."

After seeing that the Oneata warriors had everything they needed for the evening, Amita and Allison excused themselves to Allison's house, leaving Amita's home to the warriors. They debated briefly about sneaking away to check on their children, but decided against it. "I know they are my kinsmen, but I don't want to risk someone following us to our children," Amita had said.

They knelt on the dirt floor inside the house and prayed together for a long while. Finally, exhausted from the day's events, they fell asleep.

Allison startled awake when she felt Amita flail next to her. Terrified that one of the Oneata had tired of civility, she sat up to help fight off her friend's attacker.

A hand clamped around her mouth, cutting off her scream. "Shhhh! Imeshina, it's me!"

In the dim light she could barely make out Majiro's face above her own.

"Amita, it's okay. It's Majiro!" she hissed, and the other woman's struggle stopped. She turned to Majiro, "How did you get back so soon? We weren't expecting you until the afternoon at least."

"We killed a deer yesterday morning, so we decided to camp for the day. Rafi found us in the evening, and we ran all night to get here—"

Another form suddenly appeared in the doorway. "Chief, we have to go get my wife and children! The Oneata are in my house."

"I'm right here, husband."

Hearing his wife's voice, Manitari, rushed to kneel next to the platform. "The children?" he asked, his hand moving to Amita's face.

"Safe in the garden. We knew they were coming, so most were able to leave the village first."

"Good." Relief was evident in his voice.

"Why are the Oneata still here?" Majiro asked.

Allison replied, "They had no reason to hurry since you were gone, and we invited them to stay."

Majiro gaped at her. "You invited... Are you crazy?" Before she could reply, he held up his hand. "I don't even want to hear it. Right now, we need to gather up the other men. Daylight is coming soon, and we need to be ready when the Oneata wake up."

"What are you going to do to them?" Allison asked.

"What do you think?"

"You can't!" Amita cried. "That is my father and my kinsmen in there."

Majiro said, "They came to raid my village. We have no other choice. Come, Manitari. I'll alert the warriors to the north. You go south."

"Yes, Chief."

Crestfallen, Amita watched as her husband followed Majiro into the night. Allison asked. "What should we do? Should we wake the Oneata?"

Amita shook her head. "Then they might kill our husbands. No. We just have to wait." She grabbed Allison's hand, and they took turns praying as they waited for the sun to rise on what promised to be a very bloody day.

When the shouting began an hour later, the women ran outside. They found Amita's home surrounded by Shampiri warriors, all with arrows drawn and looks of glee on their faces.

"Throw your weapons out the door, and then come out one by one! You are surrounded, so don't bother fighting back," Majiro called from his position near the door.

Slowly, hands appeared in the doorway tossing bows, arrows, and clubs into the yard. Shintsi was the first man to appear, his hands held at his chest, palms facing out. Allison wondered absently how his still-slung shoulder was feeling.

"You are early," Shintsi said, as he moved aside to allow the rest of his men to walk past him.

"And *you* are in my village," Majiro returned.

"I hear that you never made it to mine."

"Maybe next time." The chiefs glared at each other as the last of the warriors appeared in the doorway.

"Everyone in the center of the yard," Manitari ordered, motioning with his bow. The Oneata complied and stood back-to-back in a circle. The Shampiri warriors made a wide ring around them. Moving into the circle of men, Allison stood between Shintsi and Majiro.

"Majiro, this doesn't have to end in blood," she said calmly.

"Woman, get out of the way, or I swear I will shoot you too!"

"Would you just listen to reason?" she pleaded.

"There is nothing to say."

"They've done nothing wrong here."

"These men are our enemies, and they will die."

"Why are they your enemies? They are only men like you, doing the very same things that you do," she pointed out.

"Any Oneata that comes into my village deserves death!"

Allison motioned to Amita. "There is an Oneata living here in peace right now."

Maapi interjected from his position in the inner circle, "And she was kidnapped! We will be happy to take her back home where she belongs." He took a step toward her, but Manitari planted himself between them.

Pointing his arrow at the man's chest, Manitari growled, "Touch my wife, and I will watch you bleed to death."

Maapi scowled. "So you are the one who took her from Paamari that day. I always hoped we would meet. It's unfortunate that I am not armed, or I would have killed you already."

"Cousin, please!" Amita said.

"You defend this man?" Maapi asked incredulously.

Amita's chin rose. "He is my husband, and this is our home."

"And you are glad about that?"

Amita replied calmly, "This is not the life I expected or hoped for, but I am glad that it is mine. Even if I could change the past, I wouldn't. I am happy here." Maapi said nothing.

Seeing the chance to drive home her point, Allison spoke again. "Majiro, do you not see that this is your opportunity to gain peace for the Shampiri?"

"We owe these men no peace," he retorted.

Shintsi inclined his head in agreement. "We would not accept it if it was offered."

"Are you kidding me?" Allison looked from one chief to the other, exasperated that they could not see what was so clear to her. "Shintsi, these warriors ambushed you while you slept, and yet no blood has been spilled. Majiro, the Oneata attacked our village when we were defenseless. They could have taken everything and everyone, but no one has been killed or raped, nothing has been stolen. I think that is a pretty strong foundation on which to begin building peace."

The two groups of warriors glared at each other, though uncertain looks were occasionally shot at the chiefs. Majiro and Shintsi still stood facing one another, each waiting for the other to speak.

"Chief Shintsi, did you not say just yesterday that peace between the Oneata and Shampiri would be 'wonderful'?" she pointed out.

The Oneata chief took his eyes off Majiro long enough to give her a dirty look. "I also said that it was impossible. We must take vengeance for what has been done to us!"

"It seems that you are on pretty even ground now. Maybe before someone starts this cycle of blood spilling again, you can lay down your weapons."

Shintsi scowled at Majiro. "Are you aware that your wife is the most meddlesome, disobedient bee of a woman that I have ever known?"

Majiro's eyes flickered for a moment and his lips began to twitch. He burst out laughing. "You don't know the half of it! Why do you think I go to Paamari to raid? Not because I want your women, but because I am trying to get away from mine!" Howling at his own joke, Majiro tossed his bow in the dirt and held his sides as he roared with laughter.

Allison rolled her eyes as the other men began snickering around her.

Finally regaining control of himself, Majiro said, "As irritating as she can be, perhaps there is some merit to what she has to say. It is true that you have not harmed any of my people when you came to raid our village. I do not understand why you have done this, but because you have, I will spare your lives." Shintsi watched him, his face unreadable, and Majiro continued, "Perhaps because we have spared your lives, you will agree to never return to our village as enemies again."

Shintsi replied solemnly as he offered his arm to Majiro, "I will give you my blood vow."

Majiro grasped the other man's forearm. "I accept."

Loud whoops filled the air as the Shampiri raised their weapons over their head in celebration. The Oneata warriors smiled at one another.

Allison joined Amita away from the men as they crowded around their chiefs. "What just happened?" she asked, bewildered.

"A treaty. I can't believe it! The chiefs are proposing a peace treaty between our tribes!" Amita bubbled, clapping her hands in delight.

It did not take long for someone to produce a knife. Allison winced as Majiro pushed the knife deep into the palm of his right hand. Clenching the cut hand over a wooden bowl, he waited as drops of blood splashed into it. After a few moments, Manitari handed him a strip of fabric with which he bound his hand.

The knife was passed formally to the Oneata chief, who repeated the process on his own hand. Once Shintsi's blood was added to the mixture, he held it to his mouth and sipped. Allison wrinkled her nose, but no one else seemed put off by observing the custom.

Majiro took the bowl and drank from it as well. The bowl empty, Majiro declared loudly, "Now your blood flows through my veins, and mine through yours. We are one body. As long as we both live, we will live in peace, for who would declare war on his own flesh."

"It will be as you say," Shintsi said, and the rest of the warriors erupted again in celebratory cheers.

"Help me, Imeshina. They will want to eat now." Amita turned to start her fire. Shaking her head in wonder, Allison joined her.

The men of Paamari stayed until the afternoon, drinking and celebrating the shocking turn of events. Allison marveled at how quickly the sentiments of the men had changed. One minute, they were ready to annihilate one another and the next they were toasting to friendship and reciting genealogies to figure out who was related to whom and how.

Majiro and Shintsi, now behaving like long-lost brothers, sat together swapping funny stories. "I must tell you about when my wife got lost in our garden. Can you imagine? Getting lost in your own garden!" Not wanting to hear the rest of the embarrassing tale, she crossed to the other side of the fire where Amita was sitting near her father and husband.

Her friend nudged her with an elbow. "You aren't upset that they are laughing at you, are you?" she whispered.

Allison shook her head. "No. If it's a choice between making fun of me or poking holes in each other, they can laugh at me all they want!"

Amita smiled and turned back to her father, her joy evident in her face. Soon enough, however, it was time for the Oneata to go. As they rose to leave, Amita hugged her father one last time.

Manitari grasped his father-in-law's hand and said, "Perhaps after the harvest, we will visit Oneata. My children would like to meet their grandparents, and I am sure that my wife would love to see her mother again."

"My fire will be lit for you," he returned.

After another round of farewells, the Oneata headed toward the trail. Ironically, they were laden with gifts from the Shampiri warriors' households as well as food for their trip home. However, they were, thankfully, leaving without any women this time.

As soon as they were out of sight, the Shampiri also disappeared in different directions into the jungle, eager to reunite with their families. Only Allison, Amita, and their husbands remained.

Majiro yawned and arched his back. "I would have never believed that this day could end without bloodshed."

Allison gave him a pointed look. "With God, anything is possible." she stated.

Manitari and Amita looked between the other two as if waiting for an eruption, but it never came. Majiro yawned again and said, "I am going to bed, but do me a favor, Imeshina. The next time you tell your God to do something of this magnitude, give me a little warning first."

He left, and Allison grinned triumphantly at Amita. "With God, anything really *is* possible. Even changing a heart of stone."

Manitari commented, "Something tells me that you did not have much to do with what happened today. No woman could have made that kind of an impact on men like Majiro and Shintsi."

"You're right." Allison agreed. "That is the thing about God, Manitari. His purposes will never be thwarted, not by you or even the chief. He is God, and we are His creation."

Manitari nodded slowly. "I am beginning to think that you might be right."

CHAPTER **TWENTY-TWO**

Eric's stomach lurched as he stepped gingerly out of the roller coaster. He followed Julia's bouncing steps down the exit ramp. "That was so great! I think that is my favorite ride in the whole park!" she said enthusiastically.

"You said that about the last one."

Julia eyed him critically. "You look kind of green. Are you okay?"

"I think I need to sit down on something that doesn't move for a few minutes. Seven roller coasters in a row is my limit."

They found an unoccupied bench around the corner and sat down. It was a Saturday right at the end of the school year, so Six Flags over Dallas was crowded with families and groups of teenagers and college students.

Eric had planned the date as something different from the usual movie and dinner routine, but he had not realized that Julia was such an adrenaline junkie. As soon as they had arrived, she had scorned all the "lame" rides and rushed straight for the biggest roller coasters in the park.

"We could ride the carousel," she offered.

He groaned. "I don't think so. I think something like sitting in a chair and watching a show might be a better idea."

Julia pulled the park guide brochure out of the back pocket of her jean shorts. She studied it for a moment and then tapped a spot on the map. "There is one here in a half hour. Not nearly as cool as Mr. Freeze, but I really don't want you to puke on me."

"I'll make a deal with you. Watch the show with me, and then I'll stand in line with you for Mr. Freeze one more time before dinner."

"Done."

They stood up and weaved their way quickly through the crowd. Luckily, they made it to the stage well before the show started because the seats were already filling up quickly. Finding an empty bench toward the side of the stage, they settled in and watched the people streaming by.

Julia said, "This was a great idea. I love amusement parks."

"I noticed," Eric replied with a grin.

"Don't you?"

He shrugged. "Sure. Though I think it is more about the company than anything else."

She smiled, but did not answer. Instead she motioned to a family nearby. The young mother had all three of her young children sitting along a low wall eagerly watching their father approach with two ice cream cones in each of his hands. The children waited patiently while their parents handed out the treats and then wordlessly began licking the ice cream until sticky streams ran down their chins and hands.

"They are so cute, but that is going to be one mess to clean up!" she said.

"No kidding. That little one has ice cream in her hair. If I was the parent, I think I'd just go on one of the water rides next and make sure they sat in the soak zone."

Julia laughed. "Parenting wisdom 101. Maybe you should go let them know."

"Nah. I think they have it under control."

Just then the show began. It was a simple comedic act by a dozen men dressed as cowboys, but it was well done. There was enough physical humor to delight the kids and enough subtle wordplays to keep the adults in the crowd entertained.

Eric glanced over at his companion. Her laughter was genuine and joyful, and it made his chest tighten with pleasure just to watch her. Reaching over, he pulled her hand off her lap and held it against his knee. She squeezed his hand in reply, but did not take her eyes off the stage.

As promised, after the show was over they walked back toward the huge blue roller coaster. The line was shorter than the last time, but it still stretched in a long zigzag outside of the building that launched the coaster.

"Are you sure you don't mind just waiting with me?" Julia asked. "We could do something else instead. I don't have to go again."

"I don't mind. Besides waiting in line means I have a captive audience."

"Are you going to do a little dance or something?"

"I might if I get bored, so you'd better keep me entertained," he warned, as he grabbed her hand and twirled her under his arm.

Julia said, "Look. There are those kids again. It looks like they're still pretty sticky."

"Why are you so fascinated by them?" he asked.

"Well, they are adorable for one thing. I don't know. I guess I just hope my own family is like that one day."

"Sticky?" he teased.

She smiled. "No. Sweet. Well-behaved. My sister and I were holy terrors."

"You? Not possible."

Catching his sarcastic tone, she punched him lightly in the arm. "Absolutely. At one point, my grandma told my mom not to bring us over again until we weren't so wild."

"Wow. Banned by your own grandmother… You must have been a sight to behold."

"We did get better after my parents got divorced. When my mom moved us here and life got a little more stable, she cracked down on us, and we shaped up. Before the divorce, I think she must have been so overwhelmed by her own problems that she just couldn't handle two little girls on top of it all."

"How old were you?"

"I was eight, and my sister was ten."

"Rough."

"Yes. But also good, in a way. My dad was—*is* a workaholic, so we never saw that much of him anyway. When he was around, it was so tense. I still remember just wishing that he would go back to the office. In some ways, their divorce was a relief to us all."

"Did you see much of your dad after that?"

"Every other Christmas and two weeks in the summer. It was enough for him." Julia's eyes clouded with emotion. "I think he was always disappointed that we weren't boys. No matter how successful we were, it was never quite enough."

Eric put his arm around her shoulders comfortingly and kissed her temple. "I can relate to that. My dad is a very hard man to please. I never doubted that he loved me, but I was consumed with trying to make him proud of me. At some point, I just realized that I had to stop living merely to meet his expectations."

Julia looked up at him. "The idea of having my own kids freaks me out a little," she admitted. "I'm scared I am going to mess them up. I mean, my mom was a great, Christian lady, but I still have issues. I guess instead of a college fund, I'll have to set up a future therapy fund for my children."

"You'll be a great mother, Julia," he said.

"It's nice of you to think that."

"No. I know it. Take it from a dad. You'll handle parenthood with a load of grace and a sense of humor."

"A dad… That's true. Sometimes I forget." She searched his face. "It must still be so difficult for you."

"It's strange," he said thoughtfully. "I still think about Isaac often, but the horrible pain of it isn't quite so bad now. Now I can actually remember him and smile instead of weep."

"I'm glad."

The line moved again, and they were close enough to watch the riders going on and off the roller coaster. Julia had moved on to a new topic of conversation, but Eric's thoughts were still on what he had said a few moments earlier. It was true. The pain of loss was not constant anymore, and as he looked at Julia's smiling face, he knew that she had much to do with that change.

Completely ignoring the fact that she was in the middle of a sentence, he leaned down and kissed her.

Julia looked back at him, her lips slightly parted and her eyebrows raised in surprise. "We've been dating for a month and a half, and you haven't done that before," she commented.

"I was just thinking about how happy you make me. Hope you don't mind."

"Hmmm. Can you run it by me again? I think I missed it the first time." She pulled his head down, and, this time, kissed him back.

"Are you sure you are up to this?" Eric asked, "We can go somewhere else."

"Not a chance. I've been looking forward to this picnic for a week. As long as you can carry the basket, I can hobble just fine on my fancy crutches. I'm almost a professional with these things now," Julia assured him.

Only two days before, Julia had reinjured her ankle during a church league softball game. The doctor told her that it was a worse sprain than the time before, but she declared it worth it since the slide into home plate that had caused the sprain had also won the game for her team.

"If you say so," Eric conceded. They loaded up their gear into his car and drove for nearly an hour to get to the national park they had chosen for their picnic.

Eric drove through the entrance, and, having done a little research, headed to a smaller parking lot farther into the park. They would still have a bit of a walk, but at least it would not be as far.

Once parked, they got out of the car, and Julia pulled her crutches from the backseat. "I can carry a backpack or something," she offered.

"I've got it."

"Give me something! You're making me feel useless."

Eric looked at her and smiled. "All right. How about I drape the blanket over your shoulder?"

"I guess that's good enough."

Eric grabbed the picnic basket and backpack from the trunk and slammed it shut. Slowing his pace to the swing of her crutches, they strolled leisurely up the trail. The park was fairly empty, and they encountered only one other pair of hikers. After just a few minutes of walking, they were far enough into the park that the sounds from the highway had faded away, hushed by the tall red oaks. Farther up the path, they could see an open forest floor beneath a cluster of fat elm trees.

"How about over there?" Eric asked pointing.

"Perfect." They ambled off the trail into the woods. When they reached their spot, Julia handed him the blanket, which he spread out at the base of one of the trees. He helped her settle onto the blanket, her back to the tree and her wrapped ankle stretched out in front of her. He then unpacked their lunch of turkey sandwiches, potato salad, fruit, and brownies. A thermos of lemonade completed the meal.

He sat down next to her and reached for a sandwich. "It's so beautiful here. So untouched. It's almost like we aren't even in Texas."

"Is this what Peru looks like?" she asked curiously.

"No. Not at all," he replied. "The forests here are full of pines and oak trees. In the Amazon, most of the trees are very different looking—incredibly tall. But the jungle floor is dense with bushes and tangled vines. In many places, you can't just walk through the trees like you can here. You literally have to cut your way through if you want to go anywhere."

Julia popped a grape into her mouth. "Living there must have been quite an adventure," she remarked.

"It was, for the most part. Allison always said that it was a man's playground." Eric smiled at the memory. "Living out there, you learn to do all sorts of things that you never do here. Cutting an airstrip into the jungle, hunting for your next meal, building your own house from the ground up… It was hard, but it was fun."

"Did your wife enjoy it as much as you did?"

"I think so. I mean, she had her moments when she wanted to quit—especially when she was pregnant with Isaac. But we all had times like that. That's why we went as a team. When one of us was discouraged, we could turn to the others to remind us why we came."

"Want another?" Julia offered the plastic container, and he pulled out a sandwich. They quietly chewed their food until she said, "She must have been quite a woman."

The comment was made sincerely and not as an attempt to probe, but Eric felt compelled to open up a little to this woman who was quickly making her own place in his heart. "You would have liked each other. She was more serious than you, not as outgoing—"

"That's hard to do."

"No kidding." He took her hand. "But both of you have this ability to make everyone feel wanted and loved. I've met beautiful women before that make the people around them feel insecure, but both of you have the opposite effect on people. On me."

Julia traced the pattern of the blanket with her finger. Not looking at him, she admitted, "I'm afraid I don't measure up to her."

Eric watched her, surprised by what she said. Confidence never seemed like something she lacked, but he was not about to give her a pat answer to soothe uncertainties. She would not accept that kind of answer anyway.

"Julia, look at me." She turned her deep brown eyes to his. "I can honestly say that I have not compared you to Allison before today, other than to note some of the similarities that I just told you. There is not some kind of a scorecard for my affection. I adored my wife." Her eyes flickered away, and he waited until she looked back into his eyes again before continuing. "I am also beginning to feel things for you that I didn't know I *could* feel again. But this is new territory for me, and it's scary. There is a lot I still have to work out in my own heart—ways I feel I failed as a husband that I have to come to terms with, but I am willing to keep moving forward if you are."

Biting her lip, Julia nodded. "I would like that… And, Eric, I didn't know Allison nor have I seen you in the role of husband, but I can hardly believe that she found you inadequate."

"Probably not, but that doesn't change what happened or how I feel about it now. You'll just have to give me time to sort it out," he said.

She smiled at him gently. "Take all the time you need, Eric. I'm not going anywhere."

CHAPTER **TWENTY-THREE**

Bending down to retrieve the yucca root that had rolled under the sleeping platform, Allison changed her mind. If she got down that low, she might not make it up again. She would wait until Isaac was around and have him get it for her. At five, he was as big as most of the nine-year-olds in the village and happy to run after them all day, often coming home only to eat or show Allison some newfound treasure.

She arched her back and rubbed her spine with her knuckles. Her pregnancy was in its final stages, and every move was uncomfortable at best. However ready she was physically to be rid of her burden, she was not so sure that her heart was prepared to meet the product of her union with Majiro.

Since the treaty with the Oneata, Majiro had treated her with grudging respect. Though he clearly held her beliefs in derision, he no longer reacted violently when she spoke of her faith. Instead he avoided her when he discovered her in the middle of a spiritual conversation and looked on with unveiled disinterest when he could not escape from it.

She was glad that she no longer lived with the dilemma of having to keep her faith from him or risk punishment, but she was most

215

thankful for the opportunity to teach Isaac freely. He, like any other young child, was delighted by the stories she told him from her memory of Scripture and soon began to ask questions about their deeper meaning. It was all the more satisfying when Majiro was around to hear her explanations.

Deciding that she had done all the chores she could stand for the morning, she left her house. A visit sounded like a good diversion, so she headed for Inani's home.

"Come inside. I will make some tea," the older woman coaxed when Allison appeared in her yard a few minutes later. Happily accepting the invitation to rest, she followed Inani inside and settled herself in the woman's hammock.

Inani ground some leaves in a wooden bowl with a rock and added boiling water. The fragrance of passion fruit tea filled the little room. "Here," she said, pouring off some of the tea into a smaller bowl. "This will help you relax."

"Thanks," Allison replied and blew on the tea to cool it.

Inani studied her for a moment from where she sat on a bench against the wall. "Your time is near, I think."

"I do too. I've had a few contractions this week. I can't imagine it is possible to get much bigger than I already am!"

Smiling, Inani said, "I remember that feeling—like an overripe melon ready to split down the middle."

"Was Majiro a large baby?" Allison asked, peering over the top of her bowl.

"No. He came early. We did not think he would survive, but he was just as stubborn at birth as he is now." Allison laughed, and Inani continued, "I had three children after him before my husband died. Both of my daughters died as children, and Majiro's brother was killed in a raid several years ago."

"Did he have a family?"

"A wife and daughter. She married and moved away from the village. I have not seen my granddaughter for years."

Allison reached over to squeeze her mother-in-law's hand. "I'm sorry."

Inani's eyes brightened, and she gripped Allison's hand tightly. "Your coming here has brought me much joy, for now I have a daughter, a grandchild, and another on the way. You have been good for our family."

"You are a wonderful mother-in-law. When I came here there was so much that I couldn't do. You were very kind to teach me all that I needed to know."

Still smiling, Inani rose. "Why don't you rest here? I will keep an eye out for Isaac." She patted Allison's arm and quietly went outside. Not able to resist the suggestion, Allison set her empty bowl down on the ground and leaned back into the rough hammock fabric for a nap.

She awoke with a jolt, unsure about what had awakened her, but the tightening in her midsection revealed the answer. Laying her hand across the top of her abdomen, she groaned. Ready or not, it seemed that her time had come.

She waited until the contraction had passed and the hard sphere in her middle had softened again. Getting out of the hammock was not nearly as easy as getting in had been, and by the time she struggled to her feet, she could feel another contraction was on its way. If they were already coming this quickly, she must have slept right through early labor.

Inani's yard was empty, so she walked as swiftly as she could manage to Amita's house. There was no one home. Feeling desperate, as another contraction swelled, she grabbed the edge of the house and panted.

God, help me! I am not ready for this.

She noticed a group of children walking toward her carrying firewood on their backs. Micheli was with them. "Micheli, come!" she called, waving her hand in earnest.

The girl broke into a sprint with the heavy load of firewood still across her thin shoulders. She dumped the wood next to the fire pit and ran to Allison. "What is it?" she asked.

"Where is your mother?" Allison gasped.

"Back at our garden."

Oh no! So far away.

"Please, run and send her to me. The baby is coming." The girl's eyes widened. Without another word, she whirled around and ran back in the direction she came from.

Allison closed her eyes and rested her forehead against the bamboo wall. *Not yet, not yet. Just wait a little longer.* But as she counted the seconds between her contractions, she realized that a little longer was all it would take. Her pains were only five minutes apart and getting closer. Surely the baby would not come before help arrived. Her labor with Isaac had been nine hours long. She knew second babies usually came more quickly, but surely not this fast!

A gentle hand rested on her back. She turned expecting to see Amita, but it was Majiro's face she looked into. His forehead was dotted with sweat, and his chest heaved with exertion. "I saw Micheli on the trail... are you okay?" His eyes were clouded with concern as another contraction took its hold, and her face twisted into a grimace.

Allison gripped his arm for support; her eyes squeezed shut against the pain. The contraction passed. Opening her eyes, she offered him a weak smile. "I'm just fine. Never been better."

Apparently not appreciating her attempt at humor, Majiro rolled his eyes. Without warning, he stooped and effortlessly scooped her into his arms. "I'll get you home quickly, Imeshina. Tell me if we need to stop for another pain."

"You're going to break your back!" she protested against his chest as he hurried back toward their house.

He scoffed. "I've carried game much heavier than you for miles. I think I can manage to get my own wife home to deliver my child."

In truth, she was glad for the help. She quite possibly would not have been able to get home on her own. Majiro kicked open the front door and set her gently on the sleeping platform. She leaned back against her outstretched arms, her legs splayed in front of her.

"Where is my mother?" he asked.

"I have no idea. She said she would look after Isaac, but he was down at the river. Maybe she is there with him."

"I'll go find her."

"No!" Allison stretched out her hand to him. "You can't leave me, Majiro. This baby is coming fast, and I need help."

Majiro looked between her and the door. "I don't know anything about birth. That is a woman's job."

She hissed, "If you want your child born in the dirt, then go ahead and leave. Otherwise, help me!"

Majiro hesitated for a moment longer, then lifted his shoulders in defeat. "What do you want me to do?" he asked.

"Get two pots of river water on the fire to boil and put the knife in one of them. Wash it first. Cut some banana leaves from the tree behind the house and lay them on the floor over there." She continued issuing orders between contractions, and Majiro scurried around retrieving supplies and setting up a birthing area.

"Help me stand," she said, reaching up her hand.

He looked at her doubtfully. "Shouldn't you be lying down?"

Allison glared at him. "How many times have you given birth?"

Dutifully, he hauled her to her feet, but she doubled over as a powerful contraction nearly knocked her to the floor. "I think you should lie back down," he said.

"I want to walk. It will help the baby come down more quickly."

Majiro swore. "Then *lie down*! Give my mother or Amita time to come back to help you."

"I. Want. This. Baby. Out. NOW!"

He gritted his teeth, but did not argue. Clenching his forearm, Allison waddled around the room. Sweat trickled down her back. Her legs buckled a few times, but Majiro's firm hold around her waist kept her upright. They circled the tiny room over and over again, each rotation taking longer than the one before as her contractions increased in frequency and duration.

A splash on her feet startled them both, and Majiro jumped back. "What was that?!" he asked, staring at her as if she had grown horns.

"That was the bag of water around the baby breaking open."

Majiro swore again. "Disgusting!"

"You're going to see more disgusting than that before this is over," she snapped. "Help me sit down on the mat. I'm getting dizzy."

Stepping gingerly over the muddy puddle on the dirt floor, he led her to the birthing mat. However, instead of sitting she rocked back on her hands and knees.

"What are you doing?"

"I am trying to get comfortable, Majiro. This isn't exactly a pleasant experience, you know! My back is killing me, and this position relieves the pressure," she explained. *Oh God, what I wouldn't give for a hospital, an epidural, and someone that actually knows what he is doing next to me!*

"How can I help?" he asked quietly, and her exasperation eased a little as she realized that he was much more frightened than she was.

"Would you rub my lower back?"

He reached over and began rubbing his thumbs next to her spine, and she arched to meet his hands. "Harder."

"Any harder and I will bruise you."

"I don't care."

All of a sudden, Allison screamed and flopped onto her back panting. One contraction rolled on top of the other in never-ending waves. She struggled to catch her breath in between.

"I have to push," she grunted.

Majiro's eyes widened like a trapped animal's. "No! You can't. You have to wait until someone is here to catch the baby. I can't do it!"

"You have to do it, Majiro. No one else is here, and this baby is coming whether we want him to or not."

He gulped. "What do I do?"

"First, help me take off my dress." She lifted her arms, and he pulled the rough fabric over her head. Wadding it into a ball, he tossed it into the opposite corner.

"Now what?"

"Now be ready. I don't think this will take very long." Another contraction began, and she pressed herself up into a half-sitting position as her body took over and instinctively did what it was made to do. Perched next to her leg, Majiro alternately called out encouragement and checked her progress.

After twenty minutes of pushing, he said excitedly, "The head is coming out!"

"Then be ready to catch the baby. But don't pull him out. Just wait until he comes on his own."

Majiro nodded and squatted between her knees. With the next contraction, Allison felt the so-called ring of fire and shrieked as pain ignited every nerve in her body.

Now immune to her screams, Majiro described his view as if she had no idea what was going on down there. "His head is almost out… It's out now! Is he supposed to be that color?"

Ignoring him, Allison instructed, "Is the cord around his neck?"

"I don't think so."

"Good. Then put your hands underneath me. He will be out with the next push."

As promised, when she bore down again, she felt the baby's shoulders squeeze through, and the child slid the rest of the way out.

"She's out! It's a girl, Imeshina!"

Allison sat up and looked at the slimy baby between her legs. Grabbing a rag, she wiped the goo from her face.

"She's not breathing!" Majiro cried in a panicky voice.

"She will." She turned the baby sideways and rubbed her back. A weak wail filled the room. With a sigh of relief, she laid the baby back on the mat. Little feet kicked the air defiantly. The baby's eyes opened, and her whimpers died down. Her parents laughed.

"She's beautiful," Allison said in awe, as a powerful, unexpected love for her new daughter filled her heart, and tears spilled unchecked down her cheeks.

"She's perfect," Majiro confirmed. "You did well, Imeshina." He leaned over and kissed her forehead, and she smiled softly at him. Despite all the abuse she had suffered from this man, he had given her a daughter, and she was thankful.

The door banged open, and Amita burst through. "I'm so sorry! I came as fast as… Oh." Amita stopped short when she saw the baby bundled up on the leaf-covered floor, her parents watching her with the fascination that only a new baby can command.

Quickly sizing up the situation, she reached carefully into the cool, boiled water for the knife. "Chief, I can finish here. Go on out."

Majiro stood. Looking down at Allison and his daughter, he asked softly, "Are you sure you don't need me anymore?"

"Amita can take things from here." Still he hesitated, so she added, "After the cord is cut, I will send her out to you." Satisfied, he walked out of the house, a big grin plastered to his face.

Amita knelt next to the baby for a look. "Congratulations! What an adorable baby! Where is your string?"

Allison pointed her to the lengths of string she had set aside in preparation for the birth, and Amita busied herself cutting the cord.

After the baby was cut free, Allison lifted her from the mat and placed a soft kiss on her cheek. "Here," she said, placing her in Amita's arms. "Give her to Majiro to hold. I'm contracting again; I think it's time to deliver the placenta."

Amita hurried from the house with a promise to return quickly. Sighing, Allison laid back on the mat, her eyes closed and a contented smile on her face.

That evening, Allison sat outside by the fire with a crowd of people around her. Word had spread that the chief had a new daughter and many stopped by throughout the afternoon to offer well wishes.

Majiro's misfortune of delivering his own daughter was a source of endless amusement, and he was forced to retell of his participation in her birth with each visitor that arrived. Though he seemed to be properly embarrassed at being forced into a role normally reserved for women, he was able to laugh with the rest at the unlikely story.

Allison's eyes were growing heavy from the long day, and she was glad that as the sun's final rays lit the sky a brilliant red, the visitors returned to their own homes, unwilling to be caught on the trails in the dark. Finally, only she and Majiro were left with their children.

The baby fussed in Majiro's arms, and he walked around the fire bouncing her lightly. Soon, however, she began to cry in earnest, and Allison held out her arms. "Let me take her." Majiro reluctantly relinquished his burden, and she pulled a blanket over her shoulder so that she could nurse privately. He watched her curiously. She knew that he thought it was an odd thing to do—most of the women wore no shirts at all and nursed wherever it was convenient, but she could not bring herself to go completely native.

Isaac tugged at her sleeve. "Mommy?"

"What, sweetie?"

"I can't see her."

"She's eating right now. You can see her when she is finished."

"Can I hold her then?"

"Of course. But you'll have to sit down and let a grown-up help you."

"Okay…What's her name?" he asked.

Allison glanced at Majiro. They had not yet discussed a name, since naming a child usually came weeks after birth in the Shampiri community. "Well, I don't know. We haven't decided yet," she responded. "I was thinking that we should call her Grace."

"*Grace*?" Majiro tasted the English name and made a face. "What does that mean?"

"It means a lot of things. I guess the definition I am thinking of is 'undeserved kindness.'"

"I don't think so. I can barely even pronounce it."

Allison looked at her daughter, now contentedly sleeping in the crook of her arm. An undeserved kindness she was indeed. A beautiful gift in the middle of painful circumstances.

"It also means 'lovely,'" she said hopefully.

Majiro nodded in approval. "Well, she is the most beautiful child I have ever seen," he said with fatherly pride, and Allison chuckled. "Her name is *Cameetsa.*" Allison cocked her eyebrow. Only Majiro would have the audacity to name his daughter "beautiful."

"You can't name her that."

He shrugged. "You call her whatever you want. The rest of us will call her Cameetsa." It was a compromise of sorts and likely the best she could get. She rolled her eyes, but agreed.

"Come on inside now, Isaac, and you can hold Grace before bedtime."

Isaac hopped off the bench and led his mother into the house. Majiro followed them inside.

The third time Grace cried in the wee hours of the night, Majiro rolled over and griped, "Can't you keep her quiet for a few hours? I can't get any sleep." Isaac sighed from his own sleeping mat in the corner.

Fearing that her son would awaken as well, Allison got up and tiptoed outside into the cool night air. Wrapping the baby tightly in a blanket, she sat on the ground next to the wall to nurse.

Grace latched instantly and began the cycle of eating and napping. Yawning, Allison rested her head against the bamboo. She had forgotten how exhausting it was to have a newborn. But her daughter was worth it. She studied the thatch of black hair on her tiny head and the button nose that reminded her of Isaac. Perfectly shaped, pink lips quivered incessantly on her breast even as the baby dozed. Majiro had it right: she was breathtaking.

She marveled at the change that had taken place in her heart in just a few short hours. A day ago she had dreaded the impending birth and still shed tears as she thought about being the mother of

Majiro's child. Amita had been right all along. When she looked at Grace, all she could see was her own flesh and blood. Her daughter.

"You are a miracle, Grace." she whispered as she traced the curve of her soft cheeks. "God has turned my sorrow into joy and given me beauty for the ashes of my life."

God, make me worthy to care for this precious one. Give me wisdom and, more than anything else, let me point her to You. As You have given her to me, so I give her back to You.

For a few more minutes she remained sitting, holding her daughter close and watching her sleep. Finally, practicality won, and she went back inside to salvage what she could of the remaining hours of darkness.

CHAPTER **TWENTY-FOUR**

Majiro was pleased to have their daughter in his arms during the daylight hours, but after the sun went down, Allison was on her own. Unfortunately, Grace was not a good sleeper, and by the time she was a month old, Allison's eyes were a permanent red for lack of sleep. She struggled to keep up with her daily chores as she learned to shuffle being the mother of two children. At times, she felt like she did in her early days at the village—positively drowning.

Amita had offered to come and help her prepare a batch of *cachojari,* since she had neglected that chore long enough that Majiro was nagging her daily to make the pink beer. Allison was already at work peeling an enormous pile of yucca in the front yard when her friend arrived, her own infant daughter in a sling at her hip and Micheli at her side.

"You get to play with Cameetsa, my love," Amita said as she sat the six-month-old down on the blanket in the shade where Grace was lying. The women laughed as Amita's baby began screeching in protest to being left alone.

"I don't think she is very impressed with my daughter," Allison remarked.

"When they are older they will be great friends, I'm sure. Micheli, mind the babies for us while we work." Amita surveyed the yucca stacked on the ground, one pile peeled and the other with the dirty outer layer still attached. "I'll get this first batch on the fire to boil." She grabbed Allison's largest pots and a jar of river water. After halving each root, she chopped them into four-inch lengths, rinsed them, and tossed them into the pot. Once the pot was full, she set it on the flame and sat next to Allison to finish peeling the rest.

Thankfully, the yucca roots were mercifully easy to peel. After slicing longways down the root, an inserted finger underneath the skin detached it easily in a wide ring. The pile of peels looked like dirty scrolls rolled around themselves.

Amita looked over at her. "You look tired," she observed. "Rough night?"

"Same as always. She doesn't sleep for more than three hours at a time. I had forgotten how tiring it is to have a newborn."

"Do you want me to take her this afternoon so you can nap?"

Allison threw the last of the cut yucca into the pile with the rest and stood to check on the pot on the fire. The water was boiling rapidly and a poke into the center of one of the roots assured her that it was tender. She wrapped her hands in the hem of her skirt and moved the pot to the ground, replacing it with the next one.

She replied, "No. The issue is more me remembering to sleep during the day instead of trying to get things done. Majiro likes to tote her around during the day."

Amita laughed. "I have never seen any man so interested in his baby. Most men barely seem to notice them until they start walking and talking."

"I've heard some of the other warriors making jokes to him about it, but he just laughs along with them. It hasn't stopped him from wanting her around most of the day… He must have been devastated when his wife and child died."

Standing above the drained, cooked yucca, Amita shoved a short wooden paddle back and forth into the pot to mash the root. She nodded. "He was. His wife got sick after she gave birth. At first she was fine, and then a week later she started getting fevers. A few days later, she was dead. Majiro tried to find a wet nurse for his son, but there was no one nearby with enough milk for their child and his. The baby died a month later."

"That's horrible." Allison shivered. "He never talks about either of them."

Holding out her hand for the small purple sweet potatoes Allison was pulling out of a basket, Amita said, "No doubt. After his son died, he disappeared into the jungle for several weeks. When he came back, he would just walk away anytime their names were mentioned. We all learned not to say anything to him about them."

Allison broke off a piece of peeled sweet potato with her teeth and chewed it thoughtfully for several minutes, being careful not to swallow. She leaned over and spat the contents of her cheeks into the hot, mashed yucca.

Amita took a bite of her own sweet potato. "How about Isaac? Is he still enjoying having a new sister?" A line of purple juice slid down her chin, and she brushed it away with the back of her hand.

Spitting out the next mouthful, Allison replied, "Oh, he adores her! No signs of jealousy yet, though her birth has prompted a lot of questions about his own birth and, consequently, his father."

"Does that bother you?"

"No. I love it when he asks me questions about Eric. I only wish that he could remember him. He was such a great dad and a wonderful man."

Amita glanced sideways at her. "You still miss him."

It was a statement, not a question, and Allison smiled at her friend's keen observation. "Especially since Grace was born. I keep thinking about when Isaac was a baby and how much we enjoyed becoming parents together."

"I'm sad that you were taken from your home and family, but at the same time, Imeshina, I am so glad that you are here. And not just because you taught me about Creator God; you are like my sister too."

"Thank you," she replied softly. "I could say the same for you."

The two lapsed into silence for the next hour as they worked on the messiest stage of the beer making process. The pile of sweet potatoes dwindled slowly as each was peeled, chewed thoroughly, and added to the mashed yucca. When they finally finished the last of the sweet potatoes, they stirred the mixture and took handfuls of it to continue chewing. By lunchtime, the contents of the pot looked like smooth pinkish-purple creamed potatoes, and they were finished with the chewing part. Amita sighed and smiled wide with her eyes crossed, and Allison laughed at her friend's purple teeth.

She stood and filled two wooden bowls with water for them to rinse their mouths with, and afterward pulled another jar of boiled river water from beside the fire. They poured the cooled water into the two heavy pots of mashed yucca and sweet potatoes. Reaching their hands into the pots, they slowly stirred in the water, squeezing the mixture between their fingers. Using a loosely woven cloth, they strained the chunks from the beverage and tossed them behind the house.

"So, guess what Manitari said to me last night?" Amita said, as they returned from their last trip to toss out the unwanted pieces of yucca and sweet potato.

"That he wants another baby?" Allison teased. "Seriously, Amita, tell him you need a break!"

Amita giggled, blushing bright red. "No! He told me that he has been thinking about Creator God and Jesus."

Allison's mouth dropped open as she reached for a jar of Amita's old *cachojari*. She added it to the new batch to speed the fermentation along, otherwise she would have to wait out several more days of Majiro's complaints. "No kidding," she said. "What did he say?"

"He said that he can't deny the power of the spirit that we have. And I don't think he was just talking about the treaty with the Oneata. He's seen the change in my heart too."

"That is incredible! Of course, I am not surprised. It's obvious to anyone with eyes that following Jesus has made all the difference for you."

"Well, don't get too excited," Amita admonished, as she stirred the beer one last time. "He also said that he cannot follow Jesus because to do so would be disloyal to the chief."

"What did you tell him?"

"I asked him who deserved his loyalty—the chief of his people or the creator of all. He didn't have much to say after that."

They chuckled. Allison said, "God has given you great wisdom, my friend. We will keep praying for Manitari because it seems that God is after his heart as well."

Finally finished with their arduous chore, Amita left to find her daughters while Allison woke Grace up to nurse. "No wonder you don't sleep at night," she cooed to the yawning infant. 'You can't stay awake at all during the day. We're going to have to work on that, little one, because your mama needs to sleep sometime too."

CHAPTER **TWENTY-FIVE**

"I was thinking maybe we should just order some Chinese and watch a movie at my house," Julia said as she climbed into Eric's car after work. "I'm so tired from trying to get my lesson plans done."

Trying to keep the panic from creeping into his voice, Eric said, "Um. I was really craving Italian, and I already made reservations at DaVinci's. Tomorrow is Saturday. Maybe you can sleep in."

Julia yawned. "Okay. DaVinci's it is, but I am not promising to be good company. I might be asleep under the table before we get our food."

Smiling with relief, he reached for her hand. "I thought you were going to wait until you were finished working at the church before doing lesson plans."

"I was," she admitted. "But then I panicked. I only have a week between my last day at the church and my first day at the school. What if I get sick or something? Or what if my students plow through my lessons so quickly that I need to make more? I don't want to be unprepared."

"I think even if you were caught unprepared, you would do an amazing job. Those kids don't know how lucky they'll be to have you as a teacher in a few weeks."

Julia smiled at him and said, "Thanks for the vote of confidence. I'm more nervous than I was during my student teaching."

They rode in companionable silence the rest of the way to the restaurant. Parking in the back of the full lot, they made their way into the crowded restaurant lobby and waited in line.

"Hi! Welcome to DaVinci's," greeted a teenage hostess when they finally reached the front.

"We have a reservation for Eric Carter please," Eric said.

The hostess' eyes brightened. "Yes, of course! Right this way." She led them past the main room of the restaurant and toward a pair of gigantic, wooden doors in the back with a bronze plaque declaring "Banquet Room" mounted on the adjoining wall.

"Why are we going in here?" The question died on Julia's lips as the hostess swung open the door, and a crowd of familiar faces turned to them grinning.

"Surprise!" everyone cried in unison when they saw who was at the door.

Julia's mouth dropped open, and she looked back and forth between the crowded room and Eric, who was at her side laughing at her expression.

"What... what? Is this for me?" she asked.

"It's for you," Eric confirmed. "It's a belated happy-graduation party plus a goodbye-from-the-office party plus congratulations-on-your-new-job party. Surprised?"

"Stunned."

"Good." A wave of friends descended on them, hugging her and congratulating him on a secret well kept. Julia was swept away from his side, her fatigue seemingly evaporated into the garlic-scented air.

A firm hand pounded his back, and he glanced at his father who came up behind him. "It looks like you pulled it off, son. Well done!"

"Did you see her face? I don't think she saw it coming!" His mother approached them, and he pulled her into a side hug. "Thanks for coming, you two. I know it was a bit of a drive from Dallas."

Jean replied, "Oh, we wouldn't have missed it. We will take any opportunity we have to get to know our son's lovely lady better."

"She will be very glad to see you too."

With a twinkle in her eyes, Jean asked, "You're not proposing tonight, are you?"

"Mother."

She put her hands up in defense. "I was just asking."

David put his arm around his wife's shoulders. "Now Jean, leave him alone. I'm sure we'll be the first to know when he decides to pop the question."

The two of them chuckled at their own joke and walked away, leaving a bewildered Eric in their wake. *Propose? Is that what everyone thinks is going on here?* His chest tightened a little as he looked around the room trying to ascertain hidden thoughts.

Just then, the doors opened again, and he was distracted by a line of servers entering the room with huge trays of steaming food. They carried the food to the long table at the back of the room and quickly set up a mouth-watering buffet of lasagna, steak Gorgonzola, and shrimp scampi.

Eric noted with satisfaction that everything looked exactly as he had requested. Big tables around the room were set up with cutlery and drinking glasses. Vases filled with gardenias—Julia's favorite—were centered on each table. Waiters in black slacks and white button-down shirts circled the room filling drink requests, while others inconspicuously cleared dirty glasses and replaced dropped silverware.

Tapping a glass with a spoon, he soon had the attention of all the guests. "Welcome, everyone," he said loudly. "Thank you all for coming tonight to celebrate Julia's accomplishments and what I know will be a wonderful transition to a new career for her." He paused until the scattered applause died down. "I've asked Pastor Denny to say a prayer for our meal and our evening before we eat."

Without further prompting, the pastor began an eloquent prayer of blessing on their evening and on Julia. Feeling a soft hand slip into his, Eric peeked open an eye. Julia beamed at him. "Thank you," she whispered, and bowed her head. He squeezed her hand tightly in response.

"Amen!" came the chorus of voices at the end of the prayer, and the room came alive again with the low roar of conversation. Eric and Julia were ushered to the front of the buffet line where they quickly filled their plates before finding seats at one of the tables.

"This is amazing, Eric," Julia gushed, leaning over for a whiff of the gardenia blooms. "You thought of everything."

"You deserve it. I am really proud of you, sweetheart." She kissed him on the cheek.

Before they could start eating, Roger and his wife, Lydia, approached with loaded plates in their hands. "May we join you?" Roger asked.

"Of course."

Lydia shook out her linen napkin and placed it in her lap. "When is your last day at the church, Julia?" she asked.

"Wednesday. The new secretary starts on Monday, so I will have three days to train her."

"Are you sad to go?"

"Maybe a little." She leaned across as if to share a secret. "I'll miss having Eric at work with me."

Eric added, "I think she likes to keep an eye on me to keep me out of trouble."

Roger smirked. "I don't think that's what she meant, buddy." They all laughed.

Other friends joined their table, all eager to talk to Julia about her plans for the fall, which she happily shared. Her enthusiasm and humor were contagious, and the meal was scattered with bouts of laughter.

Roger set his fork on his empty plate and leaned back in his chair. "Great food, great company. I have no complaints."

Julia said, "I can't wait to call my sister to tell her about it."

"Your sister lives in Chicago, right?" Lydia asked, wiping her mouth with her napkin.

"Mm hmm. With her husband."

"Have you had a chance to meet her yet, Eric?"

Julia answered for him. "No. He doesn't know this yet, but I am going to try to talk him into flying up there with me for Thanksgiving this year to meet them."

"Sounds like a great idea to me," Roger said. Leaning toward Eric, he advised, "That's the way it works, you know. One holiday with her family and the next with yours. Might as well start the routine now because once the babies arrive, everyone thinks you should spend the holiday with them."

"So true," Lydia agreed.

Julia glanced at Eric, and he smiled back uneasily. Before anyone could say anything else embarrassing, he escaped with the excuse of wanting to refill his plate with more shrimp scampi. When he returned, his parents had pulled up chairs next to Julia.

Jean pulled a small box out of her purse and handed it to her. "Just a little congratulations gift," she said.

"You shouldn't have, Jean."

"Yes, we should. David helped me pick it out."

Julia unwrapped the box eagerly and pulled out a pair of crystal chandelier earrings amid the admiring exclamations from around the table. "Oh my goodness, these are gorgeous. I love them! Thank you so much!"

David said, "You're welcome. We thought they would go nicely with Eric's gift."

"Dad, I haven't given it to her yet."

"No time like the present."

Eric looked around the table at the expectant faces, including Julia's, and realized that they were all anticipating the wrong thing. His gift was a bracelet, not a ring. The last thing he wanted to do was embarrass or disappoint her in front of all of their friends. At last, Julia saved him. "You can give it to me later, Eric. In private."

The matter settled, the conversation moved on to other things. His mind, however, continued to whirl as he tried to think a way out of the impending conversation with Julia. He had never been one to be afraid of commitment before, and the Lord knew that Julia was everything that he could want in a wife. Yet the thought of taking the next step filled him with inexplicable panic. At the same time, he knew that women not uncommonly gave an ultimatum if they felt that their significant other was dragging his feet. He hoped that Julia was not one of those because, if she was, he had no idea what he was going to do.

It was very late when Eric finally drove Julia home. They had been the last to leave the restaurant, and many of the guests had wanted to stay late into the evening. Luckily, she was happy to carry on a mostly one-sided conversation, needing him only to grunt at the appropriate moments.

He parked in her driveway and got out to help her carry in bags of leftover food, gifts, and a vase of gardenias. She unlocked the door and flipped on the light in the entryway.

Dumping her purse and the flowers on the table next to the door, she reached down and scooped up the calico kitten Eric had given her for her birthday the month before. "Hey, Nala, I bet you are starving." she said, rubbing her nose into the soft fur of Nala's back.

"She's getting big," he said.

"That's because she eats like a grown man. Don't you, baby? You want some steak?"

Eric laughed. "Steak? No wonder she's so big."

"It's protein. It's good for her."

He followed her into the kitchen and sat on a stool at the counter, watching as she unloaded the plastic containers onto the counter. After finding the one with the steak Gorgonzola, she put a little into a cereal bowl and popped it into the microwave.

"You are coming over for dinner tomorrow night," she said.

"I am?"

"Well, someone has to help me eat all this, and even Nala won't be up for that task." She pulled the warmed food out of the microwave and scooped it into the kitten's food dish. Nala mewed from the floor until Julia set the dish in front of her.

"I guess I ordered too much food."

Julia walked behind him and put her arms around his neck. "Tonight was perfect," she whispered into his neck. "It was so sweet of everyone to come just for me—even your parents."

He squeezed her arm gently. "Aw, we all love you, Julia."

"I love you too."

Suddenly it felt like all the air got sucked out of the room, and he was very glad that she was standing behind him and could not see the blood rushing into his face.

"Eric?"

"Y- yeah?" he sputtered.

"It's okay. I know you aren't going to propose."

"You do?"

She laughed and led him by the hand to the living room couch. "I saw your face when people kept saying stuff tonight, and I knew that you thought that was what they were thinking," she said.

"Weren't they?"

"Well, maybe. But what matters is what we think, and we both know that it isn't time. I mean, we've known each other for almost three years, but we've only been dating for a few of months."

He looked at her beautiful, sincere face and traced her jaw with his finger. "You aren't mad?"

"No. Not at all."

"It's not that the idea of getting married doesn't hold some appeal. It's just... it scares me a little, I guess. I don't know why."

Julia shrugged. "Makes sense to me. The last time didn't end so well. I think I would have become a nun in your position."

He grinned. "They don't let men become nuns."

She rolled her eyes. "You know what I mean. Seriously though, Eric, you don't owe me an explanation. It's completely fi—"

"I love you, Julia."

She raised one eyebrow. "You're being a little schizophrenic."

Laughing, he planted a kiss on one of her palms. "I am not ready to ask you to marry me yet, but I do love you. Very much. You make me laugh more than any other person I have ever known, and I would hate not having you in my life."

Pulling his head down, she kissed him firmly on the mouth. "I adore you, Eric Carter. Now get out of my house before the neighbors start wondering what the local pastor is doing here at one in the morning."

She walked him to the door and wiggled her fingers at him as he headed to his car. They were both smiling.

CHAPTER **TWENTY-SIX**

Allison opened the front door in response to a knock and saw Manitari and Amita standing in the doorway. "We would like to talk to you," Amita said.

"Sure. Do you want to come over for dinner later?" she asked. "I am hoping that Majiro will return from his hunting trip this afternoon with something good. I told him to look for some turkeys."

Manitari replied, "Actually that is why we came now. We wanted to talk to you without the chief around."

"Oh. Well, come on in." She held the door open, motioned for them to enter, and then called to Isaac who was playing in the yard. He jumped up and ran inside.

She asked him, "Can you take Grace with you to play outside? Stay close to the house and don't let her get too close to the fire."

"Okay. Can I have a snack too?"

She handed him a bowl from the small side table in the corner. "Here is some pineapple. If you're still hungry, you can have a banana from the basket by the front door. Share with your sister."

Taking the bowl with one hand, he reached for Grace with the other. Matching his strides to her hesitant toddles, he coaxed her toward the door with a promise of a snack. Allison watched them go, a content smile on her face. Isaac was a fabulous big brother to Grace, who continued to charm everyone as she had in infancy.

She offered another bowl of pineapple to her guests and motioned for them to sit on the sleeping platform, while she sat across from them on Isaac and Grace's reed sleeping mat. "What's up?" she asked when they were settled.

The couple looked at one another, and Manitari cleared his throat. "Imeshina, you know that I put away my old spirits a few weeks ago in order to follow Creator God," he began.

"Yes."

He continued, "It's just that when I traveled to Iquitos before I met my wife, I was invited to a ceremony. I went, but I didn't really understand what was going on. But I think it was a ceremony for Creator God. I want to know what it was."

"Can you describe it to me?" Allison asked.

"Sure. We sat and then we stood and then we sat again. Everyone sang songs together, and some people prayed—I know that was what they were doing now, but then I just thought they were crazy, talking to the air with their eyes closed. At the end, one man stood in front of everyone and spoke until my back hurt from sitting on the hard bench for so long. So am I right, was that a religious ceremony?"

Laughing at his description, she replied, "Sort of. God's Word admonishes His followers to meet together to worship Him, study from His Word, and to encourage one another. We call it a… *church* service." She used the Spanish word since there was none that she knew of in the Shampiri language.

Amita asked, "Does it happen every year?"

"Actually, in most places it happens every week."

"We should have a church service as well," Manitari declared.

"Um, I'm not sure that would go over so well with Majiro," Allison said. "He has been lenient with me since the treaty, but I am not sure if he would allow us to meet as an organized group."

"But you said that Creator God tells us that we must meet together this way. If we are true followers, we must obey everything He says, not just the things that we like," Manitari pointed out.

Allison nodded her head thoughtfully. "You're right." she said slowly. "I can't argue with that. When do you want to hold the service?"

"How about in three days at our house after we get back from our garden?" Amita suggested.

"Works for me. Bring your children too. And can you have your drum ready, Manitari?"

"I haven't played my drum since I gave up my old spirits!"

Allison smiled. "You played for your old spirits before, now you will use it to make music to worship Jesus."

"Is that okay?"

"Why not? God created music too, didn't He? There are many stories in His Word about people using drums to sing and dance for Him."

A smile lit Manitari's face. "I would love to play for Creator God. I will work on making some new songs for Him this week!"

Her friends soon left, both of them bubbling with excitement over the prospect of a public worship service. Allison was excited but also apprehensive as she wondered how Majiro would react to the news.

That weekend Allison realized that she had been worried for nothing. She broached the subject of the upcoming church service to Majiro on Friday night, and he listened politely but dismissed the whole thing casually. "Whatever, Imeshina. Just have dinner ready on time."

On the afternoon of the scheduled service, Majiro had gone to make his chiefly rounds around the village, checking to make sure that everyone was healthy and that no one had complaints or concerns that needed to be addressed. She had put Grace down for a nap, but she had awakened by the time Micheli came to the door to announce that her parents were ready. Calling for Isaac to join her, she settled Grace onto her hip and followed Micheli home.

When she entered the house, she was surprised to see several people besides Manitari, Amita, and their children. Tsipavi, the man who had found Isaac when he had gone missing years ago, was there along with his wife and teenage daughter. Inani was also in attendance with her sister, Tentega.

"Come in, Imeshina," Amita said, "We've been waiting for you. You can begin when you are ready. We are all here."

The conversation in the room came to a halt when Allison entered, and all eyes turned expectantly to her. Manitari had set up benches around the small room for the group, and everyone was seated politely, even the children.

Taking the empty spot next to Inani, she cleared her throat and said, "Um. Well, I guess before we start, I should just tell you what the purpose of our service is. I am a follower of Creator God and His Son, Jesus, as are Amita and Manitari. We wanted to meet together along with anyone who wanted to join us to worship the Creator and pray to Him about our needs. I can also answer any questions anyone has about what we believe as His followers." It was not an eloquent speech, but the nods around the room indicated that it had been well-received. Now, however, she had no idea what to do or say.

Manitari stood with his drum underneath his arm. "I would like to start today with a song that I made to honor Creator God." Without further prompting, he began a slow cadence on the drum.

After a few beats, he began to sing with a surprisingly beautiful voice. The warm tones of his song were enchanting, and everyone listened intently as he sang about the biblical creation story as Allison had explained it to him a few weeks ago. As he described the dark world becoming light and the emptiness becoming full, the song increased in tempo and volume. He sang about the birth of the heavenly lights and the creation of the jungle and the creatures that were in it. Finally came the crescendo as he described the Creator's greatest work, man and woman, who were made in His image to know and love Him.

When the last note of the song faded away, the room remained silent for several minutes. Allison was surprised to find her cheeks wet with tears, and she realized how much she had missed spending time worshiping with other believers. It was one thing to sit and talk to Manitari and Amita or to answer questions and explain what she knew about God's Word; it was another entirely to be ministered to herself.

"Is that how the world was really made?" Tsipavi's daughter asked in awe.

"Yes," Manitari answered. "Everything seen and unseen was made by God's hand. He alone created all that is in the heavens and earth. He made it all perfect."

"What happened next?" the girl asked.

Manitari looked to Allison. In that moment, clarity struck, and she whispered a prayer of thanks. "Maybe that is where we should begin," she said. "In the beginning..." For the next hour, the group listened reverently as she told the story of Adam and Eve and their fall from grace; of their son, Cain, who committed the first murder; and of Noah, the one righteous man left on the earth, who, along with his family, escaped God's judgment in the earth-wide flood. She ended with the tale of the tower of Babel, which had everyone smiling as she described how they all showed up to work one day unable to communicate.

Tsipavi said, "Is that all? What about Jesus? Manitari has told me about Him, but I want to hear more."

"You will. That was only the beginning. To really understand Jesus, you have to understand His history and who God is."

Tsipavi seemed pleased with her answer. "We will come back again to hear more."

Manitari suggested meeting five days later, but Tentega was not sure she could get away that day. They settled instead on the day after that.

"Before we go," Allison said. "I think it would be good if we could share any of our concerns and pray together about them. Prayer means talking to Creator God. We can ask Him about anything because He hears and He cares about what is on our minds. It also means listening to Him. Often when we pray, we can feel Him leading us to do something." Other than Amita and Manitari, everyone looked at her doubtfully, but she pressed on. "I'll start. I would like to pray for Majiro that God would help him lead the Shampiri well and also that He would recognize the truth of who Jesus is."

For a moment the room was quiet, and then Amita quietly requested. "Please pray for my father in Paamari. When we went to visit him a few weeks ago, he was ill."

Tsipavi said, "If what you say is true, then Creator God holds the power over nature. My garden has been eaten up this season by caterpillars. I would like for God to protect my crops so that my family will have food."

After waiting for a few more seconds to see if anyone else had something to add, Allison closed her eyes and prayed a simple, sincere prayer for the things that had been mentioned. When she finished, she sat silently for a few minutes, her eyes still closed. Grace began wiggling in her lap, so she looked up. "Tsipavi, as we were praying, I had an idea," she said. "I remember that my mother used to use ground pepper to keep pests off her plants.

It's not the same kind of pepper that is grown here, but it might work."

"I'll try anything," he said eagerly, and she quickly gave him instructions for grinding hot red peppers and mixing them with water to sprinkle over his crops. In Texas, her mother had used a spray bottle, but maybe this would work too.

The gathering broke up on a happy note as Tsipavi's family went back to their home at the end of the clearing and Tentega and Inani headed off into the jungle. Allison was the last to go.

"I am really glad that we did that," she said. "Your song was beautiful, Manitari."

"Thanks. Next week I will teach it to everyone."

"That would be wonderful." She hugged Amita on her way out the door. "I will be praying for your father. How long until you might get some news from Paamari?"

She replied, "Maapi mentioned traveling through here sometime soon. Hopefully, we will know something then. I have been praying for the chief, and I will keep doing so."

"Me too. I know that God will get his attention somehow."

Noting the shrill whistle coming from the front door, Manitari grabbed his bow and a handful of arrows to go meet the chief outside. They had decided to hunt together this morning as they often did when there was no work to be done in their gardens.

He paused to kiss the top of his wife's head before he left the house. "Pray for me." he said.

Amita looked up at him. "Are you sure you should talk to him about God? He won't be open to it."

Her worried eyes did nothing to sway him from his resolve. "Nor was I when you first spoke to me. Someone needs to speak of the Lord to him, and he will listen to me better than others."

"Then I will pray for you."

Thankful, he went outside and greeted his friend. They walked wordlessly into the jungle, though they did not expect to see much in the way of game until they were farther away from the village. The animals had long since learned to steer clear of the area. Only those stupid enough wandered nearby, and they did not live very long.

"If we don't kill anything, I am going to go fishing later today," Manitari said. "There is not much food in my house right now."

Majiro laughed. "If you didn't have so many kids, you might be able to keep your family fed a little easier."

"Not much I can do about that." He grinned. "My wife is pregnant again."

"Again? Is your youngest even weaned yet?"

"She will be soon."

"The two of you are like teenagers just discovering passion. I don't know of any other man that looks at his wife like he just discovered a thicket of wild berries."

Manitari knew enough to be embarrassed. Men simply should not display that kind of emotion over anything, much less a woman. Nevertheless, he conceded, "She is the best part of my life. But we were not always so happy together."

"No?" Majiro raised an eyebrow.

"Until just a few years ago, she hated me."

"What happened?"

"She started following Imeshina's God."

Majiro snorted in derision, but said nothing. Manitari continued, "It changed her. She was aloof and angry, and then, all of a sudden, she was warm and happy."

248

"You should beat her. Shampiri should have nothing to do with a foreign god. She would change her mind quickly enough."

"Why would I want her to do that? She is happy now; *I* am happy now."

Understanding the hidden message, the chief asked incredulously, "Surely, you do not believe my wife's stories about her God?"

"I do."

Majiro's face reddened in anger, and Manitari waited for the explosion. At length, the chief stood and motioned for him to follow. "Because you are my friend, I will pretend that we did not speak of these things today. There is nothing that I can do to keep Imeshina from speaking about her God, but I never expected you to abandon our traditions. I don't want to hear anything about it again."

The message understood, the two resumed their hunt. However, the tension between them remained, and they were both glad to go home later that morning, even empty-handed.

CHAPTER **TWENTY-SEVEN**

The blast of cool air was a welcome relief from the muggy Texas heat when Eric and Julia walked into the office of a local nursery. "Explain to me again why we are here," Julia said as she lifted her sweaty hair off the back of her neck and fanned her face with her hand.

"For flowers for your backyard," Eric replied. "It's a shame not to do something with such a big yard. Besides, school is out for the summer. What else are you going to do?"

She held up her right thumb. "See this? You might not be able to tell in this light, but it's black. Seriously, Eric, I have never been able to grow anything. I even killed a cactus once."

Eric laughed and put his arm around her shoulders. "That's okay. I'll do the work. You'll just get to enjoy the results."

A friendly nursery employee in a green apron stepped out of the back room and greeted them. "What can I help you with today?" he asked.

"We have a naked half acre that we want to fill with flowers—"

"Easy-to-take-care-of flowers," Julia interjected.

"Hmmm." The employee tapped his finger against his chin. "You might want to take a look at cosmos. They come in a ton of colors, require almost no work, and they don't mind heat."

Julia nodded. "That sounds about right," she said.

"Come on out to the greenhouse, and I will show you a good selection," he said, leading them out the back door into an enormous greenhouse overflowing with flowers of every color and shape. Pointing out a few rows of plants, he prattled on about the pros and cons of oxblood lilies and ruellia. "Have you thought of planting any trees? The Okame cherry tree does very well around here, and it blooms for months."

"That's a good idea," Eric said eagerly. "Don't you think so, Julia? We could plant one on the west side of the patio for shade. Once it grows, it might even be visible from the street. How tall do they get?"

Eric and the nursery employee walked down the aisle discussing different trees. Julia trailed behind, uninterested in their conversation, but enjoying the heady fragrance of the greenhouse. She might be incapable of growing flowers, but she sure liked them.

She wandered around the corner and found the two men bent over Eric's sketch of her backyard pointing out the best location for each plant. "I don't know why you are getting so excited about this." she said. "It's not even your house."

"Well then, we are just going to have to have lots of summer parties there. I'm buying you a grill too."

"A grill?"

"Sure. My apartment won't let me have one, and I make awesome grilled chicken."

She shook her head but smiled at his enthusiasm. "Okay," she relented. "Do whatever you want. I am going to look around." She left Eric in the employee's capable hands and strolled through the greenhouse, making sure to walk up and down each row of plants. Near the end of her tour, Eric appeared in front of her with a potted gardenia, overflowing with blossoms.

"I have to be honest with you," he said, handing her the flowers. "My motivation for landscaping your backyard is not entirely selfless… I was hoping that soon it would be *our* backyard."

She looked at him warily, and he motioned to a small, red velvet box tied to the gardenia. She reached for the box automatically, her hands shaking as she untied the white satin ribbon holding it to the plant.

The glitter of the diamond inside nearly made her drop the gardenia. Suddenly, Eric was on his knee, his hopeful eyes watching her reaction.

"Julia, six years ago, I wanted to die. Then I met you. You revived me, and your love healed my heart. I want to spend the rest of our lives together, loving you and making a life with you. Will you marry me?"

Too overcome with emotion to speak, she nodded her head. Eric pulled the engagement ring from the box and slipped it on her finger. Standing, he kissed her softly. When he pulled away, she looked down at her hand. Very calmly, she set the gardenia on the floor at her feet. Then she squealed and launched herself into his arms.

Her kiss left them both breathless, and Eric laughed as they drew apart. "So you like it then?" he asked.

"Ohmigosh, Eric! It's the most fabulous, amazing, perfect ring I have ever seen!" she said taking another peek at the sparkling princess-cut diamond sandwiched between two smaller marquises.

He pointed to the gardenias at her feet. "I meant the flowers."

She giggled. "I love you!"

"And I love you." He kissed her again. "Let's go finish planning our yard." He pulled the sketch of the backyard from his pocket and showed her what he had come up with. This time she did not have to fake interest.

CHAPTER **TWENTY-EIGHT**

One of the benefits of raising a child on a jungle river was that swim lessons were never really necessary. It seemed that all of the Shampiri children were born able to swim—or at least had it figured out very soon after learning to walk. Isaac was no exception. Perhaps because he was so much larger than the children his own age, he tended to run after the older children and learned to climb, run, and doggie paddle before he could speak in complete sentences.

Allison loved watching him in the river, the water rolling off his naked back like one of the river otters that lived in the area. On this particular day, Isaac managed to talk her into joining him in the lazy water. It was not too difficult to do. The weather had been particularly muggy and hot over the last week as the dry season came to an end and the increase in humidity announced the coming rains.

The two splashed and chased one another for a while until Allison called for a break. She flipped onto her back and floated, and her son did the same. About the same time, they spotted a pair of red macaws flying above them from treetop to treetop. "Look, Mommy!"

"Do you know why you always see two macaws together?" she asked.

"No."

"It's because when the babies grow up they find another special macaw to be their mate, and they stay with that other bird for the rest of their lives. So they always fly together, wherever they go."

"Like Father found you?" he asked innocently.

Allison hesitated. She had vowed to always speak the truth to her son, and so he knew some of the history of their arrival into the tribe. But she also had always been very cautious about criticizing Majiro to him, mostly because she feared his being punished for repeating what she said. Standing back up, she carried him back to the shallow water on the edge of the river. "Isaac, I need to explain something to you." He regarded her so solemnly that she had to smile. "You know how I told you that you had a different daddy when you were a baby?"

He nodded and she continued, "Mommy married your daddy, and a few years later you were born. But not too long after that some of the warriors came into our village. They killed your daddy and brought us here. That is when Majiro became your father."

"Did you cry?" It was a sweet question from a tenderhearted little boy, and she loved him all the more for it.

"I cried because I missed your daddy and because I wished that you could have known him. He loved you very much!"

"But now you are happy!"

She laughed. "Well, most of the time. I still have to pray to Jesus a lot, and He helps by reminding me about all of the things I have to be happy about."

The answer seemed to sit well with Isaac, and he was content to go back to his play. Allison heaved a sigh of relief that the conversation was over. Luckily, her son did not seem terribly impressed by what she had said. He had just taken it all in stride like it was normal. Of course, to him, maybe it all really was normal. It was just a matter of perspective.

Allison knelt in front of her house scraping the ground with a knife. It was by far her least favorite chore, but a necessary one to keep the jungle from growing up around the house. Every month, sometimes more often in the rainy season, she would set aside the better part of a day to pull up all the grass and weeds that were working their way up through the soil. For the moment, Isaac and Grace were off playing with other children, and Majiro was chatting with Manitari nearby, so it was a perfect time to get her work done.

Sometimes it seemed like life was filled with drudgery, but she supposed that was true for anyone, no matter where they lived. She had to constantly choose to see the joy around her, and she often watched her children to learn how. It seemed that they delighted in everything around them and were impervious to bad days. All it took was a new morning full of promise to make them ready to leap out of bed and discover what the day held.

Just now, in fact, three-year-old Grace was bouncing down the clearing toward the house, her shiny black hair reflecting the bright sun. Allison smiled as she watched her clamber onto her father's lap and lay her head back against his chest.

"Where's your brother?" he asked.

"I don't know. I was with Sema." Her ears perking at the name, Allison stood to listen.

Majiro questioned, "What were you doing with Sema?"

"He showed me the eagles. They were flying so high, like this." The little girl spread her arms open wide.

Allison did not miss the look that passed between the two men. Majiro turned Grace to face him. "Are you sure it was eagles that he showed you?"

"Yes. He told me they were eagles," she said solemnly.

Majiro bolted to his feet. "Imeshina, come! Take the girl to my mother. Maybe she can help."

Allison's brows knitted together in confusion. "Why? I don't understand— "

"Just do it!" he roared.

Allison rushed to take Grace, who was looking back and forth between the two of them in confusion. Obeying his demand and leaving her knife sitting in the dirt, she walked quickly to Inani's house. Her mother-in-law was inside, and Allison quickly told her why she had come.

"What does it mean? What's wrong with eagles?" she asked.

Inani looked as distressed as Majiro and looked carefully at Grace. "Eagles bring curses on children who look at them," she explained. "We shield our children's eyes when we see eagles lest they look at them and die."

"Then why would Sema do that?"

"Perhaps he thought no one would know, that Cameetsa would die and no one would know why. It was stupid. He has invited the wrath of the chief."

"What will Majiro do?"

"If she dies, he will kill him."

Allison's hand flew to her mouth. "No! He can't. That would be murder."

"No. It would be justified. It would make Sema a killer. Whether to kill with weapons or magic, it is murder to kill a kinsman. The Shampiri do not allow murderers to live."

Allison looked down at her daughter on her hip. Grace was chewing on her thumb, totally oblivious to the women's discussion. "She won't die," she declared.

"I will do what I can, but no one can reverse a curse like that. We will hope the spirits will be merciful."

Allison marveled at the older woman's acceptance of what she believed was an irreversible dilemma. It was clear that Inani was distressed, but equally clear that she had little hope to change the inevitable. As the older woman turned away and began pulling dried herbs from the rafters. Allison knew that she meant to make some kind of a brew for the little girl.

God, what do I do? I don't believe all this stuff about eagle curses killing children, but I also know that the enemy works hard to keep a hold on the Shampiri through fear. Protect Grace, and make Yourself known through this situation.

Reaching out a hand to still her mother-in-law's arm, she said, "Don't do anything. I'll pray that Creator God will keep my daughter from harm. That will be enough."

"You don't know anything about such things, Imeshina. This is very serious."

"I know, but you said yourself that there is little that you can do anyway. Will you watch and see what God can do for His children?"

Inani nodded hesitantly. "I will do as you say. I hope your God is as powerful as you think He is."

A few hours later, the door of Inani's house banged open as Majiro stormed in, a wooden club in his hand. Sema entered behind him, clearly unhappy to do so.

"How is she?" the chief demanded.

"She's fine. She's sleeping." Allison motioned to Inani's sleeping platform where Grace was nestled on a pile of blankets. "Come. Let's go outside so she can nap."

Squinting in the afternoon light, she saw that a crowd was gathering in the clearing, as rumors about what had happened ran through the village like a wildfire. Most of the faces she saw held fear.

It seemed that everyone was talking at once, trying to figure out what had happened and offering their opinions on the situation. Finally Majiro silenced them all by raising his hand. "It would seem that this warrior has put a curse on my daughter," he declared, motioning to Sema.

Sema protested, "Chief, I would never do such a thing! What proof do you have? You must have the testimony of another to accuse me!"

"Manitari was with me when Cameetsa told us that you showed her the eagles."

"It's true," Manitari spoke up from his place in the crowd. "I was there."

"That is not what happened. I told her *not* to look at the eagles. I tried to protect her, but she looked up anyway. "

"That is not what my daughter said."

"She is confused!" Sema insisted. "You cannot place a little girl's word over a warrior's."

Allison watched Majiro's rigid face. She knew that he did not believe Sema, but she also realized that he was bound by the laws of his people. He could do nothing, and Sema knew it.

The crowd began talking again, but she heard Majiro utter to Sema, "If my daughter dies, I will hold you responsible. Even if you didn't point out the eagles, you didn't keep her from looking." The chief spun around and marched back inside, unaware of the malevolent glare of his kinsman. Sema turned his gaze to Allison, and she felt her stomach lurch as his hatred washed over her.

A soft hand touched her arm, and Allison smiled at Amita and Manitari. "How is she?" Amita asked.

"Sleeping peacefully. She's not going to die. God will protect her from this curse."

"I have been praying for her since the moment she told the chief what happened," Manitari said.

"Thank you. We must pray that God will show His power and love through this situation."

Manitari offered, "Let's go pray for her now."

"But Majiro is in there," Allison protested. "He won't allow it."

"Yes, he will. He is terrified for Cameetsa's life. He will do anything to protect her—even pray to Creator God." Manitari was confident, and, though she was still hesitant to cause strife between the two men, she acquiesced and led them back into Inani's house.

Majiro was standing against the wall opposite the sleeping platform, watching Grace intently. His expression showed none of his feelings, but his presence there revealed his fear.

Without looking at her, Majiro said, "My mother tells me that you would not allow her to treat my daughter." Allison remained silent, and he continued, "Now she refuses to do so. She says that she thinks your God will help my daughter more than she can."

Allison looked at Inani in astonishment. It was the first time she had ever heard Inani suggest that God's power might be greater than that of the spirits. The older woman regarded her solemnly.

Manitari stepped over to Majiro and said, "We would like to pray to Creator God on behalf of your daughter. Would you pray with us?"

"No. He is not my god, but I will not stop you."

Allison, Amita, and Manitari stood next to the sleeping girl, while Majiro and Inani watched. They laid their hands softly on her arms and feet, and Manitari began to pray quietly.

Allison tried to focus on his prayer, but her mind was whirling with what had happened. Inani's quiet offering of belief, Majiro's capitulation, and now Amita's and Manitari's demonstration of their faith in front of the chief. She wanted to throw her hands up in praise and dance around with joy. Instead, she listened to the quiet petitions of the gentle man next to her and joined in prayer for her daughter, and that God would continue to do miracles among them.

Majiro quietly watched his daughter for the next two days, almost as if waiting for her to become ill. At the end of the third day, he gently tucked a blanket around her as she slept next to Isaac on their sleeping mat on the floor and then walked outside to sit across from his wife by their dying fire.

"She sleeps peacefully. I guess she really is going to be all right." He said it as if to comfort his wife, but really it was to reassure himself. She smiled.

Majiro, full of nervous energy, jumped up from the bench. He stoked the fire for a moment, and then began pacing in front of it. Finally, he sat back down and looked at Allison through the smoke curling between them. "How did you do it?" he asked.

"Do what?"

"How did you keep the spirits from harming our daughter?"

Allison explained, "It wasn't me. I have no power of my own. Creator God protected her from whatever curse was put on her."

"Why? Spirits always have an ulterior motive. What could your God have gained through protecting her?"

"He loves her. And maybe it was a way to get your attention so that you would know that He loves you too."

Majiro scoffed, "Spirits don't love."

"God does," Allison replied simply. "He tells us in His Word that He loves the whole world enough that He sent Jesus to die for us—to pay the price that justice demands for our sins."

Her explanation confused him, made him angry. "Wait. What do you mean 'His Word'? And who is Jesus?" he demanded.

"A long time ago, followers of God wrote down the things that He told them to. It's a record of the history of God's people, and it tells about Jesus and all He said and did. Jesus is God's Son, God Himself in human flesh. He came from heaven to make a way for us to be forgiven."

"That's ridiculous. Why would He do that?"

Allison spread her hands, and he could see the frustration on her face as she tried to think of a way to explain. "Majiro, you are chief of the Shampiri, right?"

"I am."

"And you govern the Shampiri according to certain customs and traditions that your people have lived under for generations. Certain crimes require certain punishments, right?" Majiro nodded, thinking with fresh anger about Sema.

She continued, "If God is real, He is the Creator of all things. What would be the just punishment if His own creation mocked Him, scorned Him, and declared that He doesn't even exist?"

"If I were Him, I would obliterate them. They would be worthy of death."

"Exactly! But at the same time, God calls us His children, and He loves us as a father loves his children. Yet our crimes still demand justice. He offered to take that punishment upon Himself by giving it to Jesus, the only perfect Son of God."

"You are saying that He allowed His Son to die as a punishment for the evil of others?"

"Yes."

Majiro was incredulous. What kind of father was that? What kind of ridiculous justice was it to allow the innocent to pay for the crimes of the guilty? But she seemed so confident about it, so peaceful.

She said, "Majiro, Jesus was not murdered unaware. He knew full well what He was doing and that it was the only way to make us right before God."

"He was weak."

"He was willing."

A chill crawled down his spine, and he stood. His head pounded, but he had one more question. "You say that His words are written down. Where are they? I will find out for myself who this God is."

"I'm afraid all you have is me. I didn't bring God's Word with me when I came, but I will tell you all that I can remember."

Majiro waved his hand in dismissal. "We won't speak of it again," he said. But as his wife turned to go inside, a weight pressed against his chest. He needed to know more.

It was not until a few days later that Majiro found the opportunity to speak to Manitari about his conversation with Imeshina. The two had gone hunting again, this time near Majiro's garden. They stopped mid-morning to eat some ripe bananas and rest in the shade for a while.

They talked about various things that men usually speak of— the weather's effect on the gardens and old, embellished war stories—but Majiro's mind still whirled with thoughts of his wife and her strange God.

"What has my wife told you about her God?" he asked abruptly.

Manitari sat pensively for a few moments. "She says that He is the only God, the Maker of all things, and that He came to bring hope and healing and set us free."

"Free from whom? No one rules over the Shampiri."

"We have no human master," Manitari agreed, "but how long have we been held captive by our fear and hopelessness? How long have we lived in subjection to the will of evil spirits, working to please them in order to escape their wrath? With Jesus as our God, we live under His protection."

"It seems like a woman's religion to me—to cower under the protection of someone stronger. We are warriors. We need no protector," Majiro insisted. The idea of weakness left a bitter taste in his mouth. No one had ever accused him of weakness, and no one ever would.

"To align ourselves with the most powerful of beings is not weakness, Chief. It is wisdom."

Majiro lay back against the shade tree with his eyes closed, musing on Manitari's words. The man had merit, for he was a mighty warrior among the Shampiri and had proven his bravery many times. "To follow her God is an insult to our traditions. Our customs are what make us Shampiri. How could I abandon them?" Majiro asked.

Manitari shrugged. "Our traditions change. Long ago, neither my wife nor yours would have ever found a place here. When sickness took so many of our women, we changed our way and allowed foreign women to become Shampiri. The true question is, which of our customs do we hold on to and which of them do we let go of for the good of our people?"

"You think denouncing our spirits is good for the Shampiri?"

"I know it." Manitari spoke with such confidence, the same peaceful assurance that Majiro had observed in his wife for years. Doubt rose in his heart as he thought of so many rituals he had partaken in as a means to manipulate the spirits that manipulated them. He had seen with his own eyes the death and suffering of his people afflicted with curses and left without hope. He knew all too well what fear felt like. Was it possible to free his people from such pain? Whether true or not, he knew it would have to start with him.

CHAPTER **TWENTY-NINE**

Allison awoke before it was fully light outside. She had a mountain of chores to do that day and needed to get them out of the way before the scheduled church service. Rising quietly, she grabbed her water jar from its place next to the front door and eased out into the fresh, early morning air. Even though the day had barely begun, she could see signs of life in the little village. Several women were in their front yards waking their fires, and two men headed off into the jungle with their bows slung across their backs.

She quickly walked down the trail to the river, marveling at how she could navigate it easily with so little light. Having taken the same path hundreds of times over the past six years, she thought she could probably do it blindfolded without stumbling. Amita was not at the river yet, but a few other women were. Stopping to chat for only a few minutes, she was soon back on the trail to the village.

By the time she arrived at home and set her jar under the eaves, Majiro and the children were awake. They were seated on the sleeping platform and in the middle of a breakfast of cold yucca. Even after so much time, she could barely tolerate the stuff, but they ate it like it was a pancake buffet. She grabbed a handful of bananas and tossed them between Isaac and Grace.

"Eat some fruit too," she told them. "Plain yucca isn't good for you."

Majiro snorted. "Who told you that? That's ridiculous."

"No, it isn't. Fruit has stuff in it that yucca doesn't. Stuff that helps you grow and stay healthy."

He stuffed another piece of yucca in his mouth pointedly. "I don't think so."

"Then why are my children so much bigger than the others?"

"Because their mother is a giant?" He and Isaac snickered at the joke, and Grace giggled too.

Rolling her eyes, Allison asked, "What are your plans for the day? Are you going to the garden?"

Avoiding her eyes, Majiro said nonchalantly, "I was thinking about going with you to this church thing."

Her jaw dropped. "Really?"

"You don't want me to go with you?"

"Of course I do," she rushed to say. "I just… didn't think you were interested."

Majiro stood. "I am the chief, and it is my responsibility to make the best choices for my people. It's only logical that I take into consideration what *all* those choices might be." He picked Grace up and swung her around so that she hung on his back with her arms clutched around his neck. "Come on, Isaac. You two need a bath." Isaac stuffed the last half of his banana in his mouth and scrambled up to follow Majiro outside.

Still stunned, Allison put away the breakfast food and tidied the little room. After she revived the fire, she washed a few small squash and laid them in the hot ashes to roast for lunch. All the while, she prayed.

When Majiro followed her through Manitari's front door later that morning, everyone seemed as shocked as Allison that he had come.

Tsipavi, after regaining his composure, jumped from the bench and gestured for Majiro to sit. "Please, Chief, sit here," he offered. Nodding his appreciation, Majiro sat with Isaac and Grace at his feet.

The little congregation had grown by a few members, though Tsipavi's wife was rarely in attendance nor was Inani's sister often able to come. Today, however, Tentega was there along with two of her children. Since all of the benches were taken, Allison stood back against the far wall next to Amita and Micheli.

Manitari started the service with a welcome and a short prayer before asking Tsipavi to join him in leading a song. Both men tapped their drums, and began singing one of the songs that Manitari had written. By now, the song had become familiar and nearly everyone present knew the lyrics. Allison watched Majiro inconspicuously during the song, but his face was indiscernible.

Once the song was over, Manitari said, "God's Word says that we must learn His words so that we will not sin against him. I hope everyone has practiced the verse that Imeshina shared with us last week. Would anyone like to start?"

Isaac stood up and said eagerly, "I will. I practiced all week." At Manitari's nod, the boy began reciting slowly, "God is light, and in Him is no darkness at all." He smiled proudly as he successfully finished the verse, and sat down quickly. Majiro reached down to pat his shoulder in recognition, and Isaac's face glowed with pleasure.

After Isaac, most of the congregation took a turn to recite the verse as well. When Manitari was satisfied that everyone who wanted to do so had a turn, he began. "This week, my wife and I had an argument. It was about something silly, but we fought. I even went so far as to yell at Amita and call her a terrible name."

The group shot one another uncomfortable glances. Public confessions like this were simply not done among the Shampiri.

However, Manitari continued, "I felt terrible about it because I know that a follower of Jesus should not act this way, and, even though I had already asked Amita to forgive me, I thought that maybe I wasn't fit to be a part of God's community here any longer. I decided to talk to Imeshina about it to see if she knew any of God's Words that could help me. She remembered some that she had learned a long time ago. I cannot remember them all now, so I would like her to tell them to us now."

All eyes turned to Allison, and she was glad that Manitari had told her ahead of time what he wanted her to do. She closed her eyes in concentration as the words from long ago swirled in her head. She had already worked to translate them as well as she could into Shampiri, and she spoke the verses slowly.

"The Lord is compassionate and gracious,

slow to anger, abounding in love.

He will not always accuse,

nor will he hold his anger forever;

He does not treat us as our sins deserve

or repay us according to what we have earned.

For as high as the heavens are above the earth,

so great is His love for those who fear Him;

as far as the east is from the west,

so far has He removed our sins from us.

As a father has compassion on his children,

so the Lord has compassion on those who fear Him;

for He knows how we are formed,

He remembers that we are dust."

Allison finished, and Manitari began speaking again. "When I heard these words, my heart was glad because I realized that our Creator knows His creation. He knows that we are weak people bent toward doing wrong. His Word says that He does not give us what we deserve, but instead He offers us love and forgiveness. I want you all to know that even when you forget who you have chosen to follow, and dishonor Him with your choices, He forgives you and still accepts you as His child." Murmurs of approval trickled around the room as the small group of new believers absorbed what he had said.

Tsipavi's daughter asked, "Imeshina, will you teach us that verse? The one about the Lord having compassion on his children. Maybe we can learn that one this week."

Manitari said, "That is a great idea. We will practice it now and think about it this week until we have our next service."

Allison led them in the memory exercise for a few minutes until it seemed that everyone could easily recall the words. Then they shared a few prayer requests, and Amita concluded the service with a prayer.

As everyone stood and began chattering, Tsipavi called out, "Don't forget! If anyone wants to join us, my daughter and I pray next to our fire at sunrise every day. You are all welcome to come and pray with us whenever you like."

Seeing that Majiro was quickly making his way to the front door, Allison followed. Fortunately, everyone was eager to greet their chief and ask him what he thought of the service, so she was able to catch up to him outside.

She heard him say to Inani, "I didn't realize that this was such a large group."

"Well, there were more today than usual, but the group is growing," Inani replied. Majiro grunted, and she continued, "When people join, they seem to find peace. It's hard to keep them away after that."

Before Majiro could reply, a group of several men stepped out of the jungle on the trail next to Manitari's house.

Majiro called out, "Did you have any luck today?"

Sema held up two black monkeys by the tails. "There was a family of monkeys half drunk on fermented fruit. They were easy targets." The other hunters laughed and showed off their own trophies.

"What is everyone doing here?" one of the men asked curiously.

Manitari answered, "We meet every week to learn about Creator God and to encourage one another. We just finished today, but you should come next week."

The warrior looked intrigued, but before he could answer, Sema shot Allison a dirty look and demanded. "Wait a minute! Are you talking about the *foreign* God? The one this woman talks about?"

"Imeshina was the one to tell us about Him, but He is not a foreign God. He is Lord over all."

Sema's eyes blazed with anger as he looked around the group. "Surely not all of you are ignorant enough to believe her stories!"

Calmly, Manitari stood in front of the other warrior. "We believe because we have seen the evidence that proves that Creator God is the greatest spirit—even greater than the ones we served in the past."

Sema sputtered as if fitting words escaped him. Finally, he spun on his heel and walked away. Manitari sighed. "I don't think that is the last that we have heard from Sema about this."

Majiro agreed, "Not by far."

Allison did not have a chance to talk to Majiro privately about the service all day because he had disappeared shortly after they got home, not returning until right before dinner. She ladled bowls of soup made with dried fish, squash, and corn from the pot on the fire and set them aside to cool while she filled smaller bowls with their drinks, beer for Majiro and banana juice for her and the children.

Majiro was in a cheerful mood, teasing Isaac and Grace, so she was hesitant to bring up the delicate subject of church and faith. She would try to talk to him after the children were in bed.

However, that conversation would be a long time coming because before they could even finish dinner, visitors arrived. Sema led the pack of Shampiri men, several of whom had been with him that morning. Allison recognized the others as living closer to Sema, farther out of the village, but she had never had much contact with them.

Majiro stood and greeted each man casually, though she recognized the wariness in his eyes. She hurried to offer them beer, soup, and a place by the fire, and was surprised when the hospitality was refused. This must be serious.

Without bothering to make small talk, Sema launched into the purpose of his visit. "Chief, after what I saw this morning, I am concerned."

"Concerned about what?"

"I am concerned about your ability to lead the Shampiri. A good chief would never entertain foreign customs, and I saw with my own eyes this morning that you have been led astray."

Allison winced at the words, fully expecting that the confrontation would escalate to physical violence. She had never seen anyone get away with offending Majiro, especially when it came to his role as leader of the tribe. To her surprise, Majiro answered calmly, only the twitching muscle in his jaw giving away his agitation. He said, "It would take more than just a group of seven men to change the leadership of the tribe. I am chief because my father was chief and his father before him."

"Then we will hold an assembly for everyone to discuss whether or not you are fit to continue as chief," Sema replied, and the men around him nodded in agreement.

"Fine," Majiro said. "But it is already getting dark. Go to all the houses around the village, and tell everyone that we will meet tomorrow at mid-morning. Everyone must be there."

Sema agreed and left quickly with his posse. Allison and Majiro stood in the twilight, watching the men scatter to different houses to inform their tribesmen of the coming meeting.

"You shouldn't have let them be the ones to announce the assembly," she told him. "This gives them the chance to sway the others to their side."

Majiro glanced sideways at her. "That's exactly why I sent them to do it."

"You want everyone to be against you?" she asked, confused by his comment.

He said softly, "If change is coming to my people, it must be because they want it as well. I am the chief, but I am not a dictator. I will not force anything on my people no matter what I believe."

Sitting back down by the fire, Majiro began eating his soup again. Isaac and Grace, who had both been silent through the confrontation, took their cue from him and began talking as if nothing had happened. Allison also finished her dinner, but she could not concentrate on the conversation around her. All she could do was wonder what exactly Majiro meant. What *did* he believe?

Later that night, once the kids were tucked in bed after their nightly song and prayer, Allison washed her face from the jar by the front door and turned to go to bed. Majiro was already lying there with his hands behind his head. Even in the dim light, she could see that his eyes were wide open.

She crawled in next to him and lay quietly on her back for a few minutes. Finally she asked, "What's going on, Majiro? What are you thinking? Are you worried about tomorrow?"

He chuckled softly, "Which question would you like me to answer?"

"All of them! It's just that I have never heard you say some of the things that you said tonight… I expected you to fight Sema, not agree with him."

"He was saying nothing that I have not thought myself."

She rolled over to face him, propping herself up on her elbow. "Since when?" she asked.

"Awhile. I've watched the changes in Manitari and Amita, in my mother, and even in you. I've seen my daughter avoid a curse that should have killed her, and I have seen my people come to peace with an enemy of many generations. There is power in your God that I can't deny—more power than that of our own spirits. I would be a fool to be an enemy of that kind of power."

Hope rose in her heart, and she worked hard to keep the excitement out of her voice. "Do you want to be a follower of Jesus?"

Instead of answering her question directly, he went on as if she had not spoken. "I was thinking about our treaty with the Oneata. It has brought our people greater peace than anyone can remember ever having before. We are free to travel and free from fear of being raided—at least by them. I would like for you to help me make a treaty with your God."

"I don't think it works the way you are thinking," she said slowly.

"What do you mean?"

She mulled the question over for a few moments before explaining, "The treaty with the Oneata works the way that it does because both parties are equal. No one is claiming to be better than the other, and neither tribe is subject to the other. Both are independent. The treaty just implies mutual respect and an agreement to friendship. God won't agree to that kind of relationship with anyone."

"Go on."

"He's *God*, Majiro, the Maker of all things, the sustainer of life. He knows everything that has happened and everything that will happen. He knows your thoughts before you think them and every motivation in your heart. He does not enter a covenant as an equal; He requires humility and submission."

"And if I refuse to submit?" The words were spoken roughly, but there was no venom in them, only curiosity.

She shrugged. "You may refuse to submit in this life, but make no mistake. One day, every knee will bow to Him and recognize Him for who He is."

For a long time they were silent. So long, in fact, that she had just started to doze off when Majiro spoke again. "Tell me how to make peace with God."

Rousing herself, she explained the concept of sin and the need for grace. She told him about Jesus Christ and His role in God's plan for redemption, and the need to simply believe and accept the forgiveness that He offered. To her surprise, he listened quietly, lying on his side facing her. For once, his expression was open, and she could see the longing in his eyes. When she finished her explanation, he closed his eyes, and she thought that he had fallen asleep. Then he opened them again and smiled. "It is done," he said and rolled over to sleep.

Despite the importance of the day, Allison struggled to stay awake the next morning. Even after Majiro had fallen asleep, she had lain awake, stunned by the turn of events. She had finally slept in the wee hours of the morning until Grace woke her up needing help to go to the bathroom. At that point the sun was already beginning to make its ascent. She knew that if she went back to bed, she would be groggier for the extra half hour of sleep, so she sent Grace back to her sleeping mat and decided to go to Tsipavi's sunrise prayer gathering.

When she reached the little home at the end of the clearing, Tsipavi, his daughter, and Manitari were sitting around the fire with their heads bowed while Tsipavi prayed. She quietly took a seat next to him, but he stopped praying as soon as he noticed her.

"Imeshina!" he said. "What happened yesterday? Why is the assembly being called?"

She desperately wanted to tell them about Majiro's decision last night, but she felt that it was really his news to share, when and how he wanted. Instead she described the scene at her house the night before and Sema's insults.

Tsipavi's daughter asked in amazement, "He said that to the chief? And Majiro didn't throw him out for it?"

Allison answered, "No. He was very calm. He just told them that the whole tribe would need to be gathered to make any kind of decision of that magnitude."

"We should spend the rest of our time praying for the chief and for the assembly today," Manitari stated. "Majiro has been very lenient with us thus far, but if someone else leads our people, someone like Sema, we all may suffer greatly for being followers of Jesus."

They all agreed and returned to their prayer time. They prayed without pausing until the sun was blazing and the cooler night temperature had been driven away.

Realizing the time, Allison stood. "I had better get going. Majiro will be wondering where I am," she said.

The kids and Majiro were gone when she got back to her house, so she puttered around gathering the few items of clothing that they had to wash later. Since she had never actually learned to weave with any success, Inani had been kind enough to make a couple of pairs of shorts for the children, another skirt for her, and baggy shirts for all of them. They were certainly not typical Shampiri dress, but the idea must have appealed to some villagers, for she had seen several other people wearing similar outfits.

She was standing on the small table trying to untie a strip of smoked meat from the rafter when Isaac and Grace bounded inside, Majiro behind them. "Let me help you," he offered.

"Thanks." She hopped off the table. "Did you go to the river?" she asked, seeing the evidence of their hair dripping water on the dirt floor.

"Yes. The otters were swimming this morning!" Grace replied gleefully.

"It's a good omen," Majiro commented, handing her the meat.

She smiled. "We don't need a good omen, just a strong God. I went to Tsipavi's this morning to pray with them about the assembly."

"Good." They smiled at each other. For the first time, Allison felt united with this man over something that did not involve the children. It was strange and… nice.

The family ate a quick breakfast and then headed toward the center of the village. It was not nearly mid-morning, but Majiro wanted to be the first to arrive. However, there were already several people sitting on benches that had been brought outside and leaned against the closest houses under the trees.

After sending her children off to play, she sat down alone on one of the benches, while Majiro walked around chatting casually with the early arrivals. He did not seem at all anxious, but she could already feel nervous tremors in her stomach.

Within an hour, it seemed like the entire tribe had convened in the clearing. Even those who lived several miles outside of the village had somehow heard the news and were there. Sema arrived along with two of the men that had been with him the night before, strutting into the village confidently. His timid wife trudged behind him with a baby in a sling across her chest and her two small boys clinging to her skirt.

A little while later, Majiro walked to the middle of the clearing, and the chatter immediately died down. "It seems like everyone is here now, so we are going to begin," he said. "Last night it came to my attention that some people have concerns about my ability to lead the Shampiri. As our custom dictates, we will hold an assembly for these concerns to be addressed and decided on by everyone. Any married adult who wants to speak may do so."

Before Majiro even sat down, Sema took his place in the middle of the group. He quickly launched into a lengthy monologue about Shampiri traditions and his own father's warnings against outsiders and the many ways that Majiro had invited harm on their tribe by marrying a foreigner, allowing his children to be taught in a foreign language, and finally even participating in foreign ceremonies such as the one the day before. He droned on and on, and Allison fought the urge to roll her eyes at his exaggerated descriptions.

As she looked around, she was surprised to see many people nodding their heads in agreement and even some disapproving glances shot in her direction. Her stomach knotted. Maybe this was an even bigger deal than she had thought.

Finally, Sema seemed to run out of things to say and stood under a tree as one of his friends took his place. For the next hour, one after another, Sema's men stood up and essentially repeated all that Sema had said. Allison hoped that when the last man had spoken, Majiro would have a chance to defend himself, but several others stood to criticize the chief and the others who were foolish enough to denounce the ancient spirits of the Shampiri.

At a break between witnesses, Manitari walked carefully to the center of the clearing. "You all can probably guess what side I'm on," he began, and there was a smattering of chuckles from the crowd. "I think that it is important to remember that this assembly is not about assessing whether or not my beliefs or the chief's beliefs are accurate. It is about deciding if our chief has been doing an adequate job and if he can continue to lead effectively. I, for one, cannot question Majiro's leadership. He is an able man, strong in body and spirit, and has done nothing to weaken our tribe since the day of his father's death. He has my loyalty regardless of what his personal convictions are." Manitari sat down, his head held high.

To Allison's relief, a few others also stood to throw their support behind Majiro. Tsipavi's wife was the last to rise. "I do not share my husband's faith in the foreign god, but I also think that the chief has earned our support. Three years ago the Oneata came to raid our village while our men were away. Even though we were warned, I tried to gather some of my things before I ran away. Before I could leave, the Oneata arrived, and one of the men came to my house. I fought him because I did not want to be kidnapped, and he began to beat me. Manitari's wife and the chief's wife were brave enough to stop the man from killing me, and I was able to escape to my garden. When I returned a few days later, I expected to see our village raided and some of our women and children missing. Instead, I heard that Chief Majiro had made a treaty with the Oneata. At first, I was angry because I wished that our warriors had killed theirs, but now I am glad for the treaty because I can live without fear that my daughters will be stolen from me or that my husband and sons will be killed in a raid. Chief Majiro did this, and he should be honored for it." The woman sat down to a chorus of approving comments, and Majiro stood in her place.

He said, "Sema is right about one thing: foreign beliefs will change our tribe. He is also correct in saying that I have put away my old spirits and now follow Creator God." Surprise and even disgust filled most of the faces in the crowd, except for the small band of Christians who were sharing joy-filled glances with one another. Majiro went on, "Before I decided to put away my spirits, I thought of our people and what those changes might be. I realized that though there will be changes for anyone who wants to follow Creator God, they are good changes. I have seen my wife's God protect His people, and I have seen His power to overcome things that I could never do on my own. Even the treaty with the Oneata, I give Him credit for. A good leader must make the best decisions for his people, and I believe that having the Creator God as my only spirit guide will make me the best chief that I can be—though it is up to you all to decide if I am the chief that you want."

Someone called out, "I see no reason for the chief to step down." Others disagreed, and debates for both sides ensued all around the clearing. Soon, however, it was obvious that the vast majority of the Shampiri were happy with the leadership of their tribe and willing to overlook Majiro's personal beliefs. The assembly unofficially closed, as those who sided against Majiro realized that they were outnumbered and stopped arguing.

Majiro made his way through the group to Allison's side. She smiled at him. "I'm glad that it worked out this way," she said. "You are a good leader, and I am happy that everyone recognized that."

Manitari and Amita joined them to congratulate him as well, and the chief thanked his friend for speaking up for him. "Of course," Manitari replied. "So is it true what you said about giving up your spirits?"

"Yes. Last night."

Amita clapped her hands together in delight. "We have been praying for this for so long!"

Majiro smiled. "I still have a lot to learn."

"So do we all!" Manitari replied, slapping him on the shoulder with masculine affection.

Majiro looked across the clearing, and the others followed his gaze. Sema was marching toward them. "Sema." Majiro acknowledged him pleasantly.

"You won today, Chief, but this battle is not over. What you are doing will destroy our people and our way of life."

Majiro replied easily, "There are some things worth destroying."

His answer only seemed to infuriate Sema further, but the angry warrior was wise enough to back away rather than risk shaming himself by getting into a public confrontation.

After he was gone, Majiro sighed. "He's right. This was not the end of this fight." Allison hoped that they were both wrong, but she had the feeling that there would be another, bigger battle soon.

CHAPTER **THIRTY**

Nearly every night for the next couple of weeks, Majiro asked Allison to join him by the fire after the children were asleep. There he asked her every question he could think of about his new faith, and they talked deep into the night. She recited the same journey through the Bible that she had shared with the church in the beginning. It seemed only to whet his appetite for more.

On the tenth night, after the children were in bed, she went outside where he was waiting patiently. Not bothering to cover her yawn, she said, "Majiro, I am exhausted. I can't stay up with you again tonight. I need to get some sleep."

He frowned. "If you aren't going to teach me, who will?"

Refusing to feel guilty, she replied, "Talk to Manitari if you don't want to wait for me, but I have to rest. I can't function on so little sleep for so long."

"I need to hear God's Word for myself, and you are the only one of us who has ever read it. All Manitari knows is what you have told him… And I have a question."

She sat down heavily on the bench next to him and sighed. "Fine. A few minutes, and then I'm going to bed."

Satisfied, he launched into the subject that was on his mind. "You have told me that the Creator God speaks to His children, that if we just listen to Him, He will guide us and tell us what we need to know."

"Yes. You've experienced that yourself."

"Right. So what is the difference between those words of God and *the* Word of God?"

"Ah. Good question. I told you before that God's Word is written down in a book, and in there He explains a little about how those words became Scripture. It says that men were inspired by the Holy Spirit to write down the actual words of God. Some of the words are histories of God's people, some are poetry, and some are instructions to believers for how we should live; but all of them come straight from the heart and mind of God. Does that make sense?" she said, watching his face to see if he was following.

Majiro stared absently into the fire. "Kind of. But aren't the things that God tells me personally from His mind and heart as well?"

"Sure. But sometimes our sinful nature gets in the way and what we are hearing isn't really God at all, but ourselves or even evil spirits trying to deceive us. That is why when we think God has spoken to us, we need to measure that message against what we *know* is God's word."

"It worries me that you are the only one who has read God's Word," he said. "What if something happens to you? Who will teach us then? We are too reliant on you."

"I don't want you to be," she said defensively. "I am trying to tell you all everything I know so that you will have God's Word in your hearts as well. Manitari is the one leading the church—"

He patted her knee. "I am not angry with you, Imeshina. You have done well. I am just trying to be practical. I mean, if you are gone, what will keep us from distorting the things that you have said or misinterpreting what we have been told. For that matter, how do we know that you haven't done that and are leading us astray."

Though she felt a little insulted by his musings, she understood his point. "I don't know. That's a very real problem. I can promise you that I am teaching God's Word as accurately as I can, but at the same time, I know that my understanding of it isn't perfect. The depth of Scripture is endless. One could study for an entire lifetime and still not understand it all."

Majiro nodded and was quiet for a moment. Then he sighed and pulled her to her feet. "Go to bed. We are not going to come up with a good answer tonight."

Walking toward the house, Allison realized that Majiro was still standing by the fire. "Are you coming?" she asked.

"No. I'm not sleepy."

"Okay. Good night." She went inside, closing the door softly, leaving him to his thoughts.

Allison walked around the corner of her house and nearly collided with Majiro's chest. "I need to talk to you," he said without preamble. She was accustomed to his gruff demands, but there was a certain tone in his voice that made her realize that he had something important on his mind.

She followed him into the house, her suspicions further confirmed by the fact that he chose the dark room instead of the fireside. Sitting down on the floor across from him, she asked curiously, "What is it?"

"I've been praying," he announced, making her smile, "and I need God's Word, Imeshina. I need to know the whole story, not just what you can remember of it. I need to know what Creator God wants me to do."

She replied, "You don't know how much I wish the same. I wish I could give you all of God's Word, but all I have is what I carry in here." She tapped the side of her head. "Tell me what it is you want to know, and maybe I can remember something that will help."

Majiro shook his head. "It's not good enough. I need to read it for myself."

"You don't know how to read."

"I can learn!" he said sharply.

She explained patiently, "Even if you learned, God's Word isn't in your language. No one has written it down yet. The best you could do is find a copy in Spanish or maybe Amita's language."

A stubborn man, Majiro was not easily dissuaded. "What would it take to get God's Word here?"

"Someone would have to go find a copy in another village and bring it here. Then you would have to learn to read, which can take awhile. If you wanted it in Shampiri, someone would have to come here and learn your language and translate it from a different language. That can take many years."

"I want you to do it."

"Me?" Allison squeaked.

"Of course. I'll send you with Manitari to go find God's Word in another village. Then you bring it back and translate it into Shampiri. And you can teach us all to read too."

She would have laughed at the tall order if Majiro's face had not been so sincere. "It's not that easy," she said gently. "I would probably have to go all the way to Iquitos—that's very far away. Besides, I'm not a translator or a teacher.

"You taught Isaac to read," he pointed out.

"That is entirely different. He's my child, and I taught him to read in my language, not yours."

"Is there a difference? You speak Shampiri as well as anyone here. You could teach us if you wanted to."

Opening her mouth to protest again, she clamped it shut. He was probably right. It would be a much more arduous process than he could imagine, but still, she supposed, she *could* technically do it. The question, really, was should she?

Finally she said, "Let me think about it, Majiro. There are a lot of steps to the process, and I'm not sure about it yet." She was surprised that he seemed pleased with her answer. He dropped the subject at once and did not bring it back up during the remainder of the day.

Long after her family slept that night, Allison lay awake looking at the thatched roof overhead. All day she had been unable to think of much else but her conversation with Majiro. Chaotic thoughts swirled in her head like the winds before a hurricane. The very idea of returning to Iquitos made her giddy, even though it was to be a temporary visit to accomplish a purpose.

Is this what You put me here for, Lord? Is this part of Your plan for me? To be the one to translate the Bible and teach the Shampiri church how to use it? Give me clarity! It all seems so muddled.

Even as she continued to pray and think about the situation, confusing thoughts rose in her mind. For her to translate and teach made sense. If she had really given her life for the Lord to use as He wanted for His greatest glory, would this not be a part of that plan? Why then was her hesitation so deep? Something in her spirit rebelled at the idea, and she did not know if her doubts were from God, her own fear, or a more sinister foe.

Eventually she fell asleep in the middle of a prayer, and when she awoke the next morning, the answer was clear and undeniable in her mind and heart. She knew that it had to be from the Lord because it would take a miracle for it to work.

"You want to *what*?!" Majiro roared.

"That is the only way I will do it," Allison responded softly. Strangely, his anger had a calming effect on her.

"You forget your place, woman. I am not only your husband; I am your chief."

"Nevertheless, if you want God's Word for your people, you will have to send me and the children back to Iquitos. I give you my vow that someone will return to the village to teach and translate it into Shampiri." Her voice was steady even as her knees shook. She knew what it cost him to hear her words, what it cost her to say them.

Majiro stormed around the room like a caged animal, finally picking up a clay water jar and smashing it on the packed floor of their home. Isaac and Grace, hearing the noise, peeked into the house. As Majiro picked up another jar, Isaac grabbed his sister's hand and pulled her back outside.

Allison winced as the second jar shattered next to the first. Still, she stood her ground and waited for him to get a rein on his temper. He was muttering in fast Shampiri. She could only catch a word here and there, but the bitter oaths that she did understand were full of hurt and rage.

At once, Majiro stopped pacing and stood directly in front of her. "After all this time, all these years, you still don't think of me as your husband." He flung the accusation bitterly. "You think you can go back to your people and pretend like you were never even here."

"I know I can't do that. In fact, I have a daughter to prove exactly the opposite!"

"*I* have a daughter! And a son, for that matter. Do you really think I am just going to give them to you to take away from me forever?"

There was no good answer, so Allison remained silent. His anger only seemed to increase. "You are not going anywhere, with or without my children. If God wants to send us His Word, He'll have to do it without your help!"

With that final ultimatum, Majiro grabbed his bow and arrows from the corner and stormed out. Allison dropped to her knees to begin picking up the clay shards off the floor, her tears falling on trembling hands.

CHAPTER **THIRTY-ONE**

A few days after her argument with Majiro, Allison went looking for Amita. Her house was oppressive with the strain of hurt feelings, and she had to get away. The two women walked along one of the jungle trails, absently searching for ripe fruit in the trees above.

"Is he still mad at you?" Amita asked, after Allison told her about the fight and the conversation leading up to it.

"Well, he isn't exactly speaking to me at the moment."

"Hmmm," was all Amita said.

She waited for a moment for her friend to continue, but then Allison realized that the woman was lost in her own thoughts. "What is it?" she asked.

Instead of answering, Amita pointed to a star-fruit tree set back from the trail, with the bright orange fruit hanging heavy on its branches. Snapping off long slender branches from another tree, the women made their way to it. Using the sticks, it was an easy effort to knock the fruit down. Once they had enough for their families, they gathered up the fruit from the ground into the baskets they had brought with them. Some were bruised from the fall, but would still provide a tasty alternative to their usual starch-laden meals.

Back on the trail, Allison asked, "Do you think I was wrong?"

"Yes... no... I don't know, Imeshina! You say that you feel God led you to say those things to Majiro, who am I to say any different? You've been a believer for much longer than I."

"That doesn't mean anything. God speaks to you or any other believer as clearly as He does to me. It's more a matter of listening. If you think I heard wrong, I need to know. I need to take into consideration the wisdom of others, no matter how long they have followed God."

Amita nodded and thought quietly for a second. "My spirit agrees with yours," she said reluctantly. "But I am not happy about it. I don't want you to go."

Relief washed over Allison. She was surprised at how much she needed the confirmation from another believer that the answer she had received really was from the Lord. Putting her arm around the smaller woman's shoulders, she said, "I have mixed feelings about it too. I love this village and the people in it, and I will miss you terribly, but, at the same time, it feels right to go." She laughed. "Of course, it might not even be an issue since Majiro will have nothing to do with the idea. I won't leave without his blessing."

"Then we will pray," Amita replied firmly. "If this is God's will, He will change Majiro's heart."

They returned to the village with their baskets full of star fruit, guava, and a few sour sops. Amita's oldest boys ran up to them as they neared her house, trying to see into their mother's basket for what treats she brought them. Allison was surprised to see her own children there as well, since she had left them in the care of her mother-in-law.

"Where is Inani?" she asked Micheli.

Not looking up from the long guava she was splitting open with her thumb, the girl replied, "She went to see Sema's mother. She's dying."

"Dying?" Allison glanced at Amita. The old woman had been ill for as long as she had known her, but she had always seemed stable, albeit very weak.

"That's what she said."

"Maybe we should go see her," Allison suggested.

"I don't think so," Amita responded doubtfully. "You know what Sema thinks of both of us. I don't think it is a very good idea."

"Sema's not there. I saw him go hunting in that direction." Micheli pointed toward a wall of jungle farther down the path.

Mind made up, Amita left her daughter in charge of distributing the fruit from her basket to the younger children. "We will be home soon," she said.

Allison dropped kisses on the foreheads of her sticky-faced children and hurried up the trail with Amita. It would be dark before too long, so they would not be able to stay long. She hoped that she would have the chance to at least pray for the woman and maybe even tell her a little about Jesus.

They passed Inani on the trail near Sema's house, and she confirmed that Onijaa was indeed dying. "She is very weak. It won't be long now," Inani said.

Her words echoed in Allison's head as they arrived at the home and stepped inside. Much like the first time Allison had met her, the old woman was lying on a mat on the floor, with a small fire burning near her feet. This time, however, the humor was gone from her eyes, replaced with pain and hopelessness.

They sat next to her quietly, and Amita took her hand and began speaking quietly to her about new babies, marriages, and happenings in the community. The old woman relaxed against her mat. Her eyes were closed, but the smile on her face showed that she was listening.

Knowing from personal experience that Amita was a natural comforter, Allison left the two of them alone and instead prayed quietly both for the old woman's peace and health as well as wisdom and boldness to speak to her all the things that were on her heart.

However, before she could even begin, Amita broached the subject. "Tell me, Onijaa, have you ever heard the story about Jesus?"

"Who is that?"

Amita immediately began describing the loving Creator who came to earth as a man to rescue His beloved from sin and death. Her explanation was simple, reducing complex theological tenets into pure gospel.

Onijaa listened, but said nothing until Amita was finished speaking. Then she grunted, "Humph. I imagine this foreign woman has filled your head with these stories."

Not at all insulted, Amita replied sincerely, "Imeshina was the one to tell me about Jesus, yes. But I have discovered for myself His love and power. Every day He is with me, filling me with joy and peace."

"Sounds to me like just another spirit. I should know more than most. My husband possessed the strongest spirits of anyone I have ever known."

"Other spirits may give power, but what of peace?"

The old woman regarded the younger thoughtfully for a moment before shaking her head in dismissal. "Maybe not, but my life has been what it has been. I can't change things now."

Allison broke in, "It's never too late to put aside the old for the new. There is forgiveness and restoration, even now."

"Even if what you say is true—and I don't believe it is—I am too old." Onijaa's hand fluttered up. "I need to rest." she said, motioning to the door. Understanding the dismissal, the younger women left quietly.

As they neared the village clearing, Amita said, "Why would she just reject Jesus so quickly? She did not even want to hear about Him." Her frustration was evident in her voice.

Allison shrugged. "You once said that it is a hard teaching; it's different from anything the Shampiri have ever believed. Who knows all that Onijaa has seen in her lifetime? It will take time for her, just like it did for you, Manitari, and Majiro."

"But, Imeshina, she doesn't have much time left. She's dying!"

"I know. But with God, anything is possible."

Over the next three days, Allison expected at any moment to hear the news that Onijaa had passed. She and Amita had debated about going back to the woman's house, but between their previous dismissal and Sema's presence, decided it best to stay away unless invited to return.

The morning had been excessively hot, and by mid-day everyone had laid aside all unnecessary chores to retreat into the coolness of the shade trees around the village. Allison had decided to take her children to the river to cool off, and they had stayed in the water until their rumbling stomachs sent them toward home.

She was in the middle of explaining to Isaac why she didn't want him playing active games until evening, when they walked within sight of her home and her words died on her lips. There was a mob of people around her house, all shouting at Majiro. The chief, who was standing with his back to the house, was yelling back.

Unsure of what was happening, but suspecting trouble, she said, "Kids, go to Amita's house. I'll come get you in a little while."

"But Mom-" Isaac protested.

"Go! Take care of your sister." She gave them a little shove back up the trail and turned toward whatever trouble was brewing at her house.

As she neared, she saw Sema standing at the front of the crowd, and she groaned. Sema's involvement always brought strife and division. What would it be this time?

The people were so intent on their argument that they did not notice her until she broke through the crowd to stand next to Majiro. "What's going on?" she asked, but her question was met only with an uproar of shouting voices.

"Be quiet!" Majiro's shout was immediately obeyed. "There is an accusation against you," he explained.

"Against me? For what?" she asked, her eyes wide with surprise.

Sema took a step toward her and raised his fist. "For putting a curse on my mother."

She was completely baffled. "A curse? What are you talking about? I did not curse your mother."

"Go look at my mother. She is dying. Anyone with eyes can see that she has been cursed."

"Why do you think I have anything to do with that?" Allison asked, her temper beginning to rise.

Sema cocked a finger under her nose. "Did you go see her three days ago?"

"Well yes, but—"

"And since you were there, her pain has increased. Now she cannot even open her eyes. You cursed her!"

"She has been sick for years!"

"She was healthy until you came to the village." Allison's head turned to see who had spoken the quiet indictment. Her mouth dropped open when she realized that it was Ogatsita, the quiet woman whose baby had died in the first year after her arrival in the village.

"It's true," the woman continued, addressing the villagers. "Sema's mother began to get sick after the raiding party returned with Imeshina and her son." Hearing the rustle of approval run through the crowd, a chill crept down Allison's spine.

"She must have put the spell on my mother when she came, as revenge for being taken from her village," Sema said.

Majiro broke in. "My wife is not a sorceress."

"She has bewitched you as well, Chief, blinded you to what all of us can see."

"You have no proof. What evidence do you have that it was Imeshina and not some other that cursed your mother?" Majiro demanded, and Allison was glad to see that Sema seemed to have no answer.

Ogatsita spoke again. "She was at my house when my baby died. My baby was sick for many days, but it wasn't until she came that the child died." Allison looked at the woman, confused as to why she would speak against her, but Ogatsita just stared at her, unblinking.

A man in the crowd called out, "Chief, you must send her to dig up the curse before Onijaa dies!"

Majiro looked as if he were going to protest, but the cries of his people made him hesitate. "It's our way," Sema stated quietly but with rock-hard conviction.

His shoulders sagging with defeat, Majiro nodded his consent. "Take her," he said.

Allison yelped as hands gripped her arms and she was pushed through the crowd to the trail. The mob moved like a wave, surrounding her as if they were afraid she would run away. However, the thought to flee never crossed her mind because she was so thoroughly confused. She wondered where they were taking her and what they intended to do to her when they arrived.

The crowd came to a stop and she was pushed forward. Looking around, she realized that she was at Sema's house, and everyone was watching her expectantly. Her frightened eyes turned to Sema as he approached her.

"Dig," he said, shoving a wooden spade into her hands.

"Dig?" she repeated.

"Find the curse you put on my mother, Witch!"

Bending over the ground, Allison hesitantly pushed the spade into the earth and pulled up a clump of dirt. She looked up at the stern faces above her, many of which she had called friend. But there was no compassion in any of them, only anger and fear.

She continued digging, each clod of dirt examined by one of the Shampiri, though for what she did not know. She pondered what exactly a curse was supposed to look like. The hole at her feet grew past her elbow, and she waddled in a crouch to dig a little farther up.

Already her legs were sore from squatting, and her skin was burning in the heat. She wished that she had a drink, but, unsure how the petition would be received, did not ask. It did not seem as though she would be finished any time soon, so as she moved on to make another hole, she tried to situate herself in the shade. No one seemed to care where she was digging as long as she continued doing so.

After awhile, the crowd began to thin out. Some seemed to lose interest and drifted back toward the village. Others sat in the shade of the house drinking beer. However, she was never left alone. There was always someone stationed over her shoulder, watching as she pulled each spade-full from the ground and testing it to make sure it was empty of any "curse."

Sema had also disappeared. She thought him to be inside until she saw him making his way through the jungle behind his house. In both hands, he carefully held branches of stinging nettles away from his body. Most of the nettles were placed carefully on the ground next to the crowd, but one branch remained in his fist.

As he approached her, she eyed the sharp, green leaves in dread. She had walked into a nettle bush more than once, and the memory of the cutting sting was enough to make her pale as he came closer.

Digging more quickly, she hoped he would leave her alone if he saw her intently working. She could see his feet next to her as he stood above her for several moments.

Ssswip. She heard the nettles hit her before she felt the sting on her back and neck. She could feel the plant's needles break off into her shirt where they continued to pierce her back every time she moved.

He hit her again and again. Each time she groaned, but she refused to cry out and give him the satisfaction of enjoying her pain. Finally seeming to lose interest, Sema dropped the nettle branch on the ground and returned to the others.

With his attention away from her, Allison allowed the hot tears to spill down her cheeks. She was angry, so angry, at the injustice of it all. Worse was that people seemed to believe the unsubstantiated accusation, people she had known for years.

Beloved, love them. Teach them who I am.

Allison wiped her eyes with the back of her hand. Some of her anger quieted, but her self-pity was still intact. *That is all I have been doing. I never did anything to deserve this kind of treatment. All I ever tried to do was to be kind and show the Shampiri Your love.*

My purpose will stand, and I will do all that I please.

It always came back to that. From her first days in the village, she had known that God was using her circumstances to accomplish His plan. Even in those devastating first few months when everything in her rebelled at the idea of being used by the Lord in such a way, she had the absolute assurance that God was doing something huge through and around her. But even that knowledge did not keep the nettles from stinging or her heart from breaking as life took its toll on her spirit.

Okay, Jesus. Your way, not mine.

CHAPTER **THIRTY-TWO**

As the sky grew dark, a fire was lit, and Allison continued to dig. The yard was pockmarked with shallow holes, but nothing of interest had been found in any of them. Still, she carried on, trying to ignore everything around her and focus instead on praying.

She winced as a man stood above her and waited for the sting of the nettles that had come intermittently all afternoon and evening. But the sting never came. Instead, gentle hands pulled her to her feet.

"Time to come home," Majiro said softly, his sympathetic eyes taking in the dirty tear tracks down her face.

"I can go now?"

"It's dark," he said, as if that explained everything.

Leaving the onlookers behind, she followed him up the trail to their home. The fire was glowing cheerily outside, and the smell of grilled plantains and fish made her stomach knot in hunger.

She sat, and Majiro handed her a bowl of food before sitting down next to her. He bowed his head and prayed quietly, "Creator

God, we know that you are aware of what is going on here today. Help us to trust."

He met Allison's eyes. "The children are with my mother tonight," he said. "It is better that they don't see you like this."

Allison looked down at her arms. She really must have looked terrible. Her face and neck were badly sunburned, and her arms were swollen and puffy with blisters from the nettle oil. Every inch of her was covered in dirt and her knees were bleeding from kneeling for so long on the stony earth.

Majiro continued, "If you eat quickly, the water inside will still be hot. You can bathe there, and afterward rub some of this where the nettles stung you."

She took the folded leaf he offered and opened it. A green blob of herbs mixed with what seemed to be aloe was inside. Taking Majiro's advice, she gobbled her food and went inside. A large jar of steaming water with a strip of cloth lying over the edge was in the corner on a mat of palm leaves.

Peeling off her skirt and top, she sat down and began the process of trying to clean herself without opening the sores on her arms, back, and neck. All of her muscles cramped from the hours of digging and bending over, but the hot water seemed to loosen some of the tension.

Majiro came in as she was applying the aloe poultice after her bath. Without a word, he reached for a glob and smeared it on her back and neck. "You should go to sleep," he said. "Tomorrow will be another long day for you."

Allison's head snapped around. "What do you mean 'tomorrow'?" she asked.

"You'll dig again tomorrow."

"No! There's no way, Majiro. I can't!" She burst into tears.

He sat down across from her. "You have to," he said simply.

Contemplating having to spend another day digging in the sun while the villagers took their vengeance on her for a crime she did not commit turned her sobs into wails. Majiro stared at her, a look of astonishment on his face.

"It's not fair," she hiccupped, "Whatever it was that I was supposed to have done, I didn't do it. Why do I have to go back?"

"You have to keep digging until the curse is found."

Her hysteria tempered momentarily by curiosity, she asked, "What kind of curse?"

"Whatever it is that has made Onijaa sick. Someone put a curse on her by burying something—the corpse of a small animal, a rope, or a piece of pottery. Until that object is uncovered and destroyed, it will continue to grow inside her until she dies."

"You think that burying something outside of someone's house makes it grow *inside* their body?" She cocked an eyebrow in unbelief.

"Only if it is buried under a spell of witchcraft. You saw for yourself that something has been growing inside her."

Thinking of the tumor that she had felt, she opened her mouth to argue, but stopped short. How could she explain cancer to someone who had no understanding of invisible germs, much less multiplying, mutated cells? There was little wonder that a curse was the explanation the Shampiri had chosen to describe disease and death.

"I didn't bury anything."

"I know."

"What happens when I can't find anything then?"

"They'll give up eventually, I guess. But that is not what I am worried about."

"What are you worried about?"

Majiro looked at her, his eyes deadly serious. "I am worried about what will happen if you do find something."

The next morning came all too soon. Despite being exhausted, Allison had lain awake for most of the night trying to process the events of the day. Praying had granted her peace, but she was still unsure what, if anything, she should do to combat the guilty verdict hanging over her head. Her concern was that by complying with the Shampiri demands, she was admitting guilt. However, she also could not come up with a better course of action. Finally she remembered the admonition in Philippians to dwell only on the things that were true, noble, right, pure, lovely, and admirable. Thinking instead of her children and all the things God had done over the past six years, she fell asleep.

She awoke with a praise song in her head and nearly forgot what the morning was supposed to hold for her. As she stoked the fire ashes back to life, she realized that Majiro was watching her from the doorway with a puzzled expression.

"You know you have to go back to Sema's house today, don't you?" he asked.

"I know."

"You're happy about that?"

"No, I think it is terrible. I am praying with every breath that something will happen so that I don't have to go." She said it with a smile, and the creases around Majiro's eyes deepened with confusion.

"Then why are you singing?"

She broke a thin, dry stick into pieces and added them to the embers. "I can be miserable about it or I can choose to trust God," she explained. "Nothing can happen to me that hasn't gone through His hand first. If He wants to deliver me, He will. If He doesn't, He has a good reason for it."

Not saying anything, Majiro walked around the fire and sat down heavily on one of the logs next to it. He put his elbows on his knees and held his face in his hands watching the small flames lick the kindling she had placed there.

"It's that easy, is it?" he asked.

"Easy?" she laughed. "Hardly! I was up half the night thinking about it. But it *is* the truth, and it's what I have to stand on if I am going to make it through this."

He stood and watched her for a moment longer. "I'm sorry, Imeshina," he said quietly and walked away.

She smiled as an unfamiliar tenderness welled in her heart for him. It was clear that the situation troubled him and that he felt powerless to defend her against it. Yet, she knew it was not his battle to fight. It was God's, and He would do what He would do. She only had to trust.

She realized that she would be expected back at Sema's soon, so she hurried to her mother-in-law's house to give her kids a quick hug and kiss first.

Isaac saw her approaching and ran to meet her. When he got closer to her, he stopped short with a stunned look on his face. "Mom? What happened to you?"

"Sunburn and nettles. Does it look bad?"

"Uh-huh. Does it hurt?"

"Yes. So hug me gently, okay." She knelt down on the ground, and he came carefully into her arms.

He pulled away slightly to look at her face. "Mom, Micheli says that you are in trouble. What's going on?"

She was disappointed that she had to explain things to him, but at the same time figured he might as well hear it from her. "Some people are saying things about me that aren't true. They think that I tried to hurt Onijaa."

"Can't you just tell them that you didn't do anything?" he asked.

"I tried, but they don't believe me. We just have to wait and see. God knows what is going on, and He'll take care of things. Just pray for me today, Isaac. Pray that God will give me wisdom and strength to do the right thing."

Nodding solemnly, he vowed, "I will pray all day long!"

Inani poked her head out the door and began to call for Isaac. When she saw Allison, she came the rest of the way out. Grace was balanced on her hip. "I won't even ask how you are feeling," she said. "Did the herbs help?"

"I think so. Thank you for sending them and for taking care of the children." She stayed only a few minutes longer, receiving a soft kiss on her "owie" from Grace and another hug from Isaac.

Before she left, she said quietly to her mother-in-law, "Stay close to home today. I don't want you getting caught up in this."

The older woman did not answer, but said, "I'll keep the children here tonight as well. You'll be needing your rest."

Dipping her head in agreement, she blew kisses to her kids and went on her way. The shadows from the day before seemed to creep back as she got closer to Sema's house. This time she recognized them for what they were and began to sing the songs in her heart that declared the wonder and mystery of God.

There was no crowd outside the house this time, and Sema seemed surprised when she showed up unaccompanied and without being summoned. After asking for a spade, she went back to digging, continuing to sing quietly to herself all the while.

As the morning wore on, the crowd reconvened, and Sema brought the nettles back out. At the first whip of the branches, Allison sucked her breath in through clenched teeth. She had not thought it possible for them to hurt worse than they did yesterday, but the sting on top of her already raw skin was nearly unbearable.

Sema seemed to enjoy the look of pain on her face as he continued striking her viciously. "Dirty witch," he sneered. "Find your curse so that everyone can see the evil sorceress that you are!"

Without thinking, Allison rose to her feet and stood toe-to-toe with her accuser. "I am a child of God, beloved of the Father. I was bought with a price. I belong to Him, and the evil one cannot *touch* me." Though she had spoken quietly, her words hung in the air like the mist at the base of a waterfall.

Sema licked his lips and backed slowly away from her. His eyes were as full of vengeance as ever, but this time she noted a trace of fear as well. She let out a big breath and turned back to her work.

She remained reverently prayerful for the rest of the morning, even as people approached her with nettles time and again. As she looked into their faces, she was moved with compassion, for what she saw in most was not malice, but resignation.

Sema had vanished up the trail soon after the first beating, but when she saw him return, her heart nearly stopped. Amita was with him. Allison searched her friend's face for a hint of what was going on. Holding up the spade in her hand, Amita shrugged.

"Why is she here?" Allison asked, careful to keep her voice devoid of emotion.

Sema pushed the woman toward her. "It came to my attention that your friend was with you when you came to my house the other day. If she wasn't involved in cursing my mother, she at least knew about it."

"You have no proof."

"She told me herself that she believes the garbage you teach and will follow anything you tell her to do. Didn't you, Amita?"

Her gaze unwavering, the little native woman pulled herself up to full height. "I believe in Creator God, and I trust Imeshina to do the right thing. Yes, I stand by her."

Trying another tactic, Allison said, "She's pregnant! Surely you don't intend for her to stay out in the sun all day receiving punishment!"

"It's a punishment she's earned."

Allison opened her mouth to protest again, but a squeeze on her wrist from Amita stopped her. "Be quiet, Imeshina. It's okay. It's my joy to endure this with you."

A lump welled in her throat, and all she could manage was a husky "thank you."

They moved under a tree to be out of the sun. Just like the day before, at least one other person remained with them at all times, carefully examining whatever they dug up.

Allison asked quietly, "What happened?"

"Sema came to my house this morning and asked me if I was with you the other day when we came here. I told him I was, and he told me I had to come."

"You just went with him?"

"It was better than making a scene. My kids were there. Besides, I don't think anything I could have said would have helped either of us."

"What about Manitari? He just let you go?"

"He went hunting this morning." Amita laughed briefly before her face turned serious again. "Honestly, I'm glad he was not home. He would have caused a fight and probably just gotten himself into trouble.

Allison nodded but fell silent as Sema approached with a nettle bunch. Amita received her first beating, and it was apparent that the warrior would show no mercy for her, pregnant or not. Allison bit her lip hard as the blows rained down on Amita's submissive back. With all her heart, she wanted to intervene, but she knew that to do so would only cause them both more pain.

They continued digging for hours, both gaining strength from the other. Taking turns praying quietly, they were able to maintain their sense of hope.

Late in the afternoon, Allison heard Amita's gasp and looked over, thinking that she had perhaps cut herself on the spade. Amita's hand was raised to her mouth and her eyes, unblinking, stared into the hole at her knees.

Peering in, Allison lurched back in surprise. Inside the hole, curled into a nearly perfect coil, was a small coral snake. She could see that it was dead, for the red and black bands of skin were already beginning to rot away.

The native man who was on guard duty looked over to see what had caught their attention. His dark face visibly paled as he took several steps back. He looked fearfully at the women before he turned and ran to the small group of people still congregated in front of Sema's fire.

"Amita, what does it mean?" Allison hissed.

Her friend was trembling, and she too backed away from the snake. "It's a death curse. It's very evil—the worst thing we could have found."

"Why?"

Amita explained, "Only someone with powerful magic—evil magic—can use a spell like this."

"How do you know?" Allison still could not grasp the significance of what the dead reptile must represent to the Shampiri.

Amita shot her an exasperated look. "Anyone else would die handling the snake, wouldn't they?"

"Well, if it was alive, I guess. But how do you know someone didn't bury it after it was dead or that it didn't just die and get buried by the rain?"

"Look at it! Coiled like that? I don't think so. Besides, there hasn't been any rain for weeks and this has only been dead for a few days. And look at the ground around it, Imeshina! The dirt is packed solid. No one has been digging around here for long time."

Allison looked around, and she had to admit that her friend was right, at least about the ground being untouched. It took a fair amount of work to loosen the soil enough to wriggle out a spade-full of it.

"Well then, how do they know it wasn't someone else that put the curse there?" she asked.

"Our people believe that only the one that has placed the curse can find it to dig it up again."

Allison gulped as the gravity of their situation dawned on her. Looking back toward the house, she saw the group of villagers approaching, Sema in the lead.

"So what's going to happen now?"

"Now," Amita said, "they will kill us."

CHAPTER **THIRTY-THREE**

Majiro did not bother looking up when the door to his house flew open. He was sitting in the hammock with his back to the doorway, but he knew exactly who was there. He had been expecting him.

"Come in, Manitari." He motioned at the sleeping platform.

Manitari came around and rather than taking the offered seat, stood with his arms folded across his chest. "Do you know what happened this morning?" he demanded.

"I heard that Sema came for Amita."

"That's right." Manitari's dark eyes flashed. "How could you let that happen, Chief? First your wife and now mine."

"I didn't know about until afterward."

"Would you have stopped it if you had?"

Majiro lifted his tired eyes to look at his friend. "No," he said simply.

As if all of the weight of the world had fallen on his shoulders, Manitari flopped down on the ground. "We can't just sit here doing nothing! This is ridiculous. I know my wife is no witch, nor your wife eith—Wait, do *you* think Imeshina is a witch?"

"No. I know she's not. She holds no spirits but Creator God, and our curses come from our own spirits. Onijaa might have been cursed by someone, but it was not Imeshina."

"Then what are we going to do?"

Majiro cried, "What can we do? You know this is the way of our people. If she is innocent, then nothing will be found, and in a few days Sema will find someone else to blame."

"Sema has been after your wife's blood from the moment he saw her. I myself saved her life from his arrow the day we took her!"

"Sema is still bound by the traditions of our people." Majiro stood up and walked to the open doorway. The late afternoon light was fading, for which he was thankful. He was ready for this day to end.

"And if they do find a curse? They will be blamed."

"I pray it doesn't come to that, but if it does, our people will extend them mercy. That is our tradition too."

"Mercy is only given to the repentant, Majiro." Manitari sighed and stood up. "You stay if you want, but I am going to get my wife."

As each man and woman took a turn looking at the dead snake, the roar of voices grew deafening. Some shouted for retribution, while others argued for the sake of the women. Allison and Amita stood to the side, holding hands and waiting for whatever was to come.

"Do we need any more proof that they are witches?" Sema asked the ever-growing crowd. His question was met with shouts of approval, except for one man brave enough to challenge the warrior.

"You should let them speak for themselves," the man said.

"Fine," Sema sneered, as he turned to the women. "Speak. Now is your chance."

Allison stepped forward with her palms up as if pleading for understanding. "We had nothing to do with this," she stated. "We do not follow these spirits. The God we follow is a God of love and hope."

"Hope? What kind of hope does my mother have after being cursed by you?"

"I said we had nothing to do with it. We did not curse anyone!"

"Then explain how you were able to find the death curse," Sema challenged.

Frustrated, Allison realized that she had no explanation that would satisfy them and, in English, cried out, "God, help me! I don't know how to handle this!"

"See how she calls down curses even now," Sema goaded. The crowd looked nervously at one another.

"No—"

"They are evil!" he said. "We must kill them before they murder us with their curses."

Brave men in the crowd stepped forward and held the women by their arms. Tears streamed down Amita's cheeks, but indignation flared in Allison's heart. "You don't understand—" she tried to explain, but was jerked away and half-carried, half-dragged around to the side of the house. Sema stood there with an arrow loaded into his long bow.

"Jesus, have mercy," Allison whispered from the ground as she closed her eyes and prepared for the end.

"Stop, Sema! Don't touch them!" Allison's eyes popped open, and she saw Manitari and Majiro pushing their way through the people.

"Chief, we must kill them! Their sorcery must be stopped." Sema said calmly, his arrow still aimed at Allison's heart.

"What sorcery?" Manitari demanded.

Sema motioned with his loaded bow toward the hole marked with discarded spades and upturned dirt. "They found a curse, a death curse."

"A death curse? Are you sure?" Majiro asked, and a number of his tribesmen rushed to assure him that it was so.

"That's impossible!" Majiro assured them. "The death curse is a curse of our people, our spirits. Imeshina wouldn't even know how to perform it."

"She has, Chief, with the help of the other. They are guilty, and we must put them to death. It is the only way to protect our people. It's our way."

Majiro said, "It's also our way to give the guilty the chance to repent."

Allison was surprised to see Sema's bow lower, and she let out a big breath when he nodded in agreement. Majiro leaned down and said softly, "You just have to recant of the sorcery, Imeshina. Take my knife and cut up the snake to break the curse, and this will all be over."

Mechanically, Allison took the offered knife and looked at the tarnished blade. She glanced at Amita who was still weeping and at Manitari who was standing next to her, his hand on her shoulder. She handed the knife back to Majiro and declared so that everyone could hear, "I have nothing to recant. I am innocent of all of your accusations."

"No, Imeshina—" Majiro began to say but his voice was lost in the cries of outrage around him.

"What about Amita?" someone called out.

Amita's voice was surprisingly steady for the tears that continued to fall. "I have no spirits, but the one, true Creator God. In Him there is only goodness. You can kill me if you must, but I do not regret following the One who has given me life."

"Kill them!" one voice called out. Soon the cry was carried through the crowd.

Again the women were dragged forward and pushed to their knees as Sema reloaded his arrow. Manitari was held back by several men, but the anguish on his face was evident and tears ran in quick streams down his cheeks. Majiro seemed to be too shocked by the turn of events to do or say anything.

Amita's head was bent, accepting gracefully the consequence of her choice. However Allison's spirit was at war, and she felt as if she could literally reach out and touch the evil around her. Her arms spread out, she yelled to the heavens, "Lord Jesus, open their eyes! Let them see all that You are and glorify You. Bring freedom to the captives, break the chains that hold them in bondage to fear. Open the floodgates of Your power…" She groaned and sank down with her face in the dirt.

Expecting to feel the pierce of an arrow in her back, she was surprised to instead hear Sema's hoarse whisper. "Mother?"

Allison looked up from where she was prostrated on the ground. Onijaa was walking toward them, a smile on her face and soft shimmer around her. She looked years younger than she had a few days before, but most noticeable was her stomach, flat and firm as that of a young woman.

"Don't kill them, my son. They are telling the truth," the old woman declared. As she walked through the crowd, hands reached out in awe to touch her. She pulled the bow and arrow out of Sema's unresisting hands and tossed them aside.

"Mother, how… but you…"

Onijaa reached up to pat his cheek as he gaped at her. "Creator God, Jesus. He's real, Sema. I was in pain, so much pain. I finally fell asleep, but I dreamed that the one that Amita told me about,

Jesus, came to me. He told me that He was the only way to life, and He asked me if I wanted to live. I struggled with myself, for how could I ever deserve life after I've lived so unworthily? But I said yes." Onijaa's voice broke in a soft sob, but she quickly pulled herself together and continued. "I said yes! He touched me, and it was like there was a fire in my stomach stretching to my arms and legs. Then I woke up, and I realized that Jesus really had come to me." She spread her hands across her belly. "He healed my body, and He healed my soul."

Some rushed forward to embrace the old woman, while others reached down to lift Allison and Amita up from the ground. Sema, though still visibly shaken by the appearance of his mother, was not so easily swayed as many of the others.

"Mother, how do you know that they didn't put the curse on you just so that they could take it off to show us all their power?" he asked.

"These women did not remove the curse, Jesus did."

"How do you know they aren't responsible for cursing you?"

His mother stared at him for a moment. "I just know," she said simply.

Majiro added, "A follower of Jesus cannot follow other spirits."

The old man who had first spoken up for the women earlier in the day asked, "Chief, how can we put away our old spirits so that we can have this Jesus spirit?"

"Yes, tell us!" Several men and women stepped forward from the others, eager to follow the instructions of their leader to begin their new life.

For Allison, the walk home from Sema's house that evening was surreal. Majiro, Manitari, and Amita were bubbling with excitement, each exclaiming over what had happened that day.

Majiro had his first experience with leading others to faith, and Manitari and Amita were glowing with thankfulness for their deliverance. Allison was quiet, sharing in their joy, but drained and in desperate need of a good cry.

They walked first to Manitari and Amita's house. The three natives were full of plans to meet with the new believers the next day and begin to share the things that God had taught them during their own brief relationships with Him.

As they left their friends behind, Majiro commented, "Aren't you happy, Imeshina? We've seen miracles today. Onijaa is healed, and she and six others have become followers of Creator God!"

Allison smiled in the fading light. "I *am* happy. Very happy. I am just so... full."

They walked a few more steps, and he stopped in the trail. "I am sorry that I tried to make you admit to the sorcery. You have stronger faith than I do."

She shrugged. "Not really, Majiro. God's Word says that He will give you the faith that you need in the moment that you need it."

"There are a lot of things that God's Word says that I need to know."

"That is true for us all," she replied with a laugh.

"I want you to go to your people, Imeshina, and find a way to send us God's Word. Even if you don't come back. We need it. I need it."

"With the children?"

He shook his head slowly. "I can't let you take my children away."

"Then I can't go." She reached out and touched his hand gently. "Pray about it? I can wait."

Majiro looked at her for a moment and finally nodded. "Come on," he said as he began walking again. "Your children miss you, and you need a bath."

CHAPTER **THIRTY-FOUR**

On Saturday morning Eric parked in front of the strip mall and darted out of the rain and into the building. His own errand had taken much longer than he had expected, and he was late meeting Julia at the tuxedo shop.

She was sitting in one of the chairs next to the door, calmly flipping through a bridal magazine. When he barreled through the door, she glanced up from her page and smiled.

"Hey. Sorry, I'm late."

"That's okay. I was entertaining myself." She pointed to the three tuxedos hanging on a rack in the middle of the room. "I already narrowed down the choices. What do you think?"

With barely a glance at them, he shrugged. "You know I don't care. It's up to you."

Ignoring his comment, she dragged him over for a closer inspection. "I love the tails, but that seems a bit formal for an outdoor wedding. And I can't decide if doing a white tie with a white cummerbund on a white shirt is too much white. The gardenias are white, and my dress is white… maybe I should pick out a second color."

"You're the boss."

She rolled her eyes. "Er-ric! Help me out a little. At least give me an opinion."

"Okay. I think the tails look silly, and if we are having Italian food at the reception, you are just asking for stains with all that white."

Julia looked at the tuxedos critically. "You're right. What if we did sky blue for the other color? I haven't decided on the bridesmaid dresses, but that shouldn't be too hard to match."

"Perfect," he said. Gleeful at the easy decision, Julia walked up to the counter to place the order.

"Are you sure you want to order those already? It's October, and the wedding isn't until May."

"You have to do these things ahead of time," she replied knowingly. "Besides it makes me happy because it means we are one step closer to being married."

"We could move the wedding up," he teased. "I'll marry you tomorrow."

"You can't, and you know it. Speaking of which, what did you find out today at the courthouse?" she asked. Before he could answer, she was distracted by the shop employee who handed her a stack of papers to fill out. Once the order was placed, they went outside and hurried into his car.

He pulled out a document from his briefcase on the floor and handed it to her. "I was right about the death in absentia law—I guess I remember something from law school. In Texas, a person has to be missing for seven years before someone can file a petition to have them declared dead. Since I spent a whole year looking for Allison and Isaac and there has been no contact from them, it looks like it should be a simple process to get their death certificates issued. The seven-year anniversary of the attack just happens to be next month, so I can file then."

Julia reached over and stroked the back of his neck. "How are you?"

Eric studied his hands. "Sad," he finally admitted before rushing to say, "Not that I am not excited about marrying you, of course. But it's almost like going to their funerals. It's real."

"I'm sorry."

"Thanks." He kissed her cheek. "No more sad talk today. We're supposed to be planning a wedding."

"Want to come with me to look at bridesmaid dresses?"

He groaned. "I was hoping you would ask," he said sarcastically.

"Be a good sport, and I'll take you to a steakhouse for lunch." She opened the door and got ready to dart to her own vehicle.

"Now you're speaking my language." With a satisfied smile, he waited for Julia to get in her car and pull out of the parking lot, so he could follow her to their next appointment.

CHAPTER **THIRTY-FIVE**

Allison did not bring the issue of her departure back up, choosing instead to leave it in God's hands. Though it felt like the course of her life was uncertain, she was filled with peace. The church began to grow steadily over the next couple of months as the new believers brought their own families and friends with them, and soon plans were underway to clear a section of jungle at one end of the village and construct a large roof for the weekly church gatherings. Most of the teaching that Allison did now was done privately with Manitari, Tsipavi, Majiro, and Amita as they, in turn, taught the others.

She became quieter after nearly being killed at Sema's house, feeling more keenly the need for solitude and reflection. It was almost as if she could feel that a chapter of her life had closed, and she was just waiting for the Lord to show her what the next one was.

One afternoon, she was working quietly in her front yard under a tree, weaving reeds together for a new sleeping mat for the children. Isaac had recently hit a growth spurt and needed a longer one. She had already split the reeds down the middle and lashed the first layer of the mat together, flat side down, with thin vines. Now was just a matter of easing the remaining reeds through the others perpendicularly.

She was singing softly to herself as she knelt in the dirt over the mat and not paying attention to anything around her, when she felt a presence behind her. Looking over her shoulder, she saw Majiro standing in the doorway of their house, his arms crossed over his chest as he watched her. She smiled at him, and he dropped his arms and walked over.

"What are you making?" he asked, looking down at her project.

Not pausing from her work, she replied, "A new sleeping mat for Isaac."

"Don't bother. You won't be around for him to use it." Her hand stilled, and she looked up at him with searching eyes. He continued, "I've decided to send you—all three of you—back to Iquitos."

Stunned, she sat back on the ground. For a few moments, she could only gape at him while he waited patiently for the news to sink in. "Are you serious?" she whispered.

"Yes. I don't want you to go, and if I think about it too much, I will change my mind. It's the right thing to do, and God will not let me have any peace until it happens."

"Thank you."

He laughed ruefully. "Don't thank me. I'm not doing it for you. I'm doing it for my people and the church."

Allison rose to her feet and stood in front of him. Tentatively reaching up, she laid her hand against his cheek. "Nevertheless, thank you. I know this is a greater sacrifice for you than it is anyone else."

"Just… make sure my children remember me," he said gruffly. He turned away, but not before she saw the tears in his eyes.

After dinner that night she broke the news to Isaac and Grace. Understandably, Grace could not really comprehend what her mother was saying, but she did grasp that her brother was very upset. Isaac's tears began immediately, and Grace chimed in with confused sobs of her own.

"Mom, I don't want to go! I want to stay here," he cried.

"I know, sweetheart. I know you do, but we have to go. It will be okay. I promise."

"But I don't know anyone there. They don't even speak my language!" he protested.

"You speak English too," she pointed out.

"I don't care! I won't go, and you can't make me." He crossed his arms over his chest and scowled in such a perfect imitation of Majiro that she had to smile.

Majiro, who had been quietly observing to this point, said firmly, "You *will* go, and *I* can make you."

Isaac looked at him with pleading eyes. "Don't you want me, Father? Don't you want me to stay with you?" he asked. Allison's own eyes watered at her son's broken heart, and she wished for his sake that there was another, easier, way.

Gathering the boy against his chest, Majiro let him weep for several minutes while Allison cried into Grace's silky hair. Finally, he pushed Isaac back and held him by the shoulders. "Son, this has nothing to do with me not wanting you. I wish that you could stay with me forever. I wish that your sister could stay, and your mother too. Part of being a man is doing the best thing for others, even when it hurts us. I need you to be a man too. Even though it makes you sad to leave, I need you to take care of your mom and sister since I can't go with you. Can you do that for me?"

Isaac sniffed. "I don't want to."

"I know, but can you do it anyway?"

"I guess so."

Majiro pulled him back for another hug and looked across the room to Allison. "You'll be okay, Imeshina. Isaac said that he will go with you."

Isaac peeked at her. Detaching himself from Majiro's arms, he walked over to her and put his arms around her shoulders. "Don't cry, Mom," he said, patting her back. "I'll take care of you and Grace."

She looked at him solemnly, marveling both at Majiro's wisdom and her little boy's strength. "Thank you. I feel much better knowing that you are willing to come with me even if it's hard for you."

Isaac asked, "When are we leaving?"

Allison looked at Majiro, who replied, "Very soon. The rains are coming soon, so it will be time to leave the village to care for our other gardens. I have spoken to Manitari, and he has agreed to take you as soon as you can be ready to go."

"Will you take me hunting tomorrow? I want to use my new bow again before we leave."

"Sure. We'll leave at sunrise."

Placated, Isaac went to bed early, eager for the morning to come. Majiro wanted to rock Grace to sleep in the hammock, and Allison decided to give him some time alone with his daughter.

She found herself outside behind the house where she had retreated after her first night alone with Majiro so long ago. How much had changed since that night. Then, she had entertained fantasies of her own death, and probably would have made them a reality had it not been for Isaac. All she had been able to think about for months was the overwhelming desire to get away from the village and from Majiro. Now, she almost wished that she could stay.

Though there was no love between her and Majiro, at least not the kind that she thought ought to be between spouses, she cared for the man and wished him all the happiness that could be found on the earth.

Her tears came then as the faces of her loved ones in the village paraded through her mind. How she would miss Inani's companionship, Manitari's gentle wisdom, and Amita's bold love. What had happened in the span of a few years was nothing short of miraculous, and she wondered if God would seem so near when she returned home.

A breeze rustled the leaves of the tree overhead and blew her long hair around her face. *Lord, stay close to me now. I am as scared about going back as I was when we came here.*

Beloved, I am with you now, and I will be with you for the duration.

She smiled. Some things never changed.

Reaching into the far corner under the sleeping platform, Allison pulled out her old running shoes. She smiled at the memory of them, though they were now black with seven years' worth of mold and looked nothing like they had before she had arrived in the village. She wondered if they would even fit her feet any longer. After going for so long without them—she had not actually put them on since before Grace was born—surely her feet had flattened out too much for the once-narrow fit.

She had to admit that she planned to wear them back to Iquitos not so much because she needed them to protect her hardened feet, but for her pride. She was returning to civilization and wanted to at least try to look the part.

Shoes in place, Allison went outside to the clearing where a surprising number of Shampiri had forgone their morning activities in order to watch her leave. Tears misted her eyes as she looked over the people she loved dearly. In so many ways they were her family now, and, despite her joy of going home, she felt a deep sorrow at the prospect of saying good-bye forever.

Amita broke from the group and met her, tears in her own eyes. Allison took Amita's hands, and for a moment, a thousand unsaid things passed between them. Finally, Amita drew her friend into an embrace. "May our Creator God protect you and bless you. You will always be in my heart, Imeshina."

Breaking down at her words, Allison wiped her wet cheeks. She did not reply for fear that she would begin to sob. Instead she nodded and held tight to the woman who had come to mean so much to her.

Allison continued her farewells while Isaac looked on, his face sullen. He refused to say good-bye to anyone, declaring instead that he would return one day when he was old enough to find his way back alone.

Grace was in Inani's arms, her face buried in the woman's long hair. "Come here, Grace," Allison said with her hands outstretched. Her mother-in-law gave the child up with one final kiss.

"I love you, Mother," she whispered. "Take care of Majiro. He will need your faith in these coming days."

Finally, she turned to Majiro. She was surprised at the swell of tenderness that rose in her heart. His was a face that she had looked at with loathing, fear, and, finally, affection. Now, he had taken to his new faith with the stubbornness that she had always found so frustrating, and she knew that he would remain committed to it.

"Do not forget your promise," he said gruffly. "Send back the Word of God so that we can know everything that He says."

Allison replied solemnly, "I will. Thank you, Majiro, for letting us go."

"I am not 'letting you go.' It is the will of Creator God, and I must do the best for my people. I am chief."

She squeezed his arm gently. "I will pray for you every day." He nodded, and her hand fell away. It was time to go.

With an arm around Isaac's shoulder and Grace on her hip, she followed Manitari into the jungle. Soon, the foliage closed behind them, and she stopped looking back. Now was the time to look forward.

CHAPTER **THIRTY-SIX**

The trek back to Iquitos was arduous, and by the end Allison wondered if it was even worth it. It took five days of hiking from dawn until dusk before they arrived at a river that was navigable. There they waited for two days while Manitari and Isaac went to work felling several trees and cutting them into logs. They then tied the logs together to make a raft of sorts. It was just big enough to fit the four of them, but riding down the river was a much nicer prospect than walking the entire distance to Iquitos.

She had packed what food she thought she could carry, but by the time they arrived at the river, it was gone. So while Manitari and Isaac built the raft, she and Grace scoured the area for fruit and edible roots to take with them. It was almost humorous how much more capable she was of functioning in the jungle than she had been seven years before. Perhaps things would have turned out differently had she the skills then that she had now. She quickly shook that thought off with a glance at her daughter. Given the choice, she would not change anything.

At last they were on the river. Manitari used a long bamboo pole to guide the raft along, while the others remained watchful of rocks or sandbars that could stall or capsize them. Once evening arrived, they tied the raft near the shore and found a dry spot under the stars to sleep until dawn. For four days they sat on the raft watching the river and telling stories to pass the time. Occasionally Isaac would fish with a homemade hook attached to a string on a stick, but only twice did he make a catch.

For the most part, they were the only people on the water, but as they neared the city more and more watercraft passed by them. Long, flat houseboats, canoes, and fishing boats soon filled the widening river, and Allison knew that they must be very close to their destination.

They arrived at the port of Iquitos in the middle of the afternoon, when the vendors that lined the docks were closed down for the afternoon *siesta*. With shaking legs, Allison stepped off the raft and sloshed through the murky water until she stood with her children on the dirty beach. It was the moment she had not stopped thinking about for weeks. Now that it was here, she was mystified.

"Manitari, I'll be back as soon as I can. I need to find someone who can help us."

Manitari nodded, still sitting on the raft. "I will wait here until you return," he said.

The noise and crowded sidewalks overwhelmed her, and a glance down at Isaac's pale face and the tightening of Grace's hand in hers told her that her children felt the same way. Drawing a deep breath and saying a silent prayer, she pushed away her fear and pretended to know exactly what she was doing. For her children's sake, she had to at least appear strong, even though her own heart was pounding.

Luckily, she remembered the route back to the old mission compound where she and Eric had lived when they were not at the jungle base. Surely there were still expatriates living there that could help her get back in touch with her family in America. The walk there would take a couple of hours at least, but she had no money to pay for a taxi.

She set off confidently, aware of the strange looks passing their way, but choosing to ignore them. She knew what a strange, bedraggled trio they were. Her white face and Shampiri dress made for a confusing combination. The children wore only shorts, and Isaac had refused to leave his bow and arrows in the raft.

Their long walk passed quickly as Isaac asked question after question about his surroundings. He was impressed with the size of the city, and she had to smile as she tried to see things through his eyes. Grace, she knew, was simply exhausted.

By the time they reached the main gate of the mission compound, the sky was getting dark. She rang the intercom installed on the tall concrete wall and heard a woman's soft *Si* in reply. Figuring it was one of the local girls that the missionaries hired to clean their homes, she asked to speak to the home's owner.

"*Momentito*"

She waited for several minutes, and then the lock clicked and the door swung open. A familiar face greeted her.

"K-Kyle?"

They gaped at each other for what seemed like forever until Kyle found his voice. "Allison… what are you… but… Oh my."

"I'm home," she shrugged, not really knowing what else to say.

Kyle let out a loud whoop and pulled her into a bear hug that left her breathless. "What happened? I mean, where have you been? Are you okay? I don't even know what else to…" he trailed off as his focus shifted to the children behind her.

"You remember Isaac." She pulled him forward a step and picked up her youngest. "And this is my daughter Grace."

Kyle assessed the situation quickly and greeted the children. "Come in, everyone. Sounds like you have quite a story to tell me." He motioned them through the gate and into the little house behind it.

Allison followed him in and settled on the couch while Kyle puttered around the kitchen looking for cookies and juice for the kids. Tactfully, he waited to ask any questions until she sent them out to play in the yard.

"It's amazing to see you here. Alive! We thought you were dead this whole time."

"No, just taken captive."

"By the Shampiri?"

"Yes. I was given to the chief to be his wife… that's where Grace comes in," she explained unnecessarily.

"You finally escaped?"

Allison shook her head. "No. The chief sent me back with a guide—"

"Where is he?" Kyle looked ready to dash back to the gate.

"Still at the port," she replied. "He didn't want to risk our raft getting taken. I don't think he was too keen on the idea of having to make another one."

"A Shampiri here in Iquitos… amazing! Why did the chief send you back? I mean, you were always a knucklehead, but *I* thought you were fun to have around." he teased, and she smiled back at him.

"For the Bible."

"The Bible?"

Allison leaned forward, her forearms resting on her knees. "He's a Christian now, Kyle. So are a dozen others. They want to know what God's Word says. I told him if I could go, I would find a way to send it back to them."

Kyle sat like a stone. When it finally sunk in, he bolted out of his chair. "Oh sweet Jesus!" he cried and fell to his knees. He began weeping unashamedly, leaving Allison stunned and speechless.

A few minutes later, after he had his emotions under control, he noticed her surprise. Laughing as he wiped the tears from his face, he returned to his chair across from her. "I have never stopped praying for the Shampiri," he explained. "We closed the jungle base after the attack, but I have been working from here learning to speak a language that is supposed to be similar to Shampiri. I still make some treks out to look for the tribe's location. I've been hoping for the chance to actually go into their village to work."

"Well, the opportunity is all yours. If you are willing, my guide, Manitari, will take you back. He will stay in Iquitos until you and Jamie are ready to go. "

At the mention of his wife, Kyle's face tightened. "Jamie died in the attack."

"What?" She gaped at him in horror.

"An arrow. We never even got her out of the base before she was gone."

Allison's eyes spilled over and her heart ached at the loss. "Jamie and the baby—Oh Kyle, I am so sorry. I had no idea. All this time, I thought it was you that was injured. I never once thought that Jamie could be hurt too."

"I took her back to the United States to bury her, but I had to come back. I guess I just didn't want her death to be in vain. All we ever wanted was to see the Shampiri have the opportunity to know Jesus, and I've never let go of that goal... I can only imagine how ecstatic she would be to hear your story. In fact, if she were here, I think she would be halfway back to the port already!"

"Sounds like her." Allison smiled sadly, and they both went silent, lost in their own memories.

Finally Kyle broke the awkwardness. "We looked for you for a long time."

"The village is tiny and very hard to get to," she said, making it clear that she held no one responsible for not finding her.

"Eric looked for a full year until he finally gave up."

Allison cocked her head in confusion. "Eric? But Eric is dead."

"Allison, Eric is alive."

For several moments, the blood rushing in her ears was still all that she could hear. Thankfully, she did not pass out, though her stomach churned. Eric, alive? But how could that be? She had seen him lying, bleeding on the trail.

Kyle rushed on to explain how after the warriors had taken her to the river, he and Tim had managed to drag Eric back to the strong house. There, they found Kathy with Jamie dying in her arms and the girls huddled in a corner sobbing. While Tim called for help on the radio, he and Kathy tried to stop the flow of blood from Eric's and Jamie's wounds. Jamie died within the hour, but Eric hung on long enough to get to help.

"He was back in the jungle a month later looking for you. Everyone told him that you were dead, but it took him a year to believe it."

"Where is he now?" she whispered hoarsely, looking toward the door as if waiting for him to walk through it.

"Back in Texas."

"I need to call him."

"I know. Wait until tomorrow. One day won't change anything, and from the sound of it, your little girl needs you."

Sure enough, Grace's cries grew steadily louder until Isaac walked in, carrying her in his arms. "She fell," he stated and dropped her into Allison's lap.

Allison held her daughter tightly and comforted her mechanically. All she could think about was Eric. But Kyle was right; she needed to focus on her children first. They were hungry and tired after an exhausting week, and so was she. Perhaps it was best if she sorted out the day's events before trying to move forward. Tomorrow was soon enough.

CHAPTER **THIRTY-SEVEN**

It was her day off, and as she did every week, Jean spent the morning doing laundry and cleaning the clutter that had accumulated in the house over the week. The phone rang, and she grabbed it from the receiver as she walked by with a basket of clean clothes balanced on her hip.

"Hello?"

A voice from the past floated into her ear, and the basket in her arms dropped to the floor with a loud *thud*. "Allison?" she whispered, unbelieving, "but how... you..." She listened barely comprehending as Allison explained as briefly as she could how she had come to be on the other end of the line.

After she finished recounting her story, she asked, "Eric... how is he?"

Still gripping the phone, Jean thought of a million things to tell her, but settled for, "Fine, honey. He's well. He's working as a missions pastor in a church about an hour from here."

"I was going to call him, but I thought that maybe it would be better if someone tells him in person. Do you think that's really wimpy of me?"

"No. I think it would be better that way too. I'll call him at work and have him come over as soon as he can."

"Thank you."

"I am just so glad that you and Isaac are okay. It's a miracle!" With that, Jean's voice broke, and she began weeping into the phone. Allison's own sniffles joined hers, and they cried together for a few minutes.

"Honey, there is so much to say, but I will wait until I have you and my grandson back in my arms."

"Okay."

They hung up, and Jean immediately began dialing. Eric answered after the second ring.

More than a little anxious, Eric did not bother knocking before he entered his parents' house. After receiving his mother's cryptic call, he stopped only long enough to leave Julia a voicemail telling her he was heading to his parents' house and asking her to pray. He had made it here in under an hour, dwelling on the possibilities the entire way. His mother had given away no information, saying only that he needed to come home at once.

He rushed into the living room and found his parents seated together on the couch, clutching hands. "It's cancer, isn't it? Which one of you is sick?" he demanded.

"No one is sick. Sit down, Eric," David said.

Eric slowly sank into the chair opposite them and waited for someone to explain what was going on. He could see that his mother had been crying, so he steeled himself for whatever bad news was sure to come.

David cleared his throat and began, "Your mother received a phone call this morning—"

"It was Allison," Jean cut in.

Eric eyes widened, and he sat back against the chair's soft cushion. He had thought of dozens of things his mother might tell him when he arrived, but this had not been one of them. This was a fantasy that he stopped having a couple of years ago, right about the time he and Julia began dating.

Jean went on. "She and Isaac are safe and in Iquitos right now."

"Where have they been?" he asked wondering why he did not feel the elation he thought he should. Instead he felt cold, detached.

"In the Shampiri village," David answered. "We just never found her."

Eric jumped to his feet. "I looked *everywhere*," he said, slamming his fist into his palm.

"Of course you did, sweetheart. This isn't your fault."

"It is, Mom. I should have never stopped looking. I should have kept searching until I found her." Eric was nearly beside himself as waves of guilt washed over him.

"You stopped searching because everyone around you told you to stop. This is my fault." Jean began crying. "I discouraged you from the moment you woke up in the hospital. I told you they were gone and begged you to stop looking for them. And I... I have pushed you to Julia at every opportunity. I am so sorry. So sorry."

Compassion for his mother compelled him to kneel in front of her and put his arms around her shaking shoulders. "I know you only wanted the best for me, Mom. It's okay."

David cleared his throat. "I've already taken the liberty of purchasing your plane ticket," he said, business as usual. "You leave late tomorrow night for Lima. By the time you get there, Allison and Isaac will also have arrived. The American embassy is dealing with the logistics of getting them there, but they need you to bring their passports and birth certificates."

"I have them somewhere." Eric sat thinking for a moment before getting to his feet. "I guess I had better go talk to Pastor Denny and pack." As he turned to leave, his father stood and blocked the doorway.

"Eric," David began, "I have never really seen a reason to believe in your God. Yet, the fact that seven years later my grandson and daughter-in-law are coming home safely makes me wonder if Someone has been watching out for them all this time."

Eric's eyebrows rose at the closest admission of belief he had ever heard from his father. "That's what I believe, Dad. Maybe we can talk about it some more when I get back from Peru."

"I'd like that, I think," David agreed and walked his son to the door.

Eric got into his car, shaking his head with wonder. But soon his thoughts turned to his next task, which he knew would probably be the single most difficult thing he had ever done.

He drove directly to the church after he left his parents' house. Luckily, the secretary was not at her desk when he went inside so he was able to make it into Pastor Denny's office without having to speak to anyone else.

Without preamble he explained to the older man about the call he had received and the resulting conversation with his parents.

"I'm on a flight to Lima tomorrow."

The pastor nodded, his eyes full of compassion. "You take all the time you need, Eric. This may be a bigger adjustment than it was when you thought you lost them. I will be praying for all of you as you sort this out."

"Thank you. It still hasn't really sunk it. I feel like I am just on autopilot going through the motions."

"Naturally." Pastor Denny's understanding words were exactly what he needed to hear, and he managed to smile his gratitude at the older man.

Eric thanked the pastor again and then hurried back to his car. He drove the short distance to Julia's house and parked on the street. He knew that she would not be home yet, but she would be soon. Waiting for her would give him the chance to pray desperately for the words to break the news to her.

After a half an hour, he spotted her car coming down the street. He stood from his perch on his back bumper and walked up her driveway as she pulled in.

Julia flung open the car door and launched herself into his arms. "Eric!" Looking up from under his chin, she declared, "I've been so worried. I haven't been able to concentrate on a thing since I got your message. Well, except pray. I've been doing that a lot. What is going on? Are you okay? Are your parents okay?"

"Everyone is fine. Want to take a walk with me?"

"Okay."

He waited patiently while she locked her briefcase in the trunk. It nearly brought him to tears to look at her. It was going to break her heart to hear what he had to say.

They walked in silence and eventually entered a little park at the end of the street. She seemed to understand his need to wait before revealing his news. Inside the park they found a bench in a quiet corner, set back from the trail and surrounded by maple trees.

Before he could begin, Julia stated, "I am trying not to freak out, but, I've got to say, you are really freaking me out! What is going on?"

He thought about how to phrase his answer, but the truth was that there was really no good way to tell her. He decided that quickly and to the point was probably the kindest way to do it.

"My mom called me home because she got a call from Peru this morning. From my wife."

For a full sixty seconds Julia just stared at him, as if waiting for the "gotcha" that was sure to follow. Finally she choked out, "I don't understand."

"I don't either. All I know is that Allison was captured, but apparently never killed. And just a few days ago, she walked into Iquitos. I don't know how she escaped or why she didn't do it any sooner or why I was never able to find her. God knows, I looked."

"And your son?"

"With his mother."

Julia managed a small, but sincere smile. "That's incredible. To have your son again, I mean. I am very happy for you."

"Yeah. Thanks."

Looking down at her left hand, the diamond glittering in the afternoon sun, Julia murmured softly, "So what does this mean for you? For us?"

"I don't know!" Eric cried. He jumped off the bench and paced around in a small circle. He knelt in front of her, took her hands, and waited for her to look at him. "I love you, Julia," he affirmed. "You know that. As much as I loved Allison, she has been dead to me for years. Am I supposed to just walk away from this life that I've been rebuilding?" His voice shook with emotion, and the anguish he felt was mirrored on her face.

Julia's own tears began cascading down her cheeks as their dreams crumbled around them. Knowing there was a war going on inside her, Eric waited, still kneeling, and watched her thoughts pass over her face. He had always prided himself on being able to read her so easily, but now that fact just added to his torture.

She looked up at him with grim clarity, her full mouth set in a despondent line. "You are still married." He just looked at her, so she went on, "When you boil it all down, that is the answer. You are still married. Feelings or no feelings, I can't marry you, Eric."

She pulled off the ring that symbolized all of his promises, and put it gently into his hand. Her single gesture absolved him of all expectations and made him physically ill.

He clenched his fist around the ring and felt the prongs holding the stones dig painfully into his hand. He wanted to argue, to make excuses, but he knew she was right. His covenant with Allison was still binding, regardless of the circumstances, unusual though they were.

Julia stood, refusing to meet his eyes, and began running back toward her house. Her sobs echoed off the trees and hit him squarely in the chest.

He sighed and sat back down on the bench. "Oh God," he whispered, "What are you doing to me now?"

Eric sat on his bed late the next morning, folding clothes into his suitcase. He was not sure how much he should take with him because he did not really know how long he would be gone. He had received a call late the night before from the American embassy in Peru giving him an update. The woman said that his family was en route to Lima and would be in a hotel until he arrived with their documents. She made it sound like it would not take very long to process everything and get them on their way home.

What confused him was that the woman had said, "Allison and the children." He had lain in bed awake for much of the night trying to figure out what that meant.

Whether the woman had faulty information or there was more to the story than Allison had related to his mother, he knew that there was no way to know until he was actually face-to-face again with his wife.

His wife. He tried to imagine what she would be like after such a long time. He knew that there was a very real possibility that her ordeal had been deeply traumatic and that she might carry enormous physical and emotional scars. She might be nothing like the woman he had loved seven years ago.

He wondered about his son. He would be eight years old now, a school-aged child. Would he accept a complete stranger as his father? Would he even be able to speak English? Eric mourned for the years of his son's life that he missed, but more than anything he was filled with hope at the possibility of watching the rest of it.

It was seeing Allison again that filled him with trepidation. He knew that he had changed so much, and no doubt she had as well. After his conversation with Julia, he had committed himself to staying true to his wedding vows to her, not so much because he felt like it but because he knew that it was what God wanted him to do. His greatest fear was simply that he would find in Lima just a shell of a woman that he would have to take care of for the rest of his life. If that was the case, he would do so, but he dreaded the possibility.

After finishing his packing, Eric sat down in his living room. His eyes strayed to a photo of Isaac on the bookshelf, and he could not seem to take his eyes off it. His mind wandered, and he caught himself falling asleep.

Coffee. That's what he needed. He was afraid to fall asleep and miss his flight. His dad had arranged for a car to pick him up and take him to the airport, but as tired as he was, if he fell asleep, he would not hear any honking from the parking lot below the apartment.

Before he could make his way into the kitchen, the doorbell rang. He opened the front door and took a step back when he saw who was there.

"Julia." He looked at her closely. At first glance, she looked as lovely as ever in a crimson sweater and jeans, but her eyes were dull and rimmed with red. It looked as though she had slept about as much as he had the night before.

"Hi. I was wondering if I could talk to you. Just for a minute."

He opened the door wider and motioned her into the living room. She came in but stood near the door. "Look, I just wanted you to know that I called my sister in Chicago last night, and I decided that I am going to move back there—"

"You don't have to do that, Julia."

"Yes, I do. For you and for me." Seeing that Eric was about to protest again, she continued quickly. "My sister will love having the help with the new baby, and I love Chicago anyway. And this way, you can bring your family home and rebuild your life together without worrying about running into me. It would be weird, you know?"

Refusing to give in to the impulse to put his arms around her, he said weakly, "It's not fair to run you out of town."

"It's not just you. I... -I can't be here with all the memories. And seeing you with your family—" she stopped short and took his hand. "I'm so happy for you, Eric. Honestly, I am. This is an extraordinary gift you've been given, and I wish you and Allison every happiness... -I just can't stay and watch."

He looked into her pleading eyes for a moment. At last, he squeezed her hand and bent to kiss her softly. "Good-bye, Julia."

"Good-bye, Eric." She turned and walked back through the door into the bright sunlight. Watching her go, he marveled at her strength. Her courage had always overflowed onto him, and he would always be thankful for the time she was in his life. He would miss her like crazy.

CHAPTER **THIRTY-EIGHT**

"**S**he's sleeping. She shouldn't wake up until after I get back," Allison whispered to Kyle as she closed the door between the bedroom and living room of their hotel suite.

They were in Lima now. Less than a week ago she and the children had arrived in Iquitos with Manitari, and her head was spinning from all that had happened since.

After her phone call to Jean, she and the children had gone with Kyle back to the port to say goodbye to Manitari and to introduce the two men. Kyle's jubilation over meeting a Shampiri kept the farewell cheerful as they settled Manitari with another missionary family until Kyle could return to Iquitos. Then came the myriad of phone calls back and forth with the American State Department as they made travel arrangements and told and retold the story of her capture and release.

Finally, they had landed in Lima and were whisked away to a hotel just a few blocks from the American embassy. Their first day was a blur of meetings, and this morning she and the children had undergone extensive check-ups that exhausted them all. The pediatrician had poked and prodded both children until Isaac was irate and Grace was hysterical. They were, however, declared healthy albeit underweight and with bad cases of tooth decay and intestinal parasites.

After the checkups, Allison had returned to the hotel with the children, fed them room service, and put Grace down for a nap. Isaac sat on the living room couch reading the picture books Kyle had bought for him.

"Will you be okay here for awhile, Isaac? Kyle will stay with you in case you need anything," she said, tousling the unruly curls on top of his head.

"I'm fine, Mom," he replied, not even looking up. Nodding at Kyle, she left the room quietly.

She went straight to the hotel conference room that had been reserved exclusively for the use of her case. A representative from the State Department was already waiting for her with a couple of assistants. She recognized the tall, thin man from an earlier meeting and shook his hand in greeting. "Mr. Post, sorry to keep you waiting. I had to get my daughter to sleep," she apologized.

"Not at all. Have a seat."

She sat down and tried to remember what this particular meeting was about. There had been so many in the past day and a half that she could not even remember them all.

"I hear your doctor's visits went well. Everyone is healthy. Good, good," he said, looking at the legal pad on the table in front of him. "Well, I mostly wanted to just walk you through the next few days, so that you would know what is coming."

"Okay."

"We have most of your paperwork processed. The rest will be done as soon as your husband arrives in the morning. It should be easy enough to renew the passports for you and your son since he is bringing your old documents. It will be a little more challenging to get Grace's passport since she has no birth certificate, but we are rushing it through. "

"Eric is coming tomorrow?" she gulped, terrified and thrilled all at the same time.

"On a red eye tonight. We went ahead and booked him a separate room so that he won't disturb you in the middle of the night." Mr. Post looked at her with understanding. "I also wanted your re-introduction to be done at your own pace."

"Yes, thank you. That was very considerate of you."

Mr. Post asked, "What does Isaac think about seeing his father again?"

Allison thought for a moment before trying to explain. "He has mixed feelings. For him, the Shampiri chief is his father. I have told him about my family and country and Eric since he was a baby, so there is some familiarity there. Mostly, though, I think he is nervous. So am I."

"He doesn't show it. He always seems very sure of himself."

Allison smiled. "He *is* a very confident boy, but he's never had a reason not to be. He has always been bigger, faster, and stronger than the other children his age. But his whole world has just been turned upside down. You can't imagine how different everything is from a week ago."

"And Grace? Is she having a hard adjustment?"

"Just what you would expect for a three-year-old in a new environment. She isn't sleeping well and is terrified of having me out of her sight. They will both adjust. They're kids; that's what they do."

Mr. Post twirled his pen in his fingers. "And you?" he asked casually. "How are you doing being back in civilization?"

"Honestly, I am having a harder time than I expected to. Things are so familiar and yet so strange at the same time." She paused and then pointed to her newly cut hair. "I looked at myself in the mirror this morning, and it was almost as if the past seven years disappeared. To look at me, you would never guess anything about what happened. I don't know whether to be thankful or weep."

"You've been through quite an ordeal," he agreed. "Allison, I also want you to be prepared for what is coming when you return to Texas. There was a leak about your story, and the American media is going crazy with it. Everyone is going to want a piece of you from the moment you step off the plane."

"But why?" She was dumbfounded, having not even considered the possibility of media interest.

"Why? Why not? It's a sensational story. American missionary captured and assumed dead for years, turns up not only alive but with a tribal chief's baby on her hip. It's big news and will probably stay big news for awhile."

"Everyone knows about Grace? But I haven't said anything about her to anyone, not even to my family."

"The leak was likely from my office, and I apologize. But yes, she is public knowledge."

Allison sighed heavily, her eyes burning with tears of frustration, "Then Eric probably knows too. I had hoped to be able to explain to him myself…"

She looked up, surprised by his touch on her hand. "I obviously can't speak for your husband, but it's quite clear that none of this was by your own choice. I would like to think that any loving husband would understand that."

"I hope you are right." She sighed. "I guess I'll find out tomorrow."

"Indeed. And as far as all the media is concerned, don't feel that you must share your story with anyone. If you do decide to go public with the details, I would recommend finding an agent who can shuffle through all of the requests and help you make those decisions."

"I understand. Thank you, Mr. Post. For everything." She shook his hand, nodded her head at the others around the table, and left the room quietly.

In the elevator, she looked into the troubled eyes of her reflection in the mirror adorning the back wall. She really did not know what to think. Maybe it was a good thing that Eric found out about her daughter this way. At least it would save her the pain of having to tell him herself. Although explaining everything was not what filled her with anxiety. It was watching him react to the story. She wondered if he would even want her back after hearing what she had to say.

The next morning, Allison woke up with a start just as the sun was beginning its ascent. Her heart was already racing as she thought about Eric, who was probably already checked in to the hotel and asleep just down the hall.

She sat up in the king sized bed and looked next to her to check that her children were still sleeping peacefully. Puzzled, she touched the empty comforter and looked around the room. She spotted both of them on the floor at the foot of the bed sharing a pillow. She nearly laughed out loud. Isaac had been complaining about how the bed was too soft. He must have finally had enough and taken matters into his own hands. Why Grace decided to join him was a mystery.

She quietly pulled the comforter off the bed and laid it gently across them before tip-toeing into the living room. After closing the door between the rooms, she pulled one of the armchairs to the wide window overlooking a private golf course and folded herself into its softness. No one was playing yet, so she enjoyed the peaceful view of trees and green broken only by bits of sand and water.

Taking a deep cleansing breath, she tried to quiet her spirit. Time with the Lord had been sporadic over the last week, and she felt the weight of needing to be still before Him. Especially today.

"God, I don't know how I am going to make it through today. I am so scared of seeing Eric and telling him about Majiro and Grace. I don't know if he will accept us, and I don't know what we will do if he won't."

Beloved, I am with you. I was with you in the beginning, and I will be with you for the duration.

"I know. You've never moved. You've been my rock and my salvation since before I ever stepped foot into that village." Tears trickled down her cheeks as she thought about her first moments in the village. The terror she felt as she realized the role she was forced to play as Majiro's wife and the devastation she felt when she thought that Eric had been killed came rushing back to her, filling her senses as if it were that present moment. She thought of the evil that Sema had shown himself capable of and the fear that still permeated the lives of most of the natives.

Then she thought of Amita's sweet friendship and the joy she had felt watching each of the Shampiri believers make their stand for Christ. She thought of Inani's care and of her beautiful, little daughter that God had given her, like a flicker of light in the middle of a dark night. Through all the suffering, there had always been a measure of joy. Even in the most ominous moment, God had shown Himself present and faithful.

For as much pain as she had endured, Allison realized with some surprise that she was happy with the path her life had taken. God's purpose had been fulfilled. He had used her suffering for her own good as well as that of the tribe. She was at peace.

She did not move from her chair as the sun rose higher in the sky and the city below her began to hum with noise and activity. It was as if she was surrounded by a cocoon of peace, and she did not want to disturb the tranquility of the moment.

Eventually, however, Isaac peeked his head into the living room, and she waved him into the chair with her. "Why are you up so early, Mom?" he asked, rubbing his sleepy eyes.

"Just praying and thinking."

"About what?"

"About the village and about how good God is to us. I was thinking about your dad."

"My real dad or *aapani*?"

"I mean your real dad. You are going to meet him today. Are you excited?" she inquired.

Not meeting his mother's eyes, he mumbled, "I don't know."

"What do you mean you 'don't know'?"

Isaac shrugged and rubbed a spot on the carpet with his toe. "I don't *know*. What if he doesn't like me or something?"

She smiled at him, at last understanding his apprehension. "That's not going to happen. Remember he already knows you. You don't remember because you were so little, but I remember how much he loved to play with you and hold you. You dad was so proud of you then, and I know he can't wait to see you again."

"So when is he coming?"

"I left him a message last night. He will come over this morning when he wakes up."

"Okay."

"How about we read a book together while we wait for your sister to get up?" she suggested. "Then we'll all get dressed and ready to meet him." Isaac hopped off the chair cheerfully and began looking through his stack of books on the table. His earlier fears seemed completely assuaged with his mother's assurances. Allison wished that she could reassure herself so easily.

CHAPTER **THIRTY-NINE**

Eric stared at the door to Allison's suite, trying to work up the courage to knock. His whole future rode on what he found behind the door, and he was almost too afraid to face it. Inwardly smirking at himself for dressing up, he adjusted his tie, swallowed, and knocked on the door.

"Come in," came the soft reply from inside.

He swung open the door and his heart caught in his throat at the sight of Allison standing a few feet away next to the window. At first glance she looked exactly the same. The same sparkling green eyes. The same sweet smile on her face that had greeted him so many times. Her hair was a little shorter, her body a little thinner, and there were little lines around her eyes that had not been there before. But it was Allison.

"Hi," she said, her eyes mirroring the hope he felt building up inside of him.

"Hi." For a moment, they just stood there looking at one another. Finally, Eric found his voice. "You look nice." It was lame, but he hoped she would understand all that he did not say.

Allison tugged on the hem of a faded blouse that was too big for her slight frame. "Thanks. A few friends of Kyle's were able to scrape together a wardrobe for me… I didn't come out with much." She blushed, and he was afraid that he had embarrassed her.

"I wasn't talking about your clothes. I meant you. I—I wasn't sure what to expect, but you look… perfect."

"Thanks," she repeated. "You look good too… How was your flight?"

"Good." They sat down on opposite chairs and lapsed into an awkward silence, neither sure how to proceed.

He asked, "Where is Isaac?"

"He's watching cartoons in the bedroom. I told him I would come get him when it was time for him to see you."

Eric could hear the sounds of a child's television program from the next room. "How is he?"

"He is amazing." Allison's face lit up as she began to describe the boy their son had become. "He's tall like you. And smart. He speaks Shampiri perfectly, and English too. He loves to read, but he's athletic and so sweet."

"You taught him to read?"

She laughed. "Yes. Not an easy thing to do where there are no books, but we managed."

"Allison…" He paused. "What happened?" It was a vague question, but the right one. It was as if the dam burst open, and she began telling of what she had endured from the very beginning.

She explained her capture and how she had arrived at the village. "I was given to the chief to be his wife." she explained, looking at him carefully.

The blood drained from Eric's face as he took in that bit of information.

Allison looked at him peculiarly. "You haven't seen a newspaper for the past couple of days?"

"No. Why?"

"I just assumed that you had heard about it by now. Some of the details were leaked to the press."

"No. I haven't heard anything really... Did he *hurt* you?" He knew the answer, but a part of him still needed to hear the truth from her.

"You mean did he rape me? Yes. Repeatedly." He winced at her brutal clarification. His stomach rolled, and he thought he might throw up as she went on. "I was his wife in every way, except for love. I came to respect him and even appreciate him, but I never fell in love with him."

"I should have protected you. I should have—"

"You should have what? Not gotten shot? Crawled after me into the jungle, so that they could kill you? There isn't anything you could have done differently," she said firmly.

"I should have kept looking. At least it could have been a couple of years and not *seven*!" He jumped to his feet. He was angry, but not at her, never at her. Pacing in front of the window, he tried to rein in his convoluted emotions.

"From what I understand, you spent an entire year of your life trying to find me." She stood and joined him in front of the window. Tentatively, she reached for his hand. "You weren't supposed to find me."

He looked down at their clasped hands and tears burned his eyes. "What do you mean?" he asked.

She began to tell him about Amita, Inani, Majiro, and others and their journeys to know the Lord. He listened to her description of life in the village and all that she endured to walk faithfully the path that God had laid out for her. The tears in his eyes spilled down his cheeks as she spoke about Isaac calling Majiro father and finally as she described Grace's birth.

She ended by saying simply, "I won't pretend it wasn't hard. Parts of it were awful. But, Eric, God was *there*. I saw Him work so powerfully in a thousand different ways."

"And you are okay with all of this? It doesn't bother you at all that you had to endure so much," he asked gruffly. He could not wrap his mind around the peace that she had while his own heart felt as if it were ripped into a million pieces.

"When we gave our lives so that the Shampiri would have a chance to hear the gospel, neither of us could have guessed that this was the way it would turn out. But what is this life but a tiny breath of eternity? So God asked for a few years of it. In return, He has given us an inheritance in the nations!"

He marveled at her words and the joy that lit up her eyes. He put his arms around her and held her close. "You are amazing," he whispered.

She pulled away, and they sat back down. "What about you?" she asked, "Your mom told me that you are working at a church now?"

"Antioch Bible Church. Right after I got back home, I ran into Pastor Denny."

"Our Pastor Denny?"

"The very one. He's the head pastor of the church and, long story short, I am the pastor of missions."

"Do you like it?" she asked.

"I love it. It's an amazing church, vibrant and growing. The missions program is expanding both locally and internationally."

Allison paused thoughtfully. "And personally, Eric? Are you happy?"

Eric studied the wallpaper across the room. "I wasn't at first, but now…" He looked up at her and saw understanding light in her eyes.

"You're with someone." He nodded, and Allison's hands clenched tightly in her lap. "Are you married?" she choked out.

"We were going to get married in the summer. I was pushing for sooner, but Julia—that's her name—really wanted a summer wedding outside in the wildflowers."

"Oh, Jesus, no…" she groaned. "Until Kyle told me a few days ago, I thought you were dead. Ever since then I just thought that if you could look past Majiro and Grace, then things could go back to the way they were. I never thought about you moving on with your life. But of course you have. How could you not after so long?"

"We broke up."

"What?"

"The day that I found out you and Isaac were in Iquitos, we broke it off." Seeing the question in her eyes, Eric pulled both of her hands into his and continued, "You are my wife. Thank God you returned when you did or things might have gotten messy."

Allison reached to touch his cheek. "Eric, are you sure?"

"Positive. We'll make a new start together. It will take some time to get all the wrinkles ironed out, but I'm in if you are." He had barely finished his sentence when Allison threw her arms around his neck and wept.

They remained unmoving in each other's arms for a long time, until a cry from the other room brought both back to the present moment. They listened as Isaac spoke to his sister in comforting tones. Allison looked up at him with a question in her eyes.

Eric smiled down at her. "We always wanted a daughter, didn't we?" She beamed and called for Isaac to come in with his sister.

The pair entered the room timidly. Grace ran for her mother, who lifted the child easily into her arms. The little girl was a perfect doll with chubby cheeks and a rosebud mouth. Eric smiled at her, and she offered a shy grin in return.

Turning his attention to his son, who remained just inside the doorway, Eric hunkered down on one knee in front of him. "I know you don't remember me, Isaac, and that's okay. We'll have lots of time to get to know one another again. I want you to know that I am very glad to see you and that I love you very much."

"Can we go hunting soon?" Isaac asked innocently.

Eric laughed and hugged his son. "Absolutely! And I'll bet you'll be teaching me a thing or two!"

Eric stood with his arm around Isaac and grinned at his wife. "I'm glad to have my family back again. All three of you."

CHAPTER **FORTY**

"Bye, Mom. See you tomorrow!" Isaac pecked his mother's cheek before darting around his grandmother's legs and back inside the house.

Jean laughed. "I don't think we'll have any problems."

Allison's brows came together with worry. "If you do, please call me, and we will come pick them up. They've never been away from me overnight before."

"I'll call if I need to, but I don't think I will. We're going to have a great time. Right, Grace?" Jean held out her hand to the little girl. "Are you ready to go play with the doll house Papa bought for you?" Grace nodded shyly and grabbed hold of Jean's hand.

"Go, Allison. Eric is waiting for you."

Allison looked over her shoulder to see Eric leaning against the hood of their car. Leaning down, she kissed her daughter one last time before turning and walking to the driveway.

Eric stood. "Ready?"

"Yes. At least I think so." She looked back at the closed front door. "Do you think they will do okay?"

"Honestly, I do. And we need some time alone."

She sighed but got into the car without another word. He was right; they did need time to themselves. It had been over a month since they had returned from Peru, and the chaos just now seemed to be slowing down. The calls from the media were tapering off as they continued refusing to answer the phone or talk to reporters on the street. Eric's church had been welcoming, but curious, and they had felt obligated to accept the unceasing dinner invitations from members. The remaining evenings were mostly spent with friends or with Eric's parents, who could not seem to get enough time with their grandchildren.

Glancing over, she studied Eric's profile. Sometimes when she looked at him she was nearly brought to her knees. Having him in her life again was beyond any dream she had allowed herself to have. That he was there, in flesh and blood, still astounded her. Unfortunately, she was unsure if he felt the same way.

"So what's the plan for tonight?" he asked.

"I have dinner already prepared. I just have to pop it in the oven."

"What is it?"

"Chicken parmesan, your favorite… or at least it used to be."

"I still like it. You always did too. I guess it'll be nice for you to have it again."

She shrugged. "I guess. The food here seems too rich to me. Sometimes I get nauseated when I try to eat."

"You should still eat what you can. The doctor says you're underweight."

"I know."

They did not speak for the next half hour as Eric drove them back toward their apartment. Allison watched the scenery beyond the interstate. It still shocked her how much had changed since she had last been in Texas. The wide-open spaces that she remembered had shrunk; some had even disappeared completely as new housing developments and businesses sprang up.

They exited the freeway and soon entered their neighborhood. Noticing the park up ahead, Allison asked hopefully, "Do you want to go on a walk before dinner?"

Eric's knuckles tightened on the steering wheel. "No."

"Oh." She studied her hands, hurt by his clipped tone.

Eric looked at her and smiled tightly. "It's not that I don't want to take a walk with you. It's just that… That park is where Julia and I broke up."

"I'm sorry. I didn't know." They turned into the apartment complex, and Eric steered the car around to his parking spot in front of their building.

"Do you want to take a walk around the block?" he offered.

"That's okay. I'll just get dinner started." Without another word to one another, they got out of the car and went inside. Allison went straight to the kitchen, dumped her purse on the kitchen counter and flipped the oven on to preheat.

"Do you want any help?" Eric asked from behind her.

"I can do it. I just need to boil some pasta and get the chicken in the oven. There's not much to do."

"All right." He picked up the newspaper and walked into the living room.

Allison leaned over the counter and put her face in her arms. Why did it feel like she was living with a stranger? Eric was still thoughtful and gentle, but he no longer looked at her as he had in the past—like he knew every thought in her head and every feeling in her heart. The truth was that she did not really know him anymore either.

When they left Peru, her hopes had been as high as the stars. Isaac and Grace had been their first priority, and they had exhausted themselves easing them into their new life and trying to create a workable routine for everyone. Eric took two weeks off work just to be home and make a place for himself in the children's lives. There were still questions and occasional tears about Majiro and the Shamipiri village, but the kids seemed to have accepted the changes as well as could be expected. Her relationship with Eric, however, was another story. They lived more like polite roommates than spouses. She thought that perhaps they simply had not had enough time alone to work things out, which was why she agreed to sending the children to his parents for the weekend. Now she wondered if it was too little too late.

She set plates and silverware out on the table and filled their glasses with iced tea, and then flipped through a magazine while she waited for the chicken to finish baking. Dinner was quiet without Isaac's stories and Grace's questions to entertain them. The food was delicious, but Allison only picked at it.

Eric pushed his chair back and picked up his empty plate. "The cook shouldn't clean. I'll do dishes if you want to hop in the shower or something."

"Thank you." Allison shoved her plate back and retreated to the bathroom. When she got out of the shower, Eric was watching a football game in the living room. Not wanting to disturb him, she turned off the light and went to bed.

CHAPTER **FORTY-ONE**

Eric startled awake and slowly became conscious of the quiet sounds next to him. Allison was turned away from him, but her sniffles were loud in the quiet bedroom. He rolled over and laid his hand gently on her hip. "Alli? Are you okay?" Her shoulders shook harder, and her sniffles turned to sobs.

He sat up in bed and stared helplessly at her. "Please, Allison. Is there anything I can do?"

Taking a ragged breath, Allison rolled onto her back. In the moonlight, he could see her eyes were puffy from crying for so long. His heart ached for the pain he saw etched in her face. "I'm so sorry," he whispered.

"Why are *you* sorry?" she demanded gruffly.

He pulled away as if he had been struck. "Of course, I'm sorry. I'm sorry that you are sad. I'm sorry that you are hurting. I'm sorry that I don't know how to help you."

Allison shook her head wildly. "You don't understand. I'm not crying for me, Eric. I'm crying for you."

"What?"

She said, "It would have been better for you if I had just stayed in the jungle. My children were happy there, and you were happy here. You had a life here, a good one. I ruined everything for you, and I can't undo it."

"Stop it. You haven't ruined anything. I love you."

"You love Julia! And I don't blame you at all. I just can't make things better." With renewed sobs, Allison turned back away from him.

Eric sucked in his breath as he grasped the reason for his wife's tears. The thought of Julia still burned like acid, but worse was the realization of Allison's needless guilt. He slid down in the bed and lay behind her, pulling her tightly against him. She stiffened, but he kept his arm firmly around her.

"Listen to me, Allison," he whispered into her hair. "Yes, I love Julia, and maybe in some way I always will. Just like when I thought you were dead and gone from my life, I still loved you. What matters is where my commitment is, and my commitment is to you. You are my wife."

For a moment, they lay still, and Allison's cries quieted. Finally, she said, "I don't want you to love me because I am your wife or because it is the right thing to do. I want you to *want* me, Eric! I want you to look at me like you used to, like I am the only one that you ever want to be with."

"You think I don't want you?"

"You've barely even touched me since we've been home."

Before he could stop himself, a quiet chuckle escaped from his lips. "You think I've kept my hands off you all month because I don't want you?" He laughed harder as she turned in his arms and glared at him. "Good grief, Allison. I want you every bit as much as I ever did. It's just that I spoke to a psychologist right after we got home, and he said that I should let you take the lead in our relationship. He said that you are probably traumatized by what happened in Peru and might need a really long time to trust me again. He told me if I was too… interested that I might scare you, bring back bad memories and stuff."

"And you believed him? What an idiot!"

"I didn't want to hurt you or ruin whatever progress we've made."

Allison touched his face. "I thought you just couldn't bring yourself to see me like that again. I was afraid that you saw me as defiled."

He pulled her into his chest and kissed the top of her head. "I've never thought of you like that. Not even once. What happened between you and Majiro was not your choice or your fault, and I don't hold it against you, my love. I know that you are at peace with what happened in Peru, and I have made my peace with it as well. I don't like it, and I never will, but I believe that God used the evil that happened to us to do miracles. I certainly don't hold you responsible for what was done to you."

"And Julia?"

"I've released Julia, as she has released me." He smiled crookedly. "Lynn told me a couple of days ago that she spoke to her on the phone. She said that she is settled in Chicago and that she sounds like she is doing really well."

Allison searched his face. "I'm glad," she said. "She must hate me."

"I doubt it. She's not that kind of a person. The last thing that she said to me was that she wished us every happiness. I really think she meant it." He stroked Allison's jaw with his finger. "It would be pretty awful of us to not at least try to fulfill that."

"Eric, I love you so much. Every day that I was in the village, I grieved for you. When I found out that you were alive, the part of me that died that day of the attack was suddenly brought to life. But I know that I am different now; you are different now. Are you sure that we can make this work despite everything that has happened in the last seven years? Are you sure that you want to?"

He kissed her cheeks, her forehead, her eyelids, and finally her mouth. He brought her hand to his mouth and kissed that too. Looking up into her hopeful green eyes, he murmured, "I promise to love you, honor you, protect you, and cherish you. In sickness and in health, in plenty and in want, in joy and in sorrow, forsaking all others, I promise to be yours as long as we both shall live."

He watched a final tear trickle down Allison's face as she struggled to keep her emotions in check. Laying her hand against his cheek, she said joyfully, "Now I feel like I am finally home."

EPILOGUE

Twelve years later, the Carters received an invitation from Kyle Huntington to return to Peru for the dedication of the Shampiri New Testament. After much consideration, Eric and Allison chose to remain at home with their youngest three children. Isaac, with his parents' blessing, left Bible college and returned to the jungle for a couple of weeks. He carried with him messages and gifts from his mother to her friends in the village, including current pictures of Grace, who was still as beautiful at fifteen as she had been as a child.

Majiro remained the pillar of the community and church and was instrumental in the translation of the New Testament. He took a new wife, and not a day passed that they did not pray for Allison, Isaac, and Grace.

Inani died a peaceful old woman, but not before she had witnessed the birth of three of her five grandchildren.

A few years after Kyle arrived in the village, Sema took his family deep into the jungle, vowing to have nothing to do with anyone that embraced the outsider's religion.

Amita and Manitari were now grandparents of a passel of grandchildren. The youngest was a little girl they affectionately called Imeshina.

CONTACT INFORMATION

To read more of Dalaina's writings or to connect with her, visit *DanandDalaina.com,* or you may email her at *Dalaina@ YieldedCaptive.com.*

CPSIA information can be obtained at www.ICGtesting.com
Printed in the USA
LVOW042252280113

317629LV00005B/8/P